TRUE NORTH

H. B. Kravets

authorHOUSE®

AuthorHouse™
1663 Liberty Drive
Bloomington, IN 47403
www.authorhouse.com
Phone: 1-800-839-8640

First published by AuthorHouse   4/15/2009

ISBN: 978-1-4389-6705-9 (sc)

Printed in the United States of America
Bloomington, Indiana

This book is printed on acid-free paper.

DEDICATION

This book is dedicated to all
the brave men and women who
fought and died defending
our great country

and

To the love of my life - my wife,
my son and daughter, my grandchildren,
my great grandchildren and the rest of
my incredible family whose love and
support helped make this book possible

with

Special thanks to Jim Brady
who, without his help and support,
this book would never been published.

Book One

England
94th Bomb Group
1944
The Mission

The 88 mm shell explodes in a blinding flash of orange and black followed by an earsplitting blast as the B-17 bomber's windshield implodes. He raises his arm to shield his eyes but it is too late. Shards of steel and Plexiglas slice into his face and neck. Blood is streaming out of his eyes and nose. He screams...

David's eyes fly open. His hands search his face for the blood that doesn't exist. His heart is beating so loud he can hear it. It feels like a pile driver slamming into his chest. Soaked in a cold sweat, teeth chattering, he can't stop trembling. He huddles down deeper under the rough wool army blanket trying to get warm, trying to get control. It's so fucking cold. Fragments of the dream return to terrify him. He tries to slow his breathing, stop the panic. This will be his thirteenth mission, bad luck. Is he going to die today? The rest of the crews are stirring. Shit! They're awake! Did I cry out? Did they hear me? David checks the luminous dial on his hack watch. It's 1:30 AM.

One of the guys switches on the bare bulbs, lighting up the tin hut. "Time to shit, shave, eat and get this show on the road" and good naturedly snaps one of the guys with his towel. Someone mumbles, "Fuck you, asshole."

David is still shivering; the dream is like a wild storm blowing in and out of his mind. He has to shake it. He rolls out of his bunk and reaches for his fatigues. General briefing is in less than an hour. The damn dream keeps coming back…*Sitting in the co-pilot's seat. He has the controls. Jack is…The windshield implodes, the…I've got to get it out of my mind.* He gets out of bed and heads for the latrine. *Shit, it's fucking freezing.* He pisses into a long porcelain trough with a half dozen other officers and enlisted men beside him. Unlike regular army barracks, the latrines are for enlisted men and officers alike. "Kilroy was here" and other miscellaneous scribbling cover the walls.

There is no luxury of hot water and David bitches as he scrapes off what little beard he has, knowing that his oxygen mask will chafe even with a little stubble of a beard. David runs his hands through what used to be black curly hair that is now trimmed to a quarter of an inch from his scalp, Army regulations. The latrine is filled with other crewmen shaving, waiting for, or sitting on the row of toilets. The place stinks, and the damp concrete floor makes it feel colder than outside. There's a lot of bullshit. "You making your will? Jesus, you gonna sit there all day? Stop playing with yourself, let's go."

David finishes washing, takes his turn at the toilet, and gets out of the latrine, into the cold, damp night, and back to the Nissan hut. There are six double bunks with little bombs painted on the paperboard wall behind them, each with the name of a mission completed under it. Hamburg, Berlin, Cologne. Some bunks have several bombs, some more, some less. None of the bunks have twenty-five bombs, representing the twenty-five missions needed to complete a tour of duty, and a ticket back to the States. Some of the bombs above the bunks represent a work in progress, while others short of the twenty-five are tombstones for those who never made it. There is a pot-bellied stove in the middle that could keep you warm if you sat on it. It keeps a pot of muddy coffee going and smells nice, but the aroma is soon lost somewhere in the damp mold that overpowers it. Three bare bulbs give the place a sickly glow.

David looks at his bunk; he'd like to just get back into it, cover his head, and never get out. No chance. He pulls on his electrically heated suit over his long underwear. His pants and shirt follow, and finally his leather, fleece-lined pants and bomber jacket. He walks through the blackout curtain hanging in front of the door of the hut, sloshes through the mud to the mess hall, and curses the cold English mist. The night is pitch-black, conforming to the strictly enforced blackout.

Two big pot-bellied stoves are straining to keep out the cold. There is a Christmas tree in the middle of the big

5

room. It is almost 1945. *Maybe I'll get lucky and live to see the New Year.* He gets a little white Benzedrine pill, an upper to keep him awake, along with a mumbled prayer to keep him safe from the Catholic priest standing just inside of the entrance. A rabbi or a minister will be holding a basket of 'blue bomber' sleeping pills, for those lucky enough to get back when the mission and the debriefings are over. The mess hall smells of cigarette smoke, coffee, burnt toast, bacon and sweat. He gets into line and wisecracks with the servers while they fill his tray.

David sits down at the nearest table. He chases the Benzedrine pill with black coffee and tries to wake up. Powdered eggs, which don't taste like eggs, and greasy bacon has to last twelve hours before he will eat again. This is the fourth mission in five days and he is scared and just plain beat. The dream keeps sneaking into his thoughts. *Blood is streaming out of his eyes and nose.* He stifles a scream and looks for a familiar face.

A new crew shuffles in. *Poor, innocent bastards.* They are young and have no idea what they are up against as they laugh and joke trying to cover up their fear of the mission ahead of them. David wonders if he will see their names on the MIA list posted after the mission.

He spots Jack Stevens sitting at another table; picks up the remains of his coffee and moves over to Jack's table. Jack is 23; he looks 40, haggard and worn. He is reading a crumpled V-mail from his wife. When David approaches, he folds the thin paper neatly, almost like a caress, and carefully puts it back into his pocket.

David has trained with Jack and has flown with him all through cadet training as his co-pilot. They are still together flying a B-17 Flying Fortress the crew has named "Hot Dice" after David cleaned up in a craps game with some Brits on the ship that took them overseas from Newport.

Jack is always in control, cool and confident, and David looks up to him.

"What's up?" Jack asks. He puts both hands behind his head and leans back stretching as if he didn't have a care in the world.

"My dick."

"You wish." Jack takes his hands down and leans forward. David sits on the wooden bench across from him and rubs his tired eyes.

"You get any mail, Jack?"

Jack pats the pocket with the letter in it.

"Everything okay?"

"Better than okay; my kid took his first step!"

"Hey, that's great," David says, wondering what it would be like to have a child with Jessie.

"I haven't even seen the little bugger yet, and he's walking. You get anything?"

"A letter from Jessie with her picture." David takes the photo from his wallet and gives it to Jack.

"Jesus, she's a knockout."

"Isn't she?" David takes the picture back and looks at it for a moment before putting it back in his pocket.

"Well, tell you what, why don't we just get the next boat back to the States? You can get to see your gal and I get to see my kid. How 'bout it?" Jack is always cool, never ruffled.

"Ya, just like that." David says with a look of hopelessness.

Jack gulps down the last of his coffee, gets up and starts to leave

"See you at the briefing."

"Yeah." David makes a face at his coffee mug. "If the fucking coffee doesn't kill me first."

David takes out Jessie's letter and reads it again.

Dearest David,

Every day I wait for the mailman to come. My heart stops beating until I see his smile as he waves at me with your V-mail in his hand. I can't help crying with both joy and relief. My mother hears me cry and rushes to my side with a worried look. I smile through my tears and tell her it's not a telegram; it's a letter, a letter from you.

The headlines are filled with the war and, yesterday, they reported that eleven planes were shot down over Berlin. Mother tells me not to send out the package we have for you until I get a letter after that date so that we know you are alright, but I sent it anyway. Oh, David, I am so afraid. I pray for your safety every night.

I am doing very well at school although it is difficult to concentrate when I know you are in danger. Life goes on here. People complain about the rationing but they are in the minority. Betty and I are going to help with a bond rally tonight and we are both volunteers at the Army hospital in Framingham on the weekends. Most of us can't do enough for the war effort.

The casualty column in the papers grows larger each day. I am afraid to look. I just wait for your letter. When I get it I read it over and over until I think the thin paper will disintegrate.

I am enclosing a picture of me, but it is only half of me, because you are not there beside me to make me whole. I love you so much, darling. Please come home to me safe and sound.

All my love forever,
Jessie

He carefully puts the letter back in his pocket and wonders if he will ever get back home and see Jessie again. The last time he was with her was just after he received his orders to report to the Naval Station at Newport Rhode Island, where he would ship out to England with the rest of his crew.

He waited impatiently at the pay phone, and at last it was his turn.

"Jessie?"

"David! Where are you?"

"I'm still at Biggs Field, but I'm taking a train to Newport tomorrow. I have a four-day pass, and I was hoping---."

"Oh, my God. Just tell me where and when."

"What about your father? Will he---?"

"I don't care. I'll be there."

"I don't want to start any trouble. I…"

"Listen, David, we're in love. My dad will just have to understand. I can get a train from South Station and be there in a couple of hours. You can meet me at the station in Newport."

David let out a breath of relief. "Oh, honey, that's great. I've missed you. I've missed you so much it hurts."

Jessie's voice was quivering with emotion. "I miss you too; just tell me what to do."

"Okay, here's the scoop. I'll get in too late to meet you tomorrow, so find out when the earliest train leaves for Newport the day after tomorrow, and I'll call you later for the details."

"I'm so excited. I can't wait to see you. I changed my hair. I have a long braid. I hope you'll like it." She started to giggle. "Listen to me. I don't even know what I'm saying."

David looked behind him at the line of fidgeting soldiers waiting for the phone, and said, "I gotta go now. Love you, baby. Call you later."

Jessie's train was late. David paced back and forth in the little train station like a caged tiger, chain-smoking. His mouth was dry with anticipation, and the cigarettes weren't helping. He tossed his cigarette into a spittoon. A colored woman was breast feeding an infant. A couple of white soldiers stared at her. She turned slightly away from their eyes. David sat down on the polished bench and abruptly stood again. *Where the hell was the goddamn train?* Suddenly, he heard the moan of the train's whistle. He ran out to the platform. He could hear the pulsing breath of the steam engine. There it was. His heart was pounding. The train grew closer.

David had rented a room at a little motel overlooking the harbor. It only had a double bed, and he worried he might have overestimated their relationship. Jessie had written to him daily, and each letter they exchanged brought their relationship closer, and more loving. Yet, he had never touched her beyond a few passionate kisses.

A porter was helping an old lady step off the train. A group of sailors followed. A last gasp of steam bellowed out from the big engine, blocking David's view for a moment. When it cleared, he saw an old man, struggling with a big suitcase, step off, and then, there was Jessie. He felt as if his heart had stopped. She was more beautiful than he remembered. He rushed to greet her at the steps, reached up, took her suitcase, and dropped it on the platform. Then he lifted her from the stairs, took her into his arms, and kissed her hungrily. He held her at arm's length. "God, you're beautiful," and kissed her again. More passengers pushed by. She touched his lips with her fingers, looked around, and saw a group of sailors staring at them. "Can we go someplace where we can be alone?" David's heart skipped a beat. "Sure, but aren't you hungry?"

She smiled. "Yes, I'm hungry, hungry for you, let's go."

David already had the key to his room, but, when he walked by the registration desk, a tinge of embarrassment and guilt ran through him. He had checked in earlier as Mr. and Mrs. But from the smile on the desk clerk's face, he wasn't buying it.

The room was small and dingy. There was a beat-up lounge chair, a small dresser with a mirror, and a double bed. The light from the cloudy skies outside barely crept though the brown shades. Drapes hung limply on either side of the only window. This wasn't what Jessie had imagined for her first time, but no sooner had they closed the door to the room they were in each other's arms. Jessie's body pressed against David's. He covered her face with kisses and for the first time ran his hands over her breasts.

Jessie started to unbutton her blouse.

Is this her first time? She seemed so sure of herself. Then to his relief, she said, rather shyly, "I've never done this

12

before, and I'm a little nervous." She had only opened the first three buttons when she stopped, her fingers resting on the next button. "David, I don't want to…get pregnant," her brow crinkled with concern. "Have you got one of those things, you know…?"

"You can't get through the gate without them. The Army just hands them out. I just took them…" David stumbled through his explanation, not wanting Jessie to get the wrong idea that he had planned to make love to her all along.

God, we aren't married, and I'm going to do it. David is going overseas and this might be…No, I'm not going to think about it. He will come back, we'll be married, and nobody will know the difference.

She started to unbutton the next button. *But, what if something goes wrong, and I got pregnant? It would kill mamma.*

She watched David from the corner of her eye as he took off his pants. His shirt and battle jacket lay across a beat-up lounge chair. He was about six feet tall and had a lean muscular body honed by months of vigorous Aviation Cadet training. The muscles in his arms flexed as he finished undressing down to his shorts. She thought he was beautiful. She'd never seen a man naked before, and she turned away when he began to take off his shorts.

Tears welled in her eyes, but she controlled them, stuck out her chin in defiance, and finished unbuttoning her blouse. *Maybe I should finish undressing in the bathroom.*

13

David was holding her now.

She averted her eyes. *Jesus, he's stark naked.*

He removed her blouse.

Boy, he knows what he's doing. How many other girls has he been with? Damn! Bloody sheets. What if I mess the sheets? God, I'd be so embarrassed. There would be no way I could change them. We'd just be lying there, on dirty, bloody sheets.

David took off her slip, slid down her panties, and they were both naked.

Jessie could feel his penis hard against her. The tears were trying to push their way out again, when David picked her up, placed her gently on the bed, and crawled in beside her.

"We don't have to do anything you know, if you don't want to."

Jessie thought about it for less than a moment. "No, David, I want to. I really want to."

At twenty-one, David's experience with women added up to a barmaid, a waitress, and a quickie in the park with a rather inebriated teenager. This was different. This was no wham-bam-thank-you-ma'am, this was the real thing, and he had to do it right. The married guys in the barracks were the gurus, and David had talked to them, anticipating this very day. The key words were, go slow; be gentle.

David's kiss was like the first kiss she remembered, gentle, barely grazing her lips. Kisses traveled slowly and gently to her breasts; she was beginning to relax. The fear was abating. His hand slid between her thighs, and a sensation she only remembered in her secret dreams went through her body like little electric shocks. She began to move her hips with him. Suddenly he was inside her. She'd experienced only a moment of pain, and now she was swimming in a sea of delicious sensation.

Oh God, don't stop! She moved her hips wildly. Was this really happening? Suddenly, it was as if the lights went out. No, they went on. Something uncontrollable was happening, something wonderful, and it was happening for David too.

"I want to do it again," she whispered.

David kissed her and said, "Well, I might need just a little bit of help." He guided her hand to him. She felt him grow hard under her caress.

They made love tentatively again, but as the newness began to wear off, they approached their new passion with abandon, until they lay beside each other sweating and exhausted. They slept in each other's arms and awakened later, still holding each other.

"I'm starved." David said, and he kissed her tenderly.

Jessie giggled, ignoring him, pulled the covers over her head, and said, "I want to look at the wonderful thing that made me feel so good."

"It's still sleeping."

Jessie slipped down, took his penis in her hand, gave it a little kiss and said, "C'mon, wake up, baby needs you."

David finishes the bitter coffee, leaves the mess hall with a last glance at the young flyers and drives his bike through the muddy ruts to crew briefing. Thick mist leaves a wet sheen on his face, and he is cold. He leans his bike against the wall of the Nissan hut and saunters into the briefing room, spots Charlie, his crew's bombardier, and slumps into a chair next to him. Charlie looks at him with bloodshot eyes, a semblance of a grin across his handsome face. He is tall, blond and heavily built. He has movie-actor looks and he knows it.

"You look like shit." Charlie says as he pulls a crumpled pack of Lucky Strikes from his leather flight jacket pocket and pops a cigarette between his lips.

David has bottomless dark eyes, which, at the moment, are red-rimmed from lack of sleep, a strong chin and a wonderful smile. He is a handsome man, but he doesn't know it.

"You look pretty good, yourself." David reaches for Charlie's pack of Luckies.

"Fucking blue bombers. Took one last night, can't sleep without 'um," Charlie grumbles.

"Yeah, I know what you mean, can't take the hangover in the morning. Just isn't worth it." David grimaces, thinking about rolling and tossing on his skinny mattress. Finally, falling into an exhausted sleep, only to wake in a pool of sweat, the lingering remnants of his nightmare still haunting him. He lights the Lucky with a shiny Zippo lighter, takes a deep drag and exhales a long stream of smoke.

The briefing room is filling up now with men and more smoke. The tired airmen, already pushed to their limits, will face hours of briefing and a ten-hour-long mission. If they survive, and too many will not, more hours of debriefing.

Captain Williams is standing on a raised platform. He pulls back the black curtain covering a large map of Europe. The room becomes quiet. The men focus on the big map. Thick red string held by tacks outlines the route the mission will take. David follows the red string that starts at the base, crosses the English Channel, passes over France, and into Germany. Areas where flak will be heavy or German fighters might attack are marked. David follows the red string to the last tack looking for the target. His heart sinks. It's Schweinfurt, one of the most heavily defended targets in Germany. His stomach tightens, and he looks around hoping the other men won't notice the fear that is spreading through him in a wave of heat. He feels that dying would be easy compared to showing fear or worse, cowardice. He fights back his panic, and smiles deceptively, looks around for an audience, "Just another daylight suicide mission, right?" The flyers around him break into a nervous laugh, and somebody throws a crunched up empty cigarette pack at him. He ducks, and hopes that the other men won't smell his fear.

"Attention."

The flyers jump to attention. Group Commander, Colonel Perkins, walks to the briefing platform. On his green battle jacket he wears the wings of a command pilot along with an array of decorations, including the Purple Heart. He is an impressive officer; the men respect him and feel that he is one of their own. He acknowledges Captain Williams, and picks up a pointer. "At ease."

The flyers slump back in their chairs, light up fresh cigarettes and then lean forward a little in anticipation of the briefing. The only sound is the men shifting in their seats. Cigarette smoke hangs lazily in the air, mocking the tension growing in the briefing room.

The Commander taps the pointer on the map, and turns to face the flyers.

"Gentlemen, today the target is Schweinfurt, and one of Germany's largest ball bearing plants." He pauses for the groans. "We've been here before, gentlemen. You know it is heavily defended." He paces back and forth on the small platform, his steps on the wood floor beating out a slow rhythm. "I don't have to tell you men how important this target is." Perkins stops pacing for effect. He turns toward the flyers, and speaks to them in a way that each man in the room feels as if he is being addressed personally, confidentially. "Nothing," he emphasizes, "nothing moves without ball bearings. If we can put the finishing touches on Germany's ball bearing plants, knock them out, we can bring production of planes, tanks and trucks to a halt." He takes a breath; little beads of sweat are forming on his brow, even though it's very cold in the room. "The flak will be especially heavy and the ME-109s will have plenty of time to work us over. Our P-51s and Spitfires will only provide cover for us for part of the way before they have to turn back to refuel. Unfortunately, we are still waiting for more auxiliary fuel tanks for the P-51s, but that's another story."

David knows, no sooner would their cover turn back, because of their limited fuel capacity, the deadly ME-109 fighters, hiding in sun at twenty-five thousand feet, will attack them like hungry vultures swooping down for their prey.

"Remember," the Commander continues, tapping the pointer at the map, "the integrity of the formation is our only defense. Planes will break down, get hit and there will be stragglers. You cannot, I repeat, you will not leave the formation to aid them; they are on their own." The Commander hesitates for a moment, knowing stragglers very seldom return. "Our altitude will be twenty-one thousand feet. We will…"

The briefing continues, covering the weather and other details of the mission. The men are smoking and fidgeting, wanting to get started. Get it over with. Dodge another bullet. Live for another day.

Perkins knows the flak and the enemy fighters are not the only obstacles his men will face. The temperature at twenty-one thousand feet is thirty below and, in spite of the electrically heated suits they wear under heavy fleece-lined leather flight suits, frostbite will disable more of them than wounds. Things, usually taken for granted, become major problems. Just taking a piss, well, that was something else. The relief tube is in the bomb bay. A little black plastic upside-down ice cream cone attached to a black rubber tube that exits outside of the plane and freezes with first use in the thirty-below temperature. And, God forbid, someone pisses on the bomb-bay doors below, and they freeze shut. Worse, if they had to take a shit during the long flight, they would have to be some kind of contortionist to get out of their clothes. Their toilet would be a wooden ammunition box if available; if not, their flak helmets or the clothes they are wearing.

The briefing is over and the commander looks at the crews filing out of the room; they are so young, most are still in their teens; some of them haven't ever shaved yet. They are frightened and he can see it in their eyes. They are like his children. He visits them when they are wounded. They try not to cry. There is always a little bravado on the outside, but he knows inside they are asking for their mothers, and when they die he dies a little with them. They are just boys. The colonel feels he is sending them to hell and too many won't come back. His heart is aching and a mist is creeping into his eyes. What the hell, he thinks, if these kids can't stop the Germans, life wouldn't be worth living. Good

Christ, the fucking Germans smashed the Polish army of over a million men in less than a month, kicked the Brits into the sea at Dunkirk, and the goddamned swastika is flying over Paris. Somebody had to stop them. It certainly wasn't going to be the Brits, God bless them, flying their night missions, hiding in the dark, dropping their bombs, God knows where. Dying for nothing. No, it was up to these kids, which the Army Air Force, demanding pinpoint accuracy, ordered them to fly in broad daylight. God help them; they had to do the job. Their only defense is the shreds of aluminum chaff dropped from the planes. Hopefully, it will confuse the enemy radar directing the deadly twenty-millimeter guns below. They are sitting ducks; they can't run, and they can't hide; their losses will be staggering, and yet, somehow, he knows they will prevail.

There is not much talk. The flyers slowly file out of the briefing room, eyes on the floor; prayers on their lips, a few curses, a lot of fear.

It's still dark, about four. David turns on his flashlight. It throws an eerie glow through the thick mist. He finds his rusty Raleigh bike, kicks some mud off one of the wheels, and heads for the general staging area, where heavy trucks wait to bring the crews to their planes parked far out on the tarmacs. He reaches into his pocket, and feels for Jessie's crumpled letter.

It has been over a year since he left her crying at the station, her green eyes rimmed with tears. She had clung to

21

him as if to never let him go. He had brushed back a strand of her black hair. Her father would never let her wear the tight sweaters that were in fashion, but nothing could hide her sensuous body as she pressed against him. He kissed the tears away from her eyes, the tip of her beautiful nose, then her full lips and held her tight until she stopped crying.

I'm going to get home to Jessie, get married; have kids, a dog, and a little house. Somehow he knows he will, and that's what keeps his sanity. He parks his bike rear wheels into the stand, contrary to all the other bikes for good luck. A truck is waiting to take him and a group of other flyers to their planes on the tarmac. He jumps on the back and finds a place. There are a few wisecracks but, for the most part, the flyers sit quietly as the big truck jostles them in their seats. They are smoking, staring into the darkness, deep in their own thoughts and prayers that somehow they will survive. They compose silent letters to their girls or their families, telling how frightened and homesick they are. How cold and lonely they feel, instead of the ones they really wrote. The letters telling about how easy it was, maybe not any more dangerous than crossing a busy street, shielding the ones they love from the grim truth.

The gunners have already loaded the heavy wood boxes with belts of shiny brass .50 caliber rounds of ammunition in them and are checking their guns. Five-hundred- pound bombs are being loaded into Hot Dice's giant bomb bay; one has "Compliments of the 94th Bomb Group" painted in big white letters on it. Mechanics are all over the plane finalizing last minute details. It's barely dawn, the plane and its crew of workers drift eerily in and out of the fog. The smell of gasoline mixes with the damp, earthy smell of the never-ending mud; constantly nourished by the rain and fog that plagues England for most of the winter. The dream is still nagging him. He can't seem to shake it. It's cold. David shivers and wonders if it's the cold or if Death's hand is touching his shoulder. He shudders and walks over to the plane. Jim Tigerman, nick named Tiger, the plane's engineer and top turret gunner, throws him a lazy salute, and continues to check the two-.45 caliber pistols he is never without during a mission. He is ruggedly built and the oldest member of the crew at twenty-five. His crooked nose looks like it has been broken more than once and he looks like a man you wouldn't want to tangle with. He had watched his family taken from their home, herded into an already overloaded truck on its way to hell, while he hid trembling in a small attic space where his father had hidden him. He was subsequently smuggled out of Nazi Germany by a sympathetic Christian family and vows if he is shot down, he is one Jew who will never be taken alive.

Bugsy, the crew's radio operator, drifts by in the fog. "How many Germans are you gonna kill today, Two Gun?" He needles Tiger.

"Fuck you, Bugsy."

"I will if you bend over."

Before Tiger can respond, one of the big trucks pulls up. Charlie, the plane's bombardier/navigator, jumps off and calls to Bugsy," Gimme a lift with this stuff, will ya?" and passes the Norden bombsight to him. Bugsy picks up the heavy bag and carries it to the plane. He turns to Charlie, and in a low voice says, "We're fucked, aren't we?"

Charlie takes out a cigarette, lights it, and blows out a long stream of smoke for effect. "Well, we're going in low and the fucking Krauts won't need glasses to see us."

"Shit."

"We've had worse; stop worrying."

David ambles over to the two men, puts his arm around Charlie's shoulder. "You girls look worried."

"Nah, we ain't worried, just scared shitless."

"What's your problem? Just another mission, a milk run."

Tiger passing within earshot, growls, "Milk run, my ass."

David is close to the men, in contrast to Jack, who is aloof and distant, the proper conduct between officers and enlisted men as prescribed by the military, but David doesn't buy it. In spite of this breach of military bearing, the men respect him. Although he is younger than most of the men, he has become the "old man." He is there for them and, somehow, always knows when he is needed. He might be trembling with fear on the inside, but he appears calm and controlled on the outside. Sometimes he will forgo his precious leave to sit with one of the men in the crew. They might sit for an hour without speaking until, finally, the man confides his fears or anxieties. David is their Jewish priest. The crew loves him. He treats the crew as if they were his brothers, especially Charlie, and as he turns toward the plane, he remembers the last time he and Charlie had a weekend pass, and they drove to London.

Charlie waited impatiently as David buttoned his Eisenhower jacket, wasting precious time trying to see his image in a metal mirror hanging haphazardly on the wall.

"Okay let's go, I'm ready," David said as he grabbed his trench coat. You never knew when it was going to rain in England.

"For Christ's sake, it's about time, half the damn weekend's shot," Charlie said, hiding a smile.

"Gimme a break. I'm only ten minutes late, London's not going anywhere."

"Yeah, if Hitler doesn't blow it off the map with his fucking V bombs."

"C'mon, think fun, not bombs. We've got the whole weekend."

"By the time you get your ass in gear, there won't be a weekend."

"What a crank," David blew a kiss to a picture of Betty Grable pinned on the wall as they walked out the door. "You want to hit the USO club first? Lotsa good-looking girls there."

Charlie broke up laughing. "Now you got my attention."

They jumped into an old MG Midget 2-seater they had pitched in to buy when they first arrived, and drove through the green countryside to London, hoping the black market gas they bought from the Sergeant at the motor pool will be enough to make the trip. Charlie was driving. The hum of the MG's engine lulled them both into thought.

"Ya know sometimes I wonder if I'll ever get home; see Jessie again."

"You worry too much."

"I keep thinking, you know, about getting wounded."

Charlie took his eyes off the winding road for a perilous moment and studied him. "You keep thinking about that shit and…"

"What if I lost a leg or…or I was blinded?" David continued, looking blankly into the distance, oblivious to Charlie's comments, thinking how little he knew about the politics of the war. Sure, he knew about the Jews and the atrocities, and he hated the German bastards for it, but was it really his responsibility? Did he have to put his life on the line for people he didn't know, politics he didn't understand? "Without a doubt," would be his father's answer, and so it would be his, but would his father be ashamed of him, if he knew how frightened he was? Fear he couldn't even share with Charlie. Fear he might be a coward. He had taken off his hat, and the wind was blowing through his hair. For a moment he felt free from all thought and concern, and then, the thoughts of returning home disfigured or crippled, came rushing back. Would Jessie still want him if he were a cripple? Charlie broke into his thoughts.

"For Christ's sake, stop talking like that."

"C'mon, don't tell me you never think about it."

"Yeah, sometimes I think about it." Charlie answered, not willing to face his own fears.

They sat in silence for a while. David watched the rich, green fields rush by and breathed in the fertile scent of the countryside.

"Jesus, you can be so fucking gloomy." Charlie kept his eyes focused on the road.

"I'm not gloomy; I'm hungry."

"You're still gloomy."

"I know a place for great steaks, Tiger told me about it. Probably horse meat, but Tiger said it was pretty good."

"Sounds good to me, buddy, but it's not exactly the kind of meat I'm looking for," Charlie tried to light his cigarette and steer the MG at the same time.

"You know, you keep fucking those French whores in Piccadilly, and you're gonna end up with the clap."

Charlie exhaled a long stream of smoke. It flew away from the speeding convertible. "You sleep late, get drunk, dream about Jessie, and romance. Me, I just want to get laid. Don't need the romance. Don't really care."

"You just don't give a shit, do you?"

"You know what? Just between me and you, I don't."

"Bullshit."

"Yeah."

"Yeah, bullshit!"

"Hey, you got a girl waiting for you and a father who'll think you're a big hero. I got nobody," Charlie said.

"What the hell has that got to do with it? You know, sometimes you really piss me off with that kinda talk."

"Listen; just forget it, will ya?" Charlie stared at the road.

David punched Charlie on the arm. "You know you really are a grouch today."

Charlie looked at him and smiled.

"Know what, Charlie? When this thing's over we're going into business together, and we're gonna make a ton of money."

"Yeah?"

"There's this farm in Norwood."

"Please don't tell me were going to be farmers."

"Shut up and listen, will ya?"

"Okay, I'm listening."

"It's a perfect location for a flying school."

"A flying school?"

"Ya. A flying school."

"And where does the money come from?"

David smiled, looking like he was just about to perform a miracle. "We could get government loans and buy some of the training planes the Army isn't going to want anymore. They'll probably give them to us so they won't have to junk 'em. It's a natural."

"Just like that, huh?"

"Oh yeah, and that's just the beginning."

Charlie reached over and put his arm around David and gave him a hug. "One minute you're the world's worst pessimist and next minute you're the biggest optimist. I like the optimist part of you better."

"Listen, I want us to start a small passenger route like Boston to New York. We only need one plane. One old DC-3 and we're in business." David paused and looked into the invisible past. "I'm not going to end up like my old man, God bless him. Worked his ass off as a tailor twelve-hour days just to keep food on the table. No way. I'm gonna be something. I'm going all the way to the top, old pal, ain't nothing going to stop me and you're coming with me."

"Great dreams kid, but there's a lot of space between dreams and reality." Tears welled up in Charlie's eyes. David is the closest he will ever get to family.

"Listen, we're going to make it, and as far as family is concerned, take a good look, pal, because your family is sitting right here beside you."

Charlie seemed to be concentrating on the winding road. He stared straight ahead without a word of comment. Suddenly he pulled the MG over to the side of the road and turned off the ignition. He still had both of his hands on the wheel, looking straight ahead, as if he were still driving. Finally he turned to David. His blue eyes caught the sun momentarily and David could see a shiny film of tears building only moments away from overflowing.

"What's wrong?"

Charlie put his hand on David's forearm, squeezed it and then, turning away from David, looking deep into the past he started to talk.

"While my mother strained to push me out of her womb her heart gave out. She probably never even heard me scream when the doctor slapped my behind and brought me to life. My father and mother had recently emigrated from Austria, so my father had no family to turn to. Besides, he wanted nothing to do with me. At least that was all I could find out from the orphanage where I grew up. So I never had a family. Never had anyone that cared about me. Even all the broads I fucked, not one of them really cared about me. You're the only—ah, forget it." He switched on the ignition and pulled on to the road. Then he started to laugh until the tears finally overflowed and ran down his cheeks. When he stopped laughing he turned to David, "Y'know, I love you, kid," and he stepped on the gas and hurtled toward London.

They found a place to park just off Piccadilly Circus and started looking for a restaurant. The whores flirted with them in six different languages. The blackout was so complete that David almost bumped into one of them. "Can I make you happy, baby?" she asked as she tried to fondle him.

"Yeah, you can make me happy. Tell me where I can find a good steak."

"I'll show you where the best steak, real steak, not horse meat, is…if you buy me one. And I'll give you both the best blow job you ever had for dessert." David noticed that she was so thin that her shoulder blades pushed against her dress. If she had breasts they were indiscernible. But in spite of her frailty, she had a pretty face that was almost overpowered by huge brown eyes.

David liked her Cockney accent. "Okay, lead the way. We'll buy the steaks and you can forget about the desserts."

"Hey," Charlie broke in, "speak for yourself."

She led them through the dark streets, taking lefts and rights, cutting through murky alleys until they reached a blacked-out storefront. Searchlights crisscrossing the sky, looking for the German bombers that visited the London sky on a nightly basis, suddenly illuminated it. She opened the door for them and they entered the small restaurant. It

31

was dimly lit and quite cold. A heavy man with a shiny bald head lead them to a table and took their order.

When the steaks came, and they were real beef, David watched her eat. She no sooner shoveled a large piece of meat into her mouth when she followed it with another. He wondered if she actually chewed it at all. They ate in silence and when they had finished they wiped the last bits of gravy from their plates with the heavy bread that came with the steaks.

Charlie wiped his hands on the overhang of the tablecloth, as there were no napkins, and stood. "I'm going to the loo. Be right back."

As David watched him disappear into a long corridor there was a blinding flash of light followed by an ear-splitting blast that lifted him from his chair and tossed him as if he were a rag doll into the wall twenty feet away. The restaurant was ablaze. He looked for the girl. She lay in a bloody mess, her hair ablaze. Her big brown eyes stared blindly at the fire that was consuming her. As the fire crept toward David he realized he couldn't find the strength to move away. He reached up and felt his head. He had the worst headache of his life. His hand came away from his head sticky with blood. *Why did he take the poor little whore with them? She could be alive if…where was Charlie? Was he laying somewhere, hurt, maybe dying? The fucking German bombers. But wasn't he doing the same thing? Killing innocent…* He looked at the whore again, what was left of her. He vomited. God, his head hurt. He could feel the heat of the fire. He had to get up. Head splitting. He tried to get up again. *Can't get up. Tired. Poor girl. Charlie.*

David struggled to open his eyes. They seemed to be held closed by some unnatural force. He could feel his lids straining to open. Every so often a flash of light snuck through. Finally, the weight lessened and he opened his eyes. The first thing he saw was Charlie's face. His mouth was moving and his face was animated but it was a few moments before David could comprehend what he was saying.

"-----Concussion----will be okay----couple of days----bomb----not a direct hit----lucky."

David tried to sit up but his head felt too heavy so he laid back and looked at Charlie's concerned face. "Are you okay?" Before Charlie could answer David saw that Charlie's blond hair and eyebrows were now little black stubs. There was a bandage on the side of his forehead and on both hands.

"I'm fine. Sitting in the loo when the bomb hit. Restaurant owner used it as a bomb shelter. Literally scared the shit out of me."

David looked at his singed hair and bandaged hands. "How'd you get...?"

"Playing with matches."

It wasn't necessary to ask again. David knew that Charlie had saved his life.

When David came back to the present, he knew Charlie was more than family, he was his best friend. Although they had only known each other during their months of training, they were like brothers. They laughed and cried together but, most of all, they looked out for one another. David was tough and fiercely independent. The fear of making friends, only to read their names on the casualty lists later, kept him from close relationships, but somehow, Charlie had broken that barrier. They stood back to back for all comers.

They would never let each other down.

The truck stops at the tarmac where Hot Dice is parked, and David jumps off the tailgate. The weight of his parachute and flight bag helps him to a hard landing. He has a .45 strapped to his chest and his heavy leather flight jacket is open to the cold. Sergeant "Gunny" Williams throws him a lazy salute. David smiles at him and lugs his gear to the plane. Gunny reaches up with both arms and, with great effort, pulls himself up eight feet, and in through the nose hatch of the B-17 Flying Fortress. David passes his gear to Williams and begins his walk-around inspection of the plane.

Gunny ducks low, crawls to the left into the bombardier/ navigator compartment in the front of the big plane, and plunks down in the navigator's chair besides a small desk that is flush to the fuselage. Gunny is a thin boy with a face full of pimples, and very street smart for a twenty-year-old.

"How's the bomb-dropping business?" He asks Charlie.

"Not bad, how's the tail gunner business?' Charlie answers, without turning away from his adjustments on the Norden bombsight centered in the big Plexiglas nose cone.

"Oh, I get plenty of customers."

"I'll bet you do."

"I ain't been up here in these nice digs of yours for a while." Gunny fiddles with the calipers lying on the navigator's desk.

Charlie turns, looks at Gunny for a moment, turns back to the bombsight and frowns looking for where he left off.

Gunny gets a glimpse of Charlie's bruised face. "Hey you look like you got hit with a truck."

"You should see the other guy."

"What the hell happened?"

"You don't want to know."

"Jesus you look terrible. You get in a fight or somethun?"

"Yeah, something."

"C'mon, tell Mamma. What happened?"

"Ask your co-pilot."

"Gimme a break."

"Well, we're in Piccadilly looking for someplace to eat. A couple of Marines are having a good time picking on one of the ladies of the night. You know David; he don't like that kinda thing, so he walks over to them and tells them to lay off, but they are having too much fun torturing this little girl. Shit she didn't look fifteen. David steps between the girl and the Marines. That does it; one of the Marines takes a swing at him. David ducks and flattens the bastard." Charlie takes a breath. "The other guy starts wrapping his belt around his hand. You know that little trick they use, but I figure, belt or no belt, David can take him. Then two other Marines show up. Three against one. So, I ain't gonna just stand there looking, am I?"

"Jesus three Marines."

"Well it didn't last long. Half the 8th Air Force broke it up, but not before two of the fucking Marines are lying on the sidewalk. That David's a goddamn terror."

"Where'd he learn to fight like that?"

"Beats me. Anyway, he's got a nice cut on the side of his head that's about to bleed him to death, and I'm trying to get him to go to an aid station, but no way. He has to find the little girl first and see if she's okay."

"So?"

"So he finds her, all right. The kid's crying, and David's got to comfort her, him bleeding and all that. He takes out his handkerchief and wipes away her tears, gives her money; gets her a hackney, and sends her home, if she even had one. Fucking guy cares, but you know that."

Gunny nods affirmatively. "Well, gotta get to work before I get fired for goofing off." He gets up, throws Charlie a mock salute, and heads for his position in the tail.

He passes below the pilot's compartment, a level above the nose cone, looks up at Jack and David, running through their preflight check list, takes a deep breath, and whispers, "Please God, help us." He knows he is a part of a good crew, and they are all well trained. Although the nine of them have only worked as a team for a few months, they are all bound together with a common purpose: kill the enemy; get home alive.

"Hey, Gunny, what ya doing, slumming?" Tiger asks, as he climbs down from the top gun turret, which is just behind the pilot's compartment, and a level above.

"Naw, just making sure all you killers showed up for work this morning."

"Sorry about your dad, kid. Your mom going to be okay?"

"Well, my mom's moved in with my sister."

"Good idea."

"Yeah, I'm sending most of my pay home, so at least she'll be okay until they get my orders together, and I can go home."

Tiger pats him on the shoulder, because no verbal response would do, and climbs back up into the turret.

Gunny continues through the plane; squeezes through the narrow catwalk over the cavernous bomb bay, and passes Bugsy, sitting at the radio operator's desk.

Bobby Hill almost bumps into him on his way to his position in the ball turret. At nineteen he is small and wiry, has a baby face, yet he looks like he hasn't slept for a week. Gunny doesn't envy him. He has to squeeze into a little plastic ball that rolls down hydraulically from the bottom of the plane. He is locked into the freezing bubble with only the twin .50s to keep him company. He has little chance to get out if they get into trouble. The plane can't land with the ball turret down and jutting out from the bottom so, if it jams, there is no alternative but to jettison it. Bobby knows this. He'd pissed his pants once when they'd lost hydraulic pressure and had a hard time rolling the damn thing back up manually and just in time. He's a good kid, spends a lot of time in the chapel with the chaplain and, otherwise, stays much to himself, saying very little. Gunny wonders if he could do Bobby's job.

He continues down the narrow fuselage, and stops to talk to the two waist gunners, each checking his gun, which will counter, along with the top and ball turrets, any attack from port or starboard. The guns look out of two openings on either side of the plane. The merciless thirty-below air stream from the speeding plane will rush in like a hurricane once they are airborne, and will blast the gunners, almost in protest to their deadly mission.

Billie Dean is a new kid, a replacement for the plane's original gunner, who is now in the base hospital recovering from the piece of flak that nearly took his right arm off. The kid looks like he's fifteen years old and seems very nervous. Gunny smiles at him. "How's it going, kid?"

"Okay." He fidgets with the gun; his hands flutter over the belt of ammunition locked into the breech of the gun. It's like his hands are disconnected from his body. He doesn't look at Gunny who can feel the mounting tension in the kid, as takeoff time grows closer. He can smell his fear, the kid is sweating and he stinks. It's the kid's first time in combat. Gunny signals Mooney, the other waist gunner, with a nod indicating that Mooney should calm the kid down, keep an eye on him.

Gunny crawls to the tail gunner seat, the most dangerous position in the plane, where most of the enemy fighter attacks will originate. He knows he has plenty of backup. The rotating turrets on the top and bottom of the big plane along with the front turret, and the gunners on each side, make a formidable target for any attacking enemy fighters. Additionally, they are supported by the guns from the other eight planes in the squadron, all of them flying in a tight formation, making them almost impregnable. It's the "almost" that bothers him, and he has an awful feeling he isn't going to make it. He takes off his girlfriend's "lucky" high school ring, kisses it (something he does before each mission), and puts it into his jumpsuit pocket as if to keep it safe from the terror ahead. He checks his guns, crosses himself, and whispers, "Dear Jesus, help me."

At six thirty the planes begin to lumber onto the runway, waiting for the green flare to break into the foggy night to signal the okay to take off. And then, with a giant roar, one by one, they rise gracefully into the sky. It's still dark and the fog is so thick, the planes disappear from sight only moments after takeoff. It takes over an hour for the squadrons to form, and then more time to join the groups that will follow one another into the heart of Germany. Dawn breaks just as they climb through the clouds. The bright sun lights up the cloud cover, which looks like great mountains of snow, covered by an ice blue sky. It's breathtaking. The only blemish is the white fluffy contrails of crystallized vapor trailing the bombers that will hang like a highway in the sky for hours after they have passed.

While crossing the channel, under the protection of the American and British fighters, who are aptly called "little friends," Mooney walks into the radio compartment, away from the freezing wind blowing through the big open windows. Mooney is a tough Irish kid from New York. He has untidy red hair, which looks like it has never seen a comb or brush, piercing blue eyes, and a face full of freckles

"Shit, it's cold out there," he says to Bugsy, and hugs himself, trying to hold in some warmth.

"It isn't too warm in here either." Bugsy pulls up the collar of his heavy leather jacket. They are below ten thousand feet, and oxygen masks aren't required, so Mooney's mask dangles beside his face.

"How come you sit on your flak vest instead of wearing it like you're supposed to?"

"Hey, what's more important, your life or your balls, huh?"

"Never thought of it that way." Little puffs of frozen air escape from Mooney's mouth.

"Talking about balls. Hanging over the open bomb bay doors, and kicking the hung bomb loose, not to mention, it was my turn to do the dirty deed, took big brass ones."

"Don't worry about it." Mooney looks down, embarrassed.

"Last time I tried it I almost shit my pants. I'm scared of heights, and when I looked down I…"

"Forget it. It was no big deal." Mooney pats Bugsy on the shoulder.

"Well, I owe you one."

Mooney thinks about his girl back home and he remembers the straw hat with the daisies in the hatband, framing her soft face. Her sad little smile, the day they said good-bye at the train station. "Don't worry about me, baby. I'll be back before you know it." He put his hand lightly on her cheek, and saw her blue eyes fill up with tears. "I'll write you, I promise." But he hadn't mailed the first letter yet. He reaches into his pocket and takes out the V-mail letter he had been too shy to send, and hands the flimsy envelope to Bugsy. "Ya know, nothin's gonna happen to me, but…"

The fighter escort of P-51 and Spitfire fighters wiggle their wings signaling their fuel is low and it is time to turn back. David has a feeling of loss as he watches them leave. He feels alone, abandoned. He remembers back to the day his mother died…Jack's panicky voice on the intercom breaks his reverie.

"Bandit, bandit; one o'clock high!" The ME-109 German fighter screams in on a collision course with the bomber, its guns blazing, white-hot tracers slamming through the thin aluminum skin of the plane, and disappears as it rolls through the formation.

"Co-pilot to crew, damage report, over." One by one they report; no one is hit, the damage is minimal; his heart starts to beat regularly again. The B-17 fights back: a barrage of yellow and orange tracers from the B-17 find their target when the 109 returns for a second pass. It explodes in a blinding flash. Another ME-109 tears out of the sun, gets through the barrage of fire, its twenty-millimeter canons spurt streams of steel into the formation's lead plane. David sees one of the lead plane's port engines start to trail smoke, orange flames follow and suddenly the wing and the fuselage merge with the deadly flames. Two men drop through the burning plane's nose hatch. Their flying suits are on fire; one of them pulls his ripcord and the chute snaps open. The guy is banging his hands against his burning flight suit when the ME-109 turns for another pass, lines up with the helpless man in the parachute, and fires. David squeezes his eyes shut and grits his teeth. He hears himself scream, "Those fucking bastards." He can't control the hot tears flooding his eyes. Jack reaches over and puts his gloved hand on David's shoulder, and David calms a little.

The lead plane explodes when the fire reaches its fuel tanks, and David instinctively puts his arm in front of his face, as his plane momentarily lurches out of control from the blast. Fragments of the shattered plane pepper the windshield; something heavy slams into the windshield, slides off into the slipstream, and leaves a smear of blood to freeze on the glass.

David recoils. *That was their twenty-fifth; they were going to go home. For Christ's sake, why couldn't they have gotten a break?* He looks away from Jack, lifts his goggles, and wipes his gloved hand across his eyes.

The flak is so heavy it obscures the sky with great puffs of black smoke, the memories of the shells that exploded moments ago. David flinches with each new blast. Sweat is oozing from every pore and running down his body in little rivulets, leaving a cold damp trail behind, and he shivers involuntarily. His bowels feel loose, and he is worried he'll mess himself. *God, I'd be so embarrassed, to say nothing about freezing my balls off.* He turns to Jack and says, "How the hell are we going to get through this shit?"

43

"Hang in there, baby," Jack answers calmly, but David can see his hands are trembling on the controls.

They reach the "initial point" where the bomb run starts, the beginning of a gauntlet of hell, leading to the target. Jack sets the autopilot, so Charlie can take control of the plane through the Norden bombsight from here to where he will drop his lethal load on the target below. The run will take anywhere from ten to fifteen minutes, depending on the headwinds. The German guns below will be throwing everything they've got at them. Charlie has developed a certain calm now, and he is oblivious to the shells bursting around him. His only focus is the target below. He gives his commands in a calm and clear voice.

"Open the bomb-bay doors." Fragments of flak tear into the fuselage next to Charlie's head. He doesn't even flinch.

"Center the PDI." His mouth is dry, but sweat is running down his face and the rubber oxygen mask is sticking to his cheeks.

"Bombs away."

The plane rises, relieved of the weight of the twelve five hundred pound bombs. Jack lets out a deep breath and takes back the controls. Now, they must turn away from the target, and start their way back. They are over the heaviest of the artillery and most vulnerable. Another bomber begins a spiraling descent, smoke trailing. More guys bail out. David says a silent prayer for them. *I never even knew the poor bastards. Well, maybe it's better that way. I don't want to know them. I don't want to recognize any of the names on the MIA list. I don't want to mourn them. I don't want to remember them.* His mind snaps back, he focuses again, but Jack can read him; he reaches across and gives David an easy punch on the arm. He signals, are you okay, raising his gloved hand with a "thumbs up" signal and David nods affirmatively.

Below, the exploding bombs send huge black and gray clouds bubbling up toward them as they find their marks. David wonders what hell they have created below. How many have died, were there woman and children? His stomach is rolling. *I've got to stay in control; I've got to stay in control.*

They are out of the worst of the flak and what's left of the crippled formation, battered and disorganized, is an easy target for the German fighters. He thinks about the German pilots, mostly kids like himself. They haven't any choice; they are fighting for their country just like I am. Then the sympathy turns to hate when he looks at the ravaged formation. He realizes there is a difference. They are fighting for the Devil, and we are on the side of God.

David spots another ME-109. "Fighter, three o'clock level! Mooney, heads up."

Mooney lines up on the fighter and whispers, "You're mine, you little bastard, you're mine." His machine gun spurts flame, the gun kicking in his hands, shaking his entire body. The yellow tracers streak toward the enemy fighter whose guns blaze back at the bomber. The top and ball turrets' four fifty-caliber machine guns join Mooney. The deadly barrage of tracers and steel from the five machine guns find their target, and the German fighter explodes. Burning pieces of debris fall from the sky. There is no sign of the pilot.

More bursts of flak, and deadly shards of steel, from the Nazi 88 millimeter cannons on the ground, explode in black puffs of smoke filling the sky around the bomber. The dull thuds penetrate the roar of the four 1200 horsepower engines. The big bomber shudders when one of the bursts slams into the number 2 engine. Flashes of yellow flame hide in the thick black smoke that spews from the engine

"We're hit, oh shit we're…" Jack never finishes the sentence as shrapnel from another burst of flak tears into his face and neck, killing him instantly. He falls forward on the control column, sending the bomber into a steep dive. David grabs the column and pulls back, but Jack's dead weight is too much. He tries to push Jack away but Jack won't budge. The engines are screaming as the big bomber continues to dive out of control. David tries again. Jack slides partially off the column but his arm and part of his shoulder still lean on the wheel. It's not enough but it's the best he can do. With both hands he pulls back on the controls again using every bit of his strength, his arms trembling with the strain. The engines whine, the big plane bucks and shudders. The altimeter is spinning crazily as the bomber hurtles toward the ground, black smoke and flames streaming from one of its engines. David is screaming at the controls begging them to respond. He doesn't think he can hold on another second when the plane finally begins to slowly level off. There is blood all over the controls and the windshield, but David can see the number two engine still spurting flames. It would be only minutes before they reach the fuel tanks. His whole body is shaking. He cuts the fuel to the engine, and deploys the fire extinguishers, but they don't work. He pushes the throttles forward, and puts the plane into a shallow dive to try to blow out the fire, but to no avail.

"Tiger, I need help; Jack's dead." His voice chokes. "Gotta get him out of the seat." There is no response. "Tiger do you read me, over?" Again there is no response. The top turret is just behind and above the pilot's compartment. He turns in his seat and strains to look up and backward. Tiger is in a crumpled heap, an ugly oozing hole where his left arm and shoulder used to be. His head is jammed against a jagged piece of gray metal where flak has ripped through the fuselage. His oxygen mask has been torn away from his face, and dangles uselessly beside him. Blood is pouring out of his nose and mouth.

The plane shudders. Another flak burst explodes into the number 4 engine and now smoke and flames are streaming from both the number 2 and number 4.

This is his first time in control of the big bomber. The ultimate decision to abandon the plane is up to him. He quickly feathers the props on the damaged engines, and sets the automatic pilot. Then he activates the bail out signal, and presses the mic to his throat, to make sure he is loud and clear.

"Co-pilot to crew, we're on fire, this sucker's gonna blow, we're going down, we've had it. Bail out, bail out."

Suddenly, the plane shakes violently; the nose cone is hit, exploding into a million splinters of Plexiglas and bomb fragments. Charlie is blown backward; the entire compartment erupts in flames.

David feels the violent concussion. *What the fuck? Oh, God. Another hit. This is it. We're going down. Got to get out. Shit, I can't breathe. Heart's pounding so loud. Feel sick. Fucking bailout alarm's driving me nuts. Can't think. What do I do? Don't know what to do. I DON'T KNOW WHAT TO DO. God, tell me what to do.*

CALM DOWN. CALM down. Don't panic. Check out the plane; get all the guys out. Jack's dead, Jesus, Jack's dead. Too much blood. Oh, God, help him. Please, help him; help me. Slow down. Breathe in and out. Strap on the auxiliary oxygen tank. CHARLIE! Check on Charlie.

David unfastens his safety belt, moves Jack's lifeless body off the wheel and leans him gently back in the pilot's seat. *Good-bye old buddy. I'll miss you.* He stands on shaky legs and tries to disconnect from the mayhem around him. He knows he has to check the plane, see that everyone has gotten out. His entire body is trembling and he is soaked in sweat. He takes a last look at Jack's lifeless body slumped in the pilot's seat. Dark blood is still pumping weakly from his carotid artery, running down his body and finally freezing in place.

Charlie's in trouble and he has to get to him. David scrambles down to the bombardier's compartment in the nose of the plane. Charlie is lying unconscious in the flames and David tries to get to him. Another burst of flak rocks the plane, and throws David, stunned, against the navigator's desk. The frigid air blasting through the shattered nose cone revives him. A throbbing pain brings his hand to his head; he can't believe he actually sees blood on his brown leather glove, his blood. Fluid from a hydraulic line, ruptured by the same flak, has caught fire, and is intensified by a hole in an auxiliary oxygen tank. The flames force David back; he raises his arm to shield his face from the intense heat. He has to get out; his heart is pounding. *How much time do I have left? Jesus, it's freezing, and I'm sweating bullets. I'm scared. God, I'm so FUCKING scared.* His teeth are clenched so tight his jaw is aching; he has to remember to relax to stop the ache.

Charlie is face down; one arm and part of his face are in the blowtorch flames of the oxygen and hydraulic fluid. David pulls him away from the flames, and turns him over. He looks at the charred body, winces, and holds back the vomit beginning to push toward his throat, knowing he would suffocate if it clogged his oxygen mask. Blood is oozing from Charlie's stomach, and a part of his leg is torn

49

away. David knows Charlie is dead, but he can't tear his eyes away. *Dear God, I can't leave him like this. I can't leave him.*

He examines Charlie again looking for any sign of life. He takes off his glove and searches for a pulse. He can't find one, but he's not sure, and checks again. His hand is freezing, and it's almost impossible to get through Charlie's clothes to the pulse he hopes to find in his throat. His hand is shaking and he wonders if he will feel a pulse if there is one. He still can't feel a pulse. "C'mon Charlie, open your eyes, just open your eyes." The flames from the two burning engines will reach the fuel tanks in minutes. The wind is howling through the shattered nose cone. The roar of the big engines is deafening but not loud enough to blot out the scream rising in David's throat.

"Charlie, Charlie, oh God, he's dead, he's dead; those fucking bastards."

The tears freeze on his face in the thirty-below temperature that assails the cabin even as the flames engulf him. He squeezes his eyes shut to clear the tears. *I have to see that everybody gets out.* He heads to the radio compartment and the waist gunners. Passes Tiger, shuts his eyes, but still sees his torn body. He has to check every position. That's his job and somehow he is going to do it. *The fucking plane is gonna blow, and I won't get out.* The plane is vibrating violently and he can barely keep his footing as he passes through the narrow catwalk over the bomb bay doors. He passes the relief tube with its plastic upside down ice-cream cone dangling from its cradle and thinks insanely, maybe I ought to stop and take a piss. He wonders if he's going crazy.

Bugsy is sprawled across his desk, his hand still on the sender, his head now a mess of bone, brain and blood. David wrenches his oxygen mask from his face, and throws up down the front of his flight suit. There is a smell of vomit, cordite, blood and death. He wipes his mouth with his sleeve; puts the mask back on and heads toward the waist gunners. The freezing wind blows through the two gun openings, but there is no one there. He plugs into an intercom outlet and calls the tail gunner. "Gunny, over. Co-pilot to tail, over?" No answer. He tries again, no answer. He knows he is running out of time. *The ball turret is up, maybe Bobby bailed out with the waist gunners. Thank God some of them got out. Have to hurry.* Heading back through the narrow catwalk over the bomb bay his auxiliary oxygen tank gets caught, trapping his leg. He struggles to free his leg, breathing hard, eating up his precious oxygen, trying not to panic. He tries again. Nothing. His leg won't budge. He twists and yanks again. Suddenly he is free, but the oxygen tank rips off of his leg and falls to the bomb-bay doors below. David pulls off the now useless oxygen mask and heads to the escape hatch in the nose, knowing he has precious little time before he will pass out from the lack of oxygen. He jettisons the door and just as he jumps through the hatch, he looks back one last time; his vision is blurring, his body craves the oxygen

51

that is almost nonexistent at twenty-three thousand feet. He sees Charlie's body lying close to the flames and Charlie…

His consciousness leaves him as he falls into the frigid air. Something is tugging at his brain like a lingering dream, or is it a nightmare? His mind reaches back deep into the unknown shadows of his subconscious. Something is lurking there, something he is trying to remember. Something beyond the horror of the burning plane and the stench of death, something too horrible to revisit or even to imagine. He can't go there. He won't. Something else is happening; his thoughts are clouded. The wind is stinging his face, and consciousness is screaming back to him. *What's happening? I must have passed out. Oh, God, oh God, I'm falling. He starts to panic. Papa, I'm falling. Jessie, Jessie.* His mind is beginning to clear, and quick successive thoughts are jumping into his mind. *We're hit; plane's on fire; got to get out! Charlie! Charlie. Charlie. Falling! Parachute, got to pull the ripcord.*

He begins to feel for the ripcord. He is calming now and starting to think. Not yet, he tells himself. He looks for the enemy killers, the bastards. There are enemy fighters close by and they won't hesitate to fire at him, even though it is an unwritten code among airmen that that would never happen. They will be like hawks swooping down on their prey. The ground is rushing toward him, but he delays pulling the ripcord to avoid the enemy fighters. He has a feeling of unreality. He takes a deep breath. The air smells good. The damn mask isn't irritating him. He's not afraid anymore; the nightmare has faded. *Everything's going to be all right. Jessie is waiting for me. I'm going to get home and see papa. I'll wear my best uniform with my wings and, maybe, I'll have some ribbons. They'll be so proud of me. I'm not going to die; I'm going to make it.*

Below is the German countryside. The snow-covered mountains of Switzerland are glistening in the background contrasting with the ice-blue sky above. The thick German forests seem to have been planted in perfect order and symmetry. The rolling hills are punctuated by little towns, each with its own church, their steeples searching the sky, and perhaps asking God for an answer to the madness that prevails around them.

He thinks about his father again. *Don't worry, papa, I'll be alright. Take care of yourself and don't worry about me.* He wakes from his reverie. "Yes, I'm going to be alright!"

It's time. He yanks at the ripcord as his body hurtles toward the ground below; suddenly the terror is back. He is worried that he might have waited too long, and prays the damn thing will open. Something is nagging at his brain. *Goddamn it. What?* He thinks of Charlie lying in the burning plane. *Why didn't I check him more thoroughly?* He looks up and the goddamn plane is still flying, leaving a fiery trail on its way to hell.

A sharp snap as the chute blossoms; it yanks him violently from his plunge to Earth, knocking the breath out of him. There is no time to adjust the direction of his fall or to brace himself to hit the ground, and moments later he slams into the side of a steep hill. The chute falls into a puddle of white silk. A sharp pain shoots through his leg. Is it broken? He doesn't have time to investigate. People are coming toward him up the hill. He is panicky, frightened, drenched with sweat, stinking from the smell of fear. He wrenches at the chute strap with trembling hands. *I've got to get away, got to get out of here.* He feels dizzy, squeezes his eyes shut, and clenches his teeth from the pain running up his leg into his knee. Agonizingly, he starts to crawl away from the coming blur of people, but realizes it is futile. The weight of his .45 automatic presses against his left breast and he draws it, but his hand is shaking so badly it probably would be futile to use it. He contemplates throwing it away when he sees that they are already on top of him.

They are farmers, mostly old men, and a few heavily built, ruddy-looking women, armed with pitchforks and other farm implements. The first man to reach him swings his spade at David's arm. The impact knocks David's gun away, and the pain brings him from frozen fear to complete panic. He tries to get to his feet, but collapses once again when the pain from his shattered leg reaches his brain. He screams as the second man shoves a pitchfork through his thigh, and pins him to the ground.

Someone pulls the pitchfork from his thigh and yanks him roughly to his feet. The angry faces surrounding him swim in front of his eyes. He can barely feel the blows that land on his face and body as they vent their anger with their fists and whatever else they can find to beat him with. The pain that rages through his broken leg and the wounds in his thigh combine with the beating until, mercifully, oblivion takes over, and he passes out.

When he regains consciousness, he is in pitch darkness. He thinks he might be dead, until the pains that seem to pervade his entire being remind him of life.

Everything hurts. Leg hurts, probably broken? Thigh burning. Fucking pitchfork. Pain. Thirsty, very thirsty, need water. What's next? What are they going to do? Torture? Confused. Frightened. Please, God, I don't want to die here. Unmarked grave. Telegram to my father, killed in action. Gotta get myself together. Can't give these bastards satisfaction. Gotta stand tall. Shit. Can't stand at all.

He feels around with his hands, and finally realizes he is in some kind of box. He can see dim shafts of light from the roof and walls of his prison. Maybe they are bullet holes, and he is in a truck or, perhaps, an ambulance that had been strafed, notwithstanding the big Red Cross that was probably painted on its roof.

The door of his prison suddenly opens. *What the…*Bright sunlight flashes into the dark ambulance and momentarily blinds him. A loud guttural voice commands him to come out.

"Heraus, schnell, schwein."

He crawls painfully to the door, and only then does he realize his thigh has been roughly bandaged, but is still bleeding. He hesitates and looks at the blood-soaked bandage, the pants ripped up on one leg. His head is still bleeding and hurts like hell. *Jesus, I'm alive. At least, I think I'm alive.* The German soldier grabs the collar of his flying jacket, pulls him toward the entrance and, finally, the balance of the way to the ground. Then he jerks David to his feet and starts to push him toward a small farmhouse about twenty yards away. Agonizing pain shoots though his leg. He falls as it crumples beneath him. The guard screams at him to get up and, when David hesitates, the guard's hobnailed boot lands in his stomach. He retches violently. The second kick sends him sprawling. He staggers to his feet, stabbing pain shooting to his brain. He can't understand how he remains standing. The guard shoves him again and again toward the farmhouse until, finally, he lurches through the door and falls in front of two men seated behind a small table inside the room. A voice comes through to his pain-clouded brain. It is spoken softly, but with a clipped tongue in halting English.

"It is customary to come to attention in front of a ranking officer." The German officer nods to the guard.

Before the guard's boot can land again, David struggles to his feet, his head whirls, and he wavers, but he stands as erect as possible. His leg throbs and he bites his lip to stifle the pain.

"Your name?" The officer questions in thickly accented English.

"David Livingston, 2nd Lieutenant, 0133954," David answers, hoping the officer won't see the fear that grips his stomach.

"Very good, and now, Lieutenant Livingston, what were you going to do with this automatic we took from you?" He displays David's .45. "Kill some more little children or perhaps a few old women? Didn't it bother you enough when you strafed and bombed hospitals and schools? Did you come back here to see if you missed some little child perhaps?"

The officer rises from his seat and walks over to David, so close that his face is only inches away, his voice at a high pitch. "Answer me!"

David thinks of the many targets that had been planned by the top brass near schools or hospitals, and how important it was to avoid them if possible. But then, if the clouds hid the target, and pinpoint bombardment wasn't possible, blind, scattered bombardment through the clouds was necessary. Schools and hospitals be damned. They had to be ignored for the benefit of the end result.

The German's ice blue eyes bore into David. The veins in his neck bulge, his face beet red, filled with more rage and fury than David has ever witnessed. It strikes him like the breath of a wild beast. Yet, he knows that if the roles were reversed he would feel the same way. Frightened and trembling, he faces the officer and meets the German's eyes evenly. He wants to say he is sorry about the hospitals, the schools, the children, and how he had no choice but to follow orders. But the officer, filled with a hatred that smolders like an inferno within him, doesn't wait for David's answer. Instead he slaps him across the face so hard that David loses his balance and falls sprawling to the floor. As he tries to rise, the German steps forward and kicks him in the stomach. As David writhes in pain, the officer turns to the guard. "Take this Jewish pig out of my sight."

BOOK TWO

PRISONER OF WAR
1944-1945

David arrived at Stalag Luft 7 AH, a huge stone castle that had been converted into a prison strictly for airmen. It had been just 48 hours since he had parachuted into Germany. He was sure he was running a fever. The pain in his leg had peaked and, although it was not bleeding as much, infection seemed imminent.

By midday he was led to what appeared to be an interrogation room where he repeated his name, rank and serial number, and then pushed and dragged to a long flight of stone steps. There was no railing and David stumbled and fell most of the way down screaming with pain as his shattered leg bounced off the stone stairs. At the bottom of the long staircase was a dank smelling room with damp, stone walls illuminated by a single bulb, a table in the middle. A German soldier, holding an automatic weapon, sat on a chair on top of the table. Five airmen, some sitting and some lying on the straw that covered the stone floor, greeted him in silent recognition. Rats scurried about as if they owned the place, their red beady eyes catching the light now and then.

As the guard shoved David toward the others, it was made quite clear that he was to sit down, and that there was to be no talking. "Sprechen sie nicht," the guard said, in a voice that resounded off the cold walls, as he waved his ugly gun in David's direction to reinforce his order. David crumpled to the floor; his head whirled and his consciousness faded.

A guard slapped him back to consciousness and dragged him from the basement dungeon, back up the long flight of stairs, into a very large, beautifully decorated room. A huge fireplace with a blazing fire warmed the room. An oriental carpet covered most of the darkly polished parquet floor. A French desk in front of high, lead-paned windows now dark with night, stood majestically against one wall. A tall, handsome man of about thirty with rugged, hard features and blond, curly hair was leaning casually against the front of the desk wearing a black tunic, jodhpurs and boots. His left arm carried the red, white and black swastika band, and his lapels held the twin silver lightning bolts of the SS. He dismissed the two guards in harsh German. Then, in perfect English, but with a touch of a Harvard accent, he said, "Please Lieutenant, sit down," and pointed to a large leather chair with a table and lamp next to it. "Cigarette?"

David limped to the chair, sat down carefully, amazed and puzzled by the perfect English and soft demeanor of the Nazi officer.

As he put the cigarette between his lips, the German officer offered him a light from a gold cigarette lighter, "So, you're from Boston?"

David was astonished, "How'd you know that?"

"You would be surprised at how much we know about you, even about your family. I presume they're still living on Esmond Street, in Dorchester, yes? By the way, I know that area quite well. You know, I studied at Harvard, graduated in '37. Well that's another story; let's get back to you, David. Would you like a drink, Scotch perhaps?"

"Goddamn it," David almost shouted when the alcohol touched his split lip. He hadn't had time to assess the wounds that he had suffered from his first introduction to the Third Reich. He realized that his lip was split and he couldn't blink or shut his left eye. Evidently his lid was cut; at least he could see through it.

"You look pretty awful, but don't worry; a few easy questions and we'll take care of all that; you'll be as good as new. We're quite civilized, you know. You might even like it here, out of harm's way. The food's not bad, and for the right prisoners there may be a fraulein..."

David flushed with anger and hatred. He realized that this arrogant bastard actually believed he would betray his country for a warm bed and a piece of ass. He glared at the German, "Fuck you!"

"Let's start again. You're with the 94th Bomb Group, 332nd Bomb Squadron. Your first pilot's name is Jack Stevens."

David almost nodded in confirmation in his astonishment at the amount of information the polished officer had. What David didn't know was that German sympathizers in America cut graduation notices of aviation cadets out of the local papers. The notices usually read like, "Cadet David Livingston graduated and received his silver pilot wings today. His father, Robert, lives on Esmond Street…" German spies in the United States secretly sent this information to Germany for future use during interrogations. Further information was obtained from other airmen that were shot down and interrogated.

The German continued, "Listen, we already know more than you might think. Make it easy on yourself, don't be stupid. Disarming your delayed action bombs has become a problem; they keep blowing up; so many good soldiers die…"

David interrupted him. "Look, you know the score, my name is David Livingston. My rank is 2nd Lieutenant, my serial number is 0133954, and that's all you're going to get."

"David, David, please, this doesn't have to get ugly." The German's blue eyes turned to ice and his voice lost the Harvard accent to its guttural past. "Answer my question!"

David put his cigarette in the ash tray, watched the smoke curl upward, and very slowly repeated his name, rank and serial number. "According to the Geneva Convention, the only information I need to give you is my name, rank and serial number and…"

"Fuck the Geneva Convention!" the officer screamed. He knocked the tumbler from David's hand, and then, with uncontrollable fury, he pulled David from the chair, threw him to the floor, and began kicking him mercilessly. David curled into a fetal position trying to protect himself as best he could. He moaned with each kick, the pain in his leg, accentuated by the relentless beating, became unbearable. The officer screamed, "You will talk to me, you filthy Jew. You will tell me what I want to know!"

The officer was desperate for the information he knew David was withholding but, somehow, he knew the man laying on the floor, groaning in pain, was not going to give it to him.

David had the information the officer wanted. Recently, delayed action bombs had been assembled with a disarming nut that fit on a specially designed nose cone, both made out of plastic. Normally, to disarm a bomb, it was necessary to carefully turn the nut with a wrench in a counterclockwise direction. However, the new plastic head had a magnetic triggering action, so that the moment a metal wrench was put to the plastic nut, the magnetic trigger would activate the bomb, and nobody lived to tell the story. Delayed action bombs were very important as they tied up target areas for weeks, sometimes for months. Any nonferrous wrench would safely disarm the bomb, and David knew he would never give out that information. He wondered how long he could hold out, how much he could take. Maybe he should give them what they wanted, after all who would know? If they tortured him, how long would he last?

He was yanked to his feet and thrown roughly into the leather chair. The German's ice blue eyes were boring into him. "I'm not finished with you yet. Tomorrow morning we will take a sledgehammer and start with your ankles and then your knees and then, well, you get the idea. Think about it. You will talk to me, or they will hear your screams all the way back in Boston!"

David knew that he could never go home, go back to Jessie, or have any respect for himself if he talked. He looked back into those ice blue eyes, and thought about how much he hated these Nazi bastards. He knew he would never give in no matter what they did to him. He smiled the best he could with his damaged lips, and spit into the German officer's face.

He could hear the moans of the wounded flyers lying beside him. The German guard sat on top of the table, still holding his ugly gun. A rat ran over his leg. His body ached from the brutal beating the Harvard-educated officer had inflicted after David had spit in his face. "You will answer my questions, you filthy Jew or..." Suddenly the dirt floor he was lying on shuddered violently when the first shell hit. American artillery had opened up on the German battery whose guns circled the prison camp. The Germans had incorrectly calculated that the "soft Americans" would never blow up their own elite flyers.

Although General Hodges realized the Americans in the prison camp would be in mortal danger, Hodges knew that the German stronghold stood in the way of General Patton's forces crossing the Rhine, giving him no choice.

As the next shell slammed into the building three stories above him, David pressed his face into his arms. Dirt and debris fell across his body. The shriek of still another shell screeched across the night sky. The shell struck only yards from David's dungeon. The explosion was deafening and the floor trembled as earth and rocks poured over David's body. "Oh God, can you hear me?" The shelling continued all night.

He began to compare the experience of being shelled in the air, which was almost like mime. The flash would come from below and explode with a silent burst of blinding light. The whining engines and the prattle coming through the earphones that covered the crew members' ears obliterated most of the sound of the explosion. Suddenly he felt he was back in combat sitting in the co-pilot's seat of the big B-17.

"Fighter 6 o'clock high. Watch that son of a bitch; he's below you. Ball turret, 8 o'clock low. Wake up, wake up, there's another one. He's rolling through the formation. Navigator, pick up a position and count chutes; Mike's hit and he's going down." And again in mime, Mike's plane silently exploded in a terrible flash. Young bodies unseen were burnt and blown to bits. The few that had bailed out, their flying suits in flames, plunged to earth five miles below. Only one chute had opened.

It was like watching a silent film. There was no sound, no smell. It was sterile until it was you. Your plane. And then it was five minutes of horror, five minutes of the stench of burning flesh and the screams of dying men.

This was different, worse somehow, and after six hours of constant pounding his pain-wracked body stopped reacting. He wasn't thirsty, let alone hungry anymore. The rats in the corner didn't threaten him. He paid no attention to the moaning fighter pilot lying besides him. The dirt, rubble and pieces of cement pelting him would soon become his grave. He stopped praying, because it seemed God wasn't listening anyway. He fell into a numbed sleep to try to close the gap between an unbearable existence and a quiet death.

A ray of sun across his face woke him. It burst through the rubble of the three stories above him that had almost buried him. He looked up at the blue sky and at the same time heard the sound of boots crunching toward him. He squeezed his eyes shut to try to block out more terror, more pain.

A German guard stood over the wounded airmen, pointed his automatic weapon at the six flyers, and with an upward swing of his weapon motioned for them to stand up. Three of the men got up. One of the others was trying to help his comrade to rise, but the guard pushed him away, pointed the weapon at the man on the ground and motioned to him to get up. The downed fighter pilot moaned. His hip was broken, and every movement seemed to cause excruciating pain as he tried to somehow get to his feet. The guard lost patience and squeezed the trigger. At such close range, blood and torn flesh spattered in every direction. David felt sick. Cold fear crept up his spine as he witnessed the horror. He knew he had to get up or die. Agonizingly he struggled to his feet, prayed he would be able to stand and not follow the fate of the poor pilot on the ground. His head spun, sharp pain stabbed through his leg, he staggered and almost fell, but a supporting arm of one of his fellow prisoners steadied him. The guard prodded them with his weapon and they started walking. The same man that helped him stand continued to support him. In spite of the chill of the cold February day he was sweating profusely as they stumbled ahead of the menacing gun. Each step sent lightning bolts of pain through his leg and up to his brain.

"Name's Sullivan, Sully to you," his benefactor whispered.

David could only see Sully's profile. He could see one deep-set blue eye. It was rimmed with red and there was a dark swollen ring under it. His cheek was hollow and bruised and his thin lips were cut and swollen but somehow managed to smile. He had taken a good beating and David imagined the rest of his body would testify to that as well. Yet, he hung on to David like a long lost brother. David spoke through clenched teeth. "David Livingston, and thanks."

"No problem. Just hang in there, buddy, we're gonna get through this."

With each step David tested putting a little pressure on his broken leg to no avail and as the march continued his leg swelled, bled, and slowly became numb.

They joined up with a larger group of prisoners who were followed by a German Tiger tank. Those who could walk were supporting those who could not. Sometimes a pair would fall or a man would slip from the grasp of his Samaritan's exhausted grip. There was no way to avoid the fallen man as the prisoners unsuccessfully tried to step around him. It didn't matter, because at the rear of the silent column growled a huge tank followed by a half dozen captured Mongols armed with automatic weapons.

The Mongols had never been treated well in the Russian army that had conscripted them from their meager existence on the cold Siberian plain and many had switched allegiance to save their lives.

They were barely civilized, and they laughed and joked as they emptied their guns into the jumping, twitching bodies of the prisoners who had fallen and miraculously escaped the treads of the giant Tiger tank that had passed over their fallen bodies.

David wanted to lie down, just give up; let them do what they would. After all, how long could Sully hold on to him? He had had no food or water for days. It was only a matter of time. Sully was using up his own reserves to keep David alive. But David knew that he had to keep going. Somehow he had to get home, survive for Jessie. He couldn't quit now. He couldn't let her down.

He limped and stumbled, barely able to put one foot in front of the other. His swollen left foot squished in the blood that seeped into his boot with each agonizing step.

It was Sully who saved his life. For four days he had supported David and prevented him from falling and leaving him to the treads of the Tiger tank or the blood-thirsty Mongols. Finally David tried, tentatively to put weight on his broken leg and found the swollen mess was numb enough that he could actually put a little weight on it. The pain was still excruciating but, looking at Sully wasted with exhaustion, thirst and hunger, he knew it was walk or die. As he disengaged himself from Sully's thin arms, he saw surprise in his helper's eyes. Like a mother watching her child take his first steps, Sully's forehead creased with concern and anxiety. He kept his arm out in case David might fall. "Are you gonna be okay? Y'know I can still hold onto you. Jesus, I don't want you to fall."

David's leg started to surrender to the pain and he faltered for a moment but Sully grabbed his arm and steadied him. David gently reached up and moved Sully's arm away "I'm okay. Stop worrying."

"I'm not worrying. The only reason I was holding you up in the first place was that you were keeping me warm."

David hid a smile. "Yeah, well I wasn't too happy having you hold me. You know, you don't exactly smell like roses."

Sully started to answer, but his mouth was so parched by then only a gravelly croak came out.

David stumbled again and reached for Sully's arm momentarily to gain his balance. "Don't want you to freeze to death, y'know."

"Halt, halt!" the fat guard screamed at the prisoners. A wasted soldier near the head of the column had collapsed. The guard commanded him to get up but he lay there motionless. The guard kicked him but there was no response from the fallen soldier. He was mercifully dead.

They had stopped in a railroad marshalling yard next to a side-rail where a sealed cattle car waited. The stink from whatever it carried was overwhelming. David could feel his stomach turning over.

There were three SS men wearing black leather coats. Two of them had vicious-looking dogs on short choke chains. One of the column's guards walked over to them and gave stiff-armed Nazi salutes. "Heil Hitler!"

The SS men barely raised their arms in lazy, uncaring salutes. "Heil Hitler." David was close enough to decipher a few words as they addressed the guard.

"Can you understand anything?" Sully asked

"Something about the Russians…had to empty some kind of camp or something. Shit, I don't know what the fuck they're saying."

The discussion with the guard from the column finally ended when the two SS men with the dogs started to walk to the cattle car. When they reached it one of them slid a huge bolt back and pushed the big door open. What were once American soldiers stood packed tight at the door. Some of them, pushed forward by those squeezed behind them, fell to the ground, already dead. He yelled at the men still standing to get down from the railroad car and simultaneously took out a handkerchief with his free hand and held it to his nose. "Heraus, schweinhunt."

A barely human skeleton stood in the doorway as the others crushed around him. Even from where David was standing, he could see the dark hollows of the man's eyes, the horrible red lice bites that covered his face and shaved head. The man could hardly stand. The dogs were in a frenzy of barking, straining at their leashes to get to the poor thing that stood blinking from the hazy sunlight. One of the SS men with a long red scar that ran from his eye to his ear grabbed at the dirty uniform that covered the emaciated body and pulled him from the car to the ground. He fell in a heap while the dogs howled, snarling and snapping, their teeth just out of range. The man was yanked to his feet and then pushed toward David's column. He fell again but somehow scrambled to his feet as the dogs started toward him. Another scarecrow of a man dressed in the filthy rags, the remnants of an American uniform, came to the door. He got off the car on his own and was also pushed toward the column. He seemed a little stronger than the first although he stumbled a few times but he never fell. Two more appeared at the door and jumped to the ground followed by another dozen or so. Most of them fell. Some had to be bitten by the dogs in order to muster the strength or whatever it is that makes a man do something his brain and his body tells him he can't. Then nothing. The SS man, still with the handkerchief at the ready, screamed into the car again and again. "Heraus! Heraus!"

One of the last men to emerge from the car dragged himself toward the column. He was close to David and Sully when he turned and croaked out, it seemed with the last of his breath and through parched lips, "You can yell your fucking German head off, but the dead that's left in that stinking box ain't gonna come out. Ya hear that? They're all dead! You fucking murderers!"

A few more men from the cattle car stumbled or tried to crawl toward the column, the dogs led by the SS snapping at them as an incentive to move faster. When one of the men could go no further the SS man with the scar let his dog loose. David shut his eyes to try to block out the horror, but the image of the screaming man remained behind his eyelids until it disappeared in the blur of David's tears. When he opened his eyes again he saw the SS soldiers shutting the big door of the railroad car, sealing their crime with the big bolt.

The column's guards returned and gave the orders to commence marching. David and Sully tried to help the man that had joined them, but he refused. "I survived Berga and I will survive this." He coughed and then said sheepishly, "But thank you anyway. I might not refuse you next time."

Just before dark, the column was halted and the men were allowed to sit down. Sully laid down flat on the damp road. Smoke from a guard's cigarette drifted by on a gentle breeze. Sully could smell the tobacco. "I would kill that cocksucker for a smoke. On second thought I'd kill him just for the fun of it."

David looked to make sure the guard hadn't heard Sully. "Shut the fuck up before you get us both killed." Then he turned to the new arrival. "So what's your story?"

"There were sixty of us in that boxcar." He coughed convulsively, finally catching his breath. "We were wedged in so tight we couldn't lie down. I counted four days and four nights without food or water. Men pissed, shit, and died standing in place."

Some of the stink of the man was dissipating in the cold night air, but David felt like he was going to puke from the smell. "What the hell is Berga, or whatever you called it, and why ship you here?"

"Berga was a death camp, not a labor camp." He coughed until his eyes bulged. "When our platoon surrendered they separated the men who had Jewish names or looked Jewish and sent them to work there, digging a hole into a mountainside."

David focused on the man as he spoke. Running sores mingled with his lice-infested body. His eyes, black holes in his skeletal face, seemed to belong more to the dead than the living. They glazed over as if to block out the visions of the past as he continued.

"We slept on wooden beds, three tiers high, on mattresses covered with lice. There was a stinking hole in the floor in the middle of the barracks for sixty men to relieve themselves. We worked 12 hours a day with two meals of beet soup and a piece of bread. Most of us had diarrhea."

Sully sat up. "Sounds like a fun place."

"Yeah, it was fun chipping away at that fucking mountain of rocks while they beat us with truncheons or rifle butts." He coughed and spit a clump of phlegm and blood. "They knew they had turned into beasts and they tried to hide it from the Russians that were at their back door, so they shipped us out, cleaned out the whole camp."

David thought, just another German solution. Prisoners systematically starved, beaten and worked to death as a studied process of eradication.

Sully started to crawl by the sleeping men toward the front of the column. "Where the fuck are you going?" David whispered as Sully disappeared into the darkness.

David strained to keep his eyes open waiting for Sully to return. Suddenly Sully slid back besides David. He had a flying jacket that he had taken from the dead soldier the guard had kicked. He handed it to the man from Berga. "Here, put this on so you don't freeze to death. Maybe you won't smell so bad either." But the man who survived Berga no longer needed the jacket. He was very quiet and a little blood ran from his mouth down the side of his face. David touched his neck for a pulse and knew that his eyes were finally blind to the unbelievable horror that had been inflicted by his fellow man.

They started at sunrise in a cold fog that seeped into every bone of their exhausted bodies. There was still no water and only a piece of stale bread for each man standing. Those that still lie on the ground felt no hunger nor did their wounds torture them anymore. Many were curled up, knees to their chests, like sleeping children, and, indeed, they were so young most of them were not much more than children. Dead children. They were left there for the tank's treads, the Mongol's pleasure, and a feast for the buzzards. I hung on to Sully and we walked until the sun was high in the sky and the day grew warmer. I was so thirsty I would have drank my own piss.

Suddenly, an American P-51 came out of nowhere. The prisoners along with the Germans and the Mongols ran, stumbled, and crawled toward a drainage ditch at the side of the road. They fell on top of each other trying to get away from the deafening roar of the fighter's engines and the screaming barrage of lead from the P-51 swooping down on them like an angry bee, strafing the column, mistaking it for the enemy. Its six 20-mm cannons ripped up the ground behind them, the rounds tearing up the road until they found the bodies of the fleeing men and tore them to shreds.

The plane turned for a second pass and dropped one of its 500-pound bombs, ignoring the tank's 88 mm cannon pounding away, trying to blow it out of the sky. It scored a direct hit, leaving what was left of the tank crew engulfed in flames, screaming in agony, trying to scramble out of the burning tank. They were all dead before they hit the ground. The P-51 pulled up into a steep climb, banked, and disappeared as fast as it had arrived.

A big Mongol had fallen on top of David. Sticky red blood was dripping onto David's face. He pushed the man off of him, and as the Mongol rolled over his head turned with his body. There was a gaping hole through the middle of his face leaving his startled eyes staring and lower jaw open in a scream that would never be heard. David recoiled and pushed the lifeless body away, its jaw flapping as if to say something in protest. He climbed out of the pile of dead and wounded. He took a dirty handkerchief from his pocket, and tried to wipe the blood from his face, finally throwing it away in disgust. More prisoners and their guards seemed to be rising from the dead and moaning men lying in the ditch. Already flies were swarming over the torn, bleeding bodies, and the stench of death and feces was overpowering.

David looked around for a weapon, but a fat German guard approached him, his automatic weapon at the ready. David recognized him as one of the most brutal guards of the column. The guard took pleasure in beating almost any prisoner that looked up and met his eyes. He had kicked one of the prisoners to death, and then had picked up the beaten, emaciated body by his collar and had paraded him around the column, finally throwing him to the side of the road and pissing on him.

David lowered his eyes and extended his hands palms up, indicating that he was unarmed and submissive, but inside he was seething with rage. He thought that there would come a time when he would kill this sadistic son of a bitch. The guard shoved him toward an area where another German had rounded up four other prisoners who had miraculously survived the strafing. They looked like dirty scarecrows that had been misshapen by the wind. They leaned or bent in directions that would relieve them of the most pain from their various wounds and broken limbs. One of them was Sully.

It appeared that the remains of the column were being split up into groups of five or more prisoners each with two guards to continue to move them to a new camp. It was obvious that any large group would continue to attract the attention of the roaming P-51 fighters.

David limped over to Sully, who had insanely ignored the threats of the vicious guard to remain subdued and had taken a severe beating from him more than once during the march. Sully smiled with his broken lips and gave David a little salute of recognition. The brutal guard that the men had nicknamed Lardass gave Sully an icy look, mumbled something, and then indicated with his automatic weapon that the group was to start moving. The men groaned as they limped or were helped by a comrade to keep up the pace along the dusty road, while Lardass prodded them with the butt of his weapon. Sully remained at David's side, helping him when he stumbled, and supporting him when he could no longer bear the pain from his shattered leg. David loved the man.

"Fuck off, asshole," Sully said under his breath as he received a vicious thrust from the butt of Lardass's weapon.

"Don't be crazy," David whispered, as the guard gave Sully a sadistic smile that said, "I'll get to you later."

Sully looked at the guard and spat.

"Jesus, man, you're going to get yourself killed."

"Fuck him. He gets near enough to me I'll kill the son of a bitch."

Their throats were parched. They hadn't eaten and had had little water for days, but somehow they managed to walk about four miles until they came to a small, stone bridge that straddled a little brook. Lardass halted the exhausted men and motioned for the other guard to watch the prisoners while he walked down a path that led to the brook. When he returned, wiping his mouth with his sleeve, he nodded, indicating that the other guard should get a drink as well. The guard hesitated, said a few words to Lardass and looked at the prisoners, obviously asking if the prisoners could also drink at the brook. Lardass screamed at the little guard and slapped him.

Suddenly, Sully, crazed by thirst, bolted toward the brook. David watched in horror as Lardass intercepted him and hit him in the stomach with the butt of his weapon. Sully doubled over and fell to the ground. The guard started to kick him. Sully rolled into a fetal position trying to ward off the blows, but that only made Lardass kick him harder. Then, tired of kicking him, he took his weapon by the barrel and raised it over his head ready to smash it down on the semi-conscious body on the ground.

Something snapped in David's brain; he screamed at the guard, "No, no more!" He picked up a large stone, half ran, half stumbled to the fat guard, and slammed the heavy stone into his face. The surprised guard fell backward, and David landed on top of him, banging the stone again and again into the guard's face and head until it was a bloody pulp and David could no longer lift his arm. Sweat ran down his face and chest, and his breath came in heavy heaves, as he waited for the bullet to come from the other guard. Without looking up he said, "Go ahead, pull the fucking trigger, because I just don't give a shit anymore," but the bullet never came. Instead, the little German bent down and gently helped David to his feet. Then he touched the guard's bloody neck looking for a pulse. There was none. He stood up and looked down at the fat body and spat on it. "Schwein."

He waved his arm at the rest of the men to drink from the brook, and then kneeled down beside Sully and tried to comfort him. David followed the other men to the brook, but he didn't drink. Instead he took one of the prisoner's caps, filled it with water, and limped back up the hill to where Sully lay with the little German trying to help him.

"C'mon Sully, try to drink a little water."

Sully groaned. "I told you I'd beat the shit out of that cock sucker, didn't I?"

"Yeah you did a great job. He ain't never gonna bother you again." David wiped some of the blood off of Sully's face. "Think you're going to be able to walk?"

"Shit, man, are you kidding?" Sully tried to rise. He grimaced. "Hell, I could run the mile in…"

David interrupted him, "Yeah, yeah, but can you walk?"

Sully unsteadily got to his feet. He held his stomach and, through gritted teeth, he smiled. "I'll make it buddy, I'll make it."

David searched his mind for the Yiddish that he'd learned from his father and the German he'd studied in high school, and tried to thank the little German. Surprisingly, the German answered him in very accented, broken English.

"He was a pig. No one should treat another human being like that."

David nodded his head in agreement, and said in a combination of English, Yiddish and German, "Listen, you know that Germany is losing the war. Look, most of us are officers, and if you help us, we'll see that you and your family get special treatment." David reached into the bottom of his boot and took out a plastic bag that had special currency issued by the U.S. government. It was used by flyers that landed in enemy territory for bribes or whatever they needed to help them escape or evade capture. He handed the currency to the little German. "You can use this. You can use it to help get started after the war."

The German looked down at the money and pushed David's hand away. "I will help you, but not for money or promises that I know you could never keep. Go. Drink water with your comrades."

He wanted to press the German further but, with the promise of the fresh water, he turned and climbed down to the stream. He cupped his hands, filled them with the cold water and drank in great gulps until he could drink no more. When he climbed back from the stream he saw the German still standing over the dead guard. He limped over to him and looked down in horror at the broken, bloody face. He had killed a man and yet he had no remorse for killing the brutal bully. He looked away from the dead guard and turned to the little German.

"Why are you helping us?"

The German looked at David for a moment, his eyes brimming with tears. He lowered his head as if ashamed. His voice was choked with emotion. "So that I may atone for the terrible sins that my countrymen have committed, that I have committed. I was a teacher who knew better, knew the truth, and yet, I stood by and watched. A coward, too frightened to protest." He looked down at the fat guard, then back to David and said, "Well, this will be my protest, and may God forgive me for waiting so long."

The little German guard took charge of them. After weeks of evading roving bands of German soldiers looking for deserters, who refused to stand and fight for a cause that even they knew was futile, he took them to his home and hid them in the attic. His wife sent his daughters up to the attic with hot potato soup—the first real food they had had in weeks. He knew if he was caught his entire family would be murdered, so the next morning he hid them in the woods near his home. The six of them lay in the freezing German mountains, shivering in a shallow depression, the crusted ice base piercing their ragged clothing, torturing their undernourished bodies. They could see a tiny village below them. White sheets hanging from the windows of the abandoned stores and houses fluttered in the breeze in silent surrender. General Patton's tanks had rumbled through the cobblestone streets, demolishing everything: houses, fountains, barns, stores that unluckily lay in their path. They took no prisoners. The enemy was shot on sight in those few terrible minutes that it took the tanks to traverse the little town. German soldiers along with the villagers hid in the cellars and storage rooms while Patton, concerned only with beating the Russians to Berlin, thundered through.

The little German looked down on his broken village and talked about how he had seen Hitler drive through the little village while tears filled his eyes.

We couldn't stay where we were without freezing to death so we made a deal. We agreed that one of us would walk in front of our German benefactor, hands on head in surrender fashion. Then simply walk into the little town that Patton had torn through, giving the impression that the German had just captured an American flyer and was taking him in. We hoped that some remnants of Patton's charge through the town were left behind to keep control. If not, and if we were challenged, we agreed that his "prisoner" would make a break for it, to add authenticity, and the little guard would shoot; we hoped over the "prisoner's" head, maybe. We drew straws to see who would go. The only guy still in one piece drew the short straw. He was terrified. "I can't do it; I don't speak German. What if the fucking Nazis are still there? What if Patton just bombed through there and never took control. It's a goddamn death sentence."

David looked at him in disgust. He signaled to the German that he would go. He limped and stumbled down a dirt road that twisted and turned. The blood blisters burst and squished in his flying boot but his leg was so numb he could hardly feel it. They finally came to the cobblestone streets of the little town with the white sheets hanging from the empty windows in the few buildings that were still standing. The town was completely deserted. The sheets fluttering in the wind made the only sounds. Suddenly a bulkhead door swung open and three high-ranking German officers climbed out of their hiding place in the cellar. A dozen regular soldiers followed them. As agreed David tried to run. He heard the rattle of the Schmeisser blasting away, dove for the ground and waited for the bullets to rip through him, but they never did. The little German shot over his head. Once again he risked everything.

Someone was helping him to his feet. David looked up in disbelief to see that it was one of the German officers. What appeared to be the senior officer stepped forward, handed David his pistol and, in the worst English (but for David, the best he ever heard), he surrendered. David thought, he is surrendering to me, a filthy, bleeding, skinny, 2nd Lieutenant, who could barely stand up—why? Then he got it. Would they rather surrender to Patton, or me? The little German handed over his Schmeisser while the officers and the soldiers put their hands over their heads in total surrender. Their discarded weapons, rifles, pistols and fancy daggers lay in a pile at their feet. David, overwhelmed, wondered what to do next when, all of a sudden, he heard a rumbling noise. It was a British half-track with a mounted .50-caliber machine gun. There were three Brits in it. David yelled out that he was a Yank, an American officer. They were cautious and perhaps frightened when they saw the Germans, so they hung back and manned the .50 caliber. David guessed they were pretty suspicious, so he yelled, "Hey, these guys have all surrendered. C'mon over and help yourselves to some of these guns." Christ, a Luger was worth thirty-five bucks, and here was a whole pile of them. That got their attention. Two of them, weapons at the ready, started walking toward David and finally got close enough to shake hands.

David thought about how he was going to talk them into going back to get the guys hiding in the woods? He knew they'd never go for it, so he sauntered over to the half-track while they rummaged through the surrendered guns and daggers. The little German shadowed him; he wasn't going let David out of his sight. He felt that David was his protector now. David walked over to the half-track, feigned interest, and sat beside the driver. He asked about operating the half-track. The driver looked nervous and suspicious. David gave the driver a reassuring smile to try to keep him calm. "Listen I gotta get back in there and get my buddies out. You know one of them is one of yours, a Spitfire pilot." At the same time David lowered the Schmeisser so that it was pointing at the driver's crotch. "What d'ya say we could pick my guys up and be in and out of there in twenty minutes?"

"No way, mate; we're mail carriers, noncombatants. No fucking way." He was sweating so bad that David could actually smell it.

David poked the Schmeisser into the driver's balls. "Oh, we're gonna get my buddies out, oh yeah, or you're going to be talking with a very high voice or maybe not at all."

The driver tried to push the Schmeisser away. "Hey, cut the shit. Are you bloody nuts or something?"

David's face turned to stone and his eyes took on a murderous look. "Look you yellow bastard; I couldn't give a shit less. You start moving or I'll blow your fucking balls off and drive this fucker myself. So, fucking move it! Understand? Move it!"

The driver bitched and moaned and called David every name in the book, but he put the half-track in gear and got moving. His buddies started to jump up and down, waving their arms and screaming, but David gave them the finger and they drove into the forest keeping their heads low. The big half-track rolled onto a dirt road, the same road the little German and David had traversed only a few hours ago. On both sides of the road there were huge pines, their branches still heavy with snow that shrouded the road. There was nothing to see but the trees on either side. The half-track's engine obliterated any sound. It was eerie. The road was steep and heavily rutted, so it was pretty slow going. The limey driver kept looking left and right, waiting for the enemy to start shooting. He was sweating bullets even though it was freezing out. David kept the Schmeisser at his side but he manned the .50 caliber, looking for a familiar landmark and at the same time any movement from the side of the road. He had never thought about landmarks when he stumbled down the big hill holding his hands over his head in surrender fashion. *Shit*, he thought, *I didn't think I was coming back or, for that matter, living long enough to even get to the town below.* He kept looking but he couldn't find the spot where they had cut out of the woods onto the rutted road. He started to panic. *What if I can't find them?* Suddenly there was a burst of gunfire. Snow fell from the branches of the pines and bullets pinged off of the half-track. The limey driver instinctively ducked and momentarily lost control of the half-track. David was thrown to the floor. A barrage of machine-gun fire whizzed over his head. A grenade exploded in front of them. David got to his feet, grabbed the .50 caliber and fired in the direction of the attack. A second barrage of fire came from the other side of the road and he swiveled the gun toward the new attack. Another grenade exploded. Shrapnel peppered the half-track but the armored sides protected them. The limey was screaming. "You bloody fool! You're going to get us killed! I'm going back!" Suddenly he started to turn. David screamed at him. "Wait! This is the turn off. That's it, the tree, the one that's split in two."

The limey ignored him. "Bugger off, I'm going back."

Another burst of gunfire shattered the windshield, cutting the limey on the cheek. He put his hand to his face and stared at the blood on his fingers. It was only a superficial wound, but he started to scream. "Holy mother of God." He continued to turn the half-track around on the narrow dirt road. David picked up the Schmeisser, charged it, fired over the driver's head and then jammed it against the back of his neck. "Turn at the split tree and shut your fucking mouth, or as God is my judge, I'll kill you right here, right now." The driver had no doubts that David meant what he said and turned at the split tree. He had wet his pants.

When the men left behind saw the half-track, they started to cry. The little German jumped off and started to help some of them into the half-track. It took some doing, because they were so weak from their wounds, hunger and dehydration that it took every bit of strength that the German and David had. The fucking limey was so terrified he couldn't move; he just sat there sweating and trembling. The men were laughing and crying all at the same time. Sully, still under his own power, started toward David with the biggest smile and open arms. David thought he saw something move in the brush. Snow fell from a pine branch. He yelled at Sully, "Get down, get down!" Sully just kept on coming. He was almost in David's arms when the bullets tore into his back—the bullets that were meant for David.

Sully dropped at David's feet. David knew that he should hit the ground but he went crazy. He grabbed the Schmeisser and limped, stumbled, into the woods toward where the firing was coming. There were five of them. They never knew what hit them. He killed all five but even as they fell dying or dead into the blood-stained snow David kept firing. Killing them once just didn't seem to be enough.

When he got back to the half-track he saw that the Spitfire pilot had been wounded in the leg but, like a good Brit, he kept a stiff upper lip, and even helped get Sully's body into the half-track. David cradled him in his arms as his tears fell on Sully's lifeless face. David was not about to leave his friend behind.

David told the driver to get back to the road. He didn't need any urging and he took off like a kid in a hot rod.

They got back to the Brits and the Germans without another shot being fired. More Germans must have come out of the cellars, because there were twice as many of them. The Brits were screaming all kind of obscenities and threats. David just smiled, gave them back their damn half-track and watched them drive away.

They started up the big autobahn highway, the Germans with their hands on their heads. Sully's body, the little German, and David rode in a donkey cart that they found abandoned on the side of the road. They finally ran into an infantry cleanup patrol from the 101st who took them back to headquarters for debriefing.

They rounded up all the Jerries, including the little German. David tried to protect him. Tried to explain to the MP captain. "Hey this guy saved my life. Hold it…" He wanted to save him, to help him, but no way. The MPs dragged him off with the rest of the prisoners. They pushed him and pulled him toward the compound, but he broke away and ran toward David screaming something in German that David couldn't make out.

"Halt! Halt!" One of the GIs yelled as he raised his rifle and took aim.

David screamed, "Stop; wait!" But it was too late. The little German got two slugs in the back.

David sat down beside him, took him in his arms and held him like a child. "I'm sorry. I'm sorry, my friend," David said as he rocked him back and forth. David could see the life slowly fading from his eyes. He was trying to say something, but David couldn't hear him. He could only see the little German's eyes searching his face, asking why.

David's mind shut down. He remembered being interrogated but had no idea what he was asked or what information he had been able to supply. Now he was lying on a stretcher in an evacuation hospital with no recollection as to how he got there. The sound of the rain pounding on the tin roof of the Nissen huts that made up the hospital, mixed with the screams of a soldier in another stretcher. David brought his hands to his ears but he still heard the screaming. "Who stole my fucking boots?" Another voice snuck through his hands, "He won't need them jump boots anymore. They took off both of his legs." David thought about his own leg and started to cry, not for his own leg, nor the smell of the gangrene that was eating it, but for Sully and the little German and…The rest was a blur, the operating table, the air evacuation to a hospital somewhere in England to see if they could save his leg. The crumpled letter that told him his father had died before he had even opened it. The nightmares that terrified him nightly. Charlie. Charlie was dead but… Well, he wasn't going to think about that. He couldn't think about Charlie. Something happened but what was it? Why did Charlie haunt him, visit him in his worst nightmares?

David stopped responding, stopped talking, stopped caring, bordering on madness. They were all trying to help him, especially Mac the male nurse, but no one could help him. They saved his leg but no one could save him from the terror that visited him while he slept.

"Time to go home, Lieutenant," Mac said with a big smile. "You'll get more therapy there, wherever "there" is. It says on your orders Mitchell Field Convalescent Hospital in Long Island. When they get done with you you'll probably be as good as new. Jesus, man you're going home. You should be whooping for joy." David's face was blank.

David watched from the little widow beside his stretcher as the hospital plane flew by the Statue of Liberty. He touched the window with his hand as if to caress her while the tears rolled down his face. He was home and he knew if he was to see Jessie again his inner revolt had to end. He had to pull himself together. Work hard. Get better. Somehow he would do it. But then, there were the nightmares.

Therapy helped him to regain the strength in his leg so that he could walk, albeit with a distinct limp, but did little to alleviate the pain. The thought of being only a few hundred miles from Jessie and seeing her again was the only thing that allowed him to keep his sanity. He began to shower, comb his hair, what was left of it, cut his fingernails and toenails, shave daily. Most of all he tried not to limp and to stand up straight. He worried what Jessie would think, worried about his appearance, afraid that that she might reject him. He hadn't written to her. She would have no idea that he was even alive or the way he looked now; the limp, the scar across his eye, his trembling hands. He would write to her, give her a bit of a warning.

BOOK THREE

HOME

Chapter One

September 1945

After three months of therapy and psychological evaluation, it was time for David to be discharged from the army rehab center. He had a bus ticket to Boston and he knew it would be an uncomfortable ride with his aching leg, but he was going home. He was going to see his family and Jesse. Part of him was frightened to death. The other part of him was thrilled.

Doctor Sullivan dropped in to say good-bye. "I'm sorry, Lieutenant, but there's not much more we can do for you here. I think you'll be able to get rid of those crutches in another couple of months, providing you keep up with your exercises, but I'm afraid you're going to be stuck with the limp. That's just not going to go away." The army doctor chewed on his lip for a moment and then anticipated David's question. "The pain? Well, you may have to learn to live with it." He looked at David sympathetically. "I know that sounds harsh, son, but you're still one of the lucky ones. You've got a ninety day prisoner-of-war leave before discharge and you're walking out of here. You understand, don't you?"

"Yes sir, I understand." *Yeah, I understand I'm going to be a fucking cripple for the rest of my life, and, just in case I forget, I'll have this aching leg to remind me. Well, tough shit. I'll live with it. One way or the other I'll make it. Hell, I'm alive and no one is trying to kill me. I'm back. What else really matters?*

The doctor patted him on the shoulder, handed him an envelope with his orders, and a voucher for transportation home.

"Good luck, son," the doctor said, extending his hand. "And don't forget there's always the Veterans Administration. Check in with them as soon as you can and get that therapy started for the leg and, maybe, get some help with your sleep problem.

Sleep problem. You mean nightmares. Fucking nightmares. Charlie. Charlie in the fire. What happened? Why can't I remember?

"Thank you, sir." David shook the doctor's hand, and began to think about home, and that the next bus for Boston wasn't scheduled to leave until the following morning. David hesitantly touched the scar that ran through his eyelid, and then felt the crooked line of his broken nose.

What will Jessie think when she sees me like this? Maybe I should wait. It might be too soon. It was futile; he knew he couldn't wait. He couldn't even wait for the morning bus. He decided to hitchhike home.

Leaning on his crutches, he waited patiently in front of the hospital for a ride. It was a secondary road with little traffic, yet he had hardly raised his thumb when a big Buick stopped.

"Hop in, Lieutenant."

"Thanks," David said, as he pushed his crutches into the back seat ahead of him and smiled at the elderly lady next to the man with gray hair driving the car.

"Where you heading?"

"Boston."

"Well, we can get you as far as Worcester."

"That would be great. "

"What did you fly?" The driver asked, noticing the silver wings on David's battle jacket.

"B-17s."

The man glanced at his wife in the passenger seat. "Our boy's in the Marines. Getting out next Monday."

"He's okay?" Somehow David felt it would be unusual for anyone to come home unscathed.

"Oh, yeah. Thank God. He was one of the lucky ones."

They finally reached Worcester, but the Buick didn't stop; it just kept on going toward Boston.

David rang the bell to Jessie's family's apartment just as he had when he was a little boy, waiting for her mother to come to the door, so that he could ask if Jessie could come out and play. Many times he had run away before her mother answered the bell. He felt like running away now, but it was too late. Jessie opened the door. Her eyes opened wide and she put her hand to her mouth as if to stifle a scream.

"David," Jessie threw herself into his arms.

"Oh, Jessie, my Jessie." David kissed her lips and her cheeks that were soaked with tears of joy. Jessie held him tight to her breasts, and then pushed him back to get a good look at him.

David had written to her about the hospital, the treatment he was receiving and joked about his broken nose and skinny body. She took in a deep breath. This was worse than she had expected.

"Pretty bad, huh?" David asked, reading her face.

"Well, you don't look like Clark Gable, but you look pretty good to me." Yes, he looked like hell, and that's probably where he came from, but this was still David the man she prayed for every night. The man she loved. The man she was going to marry.

"My hair will grow back and I'll gain weight. I'm eating like a horse," David apologized. "I know I look like hell, but…"

"David, David, poor David?" She touched his face and gently traced the scar over his eye, ending with her hand resting lightly on his cheek. "I love you, don't you understand? I love David Livingston the man. I couldn't care less if he looks like Charlie Chaplin or Popeye the Sailor." Jessie took David in her arms again. She could feel the little sobs that wracked David's chest as he cried for joy.

Chapter Two

November 1945

"What do you mean you're going to get married? You're going to marry a cripple? Listen to me. I'm your mother," Rose said her face turning red. "You're a beautiful girl. You're smart. There are plenty of boys now that the war is over. You can do better. I…I won't permit it."

They were in the kitchen and her mother stood in front of the stove fussing over dinner. The smells from the roasting chicken filled the room.

Jessie sat down at the kitchen table. "Ma, don't you understand? I love him."

Rose tasted the soup with a wooden spoon, added a pinch of salt and then turned to face Jessie. "You love him! What do you know? He's only been home for a month. Sure he's a big hero, a fancy uniform with silver wings and lots of medals, so what? That's going to make him a good husband? That's going to make a good marriage?"

"For God's sake, Ma! I grew up next door to him. I've known him almost all my life. He was my first date, my first kiss, he…"

"Never mind, he was only a kid then. He's been gone for four years. Who is he now? He doesn't have an education; he doesn't have a job. How's he going to support you?"

Jessie stood up; the chair made a squeaking sound as it was pushed back. *Dammit*, she thought, *why can't she understand? After all, I love David, isn't that enough? The rest will take care of itself, won't it?*

"I don't care. I love him and he loves me. His friend, Melvin, is going to give him a job, and he's going to go to school on the GI Bill. C'mon, Ma, we're going to be okay."

Rose walked over to Jessie, put her hands on her arms and said, as gently as she could, "Listen, honey, you know I want you to be happy, and I only want the best for you. I want you to marry a man who can support you now…a college grad with a career who can give you a good life. I…"

Jessie pulled away from her mother, her face flushed. "Can't you understand there's no college grad with a career out there, they're all 4Fs. They couldn't get into the service because there was something wrong with them!"

"Something wrong with them?" her mother interrupted and banged the pot cover on the soup pot for emphasis, "For God's sake…he's better? A cripple?"

"Stop it! He went through hell for his country, for us."

Chastised, Rose changed to a softer tone. "Listen, your father always made a living; even during the Depression we always had food on the table. We were always warm and had a roof over our heads. I'm not complaining but I want more for you. I want you to have better. You're not going to marry that boy!"

Jessie stood up and, without another word, went to her room. Rose threw up her hands and then let them drop with a long sigh. She tasted the soup again and absently started to set the table, finally slumping onto one of the kitchen chairs. She sat for a while, mulling over her thoughts. Then, defeated, she sighed, and started thinking about where she could hire a hall and a caterer for Jessie's wedding.

Jessie knew that her mother didn't want her to repeat the same mistakes that she had made. Although her mother made the best of it, she had married a man who spent ten hours a day, six days a week, working as a shoemaker. A man who slept most of the day on Sunday, and when he did find time to be with the family, was usually irritable and cranky. Jessie understood her mother's anxiety, and at the same time felt sorry for her father. She knew that in his own way he loved her mother and loved her, and realized that he worked the long hours to support the family. What made Jessie both angry and sad was that she had never had a chance to get to know him.

David would be different. He was smart and ambitious. He would be a loving husband and father. He would play with their children, spend time with them, and they would know that they had a father.

She picked up David's picture from her dresser. His dark eyes stared back at her. She traced his square jaw with her fingertips and smiled at the little dimple in the center of his chin. He had been a handsome man then, with a strong, straight nose and chiseled features. He was wearing his cadet uniform, which accentuated his broad shoulders. He looked so damn healthy, so strong, pulsing with an incredible energy.

God, he looks so awful now. Poor David. She shivered, as she thought about his eyes, sunken with black circles surrounding them, testimony to the hell they'd seen. Then there was his broken nose and the terrible scar that ran through his right eyelid. She thought about his hard body that her hands and lips had once caressed and knew it was no more. God, his hands shook so much it was a wonder he could get food to his mouth.

She remembered her first date with David and how determined he was to succeed and be more than his father. Oh, that first date; she had fallen head over heals for him. She leaned back on the bed, closed her eyes and thought about that time, long ago, that seemed like yesterday.

It was Sunday morning. Jessie's mother's shrill voice overpowered the music. "Jessie, turn that radio off. You are supposed to be doing your homework not listening to that jigger bug junk."

"Jitterbug, Ma, and it's not junk; it's Benny Goodman and—"

"We interrupt this broadcast for a special news bulletin." The announcer's solemn voice crackled over the radio. "The Japanese have bombed Pearl Harbor. President Roosevelt…"

Rose clasped her hand to her breast. "Oh, my God!" She started to sob. Jessie ran into her arms.

Jessie thought that perhaps she should cry, but she didn't feel like crying. She was excited. Somehow she knew her world was about to change.

People were different now; even though most carried on with their lives as usual, there was a mysterious energy that prevailed. Everyone talked about the war, the draft. The older boys were joining the Army, the Navy and the Marines. School didn't seem important. They were all caught up with the war. Things were changing fast. It was as if she had suddenly grown up. She felt more assertive. She was going out on a date and that was that.

"She's just going to the movies with the girls," her mother had lied to her father as Jessie left the house to meet David at the corner of the street. David was waiting for her in Max Goldman's car and Max had brought Jessie's girlfriend, Betty. The car was a '34 Oldsmobile and had a rumble seat. It had a dent that was rusting away the left front fender and dark, smoky fumes spewed out of its rusted exhaust pipe. David helped Jessie into the rumble seat and they drove away, exhilarated and excited with the wind in their faces, Jessie's dark hair blowing behind her.

They went to a drive-in movie. David put his arm around Jessie's shoulder and she moved closer to him. He looked straight ahead, as she did, seemingly engrossed in the movie, but somehow their hands found each other in the dark. She turned and whispered to David, "This is nice," and David squeezed her hand in response. After the movie they headed for Howard Johnson on the Charles for an ice cream, where anyone between sixteen and twenty-one just had to be seen. Then, on Max's insistence and Betty's acquiescence, they went parking. They drove into the Blue Hills, and stopped in one of the many isolated areas where hikers parked their cars in the day, and lovers found privacy in the dark of the night. Max and Betty were doing some heavy petting in the front seat, punctuated with a lot of giggles and a few theatrical moans. Jessie always thought that Betty was a little fast. She was envious of her easygoing ways. Her mop of short curly hair always seemed to be in motion. She had huge brown eyes, rosebud lips and a pug nose covered with freckles. She was always making fun of Jessie, yet Jessie loved her like a sister. What she saw in Max she could never understand. Maybe it was because she could always boss him around.

Max was a giant of a man. Big and tall and seemingly fit, but within the healthy façade was a very bad heart. Still, Max played high school football with David and was an iron wall as a linebacker for the team. Max never discussed his health problem, not even with David, who was his closest friend. He was crazy in love with Betty and hoped to marry her as soon as he finished accounting school at Bryant and got a job. That is, if she would have him...

David was three years older than Jessie and she was a little in awe of him. She thought, *My father would kill me if he knew I was out on a date, especially with a boy that much older than I. Well, he'll just have to understand. I'm 16 years old and certainly old enough to take care of myself. Darn it, he just has to realize I'm grown up now. I'm going to go to college somehow, and live in my own apartment. I'm just not going to be his little girl anymore.* David interrupted her thoughts and whispered, "How 'bout we leave these two lovebirds to whatever they're up to and take a walk?"

The air was sweet with the smell of pine and the moon gave enough light for them to see a little dirt path. They walked in silence for a while and then David said, "I'm going to try to get into the Aviation Cadet Program before they draft me." He turned, faced her and put his arms around her waist.

She looked up at him a little in awe. "Really?"

"If they accept me. They don't take everyone."

"What about your dad?"

"Well, he's, he's okay with it. Besides there's the draft."

She was just getting to know him. Her head was full of the thought of him in war. "Why don't you wait, maybe they won't take you right away." She didn't say, besides I've kinda just found you even though you've been next door almost all my life.

He broke off a dead twig and tossed it away, turned to face her. "You don't understand; I want to go."

"I know but…"

"It will give me a chance to be something. I don't want to be a tailor like my father."

"You could go to school, get deferred."

He ignored the suggestion. "I'll learn to fly, maybe be an airline pilot after the war or go to college. My father could never afford to send me to college. Don't you see? This is my chance."

"But what if something…I mean you could get… killed."

"Aw, I won't get killed; maybe I'll kill some of those bastards instead—oops, sorry. I didn't mean to swear."

She looked down, not willing to meet his eyes. "And will you write to me, or will you be too busy chasing all the pretty girls away from that fancy uniform?"

"I didn't think you cared," he joked, and smiled as she pushed him away from her.

She looked up at him, paused for a moment and said in a serious voice, "You know, David, I've always had a crush on you."

He kicked a stone in the path and looked into Jessie's eyes. "Well, I guess I've had the same kind of feelings for you, ever since we moved next door."

She looked down, blushing. "You never said anything."

"I wanted to, even when we were little kids. I really wanted to, but I was too embarrassed."

"Well, it's not too late."

She moved closer and lifted her head in anticipation of being kissed and thought, *It's okay to kiss even though it was a first date because, after all, I've known him for such a long time. And look at Betty, doing who knows what with Max in the front seat of the car. Well, maybe she's right, who made up the rule that you never kiss on the first date anyway?*

David leaned over, hesitated a moment, and finally kissed her. His lips barely touched hers. He stepped back and looked at her for what seemed like forever. "I've wanted to do that as far back as I can remember." Then he took her in his arms and held her very tight and she wished she could stay there forever.

She looked at David's picture again. Did she really know this man with the brooding eyes? Where did he go when he stared into the distance, and his brow furrowed and his lips went tight as if he were in pain? What or who was buried in the deepest recesses of his mind, and would those ghosts haunt their marriage, perhaps even destroy it? Did she really know what she was doing; making a commitment for life with a man she really didn't know anymore?

Chapter Three

December 1945

Temple Beth Elam was built sometime in the late 1800's, but it was well preserved. The old varnished wood interior glowed in the candlelight and contrasted with the white roses that lined the aisle.

Jessie wore a simple white gown with a high collar that accentuated her long neck and the white gloves her mother had worn to her own wedding, twenty-four years before. She had a crown of little white flowers attached to a short veil and carried a bouquet of the same tiny flowers that adorned her head.

Rose stood at the altar in a pink lace gown, and watched her husband, smiling and proud in his rented tuxedo, walk Jessie down the aisle. "She's throwing her life away," Rose muttered stubbornly. Then she recanted and whispered, "Please, God, just let them be happy."

"I've never seen her look more beautiful," Betty whispered, as Jessie glided down the aisle. Betty's bridesmaid's gown was an emerald green, and Jessie had picked it because it was a perfect color to set off Betty's flaming red hair.

The brass buttons and silver wings on David's uniform glistened in the candlelight as he waited at the altar with Max Goldman, his best man and now, Betty's husband. This was the day he had dreamed about, but for a moment he felt alone, isolated from all about him. He wished his father could be beside him. *Papa, can you see me? If only you could be here.*

Jessie reached the altar and faced David. She took David's hand and smiled radiantly. David smiled back and mouthed, "I love you." The rabbi looked at each of them solemnly and finally spoke, "Be not like the oak, but rather like the reed." He paused and smiled. "When the storm comes, the mighty oak falls but the reed bends, and when the storm is over, the reed stands again while the oak lies broken on the ground." The rabbi paused for effect and then invoked a blessing in Hebrew.

David's mind wandered; he knew how lucky he was to be here, alive. Half his squadron was destroyed. All those wonderful men that would never come home, never see their families, get married, or have children. Poor bastards. A wave of guilt ran through him. For a moment he was with the crew, joking with them. An involuntary chill ran through his body. *Charlie's smoldering eyes were pleading with him. He...The plane's gonna blow. Got to get out.*

He trembled with the remnants of his memory still hiding in his thoughts as the rabbi leaned over and placed a glass wrapped in a white cloth in front of David's feet. The rabbi looked at David. "The breaking of the glass at the end of a wedding ceremony is an ancient Jewish tradition and serves to remind us of two very important aspects of a marriage. The bride and groom and everyone else should consider these marriage vows as an irrevocable act, just as permanent and final, as the breaking of this glass is unchangeable. But the breaking of the glass is also a warning of the frailty of a marriage. That sometimes a single thoughtless act, breach of trust, or infidelity can damage a marriage in ways that are very difficult to undo, just as it would be difficult to undo the shattered glass that lies at your feet. Do you understand this, David?"

David nodded his assent, raised his right foot and stomped on the glass. Simultaneously the guests cried out, "Mazel Tov!"

David took Jessie in his arms and leaned forward to kiss her. He looked into her eyes, thinking that this was the reality of the dream that had kept him alive. He'd crawled past death's door to be here with this one woman and now she was in his arms. *I promise I will always love you. Make you proud of me.*

He lifted her veil. Her eyes held so much trust. David kissed her and then held her close; frightened that if he released her she would disappear, and he would be lying on

116

the cold ground again with only the memory of her, praying the sun would never rise on another day of terror. He broke their embrace, but still kept his arm around her as if he was afraid she would still vanish, and led her into the party.

The accordionist played "Hava N'gilah," accompanied by joyous yelling, singing and dancing. Max and three other of the biggest men carried Jessie, sitting in a chair held high above their heads, and danced around the room with her. Jessie held on to the chair, terrified, screaming, laughing, and crying all at the same time. The guests laughed and cried with her.

David limped over to the men carrying Jessie. "Hey, be careful. That's precious cargo and besides I want to dance with her."

The men holding her shuffled away from David, teasing him. "Oh, no. Sorry you can't have her."

"Well, if you're going to keep her you'll have to support her." David smiled and edged closer.

"In that case, we'll just have to give her back to you," and the men set her down into David's outstretched arms. Jessie, flushed with excitement, threw her arms around David. "Are you really going to dance with me? Will you be okay? I don't want you to hurt your…"

David shushed her, took her in his arms and slowly, very slowly, started to dance. Jessie looked up at David and asked, "Does it hurt? I mean should we…?" David smiled, leaned closer to her and whispered, "Nothing hurts when I'm with you." He found her lips and kissed her, a long, lingering kiss, while the crowd that surrounded them went wild with shouts of approval and applause.

Yet for all the merriment there was, like the cigarette smoke that drifted in the shadows, a deep sadness that hung in the air between the shouts and the music. Between every lively beat, David could hear a quiet echo of the boys who weren't there, who would never come home. He wondered why he was spared. Why he wasn't lying in a shallow grave beside them, and guilt spread through him like the venom from a poisonous snake.

Chapter Four

January 1946

David breathed a sigh of relief when he saw that the snowplows hadn't buried his truck with the new snow that now covered the road. There was no time to shovel the damn thing out. Hopefully it would start. He'd practically spent his last dime buying it, and the last thing he needed was another repair bill. He looked at his watch. *Dammit. I'm going to be late for my meeting.*

David hoped Melvin would help him get a job at Eastern Oil, and he didn't want to get off to a bad start by being late. It was Melvin's father's company, but Melvin boasted that he really ran the show. Typically Melvin Bass.

As he drove to Eastern's offices, his thoughts drifted back to high school, and his first encounter with Melvin. He remembered that although Melvin was small for his age, he made up for his lack of size with his arrogance, and trouble followed him like a pack of angry dogs.

"What did ya call me, you Irish cocksucker?" Melvin snarled at the two boys harassing him.

"You little Jew prick, that's what I called you."

"Ya, well fuck you," Melvin said as he rushed the bigger boy, fists flying.

David rushed to Melvin's rescue. "Break it up. Break it up." He grabbed the bigger boy, who was now on top of Melvin swinging with both fists. "C'mon asshole, get off him. For Christ's sake you're twice as big as he is."

The bigger boy struggled with David, finally shook loose, and looked at David with uncontrolled hatred. "Fuckin' big deal quarterback, aren't ya. Well you're still just another dirty Jew, like your buddy there." The boy stared defiantly at Melvin, who was holding a handkerchief up to his bloody nose.

"And you're just an ignorant asshole." David whacked the boy on the back of his head with his open hand as the boy turned to leave.

David squatted beside Melvin. "You're gonna get yourself killed one of these days, kid."

"Yeah, well, no one's gonna call me a dirty Jew and get away with it."

"Hmm, I can see that," David said, looking at the blood still seeping from Melvin's nose. "You're a real killer."

Melvin couldn't help but laugh. "Well, thanks for helping me, anyway. How come they don't pick on you?"

David glared at the circle of onlookers who, just moments ago, were yelling, "Fight! Fight! Kill the bastard." David stared at them until they dropped their eyes, and then, he said, "'Cause they know they'll get the shit kicked out of them. Besides, I'm not as touchy as you."

"Why not? You're a Jew, aren't you?" Melvin asked as he explored the cut over his right eye.

David helped Melvin to his feet, and said loud enough for the crowd to hear him, "Yeah, I'm a Jew. And I'm the best quarterback this fucking school ever had. And I'm at the top of my class. And I don't have anything to prove, because, hands down, I'm better than any one of them. And they know it."

"So, what are you, his bodyguard? Why don't you let him fight his own battles? He's got a big enough mouth. Why don't you let him back it up?"

David looked at the two big boys still ready to tear Melvin apart. "Well, I'm afraid he'd kill ya, that's why."

"C'mon David, you're different than you are on the team. Stop standing up for that little shit."

"I will when you pick on him one at a time, and you aren't twice as big as he is. Then I won't have to stick up for him 'cause he'll kick the shit out of you. So, just get lost before you get hurt. Okay?"

When David entered Melvin's office, Melvin jumped up from his executive chair, and grabbed David's hand as if he were a long lost brother.

Melvin had slick black hair, combed back tightly; deep-set, black, brooding eyes, surrounded with dark shadows; and a strong Roman nose. He looked a little sinister until his ample lips parted, revealing perfect white teeth, and, occasionally, a disarming smile. High blood pressure had kept him out of the service, and stylish clothes had taken the place of a uniform. Today he was wearing a blue blazer, a white shirt with a striped blue and silver tie, and gray slacks.

"Well, you don't look so bad," Melvin lied.

"You should see the other guy."

"It's great to have you back. I mean it."

"I'm not sure I'm back yet."

Melvin crinkled his brow, a little confused. "Yeah, you've got to get out of those GI clothes."

David smiled, thinking how people thought the difference between a soldier and a civilian was a damn uniform. How could they know what a uniform stood for? How could they know of the sweat that stained it, the months of training, the years of fighting in it, the blood that seeped through it, and the guys who were buried in it? He stared into Melvin's eyes until Melvin looked down at his desk, uncomfortably shuffling some papers around.

"I need a job."

Melvin felt secure again. "Well, you came to the right guy."

"You know, I don't want to take advantage of…"

"Are you kidding? Don't even think about it."

"Are you sure you…?"

"Listen, you got a job here, whenever you're ready."

David didn't expect such a quick response. "Well, I guess I'm ready now, but…" he hesitated. "But, what would I do?"

"Let me worry about that." Melvin was sick of looking at David in one uniform or another—the jock quarterback, the heroic soldier returned home. He couldn't help but relish being the one with the handout for David to reach up and accept. And, deep down, he couldn't help but picture David in a different uniform—the overalls of an Eastern Oil apprentice, caked with grease, laboring in some dank basement installing oil burners. He blinked the image away.

Eastern Oil was a large, independent oil company. It was a second-generation company, and, although old man Bass was semi-retired, he still controlled the purse strings and remained active. He was a stern-looking man with thin gray hair, small, steely gray eyes, and the sallow complexion of a man who spent most of his time indoors.

Melvin worked with his father but was constantly reminded that his father was the boss, and made all the final decisions. They were almost always at odds with each other. Melvin, always on the losing end and Mrs. Bass resigned to there never being any real truce between the two men. In spite of their problems, Eastern had grown, and was still growing far beyond its competitors.

When Mr. Bass was informed that Melvin had hired David, he thought it was a perfect time for an object lesson. He spotted Melvin working with one of the bookkeepers. He walked over to Melvin and confronted him. Melvin knew what was coming, and he involuntarily shrunk into himself waiting for the onslaught.

"Did we, or did we not, agree that hiring of any new personnel would first be cleared by me?"

Melvin looked around the busy office, and knew this was just another chance for his father to embarrass him. "Could we do this in your office, please?" he asked softly.

Sam ignored the question. He lit up a cigar while Melvin stood in front of him as he had many times as a frightened little boy. "We're running a business here, not a kindergarten." Sam took the cigar out of his mouth to see if he had lit it properly, and that he had a proper audience.

He gestured with the cigar at the other people in the office. "No one else in here breaks the rules."

Melvin fought to control the tears welling up in his eyes. Sam took a couple of puffs on his cigar, took it out of his mouth, and exhaled with a little cough. Melvin wished he'd choke. Sam coughed again, as if on cue, shook his head, had a last disgusted look at Melvin, and left him as if he were a condemned man.

There was nothing he could do to please his father no matter how hard he tried. He started toward his office. Every pair of eyes followed him to witness his shame. He sat down at his desk, and thought about how hard he had tried for his father's approval. It seemed he had spent a lifetime looking for one little act of affection or recognition, which had never come to be. Why? It was unnatural for a father to be so uncaring for his own son. Well, it didn't matter anymore. He was through taking shit from him. He no longer cared.

CHAPTER FIVE

MARCH 1946

Three months had passed, yet the demeaning job of cleaning boilers and chimneys that Melvin had selected for him didn't faze David, in fact, he thrived on it. He gained weight and his limp improved dramatically even if the pain still remained. He knew his job held promise, especially when Joe offered to teach him to be an oil burner serviceman.

Joe was Eastern's service manager, and he was fat. His stomach folded over his belt and the layers of fat under his chin wiggled as he spoke to David. "You really want to learn this business?"

"Well, I sure as shit don't want to vacuum chimneys for the rest of my life."

"Tell you what, you take my night service calls, and I'll teach ya, sort of like on-the-job training. What d'ya say?"

"Just like that. I take your calls. Hell, I don't know squat about fixing oil burners."

Joe gave David a fat smile. "Not to worry, I'll walk you through any problems by phone."

"Shit, I'll probably blow myself up."

"You won't blow anything up, and besides, I'm gonna keep you with me for a time so you can learn a little before you go it alone. You can watch me for a while, and then I'll let you handle the calls while I supervise you."

David knew Joe would get credit for the calls, and collect the overtime money, but he didn't care. He was just grateful for the opportunity.

Most of the calls were easy to repair. If he got stuck he knew he could call Joe, who would walk him through the necessary steps to make the repair. Joe would stay warm; David would learn the business.

It was one of those cold wintry nights in March when Joe called and sent David on a service call. The janitor was standing out in front of the small apartment building, rubbing his hands together, trying to keep them warm. His breath froze into little white puffs and blew away in the cold wind. "I am glad to see you, my man."

"Damn cold out tonight, isn't it?"

"Yep, sure is. Probably colder inside than out, I guess. C'mon I'll show you the way."

David followed him into the dank basement that smelled of oil and mold. A single light exposed forgotten boxes, a rusty bicycle, and more hiding in the shadows. A big boiler, covered with asbestos, stood in the dim light, cold and useless.

"We just got the tank filled last week so we're not out of oil," the janitor volunteered.

David tried to think about what he had observed the previous weeks working with Joe, but his mind was a blank. The janitor was watching for his first move and David was sweating. He brushed the cobwebs away and headed for the relay at the back of the boiler. A spider landed on his hand, and he shook it off. "Jesus, I hate spiders." He pushed the reset button on the relay box, but nothing happened. "Shit."

"What you say?" The janitor asked

"Talking to myself," David answered, thinking that he didn't want to call Joe on his first call. He'd have to figure out what was wrong on his own. *If the reset button didn't work, maybe…there's no power.* "Where's the fuse box?"

The rusty cover to the fuse box was jammed. David had to pry it open with a screwdriver.

"God bless you," he said to the black stain on the back of the blown fuse. He changed the fuse, went back to the relay, and pressed the recycle button again. He crossed his fingers and said a little prayer. The oil burner fired up.

It was a small victory, but David was thrilled that he had actually taken a service call and completed it successfully. He'd learn this business and grow with it. This was only the beginning.

With thousands of veterans returning to civilian life, housing was practically nonexistent. As a result Jessie and David moved into a spare bedroom in Jessie's parents' house. There was little or no privacy.

"Shush, they'll hear us," Jessie whispered.

"I thought we were married."

"Oh, David, you're impossible."

"I'm not impossible. I just want to make noisy love to my wife."

"I think you've made enough noisy love for a while."

"What does that mean?"

Jessie sat up in bed and set her jaw. "Well I…I'm pregnant."

"You're what?"

Tears ran down her face. "I knew you'd be angry. I was afraid to tell you."

David put his hands on her arms, pulled her close to him, and looked into her eyes. "We're going to have a baby?"

"Yes," Jessie sniffled.

"So why are you crying? This is wonderful. I'm going to be a daddy."

"You're not mad at me?"

"You silly girl," David pulled her closer into his arms. "I love you, don't you know that yet?"

Jessie looked sheepishly at David. "What will we do when the baby comes? I mean there's not enough room here."

"Well, I guess your parents will have to move out."

"Be serious."

David had already enrolled in night classes at Boston University, majoring in Business Administration. He decided to take advantage of the housing, such as it was, available to returning veterans through the G.I. Bill. He stood in the long line at the VA waiting to apply. *Hey,* he thought, *it's only a tin hut, but with all the G.I.'s getting discharged and apartments scarcer than new automobiles, we'd better do something or we'll have to live with her folks forever. Besides it's cheap and right now cheap is important, very important, especially when you're making forty bucks a week with a baby on the way.* He checked his watch every few minutes, worried he was taking too much time, and he'd have to explain to Melvin why he wasn't on the job. Finally he reached the bored clerk and submitted his application along with a copy of his discharge papers.

"You'll hear in about a week. Next," the clerk said without looking up. He acted like he owned the place and David was a beggar who had to be dispensed with.

Thanks, yeah, thanks a lot for the dazzling respect to our returning heroes. David limped back to the truck as fast as aching leg would take him wishing he'd punched out the arrogant clerk.

He hoped the office wasn't looking for him. It was almost lunch hour anyway. *Shit, I ought to be able to goof off once in a while,* he thought. *I'm up half the night working my ass off, aren't I?* He wanted to tell Jessie about the possibility of the new apartment. *What the hell, I have to pass the house on the way to the next call anyway.* He headed for home.

"Jessie, I'm home. Jessie? Where are you?"

"I'm in the bedroom. What are you doing home? You didn't get fired?"

David flopped on the bed, kicked off his shoes, put both hands behind his head, and smiled. "I signed up for an apartment in the veteran's project; you know the one in Franklin Field."

"You didn't."

"Yes I did. We can't live in a bedroom in your mother's house forever. We've got to get out of here. Be on our own."

"Don't I have anything to say about it?" Jessie asked, putting her hands on her hips, and looking at David defiantly.

"Aw, don't be like that. I thought you'd be happy. We could be by ourselves. Just the two of us."

"They're just a bunch of ugly tin huts. I thought we were going to find a real apartment."

"Are you kidding? If there was one, the landlord would be looking for two hundred bucks under the table. Where the hell would we get that kind of money?"

"What's wrong with living here for a little while longer? Maybe something will turn up."

"Nothing's going to just turn up." David felt deflated. He thought Jessie would be excited. They would finally be on their own. Really start their lives. Be independent.

"My mother will go crazy when she finds out."

"You're not married to your mother."

"Please don't start that again. We are very lucky they took us in."

David got off the bed and stood in front of Jessie. He put his arms around her waist and looked into her eyes. "Please, sweetheart, just trust me. It's only temporary. It's a step in the right direction." He bent over and kissed her.

"You always get your way," she pouted.

David's hands slid up her waist, and he started tickling her. She started laughing and then begged him to stop.

David kicked the door to the room shut, picked up Jessie and carried her to the bed, still giggling. David kissed her, and held her close to him.

"Careful, darling," Jessie said, pushing away from him.

David kissed her neck and slid his hand under her dress and up her thigh. Jessie gave him a peck on the lips, put her hand over his. "Not now honey, I'm so tired lately; you know with the baby and everything. I'll feel better tomorrow."

"Do you know how many tomorrows it's been?" David pulled away from her, reached for a package of cigarettes on the night table, slipped one out, and lit it.

"Please don't be angry, honey."

"I'm not angry, I'm frustrated."

"I'm sorry. It's only for a little while longer."

"Well, I gotta get back to work."

"You're mad at me," Jessie said, pouting.

"No, I'm not mad, forget it. I'm just being cranky."

"Promise you're not mad at me."

"I'm not mad at you. I'm not mad at you." He bent down and gave her a quick kiss.

"I gotta run. See you at dinner."

Outside, he took a heavy drag on his cigarette and then flipped it into the dirty snow still piled in the gutters. "Fucking cigarettes!" He got into the truck, started it up, and decided to drive over to the veteran's project to take a quick look.

He pulled onto one of the treeless streets, stopped, leaned back in the seat, and stared through the windshield at the lines of tin huts with multicolored laundry hanging from the laundry reels behind them, flapping in the cold breeze. A stray dog ambled through the weeds and the remains of the snow from the last storm. A woman nudged her back door open with her shoulder and spilled the water from a big icebox pan into the street. The dog waited for her to go back in and then began to lick at the wet ground, wagging his tail. "What a shithole."

David shifted into first, heading to his next call. It was a little after noon, and he was hungry. He decided to stop at Wollaston Beach on his way to the next call, have the sandwich and Coke Jessie had packed for him, and look at the water. *Hell of a life,* he mused.

Same old routine, day after day: Jessie pregnant and untouchable and he with the same old calls and dirty hands. He held up his hands to inspect them. Then he looked down at his ugly overalls and thought about his crisp military uniform hanging in the closet. How proud he had been to wear it. He raised his right hand as if to return a salute from an imaginary private and then let it drop back to the wheel of the truck.

Well at least no one's shooting at me. He took a swig of the Coke and watched a young girl walking along the shore. She had long legs. Her hair was black and shiny. She walked with long strides; little streams of freezing breath came out with each step. She wore a short jacket that emphasized her boyish figure and flat stomach. He thought about Jessie and his life. What was it really all about? Was his youth gone before it even started? He was about to bring a child into the world. Was he really ready for that? What happened to the dreams that kept him alive during the war, the perfect wife, the house full of kids, and the job that would make all of it possible? He looked at his grease-stained hands again. The war may have stolen his youth, but he'd be damned if it would keep him from his dream.

Of course there were the other dreams. The nightmares. Waking up in the middle of the night, soaking wet, trembling like a frightened child, a stifled scream just hiding in his throat. *Charlie. What was he trying to tell me? I have to get some help. I have to get some help. I'll call the Veteran's Administration tomorrow.*

CHAPTER SIX

MARCH 1946

Dark clouds, fat with freezing rain, rolled in from the sea. Dirty piles of ice and snow edged the sidewalk and the promise of spring, even in these last days of March, seemed elusive. David parked the red '39 Ford pickup illegally, got out and tried unsuccessfully to step over the slush coursing down the gutter. "Son of a bitch," he uttered, finally getting a foothold on the slippery sidewalk. He pulled the collar of his leather-flying jacket closer around his neck and cursed that he didn't have gloves. It was drizzling and a cold mist dampened his face. *Ah, springtime in Boston.* David was conscious of the people walking quickly by toward Scolly Square. He looked down, not wanting to meet the eyes of the passers-by, not ready to know these strangers yet, and limped toward the entrance of the Veteran's Administration. The revolving doors triggered the memory of his first visit to town with his mother.

He was just eight, and it was the Christmas season. They had come to town to see Santa. Even Jewish kids believed there was a Santa. A light snow dusted the sidewalks. The Salvation Army volunteers dressed in Santa suits were ringing their bells. Store windows glistened with bright reds and greens, and silver tinsel. David couldn't wait to push through Jordan's revolving doors, where Santa would be waiting for him. He tugged at his mother's hand, and she hurried with her characteristic little short steps, until they got to the revolving door. He rushed in first and pushed until he was out on the other side, but something was wrong. His mother was still in the door, and she had fallen. He couldn't get to her through the glass that imprisoned her. He screamed, "Ma, Ma." There were a lot of people now on both sides of her. Someone yelled, "Call an ambulance!"

People stopped to gawk.

"Poor woman, is that her little boy?"

"Did someone call an ambulance?"

"Give her some air. For Christ's sake step back."

A lady stopped and bent down with great effort through her corsets to comfort him. She smelled of very heavy perfume. She held him tight against her. He struggled to get away, when the door caging his mother spun loose, and her body spilled out at his feet. A man bent over her, checked for a pulse, looked up, and said solemnly, "She's gone."

David broke loose, and ran to his mother's side. "Mama, Mama! Open your eyes. Please open your eyes. Mama. Mama."

His eyes brimmed with tears now at the memory of his mother's death. *Was it his fault?* He brushed them roughly away with the side of his hand, and pushed through the swinging doors into the low mumbling drone of the VA and the present.

He limped through the smoke-filled lobby. It was crowded with veterans, some still wearing their uniforms, trying to resolve their veteran's benefits and their new lives as civilians. The easy banter that always accompanied these men, even in the worst of times, was gone. There was no longer an enemy, a clear-cut mission. They looked confused. They stood in long lines waiting for their turn. He knew waiting was nothing new. They had all spent their military lives waiting. Waiting in the mess line. Waiting in the supply line. Waiting for transport. Waiting for the enemy. Waiting to die. Now they were waiting for the various bits of information they needed to assimilate into their new lives as civilians.

He took the elevator and got off on the fourth floor. The place smelled of stale cigarette smoke, sweat, and disinfectant. He pulled off his coat and limped down the long shabby corridor past the many doctors' offices on each side until he came to a waiting room. It had a worn leather couch and some wooden chairs. Two other men about his age, still in uniform, sat there. One read a tattered magazine, and the other looked down vacantly at his shoes. He sat down on one of the hard wooden chairs, grateful to take the weight off his aching leg, and thought about how elated he had been when he first got home. The whole country was in love with the men who fought for America. Every soldier was treated like a hero. David smiled, remembering when he had first come home, still in uniform while waiting for his final discharge, and had taken Jessie to the movies.

They stood in the long line at the Metropolitan Theater to see *Conflict* with Humphrey Bogart and Sydney Greenstreet. There was a cold drizzle that threatened to turn to sleet. David's leg ached while he waited, leaning on his crutches.

"Lieutenant?"

David looked up.

The usher touched his arm. "You don't have to stand in line, sir," he said, and beckoned both of them to follow him.

"But we don't have tickets," David protested, but the usher led them to their seats.

"Enjoy the show, sir," the usher smiled and gave him a little salute.

But that was yesterday. The uniform with all the decorations and the silver wings was in mothballs. His old clothes from before the war, no longer in style, and now too small, had taken their place. Zoot suits with long jackets, tight pant cuffs, and baggy knees that filled the racks of the local haberdasheries were the new uniforms of the day. Not a hero anymore—that was over, just John Doe looking to survive in this new world, and trying to get his head straight. He felt lost. This was a place he didn't understand. These new civilians went doggedly to work each day, complained about their bosses and waited for their cherished weekends. In combat, he always knew where he stood. That world was simple. Staying alive was the priority, but now, as a civilian, the only goal was to make money at the expense of everything else. A fat bank account took the place of medals. He thought about the many times men had risked their lives for their buddies and how here, in this new life, they trampled their coworkers and friends alike, just to get ahead. *Well, I'm not going to fall into that trap,* he thought. *I'm not going to sell my soul for a fucking car or a fancy suit.* He looked down at his muddy army-issue shoes and shook his head, thinking how embarrassed he was that he couldn't afford to buy a new pair. He laughed at himself, thinking, *Well, maybe...I might sell...a little bit of something, if I could get a new pair of shoes.*

He looked for something to read. Anything to cover his embarrassment at being on the floor reserved for treating combat fatigue and other psychiatric problems. But, before he could reach for a rumpled newspaper on the stand beside him, he heard his name.

"David Livingston?"

Doctor Richard Sanders waited for one of the three men to acknowledge his greeting. David grunted a low "Here" and pushed himself out of his chair. Even though it was a little chilly in the corridor, David noticed that Sanders was sweating. David thought he was about 30 or 31. His hair was already receding, and he needed to lose thirty pounds.

Sanders wore horn-rimmed glasses and a rumpled dark gray suit. He had an easy gait and a pleasant smile. He reached out to shake David's hand, and let it hang there for a minute when David declined to take it. With the rejected hand he directed David toward one of the small offices. There was a scratched, olive-colored desk covered with yellow folders, and a green executive chair older than he was behind it. A hard wooden chair stood in front of the desk and David sat down on it facing Sanders.

"Cigarette?"

David's hand shook reaching for the cigarette and he was grateful when the doctor lit it for him. The damn tremor was embarrassing. The Army doctor had told him his tremendous weight loss might have affected his nervous system, but it would get better with time, maybe.

"Mind if I call you Dave?" Sanders asked.

"It's David." His voice cold, detached.

"I've been reading your record, David," Sanders took a drag of his cigarette. "Very impressive."

David looked down without answering

"Purple Heart, Distinguished Flying Cross. Air Medal, POW."

"So what does it buy me?" Jesus, to think it meant something then, what a bunch of bullshit, he thought, moving his leg to try to make the ache go away. Nothing helped; it just ached.

"It doesn't buy you anything, David, but it's still a good record."

There were a few moments of silence while both men smoked. Sanders took out his handkerchief and wiped his brow. He thought that in spite of David's broken nose and scarred eye, he was a handsome man. On closer inspection he could see the pain that lay just below the surface. Was it just physical pain or was it much deeper, something gnawing at him deep inside? Well he'd work on that later. It was time to get started. He looked up at David and asked, "Why are you here David?"

"I'm not sure."

"You're not sure?"

"Well, I…" David paused, looking for words.

Sanders wiped his brow again and gazed into space.

"Can't sleep," David mumbled, expecting a comment, but none was forthcoming. Sanders looked disinterested and bored. David felt his cheeks flush with anger. "I told you, I can't sleep."

"I heard you, David."

"Then why the fuck aren't you answering me?"

Sanders just looked at David expectantly.

"I've been having bad dreams. Nightmares." Charlie's smoldering body flashed in front of his eyes, and he let out an involuntary little groan.

Sanders took another drag on his cigarette, and exhaled slowly, the smoke curling into the air. He was doodling on a notepad now.

"I'm up half the night. Sometimes, I think I'm going crazy."

Sanders stared at David, and tapped his pencil on his notepad.

"You know, this is a lot of bullshit, what the fuck am I doing here in the first place?"

"You're very angry, David."

David squirmed on the hard chair. "I'm not angry; I...I just need something; maybe some pills to help me sleep? Shit, I haven't slept good for...I don't know."

Sanders leaned forward. "No pills, David, that would just mask the problem."

"The fucking problem is that I can't sleep."

"I understand that, David, but sleeping pills just won't do it."

"So what the fuck will?"

"You use fuck a lot."

"Yeah, it's a bad habit."

"It's disrespectful."

"Are you going to give me lessons in etiquette, or tell me how to get some sleep?"

Sanders ignored the question, although his face grew red. "Therapy takes time. We both have to work hard at it." He paused for effect. "I can only help you to help yourself. Do you understand?"

David lowered his eyes without answering.

"David?"

Tangled thoughts ran through David's brain like a movie film skipping, sending flashes of memory close to the surface, and then abruptly disappearing, replaced with terrible frustration. David's mouth started to form words, but the thoughts were changing so fast, he simply shook his head.

Sanders leaned forward in anticipation. David just looked silently at his feet and didn't respond. His face was still burning. He was confused and only wanted the session to end so he could get the hell out of there. Time passed until Sanders said, "Okay, David, let's call it a day. We'll meet again next week at the same time."

After David left, Sanders leaned back in his chair and thought, *They're all the same; confused, angry, tortured with their nightmares.* So many of these kids had passed through his door, sat in the same seat with the same look of loss and confusion. God knows he tried to help them.

He stared out the dirty window of his office for a few moments, thinking that he had been spared the horror and pain these men had gone through. He was lucky, wasn't he? Yes, he was lucky, but somehow he felt he had missed something, that he was diminished because he hadn't been a part of it. Ashamed. Guilty.

What a lot of bullshit. What was he thinking? He was a doctor. He took out his handkerchief, wiped his brow, stood up and stretched. He reached for his coat and hat, and wondered what terrible secrets lay buried behind David's angry silence.

CHAPTER SEVEN

MARCH 1946

The thrill of accomplishment at work faded into a dull routine. School was the only thing that interested him. The nightmares continued to haunt him, and the meeting with doctor Sanders hadn't gone well. The guy was a jerk, and he'd be damned if he would go back. He left the VA and headed for home

David parked his truck, got out and climbed over the snow bank knowing he'd have to shovel out a place for the truck before he finally parked it for the night. It was late March, but the winter wouldn't quit. He scanned the sky, hoped it wasn't going to keep snowing. He headed for the tin hut in the Veterans project that they had finally moved into only a few weeks earlier.

They all looked the same: colorless, squat and ugly. *Hell, if you ever came home drunk, you'd never find your way home.* He walked up the wooden steps to the front door of the Nissen hut, which was divided into a home for himself and three other veterans' families, and wondered when he would be able to make enough money to afford a real home. He knew what was inside. Three tiny rooms, an oil-stove to cook on and an icebox with a huge pan under it to collect the water from the melting ice. It had an oil heater, which was supposed to keep them warm, soot staining the wall behind it, along with an oil smell and cold, drafty floors. What the hell could you expect for twenty-seven dollars a month? At least they were out of Jessie's parents' house. Hey, they had a roof over their heads and they were on their own. It was a start.

David looked at his grease-stained hands, and suddenly the grease turned to blood: black, sticky blood. Charlie's blood. He sucked in a breath of frigid air before his throat constricted. He broke into a cold sweat, struggled for air and tried to control the terror that raced through him. This wasn't the first time his nightmare came to life during the day. He squeezed his eyes shut, trying to get control, opened them as he caught his breath, and looked at his hands again. They were trembling beyond control, streaked with the oil that seemed to permanently stain them. He had to pull himself together. He squared his shoulders, took a deep breath, opened the door and wiped his feet. His next-door neighbors were fighting again. He could hear their obscenities through the thin plasterboard walls.

He knew that as soon as he'd get comfortable, the phone would ring. It would be Joe. Without as much as a hello, he would give him a name, an address, and the problem that existed. Then he would hang up. The calls could easily continue through the night, which meant shoveling his truck out of the drift the snowplow would create, each time he got a call. Not an easy life, but he was learning a trade, going to school, and that was the answer to the security he needed for himself and his little family. And he knew, no matter what it took, he was going to get it.

In the few weeks since they had moved in, Jessie had made the little hut into a home. A picture here, a touch there. She was in the tiny kitchen cooking spaghetti sauce that smelled wonderful. As he came in she turned from the stove and smiled. God, how he loved her. She searched his face. "Hard day?"

He grunted affirmatively, and put the bottle of milk he had picked up in the icebox. He turned and watched her, busy at the stove, and thought she looked like someone on the cover of the Saturday Evening Post, a figure that Norman Rockwell might have illustrated. She was wearing a red and white gingham apron, tossing her head, sweeping away the wisps of her long black hair from her eyes. The little expansion in her belly hardly showed. She wiped her hands on her apron and said, "You look beat."

She knew how hard he was trying and what a comedown this was for him. Going from hero status, wearing his uniform decorated with his silver wings and all his medals, soldiers saluting him, to a demeaning, dirty job, standing there in dirty coveralls with grease on his hands and face.

He bent over the sink to try to wash the oily grime from his hands. "I went to the doctor today." He dried his hands, walked over to the table and straddled one of the kitchen chairs.

"What did he say?"

"He didn't say much. I guess I did all the talking." He wondered how he could relive that hour with Sanders with her. What would she think of him?

"Did you get something to help you sleep?"

"No."

"Why not? I thought that was what you were going to see him about."

"He doesn't believe in pills."

She turned back to the stove, spooned a little sauce from the pot and tasted it. "Well I don't understand why…"

"Well, it doesn't matter. I'm not going back; it's a waste of time."

"What…what about the nightmares? You said you would keep going. Try to get some help, and now you're going to quit?"

"He's a jerk. He just sits there. I feel like an idiot."

"You have to give it a chance. You…"

"I gave it a chance."

"No you didn't." Jessie's face was red with frustration. "You went once and you call that giving it a chance? You…"

"Okay. Okay." David raised his hands in mock surrender. "I'll think about it." He wanted to get off the subject, especially Sanders. Forget about the war. Do normal things. Talk about how much he loved her.

"No spaghetti unless you promise."

"Cross my heart," David said, with a big smile he knew she couldn't resist.

She stamped her foot. "Oh you, you're never serious with me."

"I said I'd go back."

"Well, you'd better."

He looked up at her, his smile fading. "Have you any idea how much I love you?"

She bent down to kiss him. He pulled her to his lap and held her very close, thinking about how lucky he was. It hurt him to know how much she trusted him, and how unsure he was about himself in this new civilian world. Flying was one thing. Civilian life was another. In combat he lived by the hour, sometimes by the minute. Every night was lived like it was the last. Every trip to the target was a lifetime. Each time the wheels of his plane touched down and the mission was over, he knew he'd done his job and done it well. Now his goals seemed to be almost unreachable, and the days dragged on. The only consolation was Jessie.

She was kissing his ear, and he nipped her neck playfully.

"Hey, you'll give me a hickey." She giggled and pushed him away.

"I don't care; I just want to eat you up, you taste so good."

"Now wouldn't it look nice to have your beautiful wife walking around with a big hickey on her neck?"

He pulled her closer.

She whispered into his ear, "I do love you, David."

"Okay, prove it."

"Before supper?"

"What's wrong with before supper?"

"Sorry sir, you'll have to wait for dessert."

"Awe, c'mon baby, don't be like that."

Jessie giggled and twisted out of David's hands.

"I guess a fuck is out of the question?"

"David, you are so bad."

"I'm not bad, just horny."

She slipped into his arms again and whispered into his ear, "Well, I'm horny too, but you're still gonna have to wait." She gave him a little peck on his nose. "I'm hungry and I'm gonna get the spaghetti." She put the plates of spaghetti on the table and took the bread out of the oven. As she looked at David, her face clouded. "This morning, when I put the trash out, there was a rat as big as a cat." She instinctively put her hand on her stomach. "I don't want to have our baby here, David."

"I know, sweetheart," David said as he looked at the door, half expecting the rat to enter. He thought he would kill it with his bare hands if it threatened Jessie. "We'll be out of this dump real soon; before the baby comes." He took her hand. "I promise."

That night, sleep hadn't just eluded him; it was nonexistent. It was the rat. He couldn't get the rat out of his mind. Then it was rats, lots of rats, big rats, like the rats in the cell in the prison camp. Germany. His ran his hand over the scars on his left thigh. He could still feel the warm blood that had oozed through his fingers.

He squeezed his eyes shut and tried to stop the memories that best lie sleeping, but they slithered into his brain like a poisonous snake.

Chapter Eight

November 1946

Eight months had passed and they still lived in the Nissen hut. It was the end of November and there was an early snow. It was almost Jessie's time. He had promised they would move before the baby came, but there was nothing they could afford. He felt ashamed; he'd let her down. Yes, he'd let her down.

Something was nagging at him. What was it? Who else had he failed? Who else? It was…in his nightmares. Charlie? Charlie was dead. There was no pulse. David was sweating while his breath was freezing. The flak. The black puffs with the fire inside. A small volcano about to erupt, the panic; there was no excuse for the panic. He was too well trained to panic. Charlie was dead. He was dead. *I checked his pulse. For God's sake, he was dead.*

He took a deep breath, squared his shoulders, and walked over to the tin hut that was still home, stamped the snow off of his boots as best as he could, and stepped through the tiny threshold.

"Jessie? Jessie?"

"Oh, David. Thank God you're home. I'm in the bathroom. My water broke. We have to get to the hospital! God, I wish my mother were here. Get me some towels. Oh, shit, the floor's all wet."

David ran into the bathroom. "Okay, okay, calm down, calm down, we'll be all right. I'll…"

"Maybe you should call my mother?"

"No time." David helped Jessie up, threw her coat over her shoulders, helped her out of the door, into the truck, and tried to stay calm. Jesus, he was going to be a father. His hands were trembling; he could hardly get the key into the transmission. Finally he got the truck started.

"We should have called the doctor," Jessie said, her voice stronger.

"Do you know the number? I can call in on the radio and…"

"No, I can't remember it"

"We'll call the doctor from the hospital."

Jessie squirmed in the seat and bit her lip against the pain that seemed to be taking over her whole being. "David, I'm scared. Oh, God it hurts! Hurry, I can't…"

"Don't be frightened, honey, I'm right here. You'll be fine." *Please God let her be all right. Don't let anything go wrong,* David prayed silently.

*My God, a baby, my baby, the baby I created. How many lives, how many babies will never be born? How many bombs, killed how many...? Will God remember that I was one of the...? Will He hold me personally responsible? Punish me, the baby, Jessie? Oh, please, please God; don't let anything happen to them. I...*The truck was out of control. It skidded and finally bounced off the curb.

"David! What are you doing?"

"Shit, not paying attention." David got the truck back on the road, wheels spinning on the ice.

"Sorry, so sorry. Are you okay?"

"You almost killed us! Uh, oh!" The pain stabbed at her and she groaned. "Just get us there in one piece, dammit."

"I said I was sorry."

Both Jessie and David jumped as Joe's gruff voice came over the two-way radio and startled them.

"David, it's Joe, I been calling your house. Where the fuck have you been?"

"We're having a baby, Joe. I'm on the way to the hospital."

"Ya, well, congratulations, but I got an emergency. A big one, so you better call me when you get to the hospital."

"Joe, I can't..." Joe was off the air.

"David, you're not going to leave me, are you?" Jessie held her stomach as if that would hold the baby back.

David took a corner and the wheels screeched; the truck skidded. His hands were gripping the wheel so tight they hurt. *That son of a bitch,* he thought. Nothing was sacred. For God's sake, they were having a baby. He couldn't take his eyes off the road to give Jessie a reassuring look, but he said, "Don't be silly. I'm not leaving you."

"Promise?" Jessie said in a little voice.

"I promise."

David pulled up in front of the emergency entrance, flung open his door and opened Jessie's. She was doubled up and barely managed to say, "Hurry, David, please hurry."

Within minutes she was in a wheelchair being wheeled off to the delivery room and, although David had given her doctor's name, he doubted they would get in touch with him in time.

David stood in the lobby wondering what he was supposed to do when an elderly nurse's aid came over and, in a motherly voice, said, "Why don't you follow me. I'll take you to the maternity waiting room. You can get a cup of coffee and there are some magazines. The doctor will come out to see you as soon as he's finished." David followed her obediently.

There was only one other person in the room and he was on the pay phone. David heard him say, "It's a boy. It's a boy. Thank you, and you too."

He felt sad that he had no family to call. He didn't even have Jessie's mother's telephone number. Well, he'd look that up. He suddenly remembered Joe's instructions to call. He reached into his pocket, found a couple of nickels and muttered "Bastard" to himself as he dialed the office number and asked for Joe.

"It's about time." Joe said, and before David could say a word he continued. "I got two men out sick. Willie and Fred are over at Westland Ave. The fucking boiler finally let go. There's hell to pay there, and you're all I got left. Woodrow Apartments is out of heat and the old man himself called screaming and swearing at me. Considering he's our biggest oil account, you just better get your tight ass over there."

"Listen, my wife's having…"

"I know your wife is having a baby. She doesn't need you to sit on your ass waiting for her to deliver. Believe me, you'll be cooling your heals there for hours. Take the call and you'll be back in plenty of time." Before David could respond he hung up.

"Goddamn it!" David screamed as he slammed the receiver down on the hook. He paused for a moment and then ran out of the hospital to the truck.

Jessie had barely opened her eyes when she heard the nurse calling her name. "Mrs. Livingston, wake up. I have a darling little girl that wants to be with her mommy." The nurse leaned over and put the baby in Jessie's arms.

"Is my husband here?"

"I'm sorry dear there was no one in the waiting room, but I'm sure he'll be here shortly. He'll want to see you and his new little daughter."

Jessie looked at the little bundle in her arms and smiled. "You are so beautiful," she whispered. Suddenly she burst into tears. "Damn you, David, where the hell are you? You promised you wouldn't leave me." She wiped her nose with the back of her hand, sniffed a couple of times and turned her attention back to the baby. A bolt of panic shot through her. What did she know about taking care of a baby? Nothing! *Oh, God, I need my mother. I have to call my mother. Damn you, David.* She looked at her daughter. She was so innocent. She took in a deep breath and her eyes filled with tears.

About an hour later David came into the room; his face and hands were stained with oil, sweat running down his face. "Jess I'm so sorry I…"

"You left me, David," Jessie said and turned her face away from him. "You promised you wouldn't leave me." She turned back to him and stared into his eyes, her eyes burning into his. "I begged you not to leave me."

Suddenly her eyes were Charlie's eyes. Charlie's eyes smoldering like red, hot coals. Unforgiving. Her lips were Charlie's lips. He was trying to say something. He…

David snapped back to reality. He kneeled beside Jessie's bed and said, "Jess, please, let me explain. I'm so sorry but…"

Jessie interrupted him. "Please, I'm tired. Just go away and leave me alone." She turned away from him and David knew that he had failed her and she was not alone. There were Charlie's pleading eyes, the little German, and Sully in his nightmares. He'd somehow failed them all and now he'd lost something; something else that could never be replaced.

Jessie's mother came every day to help her with the new baby and David spent every free moment he had doing his best to help. Most of the time he was shooed away so that the women could do the job they were somehow innately capable of, notwithstanding Dr. Spock's new book on child rearing always close by.

"Bye, Mom, thanks for coming, and thanks for the chicken."

"Goodbye sweetheart, I'll see you tomorrow. Take care of my baby."

"Don't you worry."

Jessie heard the pipes bang as David shut off the water in the shower, and a few moments later David came out of the bathroom with a towel wrapped around him.

"Mother gone?"

"Just left." Jessie turned toward the little kitchen. It was hard to be angry with someone in such close quarters.

Besides it had been almost a month that she had kept David out in the cold, and he did look delicious wrapped in that towel. After all, if he hadn't taken the damn call Joe might have fired him or, worse, the big boss. He still shouldn't have left me. *Well, I can't be angry with him forever,* she thought.

"Are you hungry?"

"Starved."

"Mom brought us a chicken. I'll warm it up…"

"Jessie," David interrupted her as he held out his arms. Without another thought Jessie fell into them as David kissed her cheek, forehead and finally her lips. "I'm so sorry, honey." His tears were wet on Jessie's cheek.

"The hell with the chicken," she said, as she led him to the couch.

The phone rang three times before David picked it up, but it was too late. Sarah was awake and crying. It was half past two in the morning.

"Hello." He sat up and swung his legs over the side of the bed.

"Felton, 32 Riverway, out of heat," Joe's gravelly voice grated through the phone.

"Son of a bitch, hung up again, doesn't even have the courtesy to say hello," David mumbled to the empty side of the bed and hung up the phone. Jessie had disappeared into Sarah's room.

He started to dress when she returned, rocking Sarah in her arms. She looked out the window. "It's snowing out."

"What else is new?"

Jessie looked out the window again. "It isn't bad enough that you have to go out in the middle of a snowstorm, but to add insult to injury you don't even get paid for it."

"I'm learning a trade."

"You're being taken advantage of. You know this stuff better than he does. How long are you going to let him take advantage of you?"

"How 'bout until I see him this morning?"

"Now you're talking."

David arrived early and approached Joe, who was drinking his morning coffee and sat on the corner of his desk. Joe eyed him quizzically. "Morning, David."

"Morning. Any coffee left?"

"Nope, you're too late."

"I'm early."

"Well you're still too late."

David looked around at the other men starting their day. He needed to get Joe alone, do this just right. After all, Joe could fire him on the spot. "Got a minute?"

"Sure, what's up?"

"Well, it's kinda private, could we… ?" David nodded in the direction of the door.

Joe got up, followed David out the door, leaned on the truck parked at the curb and waited for David to speak.

"Can't take your night calls anymore."

"Why, you sick or something?"

"No, I just…"

"It's those doctor appointments…"

"No, no, it's that I need to make more money. Can't pay my bills. I need to get paid for the night calls."

David held his breath.

Joe waved his finger under David's nose. "You think I broke my ass teaching you this fucking business so you could run out on me whenever you please. You…"

David held his hands up, palms facing Joe as if to protect himself. "Joe, please, hold on; I just…"

Joe knew that he'd taken advantage of David. He couldn't really fire him because, if his deal was exposed, the big boss would fire him on the spot, but he had to salvage something. At least he could threaten the kid. "I guess you don't want to work here anymore?" He scowled.

David's heart sunk but he had to prevail. He'd have to take his chances. Hell, it wasn't as if someone was shooting at him. "C'mon, Joe, gimme a break. You know I want to work here." David paused. "I don't want to go any place else."

Joe thought there was a chance he might be promoted to assistant manager and he would need David to fill his shoes. David was the best he had and he would be lost without him. "Okay kid, I'll tell you what, I'll split the difference with you. You get half, okay?"

"Don't want to be a pig, but I…"

"You are being a pig."

"Joe, I need the money!"

"All right, just don't ask me for no more time off." Joe growled. He threw his empty coffee cup into the gutter and walked back into his office.

CHAPTER NINE

FEBRUARY 1947

Sarah had finally fallen asleep in David's arms. He put her into her crib and quietly tiptoed out of her room, closing the door behind him.

Jessie was in bed when David crawled in and put his arms around her. He kissed her neck, and she responded by kissing the arm that embraced her. Exhausted from working all day and most of the night, he found sleep quickly and, once again, his nightmares.

He was standing among the firemen watching the little house burning furiously. Flames shot out of the doors and windows like a blowtorch. Suddenly Jessie appeared in the doorway. The flames were all around her. He screamed and started to run toward her. She was mouthing the words, "Please help me. Please help me." A big fireman stopped him and said, "It's too late, it's too late, it's too late."

His eyes flew open. "Oh God. I've got to get him out; I've got to get him out; I've..." He sat up covered with sweat and looked over at Jessie. She had awakened and now pulled him to her and rocked him, trying to comfort him.

"I'm so sorry."

"Don't be silly, my love," she whispered, kissing his face, wiping the sweat from his forehead. "It's not your fault. You can't help it."

"I don't know what to do anymore. I'm so tired." He got out of bed and walked to the window. He knew there would be no more sleep this night. His hands were shaking so much that he had to fold them under his arms to quiet them. He had skipped a number of appointments with Sanders and now he had to find a way to see him again. He had to get some help.

A week later and another nightmare. David sat on a hard wooden chair. He was alone with his thoughts in the deserted waiting room. There were some outdated magazines on the scratched table beside him, along with an ashtray filled with the remains of the cigarettes from the earlier part of the day. He slipped a cigarette out of a new pack of Luckys and made a mental note that this was his second pack of the day. His mouth tasted like shit, and he was developing a smoker's hack. Fucking coffin nails will probably kill me, he thought, but he lit up anyway and took a deep drag, thinking that he'd love a cup of coffee. Well, he'd like anything better than spending an hour with Doc Sanders. What the hell made him so nervous about seeing the doctor baffled him. Most of the time Sanders just sat there doodling or looking into space. How was that supposed to help him? He took another deep drag, coughed and then in disgust smashed the cigarette out in the already overflowing ashtray. He looked at his watch. It was five twenty-five and his appointment was at five. What the hell, beggars couldn't be choosers, after all, he admitted begrudgingly. Sanders was staying late so that he could come after work. So what, he'd still sit there on his smug fat ass and waste another hour of their time.

A cleaning woman was starting to wash the floor at the other end of the corridor. The smell of the disinfectant reminded him of the months he'd spent in the hospital in England. They had saved his leg but he would always have a pronounced limp and probably always be "David the Gimp." *Okay, so I'm feeling sorry for myself,* he thought. Why not? Beside the gimpy leg, his hands shook so much that he was embarrassed to lift a glass in front of his friends. Even that was okay, but the nightmares, they were driving him crazy.

Sanders's office door opened and a pretty girl with light brown hair came out, followed a few moments later by Doctor Sanders. Sanders gave the girl a conspiratorial smile and then turned to David. He said, "Sorry to have kept you waiting," and waved David in with a hand holding his file.

"Sit," Sanders said, throwing the file on his desk and sitting himself. He took off his glasses and started to wipe them with a handkerchief. He finished cleaning the glasses, leaned back in his chair and raised his eyes to meet David's. David avoided his eyes, looked up at the ceiling and blew out a long breath. For a few moments there was silence.

"You're still angry with me," Sanders asked.

"I'm not angry, I'm pissed."

"Pissed?"

"Yeah, pissed."

"Do you want to tell me about it?"

"No."

Sanders didn't respond, but wiped the little beads of sweat on his forehead with his handkerchief, and waited patiently for David to speak. Minutes passed in silence.

David let out a long breath almost in surrender. "There you go; the silent treatment again. That's going to make the nightmares go away, right?"

Sanders sat quietly.

"They are so real. They stay with me for hours after I wake up."

"Tell me about them," Sanders asked softly.

David looked down at his shoes and then at Sanders. How could he describe the convoluted dreams that crept out of the darkest recesses of his mind, jumbled and confused? They were so terrifying that he would awaken bolt upright, soaked in sweat, a silent scream on his lips, his body trembling, hardly consoled when Jessie awakened and held him in her arms, trying to calm him.

His eyes filled with tears. He brushed them away with the back of his hand. "I can't. You don't understand. I…" He swallowed hard and brushed the back of his hand across his eyes again, avoiding Sanders eyes.

Sanders sat quietly but attentively.

David continued, "They all left me, they…" David looked away from Sanders and took a shaky deep breath.

"Go on David, who left you?"

"I couldn't move. They just looked at me and then they left. They just left me there. The place was on fire. I could feel the heat; my clothes were burning. I screamed for help but they just ignored me. Then we all left."

"We all left?"

David looked confused. "Yeah, we all left," he said very slowly, thinking about what he had said. Panic filled his chest and he looked at Sanders for help, but Sanders just continued to look at him expectantly. David dropped his eyes, his chest felt constricted, stomach queasy, bile rose in his throat, and he broke into a sweat.

Sanders saw him pale, saw the panic in his eyes. He had hit a pressure point. What was David hiding, too horrible to face? "Who left you, David?"

"I don't know. I don't remember." David's chair made a grating sound as he pushed it back. "I gotta go now." He started hesitantly to get up. His felt as if his feet wouldn't hold him.

"Please sit down, David, we're not quite finished."

David stood, hesitated for a moment, and finally slumped back down in the hard chair.

Sanders face softened. "I know this is difficult for you, but we are starting to get somewhere. We can do this, David, but I need your help."

David looked up and into Sanders's eyes. They were concerned eyes. He studied his face for a moment; it was the face of a man who cared. David knew that he needed to continue, to get the poison out. Maybe Sanders could help, but he couldn't go THERE. THERE was where the demons hid in the flames raging behind the door to the nightmares that tortured him. He knew if he opened that door, they would consume him. Panic constricted his chest. He fought for control. *Take deep breaths. Relax. Go somewhere else. That's it, a country road in autumn, red and orange leaves falling, floating slowly, very slowly, down to earth. The ground is covered with the red and orange leaves.* More deep breaths and he began to calm.

Sanders knew he would have to let David have a break. He couldn't push him any further today. He'd change the subject.

"Why don't you tell me a little about yourself, your folks, where you grew up?"

David remembered his father waking him with a kiss. Sweeping him up in his arms, blanket and all, carrying him into the kitchen close to the big black iron stove that warmed the house and provided the fire to cook their food.

"We lived in a cold-water flat in Winthrop. It was freezing in the winter. The wind blew in from the sea and the only room that was warm was the kitchen, where my father kept the stove hot for as long as the coal or wood would last."

"I was eight years old when my mother died. I felt lost, abandoned, confused. It was the first time I saw my father cry. I don't know why, but I couldn't cry, the tears just didn't want to come out. I was ashamed, because I knew I should be crying like everyone else, but I just couldn't."

"'Why, why did God do this?' my father kept asking me, or maybe he was asking God, or…I don't know. He didn't want to stay in the apartment in Roxbury that we had lived in for as long as I could remember. I guess there was too much of my mother there, so that's when we moved to Winthrop. It was lonely at first. My father was withdrawn, uncommunicative, and I missed my mother. One day all the tears that I had dammed up poured out of me." David's eyes glazed as he looked into the past. "My father took me in his arms and held me. He said no more tears. We are not going to cry for Mama anymore. She must be ashamed of us, crying like babies. We are still a family. Now wipe away those tears. We have to get on with our lives."

David took a deep breath and continued.

"By the time I was eleven, I was very much on my own. My father treated me as an equal and I was just happy to be with him. After the day was done and the supper dishes were washed, we would sit by the stove in the kitchen, and he would tell me stories about when he was a boy in Russia until my eyes would get heavy and I would fall asleep."

"What about friends, did you have any friends?" Sanders asked.

"Well, Winthrop was a poor town, predominantly Irish. It was a tough place for a skinny, Jewish kid to make friends."

David drifted back to when he was eleven. The memory of his father's voice was so vivid, he was living it again as he closed his eyes and related it to Sanders.

"David, be a good boy, take the pail with you and see if you can find some coal along the tracks. Mind you be careful of the trains.

"I went down to the tracks, filled a pail with coal and started home. Three of the Irish kids saw me. I started to run, but they caught up to me and took the coal away. I had never been in a fight before, but I tried my best, fought back, but, in the end, I got a bloody nose, and ran home crying. I told my father that they took away the coal and called me a dirty Jew. I remember my father wiping my nose with his handkerchief, telling me it was all right, don't cry. I still remember what he said as if it were yesterday.

"So you got a bloody nose, but you fought back and you hurt one of them. They will think twice before they pick on you again. Listen, I don't care if you hit them with a rock or a stick, or you kick or scratch or bite, but you must always leave your mark. The trouble with us Jews is that we never stood up and fought for what we believed in, even though the bible taught us, an eye for an eye, and a tooth for a tooth."

'And a nose for a nose?' I had asked my father and he smiled and said, 'Yes, and a nose for a nose, or whatever it takes.'"

"Tell me about your father, is he still alive?"

David looked down and frowned. "No, he died. He…" David paused, clearing the lump in his throat. "He had a stroke."

"And?"

"And he was one of the finest men who ever lived. He died broke because, whatever he didn't give to me, he gave to anyone who asked, and if they didn't ask, and they were needy, he found a way to give to them anyway. He even gave to his archenemies, the *goyim*, as long as they didn't know it was him."

"The *goyim*?"

"Yiddish word for Christians."

David paused, remembering his father's strong face lined with the history of hard work and hard times. "He worked around the clock to get us out of Winthrop into

172

a heated apartment in Dorchester so I could go to a better school." David reached into his shirt pocket and pulled out a cigarette. He lit it and leaned forward as if to emphasize his next words.

"He didn't want me to be like him, uneducated, scraping for a living. He wanted me to fight back, to be something. Well, I learned to fight. I learned to fly. I even learned to kill, and I will be successful someday and make a lot of money like he wanted me to, but I will never learn to be, nor will I ever be, the man my father was."

CHAPTER TEN

JUNE 1947

Mary Benash was one of the combination secretary-stenographers at the disposal of the doctors on the fourth floor of the Veteran's Administration. She had dark brown eyes, very full lips and light brown hair that she wore in a pageboy to emphasize her long neck. She was outside Dr. Sanders' door and tried to think of some excuse to go in. Mary didn't know what attracted her to Sanders, but she always felt some sort of excitement when they were together. He made her feel better than other men did. He had a certain charm, was always easy to talk to, and most important, he listened. He was a rogue and never stopped making passes at her, but they were not lewd like some of the other men in the department. She liked his easy manner, in contrast to the other doctors who bossed her around and seemed never to be satisfied.

She knew Sanders' appointment hadn't shown so she went in after a soft knock.

She was wearing a short jacket that had military buttons and a matching short skirt.

"Anything you want from me today, Doctor?"

He stared at her for a minute. "As a matter of fact there is." He took off his glasses. "You know, Mary, we've worked together for a long time and, at the risk of being too forward, I'd like to get to know you better. What would you think about having a drink with me after work? Just a drink and a talk, what do you say?"

She hesitated at the door and said, "Oh, I don't know."

"C'mon, Mary, be a sport."

"Just drinks?"

"Just drinks, promise." He'd promise anything to get into her pants.

The Glass Slipper looked across Beacon Street to the manicured gardens and weeping willows of the Public Gardens. Politicians from the Capital at the top of the "Hill" loved to drink and make their deals there as well as the "in-crowd" and those who pretended to be "in." It had been a small hotel but now rarely depended on the rooms upstairs. The major part of the business was the bar, although the food was often the talk of the town. There was a small dining room off the bar. Additionally, there was a smaller room, which could only be reached through tiny alcoves that led off of both the bar and the dining room. It was used for even more secluded meetings for both business and pleasure. The bar, however, was the place to go.

The pay phone was downstairs directly across from the men's room. Sanders debated whether to phone home first or go to the men's room. He decided to use the phone. "I'm sorry I didn't call you earlier, but I've been so damn busy. Listen, I've got a medical conference tonight. I'd forgotten all about it...so I guess I'll eat in town. I won't be too late, but you know how these things are. I'm sorry, baby, but what can I do?" As he hung up he felt relieved. After all, he'd been pitching Mary for months and now she was ripe. He headed for the men's room and finally the bar.

"Beefeater martini, Al."

"Yes sir, and good evening, Dr. Sanders." Al reached for the bottle of Beefeaters. Glen Miller's "Moonlight Serenade" drifted from the jukebox.

"Dr. Sanders, sir? Aren't we formal tonight?"

"Yes sir, I found my customers give bigger tips when I sir them, sir!"

"Cut the shit, and give me my martini."

"Olive?" Al asked as he poured the drink.

Sanders ignored the question and scanned the bar. "Is that a hooker?" He indicated the direction with a turn of his head. "She's not bad."

"Oh yeah...twenty-five bucks...talk about newspapers going up to ten cents."

"I'd never pay for it." Sanders eyeballed the hooker and wondered if he could fuck her and talk her out of getting paid. He turned back to Al. "Hell, chasing it is sometimes more fun than making it."

Al wiped the bar in front of Sanders again. "You gonna have dinner here?"

Sanders looked toward the door. "I'm expecting this little doll I've been playing...If she shows, I probably will."

"Aren't you afraid your wife will get wise?"

Sanders laughed. "What she don't know won't hurt her."

"Maybe, if you don't get caught."

"Who made up the rules anyway? Who says you have to live a life full of restraints and guilt?" Sanders picked up his drink, sipped it and continued. "You're whole being craves sex, something that's natural and instinctive, but it's immoral so you suppress it, and eventually end up seeing someone like me. We're all a bunch of hypocrites. We know what we want but we're afraid to take it...at least openly." He adjusted his glasses that had slipped down his nose. "Hey, this is 1947, not the Middle Ages. You know what I mean?"

"Ya, but then everybody would be screwing around."

"They wouldn't be as promiscuous as you think. Right now sex is a big deal. You take anything you can get, anywhere you can get it, but if it wasn't so hard to find and there was plenty of it, you'd be more selective, wouldn't you? Look at the people who come in here, married men and more and more married women. Why? They're looking for a bite of forbidden fruit and after they bite it they want more and more. Take the forbidden fruit away and see how fast they'd run back home."

"Is this the psychology class I missed when I didn't go to college?"

Sanders ignored Al's wisecrack, "I'll be goddamned if I'll make myself sick, conforming to a bunch of hypocrites. I know better. Believe me, my friend, people will wake up and there will be a sexual revolution."

"I can't wait." Al said, looking around the bar for another customer to escape Sander's lecture.

Sanders took out his handkerchief and wiped his brow. "They'll break all the rules; the pendulum will swing all the way to the right before it gets back to center and it may really never get back to center."

"I hope not."

"Wise ass." Sanders glanced at the door again and looked at his watch, which wasn't there, because he had left it at home in his rush to get to his office. He turned back to Al. "If you could give me the time and save the wisecracks, I would appreciate it."

Al looked at his watch. "Five twenty-one and thirty seconds. I don't know about milliseconds because I didn't go to college."

Sanders, ready for a comeback, forgot about it when he spotted Mary coming toward him. She had a nice wiggle to her walk.

Mary was smiling and, although she was not beautiful, she was appealing in the dim glow of the lights in the Glass Slipper. She hadn't changed her neat little suit, but she had fixed her make-up and put on some perfume and she smelled and looked delicious.

"Hi," she said softly, sitting beside him.

Sanders looked into her eyes for a long moment before he spoke. He visualized her in bed, naked.

"Mary, you look lovely. I mean it, without the line…I'm really glad you came."

Mary looked down, avoiding Sanders' eyes. "You know I shouldn't have."

"Why not?"

She took his left hand and showed him the ring he was wearing. He took it off and put it in his pocket.

"Feel better now?"

"Not really."

"Can I get you something?" Al asked, as he wiped the bar in front of Mary and rolled his eyes in appreciation.

Sanders ignored him.

"Yes, a Manhattan, please."

"Mary." Sanders gave her his sexiest look and put his hand on her arm. "Stay for dinner."

"And if I did what would that lead to?"

Sanders took off his glasses and leaned forward. "Why does it have to lead to anything? I like being with you isn't that enough?"

Mary thought about the long ride back on the streetcar to South Boston, the cold leftovers for dinner, another evening alone. But in spite of herself, she said, without real conviction, "Not for me, it isn't."

"Mary, just once, forget about everything but tonight… please?"

She smiled, flashed back to the cold leftovers, hesitated for a moment, and then said, "What the hell."

Mary's apartment was small and inexpensively furnished with an array of mismatched hand-me-downs from family and a few better pieces that she had managed to buy with her meager salary. She turned on the radio to a music station. Glenn Miller was banging out "Chattanooga Choo Choo." She changed the station and got Sinatra. She wondered why she was doing this. Did she just want to get laid, or was it the feeling of power that she had, knowing that sex had put her completely in control?

Mary came out of the kitchen holding a half empty bottle of cheap vodka. "I think the only thing I have to drink is vodka, okay?"

Screw the vodka; it's getting late and I don't want a drink. What I want is you naked, Sanders thought, but he said, "As long as it has ice and you serving it, it'll be wonderful."

Mary handed Sanders his drink, but he put it on the table, reached for Mary's hand and pulled her down on the couch beside him.

"For God's sake, Mary, relax. I'm not going to rape you."

She slid into his arms and kissed him hotly and whispered in his ear, "I wish you would."

Ruth was reading in bed, waiting up for Sanders when he got home. He was glad Mary had been so sensible about him leaving early. He pulled off his jacket as he entered the room, loosened his tie, bent over Ruth and kissed her forehead, hoping that none of Mary's perfume still clung to his body.

She put down her book and looked up at him. "How was the meeting?"

"You know those things," he began undressing. He wished that she had already been asleep so that he wouldn't have to go through a third degree.

"What was it about?"

"About? Oh, the deterioration of morality, the effect on the nervous system etc., etc. Very interesting, wouldn't have missed it for the world." He wondered if she really bought this bullshit. Well, he wasn't going to worry about it; after all, a little pussy on the side wouldn't hurt anyone. For Christ's sake every guy in Europe had a mistress. All he had was a stray piece of ass once in a while. What the hell was so wrong with that? Hell, he wasn't falling in love with them, he was just fucking them, just enjoying the moment.

CHAPTER ELEVEN

DECEMBER 1947

"You're on tonight." Melvin's voice echoed through David's two-way radio.

"Tonight and tomorrow night are my nights off. Big exam for me tomorrow night, remember? I took all day Sunday instead."

"Listen, school's your problem. Business is mine. Exam or not, I say you're working tonight."

David pounded the steering wheel with his fist and gritted his teeth. *Stay in control. Don't lose it. Try to make nice.* "C'mon, Melvin, give me a break. This is really an important exam. I really would appreciate it." David held his breath.

"Give you a break? You goof off every Thursday for a so-called doctor's appointment. You can't be reached between six and nine all week long because you're in school. Jessie has to take your kid to the doctor. Should I go on?"

Keep calm. "Okay, okay, you got a point. I've been a pain in the ass, but you know I work free overtime, like Sunday, to make up for it. Melvin, I really need to…"

"David, this is bullshit. You're working tonight or you're not working at all. You can take your test during your supper hour so long as there are no emergencies. Over and out."

David thought he heard Melvin snicker just before he signed off.

"You should be nice and warm now, Mrs. Pearlson. The burner is running just fine. Could you just sign here, and I'll be on my way?"

"I'll just get my glasses."

David checked his watch. *Shit, I'm already late.*

"Now where did I put my glasses? I'll be right there."

David shifted his feet, looked at his watch again.

Mrs. Pearlson finally returned. "Here they are. Oh, my, I'm so sorry. Now where do I sign?"

David took the clipboard and ran toward his truck, slipped on the ice and swore. He scrambled to his feet, got into the truck and checked in on his two-way radio. There were no calls waiting. He breathed a sigh of relief, started the truck and sped toward BU. When he got to the parking lot he started to look for a place to park. "I knew it, dammit, I knew it." There were no parking spaces. He circled the lot twice. A set of brake lights flashed. He shot the truck toward the lights, waited for the car to back out, parked, and ran toward his class. Not only was he unprepared, but he was three-quarters of an hour late.

"Not a good start, Mister Livingston," the professor said as he handed David his examination papers.

David sat down wearily, spread the exam papers out and went to work.

The bell rang, signaling that the test was over. The professor began to walk through the aisles picking up the test papers. Some of the students had already dropped their test papers on the professor's desk on their way out. In the confusion the professor skipped David, still playing catch up with his lost time. The room was now empty of students except for David.

The professor carried a sheaf of test papers back to his desk, sat down, and looked over his glasses at David. "It will take about thirty minutes to put these papers in order."

Thirty-five minutes later David brought his paper to the professor. "Thank you, sir. I just wanted to say…"

The professor cleared his throat and continued to sort his papers. "Goodnight, Mister Livingston.

The next morning David picked up his service calls from Joe and started for his truck just as Melvin sauntered by. "How did you make out on your test last night?"

Melvin disappeared into his office before David could respond.

David's lips moved silently. "I did damn good, no thanks to you, bastard."

Over the last two years oil had replaced coal for home heating at a staggering pace and Eastern's business grew exponentially. Management had trailed as it does in small family companies that grow too fast, and the need for an assistant manager was apparent.

Melvin sat behind a large antique desk that had been with the company since its inception. The desk was a mess, with papers and empty coffee cups strewn everywhere.

"What do you think about Joe as an assistant manager?" his father asked as he sat stiffly on the soft chair in front of Melvin's desk.

"Are you really asking me what I think, or are you letting me know that's who you've decided on?"

"I'm asking you what you think," Sam Bass said in an impatient tone.

"You really don't give a damn what I think and you never did."

Sam shifted uncomfortably in his chair. "Melvin, please, if I didn't care about what you thought, I wouldn't have asked you."

"Why the sudden interest in my opinion? You never worried too much about what I thought before."

Sam waved his finger back and forth in front of Melvin's face, "You see, the minute I try to work with you, you…"

"You know and I know, you really don't give a damn what I think. This is just lip service and you know it, so go tell Joe he's the new manager." Melvin looked down at his desk as if he was busy, his lips pursed.

Sam stood up, put both hands on Melvin's desk, and leaned forward menacingly. "Look Melvin, I'm asking your opinion, but you're aggravating me."

"I know I'm aggravating you. I'm always aggravating you. Did it ever occur to you that you aggravate me?"

"Watch your step Melvin."

"Oh, what's the use?" Melvin got up and started to walk to the door.

"Alright, what do you want from me…I asked you what you thought…"

Melvin turned and said, "Do you really care…would you really do what I asked?"

"Yes, yes I would."

Melvin's memories of David raged within him like a gathering storm. David at the top of his class, David on the football team, David with the prettiest girls, David the war hero, David his protector, David, David, David. It was time for David to fail, to be humbled.

"Alright then. Make David Livingston the assistant manager."

Sam knew Melvin was testing him, taunting him. There was no way Livingston, with little or no knowledge about management, could succeed. He was determined to teach Melvin a lesson. After all, Melvin would have to deal with this thing too. He'd have to take on the additional load to make up for David's lack of experience. Maybe it would teach him a lesson, make him see how obstinate he'd been.

Sam Bass looked into Melvin's eyes, measuring him for a moment. Then he reached over, pushed the intercom button on Melvin's desk to the Service Department and said, "Send David Livingston to see me." He looked at Melvin with a secret smile. There was no turning back. He had called Melvin's bluff. David Livingston would be the new assistant manager.

Chapter Twelve

MARCH 1948

Jessie paid the oilman six dollars for the forty gallons of oil that barely heated the little hut. She never felt warm enough, and as she shut the door on the bitter wind that always found other ways to sneak into the little apartment, she wondered if she would have enough money to pay the rent. Well, Uncle Sam might have to wait, but not for long, now that David had been made assistant manager.

Sarah was playing with a teddy bear, oblivious to the cold floor. Jessie bent down, lifted her into her arms and held her tight. It was time for Sarah's nap. She carried her to the tiny bedroom and put her to bed.

This was no place for Sarah to grow up. David had promised they would move to a better environment before Sarah was born; now Sarah was almost a year and a half, and they were still living in the same drafty hut. David had little time to spend with Sarah, and Jessie wondered if history was repeating itself. Had she really ever had a chance to know her own father? He, like David, usually left for work before she was awake and at best would return in time for a kiss goodnight. She wondered once again if David had really wanted a child. There was a subtle change after Sarah was born. Was the passion between them subsiding? Didn't all marriages cool down after a few years? Was she paying enough attention to him? Could he sense her fear of getting pregnant again while still living in a damn hut? Maybe he was just so tired from studying every spare moment, and the long crazy hours he worked, or whatever. She sensed something was wrong, but she couldn't explain it.

Suddenly she remembered that Betty and Max were coming to dinner and looked at her watch. "Dammit, it's four o'clock and I'm not dressed and nothing's ready. Shit." She always blushed when she swore. "They'll be here at six thirty."

Max and Betty Goldman were already there when David arrived home. David kissed Jessie and Betty. He shook hands with Max warmly.

David looked around the tiny living area: the borrowed and second-hand furniture, the oil-stained wall behind the oil heater. He was embarrassed, knowing that Betty and Max had a cute little one-bedroom apartment, while he was still living in the damn veteran's project. But he knew that it wouldn't be too long before they could afford a real apartment and get out of this rat trap.

Max slapped David on the back. "Well, how's it going, buddy?"

"Actually, things are really good. They're throwing a ton of shit at me, but I'm handling it. I think I almost like it."

"I hate what I'm doing. Sometimes I feel like quitting, but the pay isn't bad and..." Max took a sip of the drink Jessie had poured for him.

"Max, if you hate what you're doing, you should get out. Start looking around. What the hell, you don't owe those bastards anything."

"Well, I'll try for a raise one more time and if they don't come across then..." David changed the subject. "Did you get a chance to watch the game on TV?"

"No, our TV is on the blink, but the Yankees won. First time they televised a World Series and I missed it. My luck."

They talked and smoked, sipping their drinks, while Jessie and Betty went into the kitchen to put the finishing touches on dinner. Betty spoke softly to Jessie. "David's going to go places, Jessie. You're a very lucky girl."

"I am lucky, Betty. Not because he's going to make us money, but because I love him, and he loves me. Imagine, married people in love?"

Betty's brow wrinkled and she avoided Jessie's eyes.

"What's wrong, Betty? You looked funny then."

"Nothing, I'm fine."

"Come on now, this is Jessie. What's wrong, did I say something?"

"No."

"Betty?" Jessie gave her a concerned look.

"Well, it's just that…Oh, Jessie, it's such a long story." Betty fidgeted with her wedding band.

"What's wrong?"

"Nothing's actually wrong…It's so hard to explain. Max…" Betty ran her hand through her hair.

"Oh, it's Max."

"Yes and no. Maybe it's me, I just don't know. I hate to lay it on Max; believe me Jessie, he's wonderful, he's sweet and kind, but…"

"What do you mean?"

"I can't explain it, Max's just Max."

Jessie took Betty's hand. "Betty, Max's so good."

"Maybe that's the trouble. Look, don't say anything to David. Here they come, so drop it."

Jessie felt sorry for Betty, but at the same time she felt guilty, because she liked the idea that her husband was getting someplace, while Max seemed to be stagnating, and it felt good that Betty was impressed with David. She was ashamed of herself for even thinking like that, but she shrugged her shoulders and thought, well, what's wrong with feeling proud of your husband, knowing that other women admired him. Suddenly she wrinkled her brow, and wondered if she really liked the idea that other women found her husband so interesting.

Max pushed his chair back and made a show of rubbing his belly. "That was a hell of a dinner."

David wiped his mouth with his napkin. "Yeah, honey that was great."

Jessie started to pick up the dishes. "Well, since you guys are so happy with my cooking…and don't forget that Betty was just as responsible for this fabulous meal. Guess who's doing the dishes?"

Both David and Max gave out a theatrical groan.

"Just kidding. Just kidding." Jessie looked at the hand-me-down dishes her mother had given them. "And, besides, I wouldn't want you clumsy bums chipping my beautiful china."

Both men gave a fake sigh of relief. Max looked at his watch. "Jesus, it's almost ten o'clock. Got a big day tomorrow."

After the goodnights were over, David felt drained.

"You look so tired, honey," Jessie said, slipping into David's arms. "Are you okay?"

"Just tired."

"C'mon, wash up and get to bed. I'll clean up. You need some sleep."

"Sleep, huh? That would be novel."

Jessie looked up into David's eyes. She crinkled her brow. "Is something wrong?"

"No, nothing's wrong. It's just that I feel so unsure of myself. I mean, why did they pick me instead of Joe? I think I can do the job, but…" His head started to throb, the beginning of a severe headache. "What if I screw up? After all, I don't know anything about being an assistant manager, and working directly under Melvin doesn't sound like an easy deal, either."

"But Melvin's your friend."

"Yeah, we're supposed to be friends, but lately it seems like anything but that." His mind kept churning. He excused himself from helping Jessie clean up, even though he felt terrible leaving the whole mess to her, and went right to bed. He was still awake when Jessie slipped noiselessly into the bed beside him, and he started to tell her that his headache was worse, and that he couldn't sleep, but then decided not to.

Jessie knew David was still up but she pretended not to. She wanted to be alone with her thoughts. She remembered how easily she had become pregnant and how little thought they had given to that commitment. She and David had never discussed having a baby; it just happened. They had never talked about raising a child, about education or anything else; they just did it. A flutter of panic rose in her chest. Was she imagining that David had changed? When was the last time they had made love? *Stop it,* she admonished herself. David was just working too hard. And then there were his studies. She didn't know how he did it. Yet he was at the top of his class. He was trying so hard to get them into a real home, a decent place to raise their child. How could she ever have doubted him? She had loved David almost from the first time they met. He was everything that she had dreamed about. She turned over onto her side, cuddled against him and waited for the curtain of sleep to calm her troubled mind. It was a long time coming.

CHAPTER THIRTEEN

JUNE 1949

"Half a day today, David?" Melvin smirked as David headed toward his truck.

David continued walking to his truck but turned his head toward Melvin. "Doctor's appointment."

"Again?"

"No, still." David kept walking.

Melvin raised his hand with his forefinger extended as if he were admonishing a child. "You know, David, I haven't docked you yet, but..."

"But you're going to, right?"

"I didn't say that, I..."

"I'll have my ears checked."

"Well, I mean, it's like once a week and..."

"Please, stop the bullshit and just dock me. I'm late as it is." *Besides if I don't get out of here real quick, I'm going to deck this idiot,* he thought. He got into his truck. Melvin just stood there with his mouth open and surprise in his eyes.

It was a beautiful day with huge, white, puffy cumulus clouds that played tag with the sun. It was too nice to sit in Sanders' stuffy office, but he needed to talk. Sleep was still elusive and the nightmares continued unabated. He knew he shouldn't have been testy with Melvin, but the lack of sleep was getting to him. After all, it was Melvin who hired him and took all the heat from his father. And from what he had heard, it was Melvin who recommended him for the assistant manager's job. So what if he was a little chicken shit? He thought he'd make it up to him tomorrow.

Miracles still happened, he actually found a parking space. He was late. He did a limping jog to the VA, caught the elevator and stood outside of Sanders' office out of breath. *Fucking cigarettes.* Sanders spotted him through his office door and without rising beckoned him in.

David sat down on the hard chair, trying to find a soft spot that didn't exist. Sanders remained quiet and serene, waiting for David to speak. There were a few moments of silence. "This isn't working."

Sanders waited patiently.

"It's a waste of time."

"Is that what you came in to tell me today?"

"Well, yeah. I guess so." David squirmed in the hard chair.

"So, are you leaving?" Sanders started to pick up some papers on his desk.

"Goddamn you. What am I, just another fucked up G.I. that you can't wait to get rid of?" David started to rise.

"You're very angry, David."

David jumped up from his seat, his face contorted. "Goddamn right I'm angry."

"Sit down," Sanders said sternly, "and listen. You have to pick yourself up from the ashes of this war and find a way to forget. Find a way to survive and prosper." Sanders took a deep breath and let it out. "Stop being pissed off at me and, more so, stop beating yourself up."

David sat down and started to speak but hesitated. "I'm not pissed off at you.

"I...I just don't know where to start...so mixed up... really sorry."

Sanders knew he was getting to David. He would have to tread lightly. Go someplace easy again. He took off his glasses and squeezed his eyes trying to think of a starting point. "Tell me a little more about Winthrop, when you lived there with your dad." He paused, hoping for a response from David.

David hesitated. The muscles worked in his cheeks. He forced himself to relax. "I loved it there in the summer." David smiled, thinking about it. "I used to go to the beach a lot. There were huge boulders piled up to break the water. Some of them spilled farther back on the beach. Sometimes two or three of them were close together. They made the best forts. I used to pile up the sand between them and wait for the tide to come in. The little fort would hold out until the water finally surrounded it and then it would once again sink into the sea. The next day I would come back and try again. I never gave up, but the sea always won. I remember telling my dad about it and he said it was a lot like life. You could keep trying to build forts around you, but life rolled over you anyway, like the tide. I didn't really understand what he meant then, but somehow, it always stuck in my mind like a puzzle. I think I know what he meant now."

Sanders waited for him to continue.

"There were no forts to protect me then or, for that matter, now either. I had to survive on my own guile, my own spirit." David stopped, deep in thought.

"And how did you survive then?"

"Then?"

"Yes, in Winthrop."

David pulled out a Lucky and fired it up. "I fought back."

"Fought who? Why?"

"Well," David took a drag and blew it out. "First the sea, even though I knew I could never beat it. I just wasn't going to stop trying."

"And then?"

"The kids. The kids who picked on me…because I was Jewish."

Sanders took off his glasses and wiped his brow. "Weren't there other Jewish boys?"

David smiled. "Yes, but they wouldn't fight back."

"But you did."

David laughed. "Oh, I did. I fought my way to school and I fought my way back."

Sanders wiped his brow. "How did that make you feel?"

"Like the way I felt about the sea. Fighting the sea, fighting the kids, but never giving in."

"And your father, what did he think?"

"My father?" David leaned back in his chair. He smiled. "I remember my father holding my hands, taking out his handkerchief and wiping the tears from my face. His eyes were very sad, but they bored into mine and he said, 'You will spend your life fighting for what you believe in.'"

Sanders sat quietly as David continued.

"He looked at my scraped fists and then looked back into my eyes with an intensity that I had never seen before. I'll never forget what he said: 'You will bleed and hurt, but you will also make your enemies bleed, and one day you will walk as a leader with your head high and only bow your head to God. Do you understand?'" David took a breath, and ran his hand through his hair.

Sanders waited patiently.

"I can still hear his words as if he had spoken them just yesterday. He held my shoulders so tight that they hurt, and he said, 'Listen, you're only a little boy, but you are my hope. Someday more Jews will think the way I think, and they will teach their sons, and maybe, just maybe, we Jews, not one by one, but all of us, will stand tall and proud. Listen to me! I came over from Russia when I was your age. I didn't have a mama or a papa so I lived with an uncle. He told me I should look down so no one should notice me. I should learn to be a tailor like he was. School was for the rich. And so I became a tailor, and now, I can hardly keep a fire in the stove. I still look down, instead of carrying my head high and proud, but not you, you will fight back, stand tall."

David's eyes filmed over and he closed them.

Sanders voice brought David back. "And are you willing to keep fighting?"

David shrugged.

"Are you willing to stop fighting me and use your energy productively?"

David met Sander's searching eyes and waited quietly in contemplation until the session was over.

Sanders waited for an answer. The silence was electric.

David pushed his chair back, got up, walked to the door, turned to Sanders, and said, "I'll think about it."

Chapter Fourteen

April 1950

In spite of himself, Sam Bass liked David. He had been with the company for over three years. He was a tireless worker, innovative and smart, and Sam felt that he was a good example for Melvin.

Sam hated to drive, and he would often ask David to drive him, much to Melvin's consternation. David was respectful, a careful driver and a good listener.

"I'm going to the bank," Sam announced.

Melvin quickly came around from his desk. "Do you want me to drive you, dad?"

"No, that's all right. I already asked David." Sam picked up his hat and headed for the door.

Melvin looked out of his office window in time to see them drive away. He sat down, stared at the papers strewn across his desk. Suddenly and violently, he swept them to the floor. He caught his breath and tried to choke back the anger that consumed him. "Fuck him. Fuck him. Fuck them both."

Sam found David waiting in the car and slid into the passenger seat. They rode in silence for a while. He was glad David was driving. If it were Melvin, he'd be nervous. The boy always made him feel that way. He didn't know why. Well, he felt comfortable now, so he settled back in his seat and relaxed.

"How are you doing in school?" Sam asked, not looking at David.

"Okay, I guess."

"When do you get a chance to study?"

David smiled. "Every chance I get. Between service calls, during lunch, even in the john."

"I wanted Melvin to go to school."

David kept his eyes on the road.

"You still live in the veteran's project?"

"Yes sir, we do."

"Not a great place to live, I imagine?"

"It's really not that bad. At least we've got a roof over our heads, and I'm thankful for that."

"Seems like you deserve better. What the hell, you're a hero, aren't you?" Sam said, a little surprised with himself.

"No, not a hero, just lucky. The guys that didn't make it back are the heroes."

Sam studied David's strong hands lightly resting on the wheel of the old Packard, and thought how those same steady hands must have guided his bomber through his missions to hell. Suddenly a wave of guilt swept over him. He found that he liked, even admired this strong, humble boy. Yet, he thought, Melvin, the little bastard, repulsed him. Angered him. Nothing Melvin did pleased him. Everything he did annoyed him. His desk was always a mess, strewn with papers, crumpled cigarette packs, coffee cups. To Sam a messy desk was an indication of a disorganized mind. He clenched his fist, and thought, *There I go again, hating him, always finding fault with him, and I know why. It's wrong. I'm too hard on him. After all, it's not his fault. I just can't forget. I know it's wrong. I'll try. I'll keep trying, but I know I'll probably never be able to find a place in my heart for the boy. I can't, I just can't.*

When they arrived at the bank, Sam got out, told David that he would take a taxi back, and thanked him for the ride.

Sam met Will Donner in the executive dining room. They shook hands warmly, found a table and sat down. Donner was tall and lanky, well over six feet. He had steel gray hair and a hard jaw. The waiter came over almost immediately and they ordered. Sam never liked the opulence of the bank's executive dining room or for that matter the big plush offices reserved for its executives. After all, the bank always preached frugality, and yet they flaunted the opposite. It was a strange world.

They finished lunch and went over their respective agendas. Sam offered Will a cigar, but he declined.

"Mind if I light up?"

"Enjoy."

Sam fired up his cigar and leaned back relaxed.

"How is Melvin doing?"

"Well, he's still Melvin." Sam avoided Donner's eyes. There he was, putting the boy down again.

"Come to think about it, we foreclosed on a nice little house in Milton. It might be just the right thing for Melvin.

Sam wished he could take Will up on his offer and get Melvin out of the house, but Melvin was too comfortable, and he knew it would be a lost cause. He thought about David.

"You know, Will, I told you about this new kid that I made assistant manager. You met him once, remember?"

"The kid that was a POW? Sure, I remember."

"He's a good kid, and, well, I'd like to do something for him. Lives in that veterans project in Dorchester and…"

Will put his fork down and finished chewing. "Why don't you tell him to come in and see me?"

"Maybe I will."

"Might be just the right thing for him. Start him off in a nice little house. Probably the best investment the kid could ever make. And, of course, your recommendation will go a long way."

Will was all business when it came to the bank, Sam snickered to himself, realizing that he had just accepted financial responsibility for David.

Chapter Fifteen

May 1950

Jessie adjusted Sarah's comforter, blew her a kiss and quietly followed David out of her little room. It had been a long day. They plunked down on the couch, Jessie with a big sigh, David with a grunt, looked at each other and broke out laughing.

David held Jessie in his arms, and listened to the rain pounding on the tin roof of the Nissan hut. She raised her face to his, and he kissed her lightly on the lips.

"Are you okay?" Concern showed in her eyes.

"Just thinking." David gently pushed a strand of black hair from her face.

"About?"

"The rain."

"Is it making you sad? You look…"

"It's nothing." David forced a smile.

"C'mon, out with it." Jessie pushed him away and held him at arm's length, looking into his eyes.

"Just a bad memory, that's all. The rain brought it back to me. Nothing important."

"Dammit, David, talk to me! Maybe it would help me to understand. You, you never talk about it. I want to know. I'm going through this with you too. It's not fair!"

Jessie listened to the rain pounding on the roof. David remained silent. She was just about to ask him again when he looked down, away from her searching eyes, and started to tell her about the rain and the evacuation hospital in Germany.

"At first I didn't want to open my eyes. I just listened to the rain. I was afraid I had only dreamed that I had escaped, that I was free, safe again, in the hospital. Not that it was much of a hospital, but it was an American hospital, just a Nissan hut, like this one, only much bigger." David paused and lit a cigarette.

"I was lying on a stretcher, in a long line of stretchers, listening to the rain that was beating on the roof, hurting bad, waiting to get to one of the four operating tables. I was getting real close, and the closer I got, the sicker I felt."

David looked into space as if he were reliving his experience. The rain grew louder.

"The surgeons were wearing white hospital garb stained with blood. They looked like four bloody butchers. There was a galvanized pail under each operating table filled with body parts."

David smashed out his cigarette as if to crush the memory that would never fade. Then he continued, but his voice wavered. "I remember how it all started to blur, and I thought I'd be sick, but I don't know, I held it in, somehow." He looked away from Jessie, embarrassed. "Aw, you don't want to hear this."

"Please, David, I need to hear it, all of it."

David let out a deep breath. His lips trembled. Tears glazed his eyes. "There was a paratrooper who'd lost both legs, lying on a stretcher on the other side of the hut, waiting to be evacuated. He was still sedated and, I guess, he still didn't realize what had happened to him. He was delirious, blindly searching for his boots, reaching toward his feet, which weren't there. He was crying and then he started to scream. 'Where's my fucking boots? Where's my boots? Jesus my feet are killing me. Medic! Where the fuck are my boots? Medic, Medic.' My stomach turned over, feeling bad for him, thinking about my own leg. My whole body was trembling. I wanted to scream, tell them to leave me alone, but then I looked around at the other guys. Guys much worse than me. I just lay there thinking what a fucking waste the whole thing was, the war, the killing that would never stop. Hell there was nothing I could do about it, so I just waited and stared at the bloody operating table.

"Finally, it was my turn. Two orderlies picked up my stretcher and took me to the waiting barrels of legs and arms the other guys had left behind. They helped me onto the operating table. I was so scared. I didn't want to lose my leg, to be a cripple. Couldn't come home to you that way. I lay there shaking like I had malaria, while the nurse assisting the two surgeons cut away my pants leg. I could see her nose wrinkle under the white surgical mask when she smelled the gangrene rotting in the wound in my thigh. I shut my eyes and listened to the surgeon read the tag from my preliminary examination. 'Fractured occipital area, puncture left elbow, three punctures left hip, compound fracture left tibia.' After about an hour on the table, while I held my breath, the doc looked at me with eyes as tired as I've ever seen. He told me he'd immobilized my ankle, and did the best he could with the gangrene, but there was no guarantee they could save my leg. 'We'll know better when you can get to a hospital in England,' he said."

Jessie took both of David's hands in hers and held them as if she could stop them from trembling.

"I shut my eyes as if I could block out the whole scene, but I could still hear the paratrooper screaming for his boots, and calling for the medic. Then I wasn't sure if the screams I heard were his or my own."

David slumped back into the couch, exhausted.

"You need a drink." Jessie started to get up, but David stopped her.

"No thanks, sweetheart, just sit down and let me hold you for a minute, then I'll tell you the rest."

David seemed to borrow energy from Jessie's body and, after a while, he began to speak. "I was air-evacuated in a stretcher plane to a hospital on the outskirts of London. I hadn't spoken a word after I heard that I might lose my leg. I was so fucking depressed I just couldn't talk anymore. I answered questions with a nod or a grunt and, otherwise, didn't talk to anyone, not even Mac."

"Mac?"

"Yeah, he was the ward's head nurse, a good guy, about as wide as he was tall. He felt it was his duty to keep his patients happy. I guess I was a challenge, and he was determined to put an end to my depression.

"One morning he showed up with two big orderlies and a wheelchair. 'Okay, lieutenant, we're going for a ride,' he said. The orderlies lifted me from my bed, and put me into the wheelchair. Mac took over and pushed the wheelchair into the amputation recovery ward.

"Two soldiers were lying on a mat opposite each other, fighting with their stumps, an exercise to strengthen the area in preparation for prosthetic attachments. Mac kidded with them and said, 'Don't you guys ever give up?'

"A guy with one arm walked over and asked Mac what he was doing in the amputation ward, wanted to know if he was slumming, all the while giving me the once over, smiling like it was a private joke. Of course, it was, and I was beginning to get it. Mac said he just wanted to introduce me to the boys. The guy just looked at me with one of those shit-eating grins. A paraplegic rolled his chair over to join the fun and then another amputee walked over, both arms missing. They all knew what Mac was up to. I squirmed in the chair, filled with embarrassment. I started to get the picture. I turned to Mac and said, "Alright, alright, I get the message."

"Good," he said, "then say good-bye to the boys." And he wheeled me back to bed.

"When Mac got me back to bed I felt like a real jerk, but Mac gave me a pat on the back and said, 'You're going to be okay, I promise.'"

David slapped his bad leg as if to confirm that it was still there. "I guess he kept his promise."

Jessie took David into her arms, "Yes, David, you are going to be okay. I promise too." The rain stopped. David's leg ached.

CHAPTER SIXTEEN

JUNE 1950

The house, an expanded Cape, sat high on a knoll on a quiet, tree-lined street, and Jessie fell in love with it at first sight.

They walked through the house with the bank's agent, and Jessie's mouth fell open. "Oh my God, it has a refrigerator."

"And a Bendix washing machine downstairs." The bank's agent added.

"A washing machine, oh my God." She walked into the empty living room and stopped at the fireplace. She ran her hand over the smooth white mantle as she surveyed the rest of the room and wondered how many guests she could invite comfortably.

She led the way into the kitchen with David and the agent following. "An electric stove. No more jugs of smelly kerosene. This is just..." She paused and looked at David anxiously, her brow crinkling in anticipation. "Can we really buy it?"

"Well, Mr. Bass said he would lend me the money for the down payment, and we can afford the bank payments, so, if you really like it…"

"Really like it? Really like it? I think I died and went to heaven."

With Max and Betty's help, they moved in the following month, but Jessie's happiness was short-lived. Max had brought a copy of the *Boston Globe*, and he handed it to David. It read, "June 28, 1950. President Truman today ordered U.S. ground troops to Korea, a naval blockade of the Korean coast, and authorized the Air Force to begin bombing North Korea."

David put the paper down slowly as Jessie came to his side. "Will you have to…"

"I don't think so. Not with this gimpy leg." But he knew that every officer was in the reserve for ten years after discharge and, although it was highly unlikely that he would be called, he'd have to check it out.

He glanced at the headline again, dropped the paper on his lap, lit up a cigarette, took a deep drag, blew out a long stream of smoke and grimaced. Smoking much too much, he thought. *Have to cut down. I can't stop the smoking, and the world can't stop the killing.* It all seemed so futile. He mashed out the butt in the already overflowing ashtray.

Another war. Less than five years had passed since "his" war." What happened to the United Nations, all the promises of peace, of a world without war? He ran his hand over his crippled leg that he knew would never heal, and looked at his trembling hands. He thought back to the planes that didn't come back, and then the ones that did, shooting off their red flares, signaling they had wounded aboard, hoping to get a priority landing. The ambulances that either carried the wounded to the hospital or acted as hearses for the dead. He could still hear the screams of the sirens, the cries of the wounded, and the silence of the dead. Was it all for nothing? First it was the Nazis, now the Communists, when would it stop? He had no argument with the values of the democratic way of life, and understood the need to preserve it, but why was it up to Americans to try to protect it, impose it, die for it in foreign lands? There would never be an end to the politics of war.

David graduated from his accelerated course at Boston University. Although night school graduation ceremonies didn't have the fan fare that day school had, Jessie's mother and father, in an unprecedented display of generosity, took them to dinner at The Parker House restaurant to celebrate David's graduation.

It was a double celebration for Jessie. David was found to be ineligible for service. Jessie was ecstatic, but David secretly felt diminished. He thought he was no longer the man he had been. He'd lost something that he couldn't quite identify. He had become ordinary. He thought about flying. The danger faded in his memory, stripped of its terror, with only the excitement of being in harm's way remaining. He thought about Charlie. His chest felt heavy and his throat felt tight, as he fought to control the tears that were just below the surface. He stared into the past, picked up his glass in a toast, and said, "To the troops." Then, without waiting for a response from the rest of the table, downed his drink hoping no one noticed how shaky his hand was or the horror that had flashed by his mind's eye.

Well, to hell with the past. This is a new day. He was an assistant manager now and had a college degree to back it up; he would go all the way now. He thought how proud his father would have been, and looked at Jessie beaming, almost on the verge of telling her mother, "I told you so," and he was happy.

CHAPTER SEVENTEEN

SEPTEMBER 1951

David completely immersed himself in his job as assistant manager. He had spent little time at home before; now it was almost nonexistent. Many times he slept on the couch in his office. Over a year had passed and David hardly noticed until the day when Jessie, Sarah in hand struggling to keep up, swept by David's secretary. She burst through David's office door, lifted Sarah up, sat her on top of David's desk sweeping papers and other miscellaneous things to the floor and into David's lap. "Sarah, this is your daddy," she said triumphantly.

"I know that, Mom," Sarah said, a little confused.

David picked up Sarah, gave her a big hug and a kiss, took her on his lap and looked at Jessie, smiling. "Okay, what did I do to deserve this honor?"

"Well, considering that your daughter hasn't seen her father for over two weeks, I thought that you two would like to get acquainted again, especially when you promised to take her to the beach last weekend, remember?"

"Oh, sh…of course, but I thought it was next week," he lied.

"Daddy, you're such a fibber."

"You're right, honey. I've been so busy that I just forgot, and that's not right. A promise is a promise. I am truly sorry." David's brow crinkled, waiting for Sarah's response.

Sarah had never seen her father look so sad. She hugged him protectively. "That's all right, Dad, don't feel bad."

David got up, still holding Sarah, took Jessie's hand, and walked out of his office. He stopped in front of his secretary's desk. "I won't be available for the rest of the day. You can juggle whatever I have into next week, and have Joe cover for me." He smiled at Sarah and said, "I'm going to spend some time with my daughter."

"Well, you have a good time, Sarah."

"Thank you." Sarah blushed.

"Okay, princess, where would you like to go?"

"Cape Cod."

"Cape Cod?"

"Yes, one of my friends goes there all the time. They stay in a little cabin and go to the beach every day."

David was about to protest. He couldn't get away now, yet he hadn't taken a vacation for over two years, even though Mr. Bass had insisted he take one. He was due. He had built an organization that should work well without him for a few days. He looked into Sarah's pleading eyes. "Cape Cod it is. We'll go home and pack up and..."

"Oh, you are the best, Daddy!"

"Honey, this place is so adorable." Jessie's head was swiveling in every direction.

"Look, we've got a fireplace. Hey, they even left us wood."

"Logs."

"Okay, logs. Oh my God, will you look at this view." She took David's arm and led him to the little deck that overlooked Chatham Harbor. It was a perfect day. The sun sparkled on the water, and white, puffy clouds scudded by, racing the boats that slid through the water. Some of the boats sailed by without a sound; others powered along with a distant roar. The fishing boats were followed by flocks of white gulls. They seemed to mysteriously know there was a feast awaiting them as the fishermen gutted their catch and threw their entrails overboard. "Smell that air," David said as he inhaled the salt air.

"Smell what?" Sarah asked, sniffing and looking perplexed.

"The air, honey, it smells salty, don't you think?"

"Can we go to the beach now?"

"Well honey, let's just unpack a little and then we'll go right to the beach."

It was September, the shoulder season for tourists at the Cape. They laid out their towels on the white sand, and were delighted to find that the beach was practically deserted. Sarah was chasing the gulls, and Jessie was soaking up the sun, lying on her back, her raven hair flowing over a rolled-up towel supporting her head. Her eyes were closed, and she lay perfectly still. David watched her and suddenly his mind flashed back to dead soldiers laid out in a row, dog tags tied to the laces in their boot. *God, if I ever lost her,* he thought, as he felt his heart rise in his chest. *I love her so much.* He leaned over and gently kissed her. Her eyes flew open and she smiled back at him. "Y'know I love you."

"Y'know, I guess I love you too."

"Well, get down here, you big ox, and snuggle." David dropped down beside her and she molded into his body and kissed him hotly. He became immediately aroused. Suddenly another little body joined them, "I want to snuggle too." David and Jessie burst out laughing, as David rolled over onto his stomach.

"C'mon, Daddy, you're not snuggling."

The setting sun set the sky on fire. Layers of red and purple followed the last of the sun's golden glow into the reflecting sea. Slowly the dark purples and blues took over and eventually went dark as the sun drowned in the black sea. There was only a sliver of a new moon, and now a fine mist sent up from the sea enveloped it. "Okay, pal, time for bed." David swept Sarah up in his arms.

"I don't want to go to bed now; we're on vacation."

"Hey, you've had a big, big day and it's sleepy time now."

"Will you tell me a story?"

"Okay. You get ready and I'll think something up."

Later after they built a fire in the fireplace and Sarah was fast asleep, David sat down on the couch and Jessie slid into his arms. They were quiet for a long time. Suddenly, Jessie pushed out of David's arms and got up. "I almost forgot," and she disappeared into their tiny bedroom. A few minutes later she was kneeling on the floor with a little gift-wrapped box in her hand.

"What's this?" David asked, as she handed it to him.

"Open it."

"Well, what's this for?"

"Never mind, just open it."

David looked at her quizzically, opened the package and was genuinely surprised as he took a gold chain with a tiny heart hanging from it.

"This is beautiful," he said hesitantly. "But, why?"

"It's my heart on a flimsy chain. Don't ever break it, David, because I love you so much, I would just die."

David put the chain around his neck. "I'll never take this off." He pulled Jessie from her knees to the couch and into his arms. "I love you more than life itself and I will never hurt you."

CHAPTER EIGHTEEN

OCTOBER 1951

The grating sound of the garage doors, and then Sanders' car roaring to a start, wakened Ruth. Her eyes still closed; she reached over to Sanders' side of the bed. It was still warm with the memory of his body. She put her arm across her eyes and thought about the first time she had met him, her big, brainy, cuddly Richard Sanders.

It was a cold October day. Dark clouds blew by, allowing the sun to peek out for only a few moments. One could almost feel the rain hiding in the clouds, and the raw east wind that blew in across the harbor smelled of salt and impending rain. She was in Harvard Stadium for the Harvard-Yale game, wearing a turtleneck sweater over a long wool skirt, a maroon and gold scarf around her neck, and a heavy wool coat. Her two best friends, Clarice and Sylvia, were bundled as she was. "You look like cows with clothes on," she chided them.

"At least we're warm, and nobody's going to look at us anyway. They're going to be watching the cheerleaders," Clarice said.

"I hate cheerleaders." Sylvia scowled.

"Yeah, and I know why." Ruth smirked. "Come on, let's get some good seats."

Sylvia bought a Harvard banner from the nearest vendor, who was yelling, "Get yer banners, buttons, and souvenirs here."

They found good seats on the 40 yard line.

"Wow, what great seats."

"Yeah, if we don't freeze to death before the game starts," Ruth reminded them.

Two big guys sat down beside them, and Ruth wondered why these healthy specimens were not in the service. The war had started last December, and most of the boys she knew had either volunteered or been drafted into the service. The one next to her was wearing a raccoon coat. His glasses kept fogging up, forcing him to continually wipe them with his handkerchief. He had a nice smile and big brown eyes that caught her staring at him. She blushed as she turned away.

"Hi."

Ruth looked down at her hands, avoiding his eyes. "Hi."

"Hope you're rooting for Harvard." He had a beautiful smile that gave her goose bumps.

She went to an all girls school. Boy contact was a little scary and embarrassing. "Yes, I'm rooting for Harvard," she managed to squeak out.

"I bet you're a Cliffy."

"Well, yes, I go to Radcliff. Are you Harvard?"

"Medical school, thank goodness, or I would have been drafted a long time ago."

Harvard lost that day but Ruth found Richard.

They graduated in the same year. One sunny afternoon a few weeks later a justice of the peace married them. It was the sunniest day in Ruth's life, but it wasn't too long after, that the clouds began to thicken.

Although Richard wore thick, horned-rim glasses and had a receding hairline, he was a charmer, and Ruth always felt in peril of losing him. He stayed out late many nights, and he was away for days during his internship at the hospital. Then it was night sessions with patients and a thousand different excuses. When they did go out, he charmed the pants off all of the ladies, young and old. But, that was Richard, and she was willing to live with it, because she loved him, and she knew he loved her. They would stay up half the night arguing about Hume and Kant's writings on religion and morality, or whether E. E. Cummings was a fad or a genius. There was no end to their intellectual engagement, which stimulated them almost as much as

225

the sex that followed. Unfortunately, no matter how they tried, Ruth couldn't become pregnant. Richard said it would happen eventually, but it didn't.

Sometimes when he came home, he smelled of sex or perfume. She always wondered if it was her imagination. She knew most men fooled around a little, that it was innocent, and didn't really mean anything. Of course, if he had a real affair, that would be different. She would…Well, she wasn't going to think about that because it just wasn't going to happen…was it?

Ruth got out of bed and went into the bathroom. She had always slept nude, and now, she examined herself in the mirror. Her breasts were so small. Richard always said, "Who needs more? A mouthful is enough." She smiled, thinking about it. Dammit, her hips were too big and she was too damn tall. Thank God Richard was over six feet. She had a good face, sort of a peasant's face: a strong jaw, big hazel eyes, and a straight nose that she thought was a little too big, but then it sort of went with the rest of her. She washed up, brushed her teeth, put on her panties and slipped on a little housedress. She picked up the laundry from the hamper and walked barefoot into the kitchen. She started to put the laundry in the new Bendix washing machine they had bought from a door-to-door salesman. When she came across Richard's shirt, she sucked in her breath, pulled the shirt to her breast and started to cry. The lipstick stain came off in the washer, but it would stay in Ruth's mind forever.

She decided not to confront him this time, but if it ever happened again…She put the coffee pot on the stove and wished it wasn't Saturday. Richard worked all day Saturday, and she usually caught up on the ever-growing paperwork that invariably went hand in hand with a case she was given by the Society for the Prevention of Cruelty to Children. But today she couldn't concentrate. Richard kept intruding on her thoughts. After all, she was a modern, highly educated woman. Why should she just accept this, this infidelity… Well, maybe it wasn't infidelity. Richard was always hugging people, men and women alike. He was such a warm person. Maybe the lipstick was from an innocent hug from one of the many women patients he helped…Well, she was going to overlook it. *That's it,* Ruth told herself. *I'll just forget it.* But she couldn't.

CHAPTER NINETEEN

SUMMER 1952

Eastern Oil always held its annual spring picnic at Sharon Lake. Sam Bass hated mingling with what he called "the help," so it became Melvin's responsibility to make all the arrangements and to attend in Sam's place.

Melvin tackled the job each year with relish. He hired a band, made sure there were plenty of hot dogs and Coke, and rented canoes for those who would rather paddle than swim. It was the only opportunity to slip out from beneath his father's shadow and just be Melvin. That is, Melvin's interpretation of Melvin.

During the picnic, Melvin was the gracious host, the big boss, tending to his flock. He mingled and joked with "the help" and enjoyed every minute of it. Best of all, it was at a company picnic years ago that he first met Ginny.

He had a mouthful of hot dog when he realized mustard was dripping all over his hand. He had a Coke in his other hand and was trying to figure out how to get out of his predicament, when he looked up and saw Ginny. She was hiding her amusement behind her hand. She turned to her father, said something that made him frown, got up, walked over to Melvin, took the Coke away from him, and handed him a napkin. She was laughing so hard that she spilled some of the Coke on her dress.

"Hello, I'm Melvin."

"I know who you are—you're the boss's son. My father drives one of your oil trucks. I'm Ginny McGrath. The man that's glaring at us is my dad, and I'd better get back."

"Why? It's a picnic—you're supposed to have fun." Melvin looked for a place to throw the napkin.

"I know, but my dad is old-fashioned. He doesn't like me speaking to strange men."

"I'm hardly a stranger, after all…"

"Well, you know what I mean."

"Well, we can fix that." He took her hand and led her to where her father was sitting.

"Hello, Mister McGrath. I guess we've met a few times at the office. How have you been?"

"Okay," McGrath said gruffly.

Melvin looked at the lake, each ripple flashing in the sunlight, and then back at Ginny's father. "I thought I might take Ginny for a canoe ride, with your permission, of course."

"Ginny's too young to be dating," McGrath growled.

"Well I wasn't exactly asking her out on a date, I…"

"If you want to talk with Ginny, you can sit right here and do all the talking you want."

Melvin shrugged his shoulders and obediently sat down on the blanket beside Ginny. They talked the afternoon away and, when it was time to go, Melvin took Ginny's hand and whispered, "I'm going to keep asking your dad to let me take you out on a date until he says yes. That's a promise." Melvin got up, and said good-bye to McGrath. As he walked away, he looked back and caught Ginny's eye. She smiled, checked to make sure her father wasn't looking, and blew him a kiss. Melvin was in love.

What Melvin couldn't have known was, that as Ginny blew him a kiss, she thought, *He just might be my ticket out of here.*

CHAPTER TWENTY

AUGUST 1952

John McGrath was a good man. When his wife died three years earlier, he took over the responsibility of raising his teenage daughter. Not an easy task for a man alone. He had worked at the same job, driving an oil truck for Eastern Oil, for nineteen years with an exemplary record, and was looking forward to retirement. McGrath was a stern man, but with a good humor for his friends, and a marked intolerance of his enemies and his daughter, Ginny. Many commented that this was his only fault. Perhaps it was because of his huge disappointment that his only child had not been the boy he had boasted about to his friends, almost since the day his wife had told him she was pregnant. But this was not the reason at all. As Ginny grew from her diaper stage to a toddler, and then to a little girl, John loved her with a secret passion. But when she would climb into his bed on Sunday morning to cuddle up to him, he would make up any excuse in order not to have her beside him. As she got older, he became more and more distant, and the big kisses and hugs he used to receive upon arriving home became less and less exuberant until, when Ginny was eighteen, there was only a cool hello. Yet, he loved her more now then he ever did when she was a child, for now she had become a woman, and yet, this very fact provoked his greatest discontent.

Their little flat on the third floor of a three family house in South Boston had two small bedrooms, a parlor, a kitchen with a huge black iron coal stove that tried unsuccessfully to spread its warmth through the other rooms, and a tiny bathroom with an old, chipped tub. There was little privacy. Many times John would fly into a rage when Ginny, a towel barely covering her nudity and her skin still glistening from her bath, would dry herself before the warmth of the coal stove in the kitchen. John would force his disobedient eyes to his newspaper, mumbling, "For God's sake, girl, display a little modesty, cold or no cold." But when in deference to his complaints, she would reach up to towel her hair, a golden mass of shimmering curls, he would steal a glance at the high breasts and hips that belonged to an older, more voluptuous woman. Then, if not admitting to himself that he had to look at her again, to touch her perfect skin, he got up, took her arm, and forcefully led her out of the room. Afterward he would find an excuse to be angry with her. He would hate her for all his love and reproach himself for the uncontrollable feelings that raced through his mind, both conscious and unconscious.

When Ed Sullivan, who lived on the first floor of their three-family house, asked Ginny out on a date, McGrath threw the paper he was reading to the floor. His face flushed red as he turned to Ginny. "Well, you can laugh me off, girl, and argue with me like ya did with the lipstick, but I'm puttin' my foot down. No goddamn Irish bastard is taking out my little girl on any goddamn date, and that's final."

Ginny was relieved, for the thought of going out with Ed frightened her. It wasn't that he was so much older than she was, but that he was so difficult to cope with. Like the time he had met her coming home from school and offered her a ride home in his "crap can," as he called it. He had put his arm around her as they were driving and let his hand slip over her breast. She had stiffened and pushed his hand away, only to be rebuffed with, "Don't be such a goddamn kid. What d'ya think, you're the only broad in town with tits?" When he had finally let her go, she had run up to her room, crying and confused.

Two years had passed since her first encounter with Ed. To her consternation, she was still not allowed to date, but she managed to find ample opportunity to explore her sexuality with the boys at school who constantly pursued her. Ed was still on her case and determined to take her out. He came up to play checkers with her dad in the evenings. Every so often he'd bring a pint of John Jameson and, pretty soon, he became McGrath's drinking buddy.

His eyes never seemed to leave her when she was in the room, but Ginny was no longer afraid of him. She could see right through his little plan. She was impressed and felt empowered at the thought of all the effort he was expending. It was exciting to watch him flush. Once, he even spilled his precious Jameson when she bent down to replace an overflowing ashtray, purposely exposing her ample breasts. She felt the subtle power of her sex and thought, if Ed succeeded, and her father let him ask her out, she would accept. After all, he wasn't a bad-looking guy, in a rough sort of a way. In fact, she often thought about him when she was alone in her bed. She wondered how his hard body would feel to her touch. Her hand would creep down between her legs and fantasize that it was Ed touching her. At first she tried to restrain herself. After all, she was sure what she was doing must be a sin, but instead she surrendered and let her imagination run rampant.

She watched Ed go into his final act with her father. He was very polite and courteous when, upon leaving the apartment one evening, he asked her father if it would be all right to ask her for a date. McGrath reluctantly gave his permission. Two days later, when Ed asked her out, she accepted.

She had hoped that Melvin would have been her first real date, but she had only seen Melvin that one time at the picnic. He was out of her reach, but she promised herself that she would find a way. Maybe at the next picnic, which wasn't too far away.

As Ginny started to leave the flat in answer to Ed's horn, McGrath stopped her and thrust a dollar bill into her hand. She could see that he was struggling to say something, but he only mumbled, "Mad money." She put the dollar in her purse, and gave him a quick kiss. McGrath put his hand to his face where Ginny had kissed him, and watched her run down the stairs without looking back.

As she hopped into Ed's "crap can," she looked up and saw her father watching her from the parlor window.

"Where're we going?" she asked Ed jubilantly.

"How 'bout just taking a ride through the Blue Hills?"

It was a warm night with a full moon. A ride with the top down, and maybe something to eat, sounded just perfect.

Ed told her about his boyhood, his new job and his plans for the future. Even with all his gruffness, she was happy just listening to him and looking up at the stars. They stopped at a drive-in where they had hot dogs and Cokes while they listened to Rosemary Clooney sing "Tenderly" on the car radio. Ed leaned over and kissed her. His tongue slipped between her parted lips and a tingle of excitement rushed through her body.

He asked her if she had ever seen the city from the top of "Big Blue" and, without waiting for an answer, started the car. He put his right arm out, and she accepted his invitation by sliding over so that his arm encircled her shoulders.

When they reached the top, they left the car for a better view of the blinking harbor lights on one side and the city on the other, sparkling in a maze of colors and patterns.

They walked up a dirt path that led to a stone building, housing restrooms on each side and a waiting room in the middle. Ed tried the door. "It's open. Wanna see what's inside?"

"I don't care. If you want to."

They went inside. It was pitch black in the windowless room.

"I'm scared, let's get out of here. It's, it's spooky." Ginny turned to leave, but Ed pulled her close to him and kissed her. As the kiss lingered, their bodies moved against one another, and she could feel his excitement against her. She pushed him away gently, but not honestly, for her own body felt warm with a delicious sensation. He pulled her closer and kissed her ear, which sent little shocks through her. *Jesus, I better stop. Oh, that feels good.* She felt his hand on her breast. Her knees felt weak as he directed her to sit down on his coat that he had placed on the floor. They sat down, still in an embrace. He kissed her and leaned her

backward until he was lying beside her. She was trembling
with excitement. Every time his lips touched her neck or
her ear she could hardly control herself. She shut her eyes
in complete surrender until she felt his hand sliding up the
inside of her thigh. She froze, holding his hand with hers.
Panic.

"Please don't, Ed." She said it softly in a controlled
whisper.

He ignored her protest, pulled her panties down over
her hips and pushed up her skirt. She grabbed at his hand.
"Ed, stop!"

His hand broke free from hers, and slid between her
legs. She felt herself giving in, filling with desire and fear
at the same time. It was so mixed up. *Christ, stop! Stop!
I'll get pregnant. My father will kill me.* "Ed, please, please,
stop. Goddamn it, get off of me!" She tried to push him off.
"Please, Ed, I never did it before. I never did it before." *Oh,
shit that hurts. Ow! Ow!* "You're hurting me!"

When her breathing became normal again, she was
soaked with perspiration, sticky and wet between her legs.
Aghh! Ed was no longer beside her. He was leaning against
the wall, smoking a cigarette. The son of a bitch had raped
her. She wanted to hurt him, scream at him, but what was
the use? She began to cry. Ed ignored her. Suddenly she
stopped crying and she began to understand.

*So this is what it's all about. My father. Looking at me
that way. I know what he's been thinking, pushing me out of*

his life. The boys at school, always trying to get fresh, and Ed, he got what he wanted. He'll be telling about it in the corner poolroom tomorrow. Well, girl, that's okay, if you think about it. Men want to dominate you because they need to get between your legs. They'll do anything to get there. Anything. That's the simple truth. Well, so be it. Maybe it could work both ways… if a girl was smart.

Chapter Twenty-One

December 1952

The tall French windows of the Glass Slipper looked out on the snowstorm blanketing the Public Gardens. The trees were stark white against the night and the snowflakes were like tiny diamonds anointing them. A few young people wearing long, bright-colored scarves and heavy jackets were braving the storm on foot. They were laughing. Their frozen breath hung in the air as they stomped through the snow. They made Melvin feel lonely, and he began staring at each cab, wondering if the next one would have Ginny in it. She was already a half hour late. He decided he'd wait another fifteen minutes before calling her. After all, it probably would be tough to get a cab in this snowstorm.

He lit another Camel and remembered the promise he had made to date her at the company picnic. He chuckled, thinking that it had taken him three years to keep his promise, and then, only by accident, when McGrath had taken her to the company Christmas party, where they had literally bumped into each other at the refreshment table.

He looked out at the snow again. *Look at that snow come down. Thank God for David. He'll be supervising emergency service tonight instead of me.* David had, surprisingly, worked out very well, in spite of the fact that Melvin had put every stumbling block he could find in his way.

Melvin was on his second scotch when Ginny's cab pulled up in front of the Glass Slipper. The driver helped her out and even walked her to the door. Melvin left the bar to greet her. She stepped into the little foyer. A few flakes of snow glistened in her hair, and her face, flushed from the cold, set off her cool blue eyes. She had changed very little since that first day they had met. Melvin crossed the few steps between them, and took her hand. Her blond hair was piled high. A few wisps had escaped and fell across her forehead. He could smell the faint scent of her perfume.

"Hi." She kissed him lightly on the cheek.

"I was worried. Thought you might not come."

"It's pretty awful out. Thank you for worrying about me."

"I always worry about you. Remember? I love you."

Melvin took her coat, handed it to the girl in the checkroom, took Ginny's hand, and led her to a seat at the bar. "Your hand feels like an icicle. Let's get you a drink and warm you up."

"Yes, thank you, I need one." She took out her compact, looked in the mirror, adjusted her hair, wet her lips, and put the compact back in her purse.

"Al, a martini for the lady, please." Melvin downed the little that was left in his glass and added, "And another scotch, make it a double."

Ginny was glad that she had talked Melvin into meeting her at the Glass Slipper instead of her apartment. She knew he would end up drunk again, and she didn't want to deal with it at home. She smiled, thinking how easy it was to manipulate him. A little baby talk and he was eating out of her hand.

The drinks arrived. Melvin picked up his glass and held it out to Ginny. "To us."

Ginny touched Melvin's glass with hers, "Yes, to us." As she sipped the cold Martini, she looked over her glass and studied Melvin. He was a handsome man. Okay, he was a drunk, but she would fix that. He'd rescued her from the cold water flat in South Boston, helped her open her little boutique, paid for her apartment on Beacon Street, bought her nice clothes, and took her to the best restaurants. Damn right she'd drink to that.

Melvin's face turned serious. "Why didn't you want to meet me for dinner?"

"I was really busy and I didn't want you to have to wait for me. I know you like to eat early." There were other things besides his drinking. Melvin was jealous, and just about anything set him off.

"Busy doing what?"

Ginny kept her eyes locked on Melvin's. "Washing my hair, taking a bath, making myself look beautiful for you." *More baby talk. Men were such pushovers.*

"Someday you won't have to work."

"I like working. Keeps me busy. I meet nice people." She knew she had to change the subject. He had enough booze in him to start a conflagration. "Talking about work, aren't you supposed to be working or something in this kind of weather?"

"Not with good old David at the helm."

"Poor David. You're always talking about him. I can't tell whether you hate him or love him. Is he out in this storm? I feel sorry for him if he is."

"Well if you feel so sorry for him, I'll have him join us for a drink. He's in the area anyway."

Ginny turned and reached out for Melvin. "Please, Mel, don't make him go out of his way."

"Hey, he goes where I want him to." He headed for the phone.

David resented running personal errands. When the emergency operator called on his two-way radio and told him to report to Melvin at the Glass Slipper, David wasn't happy. *Dammit,* he thought, *I've got no time for this. Too many people without heat, freezing their asses off. I'll have to tell Melvin this crap has to stop. Oh yeah, just like that, and take a chance, old buddies aside, that I might lose my job.* No way. He needed this job, and he knew how lucky he was to have it. He couldn't screw up. He had to prove to Jessie, to himself, that he could cut it, be successful and be more than his father.

He parked the truck, illegally, in front of the Glass Slipper and turned on his orange flasher. It had taken him over an hour of tough driving through the storm to get there. He went up the snow-covered steps into the little foyer, stamped some of the snow off of his boots, and walked into the warm bar. As he pulled off his heavy mittens, he spotted Melvin and strode over to him. In spite of his previous thoughts, he said, "This is a hell of a time to throw a cocktail party."

Melvin frowned for a moment and then broke into a big smile. "David, David, you're not being polite, you haven't said hello to Ginny."

Even in the shadows, Ginny glistened. *God, she is beautiful,* David thought. He was quiet for a long moment, embarrassed by his informal appearance in the plush bar. "Hello," he said quietly.

Ginny extended her hand. She had a firm grip. Her smile was friendly, but with a touch of insolence. She held on to David's hand for an extra moment, and then searched his eyes, as if she might find the answer to the mystery that seemed to be hidden behind the scarred, yet still handsome, face in front of her. Her voice was husky. "Hello, David."

Melvin was annoyed. He saw the subtle change in Ginny, that certain look she saved for other men. He hid his jealousy and turned to David. "Well now, aren't you glad you came?"

David wanted to say something nice, something... clever. He was taken with Ginny and he wanted to impress her, but what was the point? Instead, he turned to Mel, who was already slurring his words. "You better take it easy on the booze. The driving is pretty bad out there."

Al put a bowl of peanuts on the bar in front of David. "Can I get you something to drink, sir?"

David hesitated. "No, no thank you. The weather, the snow, you know, just a glass of water, please."

"For God's sake, David, relax, take it easy, enjoy yourself. It's no big deal. Your people can take care of things without you for an hour, and you certainly don't have to impress me as to how dedicated you are to our wonderful customers." Melvin watched Ginny's face, looking for support. She was impassive. He downed his drink in one big gulp. "You know, Ginny, David's a big war hero...has to keep up his image. Right, David?"

David winced, but ignored the sarcasm.

Ginny turned to Melvin, her face flushed with embarrassment. "That's not very nice, Melvin. I think you owe David an apology."

"Sorry, sorry, didn't mean it." Melvin signaled Al for another drink. "They're ganging up on me, Al." He got no sympathy from Al. "Y'know, Ginny, David and I go way back. Went to high school together. Didn't we, old buddy? He was a real tiger then. Got all the girls, big fucking quarterback. A real tiger."

David caught Ginny's sympathetic eye but said nothing.

"What'sa matter, Tiger, cat got your tongue? That's funny isn't it? Y'know, tiger, cat?" Melvin laughed at his pun until he started choking. When he got his breath, he turned to Al and ordered another round.

David signaled Al with a negative nod and took Melvin by his arm. "You've had enough, fella. I'm taking you home."

Melvin wrenched his arm away from David. "You're taking me home?"

"Yup, 'cause you're not driving in this condition. Not tonight you're not."

"Since when are you telling me what to do? Ya hear that Ginny? He's telling me what to do."

David turned to Ginny. "Please, get his coat and yours too. I'll take you both home."

When Ginny returned with the coats, Melvin seemed to be worse. He had been sick in the men's room. David was supporting him, in spite of his desire to stand by himself. He was swearing at David, but David ignored him.

Melvin was the road to independence, Ginny thought, but she was sick and tired of dragging him home in a drunken stupor every time they went out. She had to try to straighten him out somehow. There he was, yelling at poor David, who was only trying to help him. And David was nice, not bad-looking in spite of that ugly scar. Well, actually it made him more interesting, sort of like a dueling scar.

What was she thinking? Melvin was her ticket to respectability and a good life; she'd just have to figure out a way to keep him sober.

It took over an hour to travel the three miles of the snow-clogged streets to Melvin's newly acquired Commonwealth Avenue apartment, and almost as long again to convince Melvin to go to bed. It was eleven thirty when David and Ginny started out for her place. Even with the heavy chains on David's truck, the traveling was almost impossible. The wind howled and drove the snow into the windshield with gale force, paralyzing the wipers. David frequently had to get out and free them, letting the snow and the cold wind into the car. Ginny laughed at his plight good-naturedly and, although David was cold and wet, her laugh was contagious, and he had to laugh with her. They got stuck twice and almost gave up until a snow plow gave them some help. David finally pulled up in front of Ginny's apartment and raced the engine to build up the amperage, so he could check in on his two-way radio.

"David to control, over," he repeated twice.

"Come back, David."

"What's up, Joe?"

"Believe it or not, all clear so far other than a couple of stuck trucks, but that's par for the course. Better go home while you still can."

"Thanks I'll think about that."

The windshield wipers, working for the moment, pushed the heavy snow back and forth. Thunk. Thunk. David could smell the faint scent of her perfume; he was conscious of her body. She exuded sexuality, and he was embarrassed that he felt aroused. They both began to talk at the same time and ended up laughing.

"So, you've known Melvin since high school?"

"Yes, and it seems like a thousand years ago."

"Were you really pals, like Melvin said?"

"Why do you ask?"

"I just don't…"

"See us as pals?"

"Well, you're so different, you…"

"Melvin was kinda small then and, for whatever reason, he had a chip on his shoulder. He was always getting into fights. Fights he couldn't win, because they were always with bigger boys, and sometimes more than one. I felt sorry for him a couple of times and, well, I sort of intervened. Helped him out."

"So you were his guardian angel?"

David blushed. "Not quite, I…"

"He talks about you a lot. I'm not sure if he says or does these things just to impress me or…Well, like tonight, pulling you away from your work. You know what I mean."

"Melvin seems to have his own demons that drive him. You know he drinks too much and he's…I don't know… bitter. Maybe it's his father…always beating on him. I don't mean physically. I feel sorry for him. I wish there was some way that I could help him but…" David shrugged helplessly. "He's sort of the poor little rich kid."

"He's very generous and…"

"Yes, he's been very good to me. Gave me my first chance. Recommended me for this job. Hell, I owe him."

Ginny wanted to say ditto, but she decided it was a good time to change the subject.

"Melvin said you were a hero."

David laughed. "No, I definitely wasn't a hero, nothing like that. Just another G.I. doing his thing."

"Somehow I don't quite believe that it was that simple."

David just smiled.

Ginny reached up with her hand and traced the scar that ran across David's eye.

"And did you get this just doing your thing?"

David took her hand from his face and held it momentarily. He felt as if electric shocks were running through his fingers. What the hell was happening? He had to diffuse the situation. He looked at Ginny with mischief in his eyes. "I got this for coming home late, and if I don't get home soon, there's no telling what will happen next."

Ginny laughed. "Oh, you're awful."

There was a long silence, while their eyes seemed to communicate a code only they could understand, until Ginny touched David's hand. "It was a real adventure. Thank you for getting me home safely." She looked at him for a long moment, opened the door, and stepped out into the storm. She walked up the stairs and, at the landing, she turned, snowflakes glistening in her hair, a glint of a smile. David got out of the truck and watched her disappear into her apartment, wondering what miracle had brought her into his life.

Ginny stopped in the vestibule and turned to the little mirror on the wall, licked her lips and smiled. "Too bad he's married; he's kind of nice in a rough sort of way." Then she said to the reflection in the mirror, "Are you crazy, girl? That's just what you need, an affair with a married man who's got nothing, and just happens to work for the guy you've been romancing for the last two years."

She walked up the two flights of stairs to her apartment, unlocked the door, took off her wet coat, threw it over a chair, and sat down. How had she come so far, so fast? She was twenty-two years old, in her own apartment, and had a business that soon would earn enough money to support her. Of course, if it wasn't for Melvin…

Still, it wasn't easy. Putting up with Melvin's drunken tantrums. Leaving her father alone with his fantasies. Listening to him call her a tramp and a whore. Threatening to run Melvin down with his truck. And finally, ending up in a drunken stupor, begging her not to leave him. She tried to call him a few times, but as soon as he heard her voice he would hang up. *Well, so be it. I am not going to let life pass me by. I am not going to be poor. I know how to get what I want. Give a little. Get a lot.*

The lights in Sarah's bedroom were on and David's heart skipped a beat. It was almost 1:00 A.M., and he knew something had to be wrong. A feeling of guilt swept over him. He wasn't paying enough attention to Jessie or Sarah.

It seemed like yesterday that Sarah was just a baby, and now she was six years old. Where had the time gone? The damn job seemed to be more important than anything else. He had been out until all hours over the last two weeks and, although Jessie didn't complain, Sarah kept asking where Daddy was. All the explanations in the world couldn't explain to a six-year-old girl why Daddy wasn't there. He ran through the snow to the door, fumbled with the keys until he was inside the vestibule of the little house, and, without removing his boots, ran to Sarah's room.

"What's wrong?"

Jessie was in her nightgown; her long hair in one big Chinese braid hung over her shoulder. She put her finger to her mouth as a signal for quiet and closed the door softly. She looked tired and she spoke softly. "I don't know what it is David. She has a temperature of 102. I called Dr. Schlossberg about eleven and then again a little while ago. He couldn't get out; his car is stuck, so we have to wait. He said he'll be here the first thing this morning; that shouldn't be too long now."

At six years old Sara was underweight and it was a constant struggle to get her to eat. She had Jessie's green eyes and dark hair, and no one could dispute that she was Jessie's daughter.

Dr. Schlossberg finally came at 5:15, and David and Jessie thanked him for braving the storm. They took him to Sarah's room, where she was now jumping up and down on her bed as if by some miracle she had completely recovered.

After Dr. Schlossberg examined her, he said, "I think this young lady is going to be just fine, but she might be a little itchy for a while, until she gets rid of these pesky measles."

David let out a long breath of relief, but then his mind raced back to Ginny, and suddenly a chill ran through him.

Was this some kind of a warning? Was somebody up there telling him that he had no right to have the feelings he had had for Ginny when she touched his hand, or looked into his eyes. He knew he was superstitious. Hell, all flyers were, but this was ridiculous, wasn't it? After all, it wasn't like he had cheated on Jessie…was it?

CHAPTER TWENTY-TWO

JULY 1953

The winter dragged by with snow day after day, and, even when spring came, the crocuses had to push their way through the snow. Spring hardly lingered when summer arrived, bringing with it a brutal heat wave. It was one of those dog days people talked about for years after. Betty was ironing in her kitchen. She was wearing an old housedress she just couldn't throw away, the one Max always made fun of. The pocket was torn, but it still held a crumpled handkerchief that she took out to wipe the sweat from her neck. She was soaked with perspiration, and she knew she probably smelled bad. She put down the iron and thought, *To hell with the ironing; it's too goddamn hot.* The radio blabbed on about Korea. Another war had ended. When would the next one start? She changed stations and found one pounding out rock and roll. But even Elvis couldn't console her, and she loved Elvis. She switched it off.

What a day to be a lady of leisure, sitting beside a country club swimming pool or maybe taking a cool shower, dressing up in something fancy, and going to some air-conditioned dinner club. Max would come home late, dead tired as usual, and the thought of staying home for another boring evening again in this heat appalled her. She started thinking of some excuse to go out, tonight…alone. She wrote him a note.

Max darling, meant to tell you this morning that I was going to run up to see mother today, and I will probably be late. There are some cold cuts and potato salad in the refrigerator. P.S. Please fix the electric fan. I think there's a short circuit in the plug or something.

Love,

Betty

It was just five o'clock when the Red Cab pulled up and honked the horn. Betty took a last-minute look at herself in the hall mirror, noticed her slip showed ever so slightly and started to adjust it. The cabby's horn sounded again. "Wait a minute, dammit," she muttered. "I'm coming." Finally satisfied, she hurried to the waiting cab.

"Where to, lady?" His question came to her as a shock. She had no idea where she wanted to go.

"Excuse me, lady, but would you mind telling me where you want to go?"

"Oh, oh, town. Take me into town."

"Lady, town's a big place. What part of town?"

"Oh, for goodness sake, just drive toward town. I'll tell you where to stop."

"Okay, lady, you're the boss." He put the flag on the meter down and stepped on the gas. As the street signs flashed by, Betty wondered where she was going, and what she was really doing. What the devil had gotten into her in the first place? She half-started to tell the cab driver to turn back and then changed her mind just as quickly.

"Driver, drop me off at the Public Gardens."

That's what she'd do. She'd take a long walk through the Public Gardens and, maybe, she'd feel better. She might even take a ride on the swan boats, or sit on a bench and think, but she had to get out of the house. It seemed forever before they got there.

The park was sweltering. There seemed to be no relief. She walked onto Beacon Street and tried to hail another cab to take her home when she spotted the Glass Slipper Bar and Restaurant across the street. A big banner that read "Air conditioned" hung above the door.

She crossed the street, stood in the doorway and peered into the dimly lit bar. She wondered whether it would be polite to sit at the bar or at one of the little tables that hugged the wall, and then decided to sit at the bar. After all, there was no one there, just two men talking to the bartender.

"Cheese and crackers are good, miss," the bartender said as he served her martini. "Help yourself."

Sanders was talking to the other man at the bar.

"Of course you can't lose any weight. You can't drink all night and half of the day, Norm, and then eat like a pig with some broad in the evening. What do you expect?"

"But I'm taking diet pills."

"You're really dieting, aren't ya?"

"Wait a minute—I don't drink like this every day."

"Look at yourself in the mirror; I'm heavy, but look at you, you're already Omar the Tent Maker's best customer. Listen, all kidding aside, you do something about that weight or, I'm telling you, it'll kill ya."

"Hey, as long as it doesn't affect my love life, I'm not going to worry too damn much." Norm chuckled. "Besides, the girls like me this way. I'm cuddly."

"Oh, what the hell's the sense, you're not going to listen to me anyway."

"Look, I know you're right, and I'm going to do something about it. Believe me; I'm going home to my last big dinner."

"Dinner! After what you've already eaten here? Goodbye, Norman."

The fat man got up, acknowledged Betty, and headed for the door. "Bye Doc, bye Al," he said as he left the bar.

Betty couldn't restrain a little giggle.

"It really isn't funny," the man called Doc said as he turned toward Betty.

"I'm sorry." She covered another giggle with her hand. "I didn't mean to laugh."

"That's all right." Sanders moved to the stool next to hers. "I haven't seen you here before. I'm Richard Sanders." He paused, waiting for her reply.

"I'm…" She hesitated, thinking that she didn't want to give her real name and then changed her mind. She needed a break, a little excitement in her life, so why not? She looked up at Sanders' face and gave him her most flirtatious look. "Betty Goldman…Mrs. Betty Goldman."

"Do we have to be so formal, or may I just call you Betty, as long as we're both stranded on this cool little island on a very hot afternoon?"

"I never thought of it that way but, now that you mentioned it, it is like an island. Of course, please call me Betty." She gave him another sexy look and wondered why this heavy man with thick glasses and receding hairline was so attractive. He certainly had a way with words and a great smile, but it was something else that attracted her. Maybe because he was the first man in a long time who seemed interested in her. Whatever, she liked the attention.

"Would you care for a fresh drink?" Sanders said as he gave her his best smile.

"I'd love one, thank you."

"Do you live around here?" Sanders motioned to Al to get Betty another drink and wondered if she was just another hooker or a real challenge. He hoped it was the latter because, after all, the best part was the challenge.

"Dorchester," she answered, suddenly worried that she had no idea who this stranger was.

"Funny, I haven't seen you around," Sanders took off his glasses.

"Not so funny, I just haven't been around."

"Oh, ball and chain too heavy for you?" He stared at her ring finger.

"No, not at all. Do you see any chains?" She cringed, thinking that she was flirting with another man, and that it excited her. A wave of panic spread over her, but it left as quickly as it had come and she relaxed again.

"Betty, this is Dr. Sanders you're talking to. Shall I rephrase the question?"

"Dear Doctor, I presume from your astute diagnosis that you must be a psychiatrist. What makes you so sure of this serious ball-and-chain ailment that I'm supposed to be suffering from?" She was becoming more animated. She liked the interplay; it was fun and Sanders was nice.

"My dear patient, any gal in her late twenties who walks into the Glass Slipper in the early evening, unescorted, on a hot summer day...very lonely...very bored...and terribly married, has a serious ball-and-chain disease." Sanders knew this line rarely failed.

"I hate to admit it, but at least you're right about the bored part." Betty saluted Sanders with her drink.

"Very honest of you to admit it, but believe me, don't think of yourself as unique because you're not. Every woman, correction, almost every attractive woman approaching her thirties, although the disease strikes at different ages, starts to wonder if her life is simply going to begin and end with dirty dishes, dusty floors, tired husbands and too much more to mention. She starts to worry if maybe her chin is sagging just a trifle, or maybe a faint touch of gray is showing, and, most of all, if she is still attractive to other men." He smiled that wonderful smile. "You can be sure that you have no need to worry about that. You are quite beautiful, you know."

"Thank you." Betty blushed and took a sip of her drink, internalizing Sanders' comments. "That's a very presumptuous analysis, Doctor."

"Isn't it the truth?" Sanders took out his handkerchief, wiped his brow, and thought, *This is too easy, but don't rush her.* She'll be ripe for next time, and he knew there would be a next time.

"Oh, I suppose if it were, a woman would never admit it. Are you married?" She looked at his ring finger and wondered why she had even asked. Then again...

He ignored her question and looked at her earnestly. "Listen, I hate to eat alone, especially since there is a possibility of dining with a beautiful woman. Will you have dinner with me? Please." Again that smile and those big brown eyes. "The food here is wonderful, the service is better." He paused for a moment and added, "I won't take no for an answer."

Betty searched the bar for, God forbid, a familiar face. The bar had filled while they were talking, but she didn't recognize any of the newcomers. She smiled at Sanders and with a little nod she acquiesced.

Sanders turned to the bartender. "Al, my check please."

Sanders made sure that dinner was served in the little private dining room. He felt safe there. After all, he certainly couldn't take a chance of being seen dining with a strange woman, especially because, at least as far as Ruth was concerned, he was supposed to be at another medical conference.

Dinner was terrific and Sanders was charming. The walk through the Public Gardens afterward was a kick she hadn't experienced since dating. Sanders was kind and understanding. When he finally put her into a cab, she hated to say goodnight. She felt like a kid again. She liked playing the game, flirting, feeling wanted again. Yet, she knew it was a dangerous game. She had had her little fling, she thought. Certainly that would be the end of it. As she rode toward home, she looked at the card Sanders had given her. *Richard Sanders, M.D. LA3-7500.* She knew she would call him tomorrow.

CHAPTER TWENTY-THREE

AUGUST 1953

The phone woke David from a deep sleep. "Joe? For God's sake, it's four o'clock in the morning. What's going on?"

"The old man had a heart attack. Like out of nowhere. Died in his sleep."

"Oh, my God."

"Mrs. Bass called me herself. Didn't know your number, and asked me to call you. They can't find Melvin. Fuckin' kid's probably lying in the gutter somewhere, drunk. Hey, it's not my problem; you're the big man now, aren't you? So, you find him."

David knew the grief of losing a parent. There was no way he would be consoled when his mother died, but he was a little boy then, and as the years of love and caring from his father accumulated, her memory faded into the warmth of her embraces and the faint smell of her perfume. That was the grief of a child.

David slowly put the receiver back on the hook. His head swirled and he thought of his own father. Funny, the first thing that came to his mind was the sweet smell of his pipe tobacco. He could see his father's face. It was the face of a fisherman who had weathered too many storms. It was a strong, hard face, yet there was always the hint of a smile that brightened it and gave whoever observed it a feeling of warmth and comfort. God, how he had loved that man. He felt a lump in his throat and tears hid just behind his eyes as he remembered the day he found out that his father had died.

He was in the Seventh General Hospital, just outside of London. The wound in his leg was killing him and he thought the back of his head was going to fall off. He reached up and touched the bandages just to see if they were still there. The nurse came over to his bedside. He didn't even know her name; at least he couldn't remember it. She had a small porcelain bowl and a white towel. She gave him a nice smile that was more professional than friendly.

"Time for a cat wash," she said. "Are you up to it? Oh, and I have a letter for you."

She put the bowl and the towel down on the little nightstand, reached into the pocket of her uniform, and took out the letter. She looked at it for a moment and handed it to David.

"Must have traveled around the world by the looks of all the forwarding stuff. Well, at least you got it. Whoops, forgot the soap. Be right back."

David examined the envelope. It was dated six weeks earlier, and it was from his Aunt Susan. He hadn't seen her since he was a kid. He wondered why she would be writing to him. Then he knew. His hands trembled as he slowly opened the envelope. His father had died. Tears sprung from his eyes.

"Oh, no. Oh, no." He felt as if he'd been stabbed with a hot blade that burned a hole all the way to his soul.

David wiped away the tears that ran down his cheeks with his hand as the memory of his father faded. He knew where Melvin was. He would be at Ginny's. He dressed hurriedly, drove to her apartment, rang the bell, and was surprised that at five in the morning the buzzer came back so quickly. He ran up the stairs and Ginny met him at the door. She was wearing a red silk dressing gown, and if she had been asleep you'd never know it. She gave him a sad look and motioned toward the bedroom. The light was on, and David could see Melvin lying face down on the rumpled bed. He was naked except for a pair of boxer shorts, and his face was buried in a pillow. His shoulders shook violently. The pillow muffled great sobs that lifted his whole body.

"Someone called Al at the Glass Slipper looking for him and Al called here, so he knows. Hasn't stopped crying since," Ginny said.

David sat down on the bed beside Melvin and put his hand on his shoulder. Melvin quieted for a moment, then lifted his head off the pillow, sniffed and started to sit up, a few sobs still choking out. He looked at David with red eyes, still wet with tears. "Why did he hate me, David? I tried so hard at first. Nothing I did pleased him. The more I loved him, it seemed the more he pushed me away. Why? Why?"

Melvin started to cry again. David hesitantly put his arms around him and gently rocked him as he would a child. "Your dad did love you, Melvin. He just…"

"No, he never loved me. For Christ's sake, he loved you more than me."

CHAPTER TWENTY-FOUR

AUGUST 1953

Services were at Temple Beth Shalom in Brookline at one o'clock. It was 93 degrees at noon when David left the office. He had worked all morning. Even though the main business was closed in respect to Mr. Bass' death, emergency service had to continue.

He adjusted the sign hanging in the door, notifying people of Sam's death, before he locked up. By the time he reached the temple he was soaked through with perspiration. He was glad Jessie was spared the heat. He knew she would be home minding Sarah.

The services were held in the large auditorium of the temple that Sam had worshiped in for most of his life. There was an altar in the front of the room and behind it an exquisitely carved wood cabinet that held the sacred Torah of the Hebrews. Below the altar was Sam's body in a light blue casket with a Jewish Star embroidered in the material draping the casket. Unfortunately the old Temple was not

265

air-conditioned and the room was unbearably hot. David stopped in front of Sam's casket. Sam had been kind to him, almost fatherly, and David felt the pain of loss once again. He touched the coffin, paused for a moment, and then turned and walked over to Mrs. Bass and Melvin.

Mrs. Bass seemed to be staring into space, her eyes were red, but there were no tears now. Melvin's head was bent too low for David to see his face. David took Mrs. Bass's hand; she simply nodded in acknowledgment. When he took Melvin's hand, Melvin continued to stare at the floor. He held David's hand for an extra moment acknowledging he was there, and David felt that it might be a signal that there would be some sort of a truce between them. He knew Melvin would need all the help he could get if he wanted the business to continue, and David was prepared to do whatever was necessary to help in any way he could. David sat down at the very back of the auditorium to wait for the services to begin. He felt a little nauseated from the sweltering temperature and the overpowering smell of perfumes and sweat from the crowded men and women. An old man with a scraggly gray beard, dressed in a shiny black suit, sat down next to him, and David moved closer to a large sweating woman on his left to make more room. He felt as if he were suffocating. He got up, excused himself to each person in the aisle, and headed for the door. He was at the door when it opened and Ginny stepped in. She looked cool in spite of the heat. All he could think of to say was, "There's no more room, Ginny."

"I want to see Melvin, David. Will you wait for me?"

"Sure."

"I've never been to a Jewish funeral. Are you supposed to do anything?"

"No, just stop at the casket and then go over to Melvin and his mother and tell them how sorry you feel."

Ginny left and David walked to the door of the vestibule that led outside. He had never been able to completely get her out of his mind, and he found himself fantasizing about her while he waited.

"God, it was hot in there," Ginny said when she returned.

David took off his jacket and loosened his tie. His shirt was sticking to his skin. Then surprising himself, he said, "Want to get a cool drink?"

Ginny thought for a moment. Then with a delicious smile, she said, "Okay, but I don't have a car." She still looked cool and fresh as a summer breeze.

"Would you mind riding in my truck? It's pretty clean."

"If it can get me out of this heat, I'll even ride in the back," she said, smiling.

"How 'bout the Glass Slipper? It's air-conditioned."

"Any place cool would be nice."

David found a parking space on a side street and they walked through the heat into the cool bar.

"Hey, Ginny, how's it going?"

"Nicely, Al, you?"

"Okay, okay, and nice to see you. What'll ya have?" Al asked, as they took seats at the bar. It was dark and cool. They both sighed with relief from the blistering heat outside.

"Something cold. Very cold."

"Couple of gin rickeys?"

Ginny looked at David and he nodded his acquiescence.

"You must come here often."

"Well, I have a little boutique right around the corner and Melvin likes to come here." She took out her compact, dabbed her face with a powder puff and wet her lips while Al brought their drinks.

David took a sip of the cold gin rickey. "So who's minding the store?"

"As a matter of fact, I just hired a really nice married lady who comes in two afternoons a week. She's a godsend. Gives me a chance to get away from the grind."

Ginny lifted her glass, said, "To air conditioning," and took a big drink, her blue eyes scrutinizing David.

"I'll drink to that." David smiled and raised his glass in a mock toast.

"Do I make you nervous, David?"

"Why? Oh you mean this?" David spread out his trembling hands. "No, it was all the gourmet food they gave me when I was Hitler's guest in Germany that left me with this."

"I'm sorry; I didn't mean to…I didn't know. I…"

"Forget it. That was a long time ago. Let's talk about you. You're much more interesting."

"No, that's what you said the last time we met. Let's talk about you."

David took a sip of his drink. "There's not much to tell."

Al came over wiped the bar in front of them. "Want some peanuts?"

David looked at Ginny. "No thanks, Al. I think we're fine." She turned back to David. "Tell me about when you were little. When you were a kid. Where you grew up?"

"Do you want to be bored to death?"

"I'll take my chances."

"All right then, here goes. I grew up in Winthrop, in the poor section, down by the wharves. We were very poor."

"We?"

"My dad and I. My mother died when I was a little boy."

"So, your dad raised you by himself?"

"Yes, we were kind of partners. We each had our own chores. My father worked as a tailor. I went to school, did

269

my homework, got the coal along the railroad tracks for the stove, and picked up the groceries."

"Coal along the railroad tracks?"

"Well, yeah. You see, when the trains came through, a little coal always fell off along the tracks, and I'd get it for the big stove in our kitchen."

"We had a stove like that." She smiled, leaned forward and touched David's hand.

"You did?" David was aware of her hand gently resting on his. Her hand was cool but it sent a heat wave through his entire being. Suddenly he wanted to take her hand in his and pull her toward him, engulf her in his arms, posses her, never let her go.

"Yes, but at least I didn't have to hang around the railroad tracks to get coal for it." Ginny removed her hand and David felt the loss of it. He wanted to reach out and take it back.

"Too bad, it would have been a lot nicer having you there than some of the guys I used to run into."

"They gave you a bad time?"

"I guess you could say that, but they didn't get off without a few bruises of their own."

Ginny's eyes searched David's scarred face, his strong jaw and bottomless black eyes. She could only imagine the strength that lay within this man. "I don't doubt that one bit," she said as she looked at David, prompting him to continue.

"When I got a little older, I worked for the grocer, delivering orders that weren't too heavy for me to carry. Got a nickel an order and sometimes I even got tips. In the winter I shoveled sidewalks and stairs for a quarter." David leaned forward and said, almost conspiratorially, "Well, I didn't always get a quarter because I shoveled Mrs. Kelley's house for free. She was so poor; I don't think she even had a nickel to her name."

David's eyes took on a far away look thinking back to his father. He continued as if Ginny wasn't there, his voice a little choked. "My dad worked very hard just to get food on the table and pay the rent. He only had this old coat that I knew couldn't possibly keep him warm, and his shoes were filled with paper to try to patch the holes in the soles. I was always worried he'd get sick." David paused feeling a little embarrassed. "Hell, I'm boring you."

"No, really, please go on." She touched his hand again. David almost flinched.

"Remember when we were talking about Melvin? You know, in the car, during the snowstorm? I said he was a poor little rich boy. Well, I was a rich little poor boy. I loved it there, just me and my dad, the boats, and the sea." David could almost smell the sea. "Have you ever been to Winthrop?"

"No."

"Well, I don't quite know how to describe the place. It used to be a small fishing village. Then business must have fallen off and the little harbor held only a few fishermen and a couple of rotting hulls. I loved to play pirates there with my friends, but what I loved to do the most was to go down to the ocean. I would build sand forts and try to beat the sea, but the tide always came in and broke down my forts. I just kept on trying and even though I knew I could never win, I didn't care. I just kept building them, higher and stronger, patching up the walls, fighting back. Never giving up." David's face flushed as the memory of the struggle to survive rushed through him. "I can't quite explain why I kept doing it, but maybe now, older and wiser, I think I understand. We all go through life knowing that we can't beat death any more than I could beat the sea. The question is how do we live each of those precious moments that make up our lives?" He paused. "Me, I'll never stop building forts. Do you know what I mean?"

Ginny squeezed David's hand, and nodded affirmatively.

David took a deep breath, memories flooding back to him. "I remember when we moved to Dorchester, so I could get a better education. I cried so hard. My dad, God bless his soul. He just couldn't stand me being sad, so he went to the pound and bought me a dog. His name was Willy and, until I found out about the opposite sex, he was the love of my life."

"I never had a dog. I always wanted one but my father..." Ginny's voice drifted away with her memories. "My father is a good man but…I can't explain it. He's just a tough old Irishman. It sounds like your father was a very kind and gentle man."

"He was, but still not a man to fool with. He killed a man who tried to rape his sister. He was only sixteen. The guy was a Russian officer. They had to smuggle my dad out of Russia. They hid him in a shipping crate with a crowbar, so he could get out, and then put him on a ship to America."

"What a story! So he was a stowaway. Did they find him? What happened when he got to America?"

David signaled Al for a refill and turned back to Ginny with a secret smile. "Sorry, you'll have to wait for the next installment. Now it's your turn."

"That's mean. I want to know what happened."

"No, I'm saving the rest for the next time we meet."

"Is there going to be a next time, David?"

David paused, looked at Ginny until their eyes met. There was no need for an answer. "Now tell me about you."

Ginny broke eye contact, hesitated, and started to pick up her drink but changed her mind. "Me, I'm just a plain old Irish girl, born and raised in South Boston. My dad works for Eastern too. Drives one of the oil trucks."

"Really? Is that how you met Melvin?"

"Well, kinda. I met him at a company picnic."

David took another sip of his drink, trying hard to keep his hand steady. "You see him a lot?" David asked, as he looked into the overwhelming blue of her eyes.

"We date. We have fun together. Well, we do when he's not drinking."

David fiddled with his glass, not responding.

Ginny looked down and without raising her eyes. "Melvin's an okay guy and he's been very good to me."

"And?"

"And, he lent me the money to open my boutique."

"And?" David stared at her.

Ginny met David's eyes and said angrily, "And, he helped me get an apartment, and helped me furnish it, and got me out of my father's house, and, yes, I sleep with him. Any other questions?"

"I'm sorry. I don't know what got into me." He took Ginny's hand, but she pulled it away and started to get off of the barstool. "I have to go."

"Please don't go. I know it's stupid but I felt a little jealous. Somehow, I kind of felt there was something happening with us. I can't explain it. I thought I felt, that you…"

Ginny stopped, her face flushed, her anger subsiding. She stood there appraising him and then she reached for his hand. Their hands barely touched, but they each knew that they had taken the first step in a long journey.

David wanted to tell her that he had thought of her a million times, but he hesitated. He was filled with guilt and confusion. He loved Jessie. What was this feeling he had for Ginny? Was it something lacking in Jessie, something that he was lacking that was making him even think about another woman? The thought annoyed and appalled him. Jessie was terrified of becoming pregnant again and their sex life had suffered because of it, but did that give him the right to cheat? *Let's face it,* he thought. *I know what's going to happen. It'll end up in a hotel room and then what?* But, even with these thoughts, he couldn't stop.

"I wanted you to kiss me that night," Ginny said. "I've wanted you from the first moment I saw you. I couldn't stop thinking about you since that night in the snowstorm. I..."

David interrupted her. "I want to make love to you, Ginny." He didn't believe his own voice. It shouldn't be that easy. You just didn't come out with it that way. He hardly knew her. And what about Jessie?

CHAPTER TWENTY-FIVE

AUGUST 1953

David rented a room upstairs in the Glass Slipper. He came back to the table, paid his bill and took Ginny's hand. He led her to the little self-service elevator.

Once inside the room Ginny was in his arms and his lips found hers. She responded passionately, holding the back of his head with one hand, her body molded to his. They separated. She looked at him for a moment, searching his eyes, then put a finger to her mouth as a signal for both silence and patience and departed to the bathroom.

David sat on the window seat and stared through the tall bay windows into the Public Gardens. He barely heard the soft roll of faraway thunder and the pitter-patter of the first drops of rain landing softly on the big window. The rain became heavier. A flash of lightning broke through the black sky. David could barely see through the pelting rain that washed over the window. Was his mind as blurred as his vision, he wondered. Couldn't he see that this would be an irrevocable change in his life? Was it too late to turn back? What was he thinking? *A stiff prick has no conscience.* He got up, undressed, undid the bed and got into it.

Ginny stepped out of the bathroom. She had showered and had a towel wrapped around her. She walked over to the bed, leaned over and kissed David.

"Get rid of that towel."

She dropped the towel on the floor and posed for a moment, waiting for his approval. The light behind her threw her into deep shadows, her hair picking up the highlights. One high breast with its pointed nipple catching the light contrasted with the darkness of the silhouette of her thighs and long legs. It was as if she were half dressed and the mystery of what lay within those soft shadows fired his imagination.

"Come over here."

She looked down at him and slowly let her eyes wander over his body. David started to sit up and reach for her, but she pushed him back down, got into the bed and straddled him. She leaned on her elbows and knees and brought her face very close to his, her blue eyes wide with excitement.

"I think I'm going to fall in love with you," she whispered. David started to say something but she shushed him, and smiled lasciviously, "Promise you'll wait for me."

Then she slid down his body, leaving little kisses on her way, and finally took him into her mouth. David groaned as her lips caressed him in a way he had never experienced before. He began to move slowly with her rhythm until he felt he couldn't wait another moment. He reached down and pulled her up so that her body molded into his. Her face was flushed and her eyes were wild. He started to adjust his body so that he could be on top of her, but she stopped him and, instead, reached down and helped him inside of her. A shiver ran through his body as he entered her. It seemed that it passed through her as well, but it was more like a charge of electricity for him. She sat astride him, arched her back, her head rolling from side to side with little moans coming from her compressed lips. She moved sinuously, her hips undulating, slowly picking up her momentum, sliding back and forth. The bed shook and groaned. "Oh, yes, fuck me, fuck me," she hissed through clenched teeth. Then with a violence that was almost primal, her body glistening with a fine coat of sweat, she rolled her hips and moved her pelvis in quick successive thrusts. Suddenly she stopped, let out a little scream and froze. David groaned from deep in his throat and with a final thrust, completely spent, lay breathing hard beneath her.

She untangled herself from her sitting position and lay beside him, the only sound their beating hearts and heavy breathing.

"Are you okay?" she asked breathlessly.

"I'm not sure yet. You?"

"I may never walk again."

"I don't want you to walk. I want you to stay right here, in this bed, beside me forever."

"Beside you? Don't you like me on top?"

"I don't know. I haven't tried you on the bottom."

"I'm ready."

"Hey, give me a break."

"Sissy."

"We'll see about that." David rolled on top of her and started to kiss her.

She pushed him away, looking at her watch. "Oh God, look what time it is. I have to close the store and Betty has to get home. I have to go."

"No, no, no, I'm not letting you go."

"David, I'm sorry." She kissed him. "Next time we'll have more time. I promise." And she slid out from under him and ran into the bathroom.

Ginny put the finishing touch to her lipstick, inspected herself in the mirror and thought, *Well, Ginny old girl, you might just as well say good-bye to Melvin and all your fancy ideas. God knows what'll happen if he ever finds out, and poor David, he'll probably hate me when he thinks about what we've done. Well, I'll never see him again, and maybe Melvin won't find out.* She peeked out of the bathroom door and looked at David, blew him a kiss and thought, *Oh, yeah, you'll never see him again. Who are you kidding, girl?*

David was still languishing in bed after Ginny left. He ran his hands down his body, thinking how good he felt and, at the same time, how ashamed that he had cheated on Jessie. He remembered one of the many quotes from the Talmud that his father had made him memorize.

"Be very careful if you make a woman cry, because God counts her tears. The woman came out of a man's rib. Not from his feet to be walked on. Not from his head to be superior, but from the side to be equal. Under the arm to be protected and next to the heart to be loved."

The clock in the Old South Church began to toll. He thought about all the hell he had endured to get back to Jessie, and now he had betrayed her.

When he got home, Sarah would rush into his arms, and after some hugs and a lot of kisses, he would put her down and kiss Jessie. He would not be able to meet her eyes and would avoid them for fear she would see his deceit.

He rushed to the shower. He felt dirty.

Chapter Twenty-Six

WINTER 1954

Melvin couldn't find sleep. He rolled and tossed, tangled in his sheets, and thought about Ginny. During the five months since his father's death, Ginny had changed. There was talk about her with David. Melvin seethed. First it was my father, now Ginny. He smashed his fist into his pillow. "You bastard," he screamed. Suddenly the phone rang, startling him. "What the fuck…" He picked up the receiver.

"Melvin, it's Joe. Sorry to bother you at home. I know it's late, but we got a big problem. See, Billy was working at the Fairmount job, you know, old lady Johnson's place, and I dunno what happened. Anyway, he cut himself pretty bad. Over at the hospital getting fixed right now and I don't know if he'll go back to the job or not after they fix him up."

"So, why are you telling me this in the middle of the night? Why don't you just call David? Isn't that his problem, or is he too big to do service calls anymore?" Or too busy fucking Ginny, he wanted to add.

"Well, I can't find him. He's not home. Jessie says his radio is on the fritz, but that he was probably on his way home, and that she would have him call me. Problem is, he won't be able to get me, because I'm working at the Sloan job, and there's no phone there, as you know. Well, anyway, I asked Jessie to have him call you, so you could fill him in."

"For God sake's, why didn't you just give Jessie the message, instead of bothering me?"

"I would have, but it's a little complicated, and I didn't want her to fuck it up. You know women. They ain't too bright, and I didn't want to take any chances. So, here's the scoop. The boiler's been running without ignition since God knows when, and the chamber is soaked with oil. Billy replaced the electrodes before he got hurt, but of course, he wasn't going to try to start the damn thing until he could get rid of the excess oil in the chamber. Shit, the goddamn thing would probably blow the roof off the building if he did. Anyway, he turned off the switch before he left for the hospital. Now, you know, the first thing David is going to see when he gets there is that switch is off. He's going to want to turn it on to see what's going on, and if he does, BOOM! So, you got to be sure to fill David in, and make sure he doesn't throw that switch."

"Okay. I'll tell him," Melvin said, as a sudden smile came to his lips.

A half an hour later David called Melvin.

"What's up, Mel?"

"It's the Fairmount job. Billy was working it and cut himself or something, and ended up at the emergency room. Anyway, you got to get down there and straighten things out before old lady Johnson starts screaming."

"I'll get right over there. Sorry you had to be bothered."

"No big deal."

"Okay, see you in the morning,"

Melvin paused for less than a second. "David! Wait! I…" But the dial tone was his only response.

"Yes I have to go out again. Dammit." David hoisted his heavy parka on and headed for the door.

Jessie was in her nightgown, her arms wrapped around her, shivering. She stopped David at the door. "Poor baby, I'm sorry you have to go out again. It's so cold." David bent down, gave her a quick kiss and said conspiratorially, "I'll wake you when I get back and you can warm me up."

David parked his truck, grabbed his heavy toolbox, and went directly to the basement door that led to the boiler room. Fairmount was an eighty-unit apartment building, and the boiler that heated it was, as the boys in the shop referred to it, a "monster." Mrs. Johnson was waiting in the basement, frowning.

"Good evening, Mrs. Johnson," David said as he put his toolbox down.

"It's not a good evening at all," she replied, tightening her robe about her. "It's a cold evening, and all my tenants are screaming at me because they are also cold. Why can't you fix this thing once and for all? I am sick and tired of—"

"Don't you worry, Mrs. Johnson, we're going to get this boiler fired up and get you some heat in a jiffy."

Mrs. Johnson turned her back on David and started back to her apartment.

David shrugged and began to check out the boiler. The first thing he saw was that the switch was off.

Melvin stared at the phone as if it had been a party to the sin he had just committed and then, slowly, put the phone back into the receiver. "The son of a bitch. Fuck him. I hope he fucking gets killed," he said through tight lips as tears of frustration came to his eyes. Did he really hate David so much that he wanted him to get hurt? David the football jock, David the ladies man, David the war hero, David, David, David. The words rushed through his mind like a flood. His face was burning with rage. *I need a drink.* He reached for the ever-ready bottle and then changed his mind. *I've got to get dressed, stop David.* But he knew it was too late for that. He would call Mrs. Johnson, tell her to tell David about the switch. Yes, he had to stop David from throwing that switch. He got out the telephone directory and started looking up Mrs. Johnson's telephone number. The pages kept slipping from his trembling hands. *Shit, there are a million Johnsons.* He finally found the number, picked up the phone and started to dial. "Hello, Mrs. Johnson?"

"You've got the wrong number, asshole. For Christ's sake, do you know what time it is?"

He checked the number in the telephone book again and dialed it. It rang ten times and Melvin hung up, swearing, checked the number once again, and dialed each digit carefully. After a dozen rings he slammed the phone down on the receiver and then, frustrated, he picked it up, and threw it against the wall.

David reached out to turn the boiler switch on when he heard Mrs. Johnson's stern voice.

"Oh, mister serviceman."

David turned and saw that Mrs. Johnson had returned or had never left. He looked at her expectantly.

"The other man that was here said that no one was to turn on that switch until he got back."

David slowly dropped his hand. He opened the boiler door and saw the fire chamber drenched in oil. He crinkled his brow, wondering why Billy hadn't told Melvin about the impending danger that awaited him. Perhaps he had told Joe and Joe had withheld the information from Melvin. He knew that Joe hated him, because he had been bypassed for David's managerial job. It certainly couldn't have been Melvin. Sure Melvin had been on his ass since he started, but Melvin was still his friend. Certainly he would have no reason to want to hurt him, unless, somehow, he had found out about Ginny. It could all be just miscommunication, and probably the best thing to do was to forget about it. Not make a big deal about it. On the other hand, he thought, he'd better be a little more aware and a lot more careful.

CHAPTER TWENTY-SEVEN

WINTER 1954

The next day Melvin sauntered into his mother's living room and looked around at the room he had spent so much time in as a boy. The old console radio had been replaced with a new TV; otherwise it looked pretty much the same. He walked over to the table with the crystal decanters and poured himself a drink, his second for the day. He flopped down on one of the antique chairs that were forbidden when he was a boy by an unwritten law and lit up a cigarette.

He was relieved that nothing had happened to David. What had gotten into him? David was practically running the damn business. What the hell would he do without him? And the talk about Ginny, the whole thing was probably just a dirty rumor. Ginny loved him. Hell, they were practically engaged.

When his mother entered the room, he noticed that she had aged considerably since his father's death the previous year. Her eyes seemed to never have recovered from all the crying and they were red and swollen. Her white hair however, was immaculately coifed. She looked at Melvin, drink in hand, and involuntarily shook her head from side to side. "Is it entirely necessary that every incident, important or not, start and end with alcohol?"

"Mother, I'm a big boy now, remember? I'm the man of the family."

"That was cruel, Melvin."

"Look, Mother, you asked me to come here. I'm here, now what is it?"

"Melvin, you're my son and I love you." She took his hand in hers. "Do we have to argue every moment we're together?"

"Mother, please, what's on your mind?" Melvin withdrew his hand.

"Darling, you are so angry, so hard on yourself."

Melvin had hurt his mother in the name of his anger toward his father. He had been cruel, yet somehow, he couldn't help himself. Now, looking into his mother's eyes, he felt ashamed. He reached for her hand. "I'm sorry, Mother; I didn't mean to hurt you. It's him. I just don't understand why. Why did he always push me away?"

Anna knew the answer, but she also knew that she could never tell her son the truth. It was cowardly, and God knows she had tried so many times, but she just couldn't do it.

"Please dear, stop torturing yourself. He just wasn't an affectionate man. He loved you in his own way. Certainly there's no need to blame yourself. He was just that sort of a man. He was hard on everyone, not just you."

Melvin saw how hard his mother was trying now, as she had always tried to make peace between him and his father. He felt sorry for her, but he was tired of getting no real answers. "Please, Mother, stop making excuses for him." He picked up the decanter and poured himself another drink.

"What did you want to see me about?"

"Well, it's the accountants. They feel there is no one at the helm. Profits are slipping and, well…"

"The accountants, so that's it. Even after he's gone, he's still in control, only now it's his damn accountants that can crack the whip."

"Melvin, you haven't been at the office very much since your father died and you know a ship without a captain, an army without…"

Another slap in the face. Jesus, he could come back from the dead to give him pain. He'd had enough; he was too angry to continue the conversation. He looked at his mother and smirked. "So go get yourself a general or a captain or whatever. I'm not interested." He downed the last of the Scotch and grimaced. "You know this is lousy scotch." He got up from the chair, and put his empty glass back on the little table with the crystal containers.

He looked at the stiff furniture, the untouched books in the bookcase and smelled a faint memory of his father's cigars. This was the room he'd be called to when his father was displeased with him, which seemed to be most of the time. Melvin would stand, while his father sat in one of the stiff chairs, looking at him or rather looking through him, while he reviewed his latest complaints about him, ending with a disgusted wave of his hand, leaving Melvin confused and in tears.

"You're not that blasé, Melvin; you couldn't be that disinterested. You don't have to work if you don't want to, but the business has to run. At least put someone in charge. Melvin, don't keep fighting yourself. Please darling, don't hate him so. He loved you, and he just wanted you to be so perfect, he…"

"Oh, maybe he loved you, but don't delude yourself, dear Mother. He never loved his son. I wanted him to love me. Do you remember when he put me on that pony and I cried because I was afraid? I put my arms out to him and he just looked at me that way he did a thousand times afterward and said, 'You take him.' Why couldn't he love me? Why was he so ashamed of me? Was it because I wasn't tough enough, big enough? What was it?"

Anna's eye's filled with tears as she listened to Melvin. Why wasn't she brave enough to tell him the truth? Her heart was breaking and she was filled with shame and guilt, but the words choked in her throat. It was too late. She could never tell him he was her illegitimate son.

She looked away from Melvin's eyes and said, "Melvin, darling, he was…"

"Mother, I don't want to hear the story all over again. I know it by heart." He was sobbing.

The doorbell rang and the maid announced David. Mrs. Bass told her to wait a few moments and then send him in.

"Please, darling, pull yourself together. I don't want David to see you this way."

David entered the room and his "Hello, Mrs. Bass" faded to a hesitant "Hi, Mel." Melvin's eyes were red-rimmed, but he didn't look as drunk as usual, and David was a little confused with Melvin's greeting: "Good afternoon, Captain."

Chapter Twenty-Eight

Spring 1954

Only a few weeks after Melvin's bitter announcement at his mother's house that David would be the new manager, David took over the big office that used to be Sam Bass's. The transition was without fanfare. He had been running Eastern since Sam's death. Now, his salary and office space became commensurate with his new position. He had never expected Mrs. Bass to relinquish an interest in Eastern, but 15%, to be paid back out of his share of the profits, was cheap insurance for good management. The excitement of his first promotion was nothing compared to this. He adjusted his tie, now part of his new uniform as manager, and thought of his father. *Papa, I wish you could be here; I know you would be so proud of me.*

It was seven o'clock at night by the time he finished moving. He sat at the big desk and surveyed the massive top. It was devoid of anything that resembled work. There was a gold pen and pencil set, a leather desk pad, a telephone, and a calendar that was turned to August 11, 1953, the night that Sam died. He was shocked to think how quickly more than seven years of his life working at Eastern had disappeared. Yet, here he was at the helm of one of the largest independent oil companies on the East Coast. There was much to do and he knew that this was only the beginning.

Before he left, he stopped at the door of his office, and turned back to survey the symbol of his new success. This was the next step up the ladder to the top, and he was going to climb it all the way. Nothing would stand in his way. He locked up, reminded himself that Jessie was visiting her mother, and headed for the Glass Slipper.

"What can I get for you tonight, Mr. Livingston?" Al asked, cleaning the bar, which didn't need cleaning.

"CC on the rocks would be nice." A celebratory drink was in order.

"Miss Ginny going to join you tonight?"

David looked up at Al as if he had suddenly disappeared, giving no answer to his question. He was inexorably becoming more and more connected with Ginny, drifting farther and farther away from Jessie and the reality of his situation. *What the hell am I doing?*, he wondered. His seven-month affair with Ginny, sneaking moments two or three times a week, was bad enough, but the deception was the worst of it. Each time he'd lied to Jessie he felt as if he had plunged a knife into her. Yet there were times he was almost successful in convincing himself that his little weakness was normal, that all the guys fooled around, and maybe it actually made him a better person, even a better husband. He rationalized that he had more tolerance for faults in other people and their mistakes, knowing of his own imperfections. He was almost successful, but not quite, and the idea that he was just plain cheating appalled him. An enormous wave of guilt swept over him. He momentarily decided never to see Ginny again. He swallowed hard, but the lump in his throat stayed as he realized how impossible it would be to give her up.

David's appetite was gone. In fact he felt a little sick to his stomach. He finished his drink, dropped a five-dollar bill on the bar, and walked out into the fog, his clenched hands in his trouser pockets. He got into his car and decided to go home. He turned the key in the ignition, listened to the engine growl, and shifted into first gear. Just as he was about to drive off, a cab pulled up and emptied its passengers.

Son of a bitch, it's Sanders with Betty Goldman. He stepped on the accelerator, hoping they didn't see him. He was sick inside. What was Sanders doing with Betty? Was she cheating on Max? The whole damn world was turning upside down. The phrase, "All the kids are doing it" sprang into his mind, along with his father's answer: "I don't care about all the other kids; you will do what is right." His father would be so ashamed of him now.

Jesus, he'd have to do something about Betty, but what? Tell Max and break his heart? Lecture Betty? Shit, she worked for Ginny; she might even know about them, and was keeping quiet about it, not wanting to interfere. He'd talk to Sanders. That's it, one hypocrite to another. What a joke! He leaned forward and put his forehead on the cold steering wheel. How could he go home to Jessie when he didn't even have the right to speak her name?

CHAPTER TWENTY-NINE

OCTOBER 1954

The doorbell chimed and Sarah ran to see who it was.

"It's Auntie Betty," she screamed with delight, as Betty leaned over and gave her a big hug.

"Look what I brought for you." Betty dangled a multicolored string of beads in front of Sarah.

"Oh, they are so beautiful. Can I put them on?"

Jessie came to the door, wiping her hands on her apron. "Did you say thank you to Auntie Betty?"

"Thank you, Auntie Betty."

Jessie kissed Betty on the cheek and then led her into the kitchen. "Coffee?"

"Can I have coffee too?" Sarah asked, already knowing the answer.

"You can have milk."

"Auntie Betty?" Sarah pouted.

Betty sat down at the red Formica table, winked at Sarah and whispered into her ear.

Jessie poured the coffee. "You'll spoil her, you know."

"Well, one of us ought to get spoiled, and it sure isn't going to be you or me."

Jessie looked at Betty quizzically, wondering if there was a hidden meaning in Betty's remark. *Is she intimating that something was wrong between David and me?* She took her coffee to the table and sat down. Not meaning to, what came to her mind spilled out in words. "David hasn't spent an evening at home in a month."

Betty took a sip of her hot coffee and sneaked some into Sarah's milk to Sarah's delight. "Max's been home every night buried in the damn, sorry Sarah, darn company books. I'm ready to scream." Betty suddenly put her coffee cup down so hard that she almost shattered the delicate saucer below it. Her eyes flashed and she tossed her curls like old times. "Let's go out tonight!"

"Are you crazy?"

"Can I come too?" Sarah asked.

Betty ignored Sarah and continued excitedly, "Why not? We could have a sandwich at Brigham's and then, maybe, go to a movie or even…a bar."

"Betty, you *are* crazy."

"No I'm not crazy. I'm bored stiff and so are you! Call your mother and ask her to sit with Sarah. Get dolled up. Have one darn night out, have some fun."

"I want to go too," Sarah pouted. "I don't want to stay with Grandma."

"Don't be late," Jessie's mother admonished them, as she mumbled, "Married women on the town. I just don't understand what this world is coming to. Come on, Sarah, get out the checkerboard. I'm going to beat you this time."

Betty dabbed her lips with her napkin. "I love Brigham's sundaes."

Jessie's eyes sparkled with the moment. "Especially the hot fudge. This is so much fun. So, what's next, the movies?"

"Let's go to a bar."

Jessie looked at Betty incredulously. "You're kidding, right?"

"Nope."

They touched up their lipstick, paid their check, and hailed a cab.

There was a cute little bar on Newbury Street and Betty gave the driver the address while Jessie fidgeted nervously. Why was she going to a bar? Women went to bars unescorted to meet men. She loved David. She wasn't interested in other men. Dammit! It was too late now. No, it wasn't; she'd have one drink and get out of there. Stupid! She should have said no in the first place.

The bar was dark, smoky, and crowded. A red, neon sign, advertising Ballantine's beer, turned the smoke into a red haze.

Jessie was visibly panicked. It showed in her face. She froze just inside the door. Betty grabbed her hand, gave her a dirty look, and then readjusted her face to a phony smile. "Over here." She pointed to two seats at the bar where two Marines had just exited.

"Ladies?"

Jessie looked up at the mustached bartender. "Excuse me?"

"Something to drink, miss?"

"Oh, yes, a Coke please."

Betty interrupted. "Uh, uh. Give her a martini. Me too."

"Betty!"

When the martinis came, Jessie tried to bolster her courage with a stiff drink of the martini and then another.

An older man with slick, black hair was sitting next to Betty. He started talking to her. His voice was as greasy as his hair. Jessie could hear Betty's voice change to fit the occasion.

Jessie looked around the crowded bar and thought, *What am I doing here? This is crazy. David would be furious.*

"Hello."

Jessie, startled, turned and looked at the soldier who was standing just to the right of her and managed to say, "Hello."

"Mind if I sit down?" He indicated the empty bar stool next to her. He was a good-looking infantryman with deep blue eyes.

"Well, I guess you can sit wherever you want." Jessie turned her back to him.

"You're married," he persisted.

"How do you know that?" Jessie's back was still to him.

"Left hand."

"What?"

"Wedding ring."

"Oh." Jessie suddenly felt ashamed. She loved David. Did this guy think she was on the prowl? Did she look like she was waiting to be picked up? She felt cheap.

"Can I get you another drink?" Blue Eyes asked.

Jessie looked at her martini. It was empty. "Yes, I mean no. I was just leaving." She grabbed Betty's arm. "We're leaving."

Betty looked perplexed. "What's wrong?"

"We don't belong here, that's what's wrong. Are you coming?"

Betty shook her head. "No. I'm having fun. You go if you want. Go back and wait for David, but don't hold your breath."

"What the hell does that mean?"

"Grow up, Jessie. Open your eyes."

"Betty, I don't know what you're trying to say, but you're scaring me."

The guy beside Betty put his arm around her. She pushed his arm away, glared at him, and then turned back to Jessie. "Forget it. I've had too much to drink."

"I want to know what you meant by that."

"Nothing, honest, nothing. It's the booze."

Jessie stormed out of the bar.

She sat in the back of the cab on the way home, wishing she had pressed Betty further. Tears filled her eyes. Is Betty telling me that David is cheating? Is there someone else? Is that why he is away so often...out half the night? Please God, no.

Jessie was still crying when the cab pulled up in front of her house. She paid the driver and headed for the front door. It started to rain, but she waited to compose herself, while the rain mixed with her tears. "Damn you, David!"

CHAPTER THIRTY

NOVEMBER 1954

Sanders opened the door to the room of the motel that was just off the main highway. Motels were great; they were out of the way and nobody cared what name went on the register. Who cared about the looks, the bed was all he needed, and it was a hell of a lot cheaper than the Glass Slipper. The room had a moldy-smelling chair, a dresser with a Gideon Bible on top, and two glasses. The drapes were heavy with dust and hung lazily over a frayed carpet. Next to the door to the tiny bathroom was a small desk with a lamp.

Betty turned on the lamp and looked at the barely covered bulb of the overhead light. As if by signal, Sanders turned it off, throwing the room into soft shadows. No words were spoken as he took off her coat, unbuttoned her blouse, slipped it off her shoulders, and unhooked her bra. She kissed him hungrily, her arms pulling him toward her. With little effort, he picked her up, carried her to the bed. She kicked off her shoes and pulled him down to her, kissing him with short little kisses that covered his face and neck. He got up and turned off the lamp. He could hear her removing the rest of her clothes as he did the same with his. Then he was beside her.

"Richard, honey, you've never told me you love me... say it."

"I love you, baby," he said without feeling, and he wondered how many times he had said the same words, and to how many women. He thought proudly, *Goddammit, I couldn't even count them all.*

"I can't bear to wait a whole week until next time. Couldn't I see you in the afternoon sometime?"

"Sure baby." He pulled her closer to him, and slipped his hand between her legs.

Betty put her hand over his, stopping him from going any further. "Tell me you love me again."

"I just told you that I love you." Sanders was getting irritated.

"But, you're not saying it like you mean it. Tell me again," Betty said kittenishly.

He wanted to fuck her one more time, but it just wasn't worth it. She was not only being a pain in the ass; she was the kind that got you in trouble. It was a shame, she was such a good piece. Well, there were plenty more where she came from. It was time to get rid of her.

He sat up and got out of bed. "We'll make love later. Doesn't seem like you're in the mood right now, anyway."

"Oh, don't be like that. I was only kidding. Of course I'm in the mood. I'm always in the mood with you. I love you. You know that." She reached out to take him in her arms.

Sanders was tempted, but he was already committed. "Let's go out, make the rounds."

"Richard, are your crazy? Someone would see us…"

"So what?" he said, thinking that this is what power really gets down to. He knew he could say anything, do anything, and she'd take it and beg him to come back. He loved the feeling; it was almost as good as sex, maybe even better.

"So what? You're kidding me."

"You just told me you loved me but all you really want is to get laid. What am I, your stud?" He looked into the little mirror on the dresser and smiled secretly.

Betty sat up in the bed. Her heart was beating wildly. "Richard, please darling, what's happened? What did I do? You know we can't go out, somebody might see us. That doesn't mean I don't love you."

Sanders was dressing rapidly. He didn't turn from the mirror to look at her. "How many guys have you had before me?"

Betty was crying. "You know you're the only one besides Max. What's wrong, what did I say? I love you. I'll go out, anywhere you say, anything you want."

He turned to her coldly, enjoying every minute of her pain. She was kneeling, naked on the bed, her head in her hands, sobbing. "Richard...Richard..."

He wanted to slap her. It was a sudden impulse but he controlled it and decided it would be more fun to whip her with words. "I don't want you to do me any favors. Stay here or, better yet, get dressed, and see if you can pick somebody else up. You can even use my room."

"Richard, I...," She sobbed uncontrollably. She could speak no more, and, besides, there was no one to speak to, because he had simply opened the door and walked out. She stayed there for almost an hour. Little animal sobs crept out, muffled by the pillow her face was buried in. Finally, she sat up, her chest in spasms, still allowing a sob to escape, almost like a hiccup. She walked like a sleepwalker to the mirror on the small dresser. Dim light from the neon sign in front of the motel crept in from the door that Sanders had not bothered to close. It threw dark shadows across Betty's face, and accentuated her swollen, red eyes. She touched her face with her fingertips and traced the lines that formed the shadows on her face. She pushed back her hair and forced a smile, but the lines were still there.

Her life had become meaningless. The days came and went without notice. Max left for work before she got up. He came home frustrated and exhausted from his office, if you could call it that. God knows how anyone could survive, day after day, in that tiny cubicle he called an office. Jesus.

There was barely enough room for his typewriter, let alone a damn picture, or anything else to make it human. All he ever got was a few rotten little raises that didn't amount to shit. And all those companies he'd sent his resume to—did they ever even read them? Then there were all his so-called friends and connections that were just more blind alleys. He's stuck there, wallowing in his self-pity, and I'm right there beside him. "Sex." She said it out loud and her mouth went tight. She reminded herself that there was little sex, and when there was, it was so quick and unimaginative, she hardly noticed. She swallowed hard. "I want a baby, Max. I want you to fuck me and make a baby. I don't care if we can't afford it. But I know you won't do it." Maybe she didn't love Max anymore; perhaps she never really loved him. She had thought about divorce so many times, but then what? How would she live? She had only been a teenager when she married Max; she had no real skills, no way to earn a living. Well, that was one thing that had changed. Working for Ginny was a good start. Ginny was smart. She could learn a lot from her. Find some independence. Get back her self-esteem.

The only spark in her life was Richard. No man had ever excited her, stimulated her like Richard. Over this last month she had been with him every moment she could make up an excuse to get away from the boredom at home. The long hours between their secret meetings were filled with fantasies about him. He was her only escape.

Sure, she loved him, but what was the use; he was married and she was married to poor Max. Richard would never divorce, especially now that he'd become so successful. He'd never even talked about his marriage. That was another life for him. That's why he'd been so cruel to her; he was trying to get rid of her. She wrapped her arms about herself as hot tears cooled on her cheeks. A chill ran through her naked body and shook her as if someone had grabbed her by the shoulders. She took a deep breath and thought, *Fuck you. You're not going to get away with treating me like this, you sadistic bastard. You can't just throw me away like some kitchen garbage.* She'd find out where he lived and call his wife.

CHAPTER THIRTY-ONE

MARCH 1955

Eastern had grown exponentially under David's shrewd management. He was obsessed with the need to build Eastern into the giant he envisioned and to have the money and power that would go with it. He didn't care what it took, or what he had to do; he only knew that he had to succeed at any cost. But, he wondered, if "at any cost" meant giving up his soul, all that he thought he stood for, and fought a war for. He mused that maybe all was fair in love and business, yet he wondered if it was okay to cheat or lie as long as you made the deal, to mislead Mrs. Bass or cheat on Jessie.

Who was he kidding? He knew that eventually he'd have to give the devil his due, but for now, success was all he could think about. He'd deal with the devil at another time.

It was 1955, the economy under Eisenhower had recovered from recession. The time was ripe for Eastern to take the next step. David knew that, somehow, he had to bring the company public, create a real value for the stock, and then use the stock and money as leverage for acquisitions.

Buying a public shell with Eastern's stock would be easy. It would give Eastern immediate stature as a publicly traded corporation. But how to get the money, that was the question. He had already used his and the other stockholder's stock as collateral to borrow money from the bank. Well, he had a plan. He would fine tune it and present it at the next meeting.

Will Donner called the meeting to order and after the usual preliminaries, turned the meeting over to David.

"Good morning." David adjusted his notes, which he had little need for because he was well prepared. "I have under agreement, of course subject to your approval, a public company devoid of all assets, basically a public shell that we can buy for stock. Moving into this shell makes us instantly a publicly tradeable corporation, which gives us the opportunity to create a real value for our stock, attract public funding, and open the door to further acquisitions and positive growth."

Bill Kelly cleared his throat and addressed David. "I'm not saying that going public isn't a good idea, but it seems to me that we already have positive growth and we ought to give the company a little breathing room before we take on any new adventures."

"Adventures, Bill? That's an interesting word. Want to elaborate?" David asked testily.

Bill Kelly turned red around his collar. Ever combative, he scowled at David. "Well, it seems to me that we have no sooner completed one of your schemes when we're into another. We…"

"Schemes. Jesus, Bill, your terminology is really something today. Schemes. Where the hell would we be today without my 'schemes'? I'll tell you where, we'd still be a little oil company fighting for its life. Instead, let me remind you, Bill, we are now one of the largest independent oil companies in the city."

"Yeah, and we're also in hock up to our ears."

David stayed calm. "Yes, Bill, and that's exactly the point. If we are public, we have the vehicle to create investment. Grow and prosper with other people's money. Know what I mean, Bill?"

"David, you're either the best con artist ever, or you're a damn genius. I'm hoping it's the latter." Bill chuckled and sat down.

The meeting continued for another hour until finally David won approval for the company to go public. Now he was ready to put his plan into action, but he had to let them digest this first stage before he spoon-fed them a new idea.

Months went by as David deftly assimilated Eastern Oil into the public shell. He was impatient to implement what he called Stage Two. He decided that he needed an ally, especially someone that Mrs. Bass would trust. He decided to call Will Donner.

Will's secretary put him through.

"Hello, Will. Hope that this isn't an inconvenient time."

"No, no, David. What's on your mind?"

"I wonder if you could find a few minutes, today, tomorrow. I want to run something by you."

"Well, I'm clear around three today. Is that…?"

"That would be great. I'll see you at three."

David parked in the bank's garage and took the elevator to Will's office. He was shown in directly, shook hands with Will, and after the usual pleasantries began to explain his plan for Eastern Oil.

"The fastest way for us to grow, Will, is through acquisitions. The problem, of course, is finding the money to do it. Well, what if we didn't need money and each acquisition could be self-financed?"

"That would be unique." Will smiled. "Go on."

"Here's how it works, and by the way, I've already tested this idea. We buy Company X by paying the owner ten cents a gallon for every gallon his company sells over the next five years, which basically represents most of our profit on those sales, but not all of it. Additionally we pay him twenty-five thousand annually over the next five years to maintain the good will of his accounts. We use the small profit on the sale of his oil to pay him the twenty-five in cash annually. In other words, we have no cash outlay and, as volume grows with each new acquisition, we begin to buy oil cheaper. Well, you get the idea. Of course these are not going to be big companies, but put enough of them together and you're talking big bucks."

"Why would he sell to us? I don't understand."

"Well, let's say his company sells a million gallons a year. With his overhead he has to work his ass off seven days a week, maybe even has to drive his own truck, to make twenty-five thousand a year. This way he gets his twenty-five grand for an easy public relations job and salts away ten cents times a million gallons or a hundred thousand a year for five years."

"I see, said the blind man."

"Not bad, eh?"

"Not bad at all." Will pursed his lips and nodded affirmatively. "And you've tested this?"

David smiled. "I've already lined up two of them."

Will laughed. "How did I know you were going to say that? Of course, you didn't mention that, since your bonus and stock options are tied to growth, this would be very good for David Livingston as well."

"I never said I would work for nothing. But, seriously, Will, can you help me sell it?"

Will studied David for a moment and was surprised that he hadn't noticed how much David had matured over the last few years. His gray flannel suit, crisp white shirt, and red-and-black striped tie gave him the very appearance of the bright executive that he had become. He smiled at David and said, "I really don't see how anyone could object. On the other hand, Anna came to see me the other day, and I have a feeling she is not too happy."

David knew that without Mrs. Bass's and Will's support his plan was doomed. "What's her problem? The company is flourishing; her stock is…"

"I can't speak for her, David. Perhaps you should sit down and have a talk with her."

"Anna, it was nice of you to come all the way down here to see me. Please sit down." David directed her to a comfortable chair, got up from his desk and sat in an adjoining chair.

She had aged a great deal since Sam's death, although she was still a proud, well-groomed lady. She spoke softly. "David, the reason I wanted this meeting in your office instead of my home is that I need you to understand that this is not a social visit. I am here to talk about Eastern Oil. I want you to know that I think you have done a wonderful job. I would never have believed that our little company could have grown to such proportions."

David smiled and thanked her. "Can I get you something to drink? Coffee? Tea?"

"No, thank you, David. I just want to talk." She smoothed out her skirt and sat forward in her chair. "Will has explained to me that you need our vote to begin to acquire small oil companies as part of a large expansion plan, and that he personally agrees that it would be a good thing. He has pointed out that the value of my stock far exceeds the value it had three years ago when Sam died, but he also told me, although I am one of the largest stockholders, I no longer really control the company. In fact, he explained that with the expansion of the business you and the board have managed to get control of the company, and we are heavy with debt. Somehow I feel that the many times you have asked me to back you with my vote were more for your benefit than mine." She took in a deep breath. "I must say that I am more than a little disturbed by it."

David's brow crinkled. He ran his hand through his hair and feigned confusion as if he didn't know where this was going. "Anna, nobody misled you. You had Will to advise you. You already know that financially you have profited and, frankly, I don't understand why you would be upset. When companies grow, debt usually goes hand in hand, and stockholders often get diluted. That's just the way it works." David held his breath.

"You, of all people, should have explained this to me. I feel that you have taken advantage of my trust."

David began to see the beginning of a storm in Mrs. Bass's dark-lined eyes, but he knew he would have to ride it out. Keep calm.

Mrs. Bass leaned forward for emphasis. "Yes, you did what was best for the company, and what was best for David. Not necessarily what was ultimately good for my son and me, whom you seem to have completely forgotten about. My son, who should inherit his father's business, who should control his father's business."

David reached out, took her hand and started to explain. He knew in a way she was right. He certainly was looking out for number one, and had manipulated her a number of times. But so be it, she was worth a hell of a lot more now. So she lost control. Did she really think Melvin would give up the bottle to take over the company? *What a laugh that would be.*

She pulled her hand away. Her face flushed, she pointed her finger at David angrily, and for the first time, raised her voice. "You betrayed me." David started to respond, but she waved her finger back and forth. "No, don't interrupt me. I trusted you and you—"

David interrupted. "I didn't betray you. I did what I thought was best for you and the company."

"No, David, what you were doing was slowly but surely taking away my husband's business, Melvin's business, and using my votes to do it! How could you?"

David sat like a chastened child. What could he say? It was true.

"You should have come to me; explained. You never once gave Melvin or me a second thought. You used us, David. That's what you did. You used us…"

This was worse than he had expected. He tried to look contrite. Dammit. His whole acquisition scheme was on the line. "You know. You must know that I would never do anything to hurt you, Anna. I have always tried to act in your best interest. I'm sorry you feel that I have not, and perhaps I should have been more attentive. I apologize for that. As far as Melvin is concerned, he has received his pay every week even if I have to bring it to his room, and clear the bottles off the dresser to find a place to put it down. You know he has barely stepped in here since I took over management, and you also know he has a position here anytime he wants it."

"I'm not interested in your apology and I'll not thank you for reminding me that Melvin is not a well man. I don't like what you have done to my family and me, David, but I know business must go on in spite of my personal feelings, so I am going to go along with your idea." Mrs. Bass stood, looked down at David, narrowed her eyes and said bitterly, "You've got what you wanted, David. You are on the way to great success, but be careful what you wish for. You just may be surprised at what you get."

CHAPTER THIRTY-TWO

APRIL 1955

David zipped up the back of Jessie's black sheath, but before she could turn toward him for approval, he slipped a gold necklace with a small solitaire diamond pendant around her neck.

Jessie reached up to touch the necklace as she turned to the mirror on her dresser. "Oh, David. It's beautiful."

David leaned over her shoulder and kissed her neck. "You're beautiful."

"So what did I do to deserve this incredible gift?"

"Soothed a guilty conscience."

Jessie turned from the mirror to look at David. "So all these nights you supposedly have been working were really spent with your beautiful mistress."

David cringed, but managed to smile. "Caught red-handed."

"If you were caught, it wouldn't be your hand that would be red."

Jessie moved into David's arms and kissed him.

Sarah had come into the bedroom unnoticed. "What would be red?"

"Nothing, honey, just grownup talk."

"That's what you always say when you don't want me to know something."

David picked Sarah up and spun her around. "Guess what I have for you."

"A present?"

"You bet." David reached into his pocket and took out a tiny ring with Sarah's birthstone gleaming in the center.

It was too big for her ring finger, but she put it on her forefinger, and stuck it out for David and Jessie to admire.

"Honey, that's beautiful," Jessie said, just as a horn sounded, noting that Max and Betty were there to pick them up for dinner.

"You're always going away. You never have time to play with me." Sarah pouted as David and Jessie headed for the front door.

David bent down and kissed her. "Tomorrow is Saturday, and I promise we'll go for a ride and stop at Howard Johnson's for ice cream and then we're going to go to the movies."

"Promise?"

"Cross my heart and hope to die. Now give me a big kiss and a hug."

As they drove to the restaurant, Max told David that he had asked for a raise and was turned down flat. While David sympathized with Max, Jessie's thoughts drifted back. Sarah was right. David had hardly been home. Their lovemaking was sporadic at best. Then there were all of the presents. Lately, there were more and more: the watch, the candy and now the necklace. Call it intuition. Something was very wrong.

At dinner Betty was as glum as Max. "What are we supposed to do? Max's been there forever. I mean, it's an insult. You shouldn't have to be put down like that, Max."

Max swallowed and wiped his mouth. "Well, what do you want me to do, quit?"

Betty put her drink down and turned to Max. "For Christ's sake, Max, do something, anything, quit, but stop bitching."

Max's answer faded as Jessie thought about David. He was on his way to the top and nothing would stop him. Certainly he would never fall into the trap that poor Max was in. They didn't have to worry about the bills anymore. She adored their new house in prestigious Brookline, the clothes, the parties, the respect that came with success, and the education that Sarah would get. But was there a price? A price she might not be willing to pay? David, out until all hours of the night, sometimes working through the weekend. Hopefully, it was work. Then, there was something missing, a certain distraction beyond work. What was it? The war had taught David how to live on the edge and somehow he thrived on it. Was it that the job wasn't enough? She wasn't enough? Did he need someone else in his life, another woman, another challenge?

Max brought her back to the conversation. "You're right. I am going to wait for the right moment and…"

Betty rolled her eyes and, looking to change the subject, asked Jessie how the plans for her housewarming party were progressing.

Jessie, still deep in thought, turned to Betty with a perplexed look. "I'm sorry, what did you say?"

"I wanted to know how the party was coming."

"Oh, well, I've got a caterer and the invitations are in the mail."

"Is there anything I can do to, y'know, help?"

"No thanks, really everything is under control." But was it? Jessie asked, her mind drifting back to her thoughts about David.

After dinner they dropped the Goldmans off, Max still defining the right moment. It started to rain. By the time they reached home it was a deluge and lightning lit up the summer sky.

David paid the baby-sitter, lent her an umbrella, and watched her run through the rain to her house next door.

Jessie touched David's arm as if to lead him to the stairs to the bedroom. "I'm exhausted. I'm going to check Sarah and go right to bed. God, these shoes are killing me."

"You go ahead, sweetheart. I'm going to read a little first."

Jessie gave David a little peck on the cheek. "Don't be too late, darling. Remember we have the Cabots' party tomorrow night. If I'm asleep when you come up, I want you to kiss me goodnight anyway."

David took Jessie's arm, pulled her toward him, and kissed her. "I love you, you know?"

Jessie's brow crinkled. "Yes, I know." She headed for the stairs.

CHAPTER THIRTY-THREE

JUNE 1955

Sanders had left the VA more than two years ago for a more promising practice. His reputation grew with his easy charm, and his practice flourished.

Mrs. Rosemond Cabot, a Boston Brahmin and former patient, who adored him, introduced him to Boston high society. Eventually, he found himself at the top of most invitation lists. Ruth refused to participate. It was just not her thing, and besides, she thought she really didn't fit in, which was fine with Sanders, who never refused an invitation.

"He's a charming bastard," Mrs. Cabot told her friends. "You just have to meet him. Well, he does say it as it is whether you like it or not, but in the end, you just have to love him."

The Cabots threw a giant party every July to raise funds for the Beacon Hill Historical Society and she hoped that 1955 would be a banner year. The funds helped keep developers from changing the historic integrity of this beautiful area of Boston. The party was held at the Cabot's brownstone just off Louisburg Square on Beacon Hill. Coincidentally, both David and Dr. Sanders were invited. Sanders because he knew many of their most intimate secrets and David because of a large donation that Eastern had made to their cause. It was the first time they had met on a social basis.

"David." Sanders said in a surprised voice.

"Doctor Sanders."

"How are you?" Sanders extended his hand in greeting.

David took his hand warmly. "I'd be terrific if I could shed this monkey suit and put on a good pair of jeans. I hate these things."

"Join the club. Well, I guess it's been...what? Four years since we've seen each other. How's it going?"

"Not bad."

"What does that mean?"

"Are we back in therapy?"

"Sorry, it's a habit."

"So what do you think about all this?" David swept his hand to encompass the entire ballroom.

"What do I think? Just look around, look at these people. Most of them are wealthy beyond your imagination. They have a home for every season, huge yachts, jewelry that could blind you, the most expensive cars, and for what?"

"Let me guess. It's nice to be rich?"

Sanders took out his handkerchief, wiped the tiny beads of sweat from his brow, and continued, "It's not necessarily nice to be rich. They spend their whole lives working for all of this, and now, with the ends of their lives staring them in the face, they're asking themselves why, what for? Most of them aren't happy, because they didn't have time to be happy; they were too busy accumulating their wealth. It's like they were pissing into the wind. Don't you see it's just so much nonsense? Hey, I'm not innocent here, I'm a part of all this, but at least I know it's just bullshit."

Jessie came over and took David's arm and smiled at Sanders. "Hi, I'm Jessie."

"So you're Jessie. What a pleasure." Sanders took Jessie's extended hand and, although hardly discernible, took in her low-cut Chinese red gown and the little diamond that lay seductively just above the deep cleavage of her breasts.

"And you are?" Jessie asked, with a big smile, slipping out of Sanders' smooth hand that held hers a bit too long.

"Oh, I'm sorry. This is Dr. Sanders, the doctor I used to see at the VA."

"Ah, the Black Knight who was going to kill my husband's demons."

"No, milady, just a squire. Your husband has to kill his own demons."

"Wait a minute," David broke in, smiling. "Leave my demons out of this."

"Right, we don't have to talk about David's demons. After all, we all have our own demons, don't we? What about your demons, Jessie?"

"But yours should be so much more interesting, Dr. Sanders'."

"Richard."

"Alright, Richard, tell us about your demons."

"I'm afraid I'll need more to drink, and more time to know you better. And I hope I will get to know you better, in order to share that with you."

"But you do have demons?" Jessie persisted.

Sanders took out his handkerchief, prepared to wipe his brow. "Oh, yes, I have them, lots of them, but it's a beautiful night and the terrace looks inviting. Why don't I refresh our drinks and meet you out there. Then we can tell the demons to go back to hell, and talk about all the beautiful things that life has to offer, for instance, you, Jessie."

Sanders left dabbing the little beads of sweat that had formed on his brow. Jessie followed Sanders with her eyes and said, "Wow, your Dr. Sanders is really a piece of work. Isn't he?"

Sanders returned with the drinks and the three shielded themselves from the babble of the ballroom by moving to the terrace. The night was cool and fragrant and the discussions, almost always led by Sanders, were challenging and exciting.

On the drive home Jessie said, "Why have you been hiding him all these years? He's nice, a little opinionated and probably tough as nails, but I liked him. I think we should invite him to the party. He's kind of interesting, don't you think?"

Yeah, he's interesting all right. He was fucking my best friend's wife. "I really don't know him socially and I'm not sure if he would want to mix business with pleasure."

"Well, I think he'd add a little spice to the party. Everyone likes a newcomer. I'll invite him and if he's uncomfortable, he just won't come."

No doubt, he'll add a little spice to the party, especially with Max and Betty there. Jesus! What if Melvin is on the party list? He'll surely take Ginny. I better see Ginny, and what? Tell her not to come? What a fucking disaster!

David looked for a space to park on Beacon Street, which was just about impossible night or day. It was his third pass and he was mumbling a few curses when he saw Ginny. He double-parked and she came over to the car as David rolled down the window.

"Did you read my mind?"

"I knew you would have an awful time parking so I came down and waited for you. Can you get away tonight?"

David leaned over and opened the car door. "Yes, but it has to be an early evening this time. I've been late every night this week and Jessie is starting to look at me like I have two heads."

"Well we wouldn't want to get into trouble with Jessie, would we?" Ginny said sarcastically as she got into the car.

"C'mon, Ginny, let's not start our evening with that stuff. You know what the deal is, so let it go, will you?"

Ginny slid over closer to David and faced him. Her eyes scanned his face as if she was memorizing his every feature and then she gently put her hand on his cheek. "It's just that I love you so much, David. I want you all for myself. I want us to be together without worrying who you might bump into that will tell Jessie; hiding in the back of restaurants, sneaking into motels, worrying about the time. I want it to be just you and me; just us."

"Oh sweetheart, don't you think that I want the same thing?" David answered, kissing her lightly on the lips, and thinking that this was no time to bring up the party. He'd just have to take his chances, and hope for the best.

"Then why don't you do something? Tell her about us?"

A horn honked from behind them and David realized he was blocking another car trying to get out of its parking space. He put the car in gear and started driving out of the city. He welcomed the interruption. It gave him a moment to think, but he knew that even if he had months to think, he would be just as tangled and conflicted. He couldn't give up Jessie. He still loved her. It was maddening. He loved two women, differently, but nevertheless, he loved them both. He looked at Ginny for a moment, then back at the road, and gave her the only answer that offered hope and yet was noncommittal. "I'm not ready yet. I need time." He could both see and feel her disappointment, but he knew that was all he could give her and he hated himself for it.

Ginny felt a surge of anger but let it subside before she spoke. "I love you, David, and I know you love me, but you are hurting me."

"I know. I know I am and it's the last thing I want to do. Just give me a little more time to sort things out."

He reached out for her with his right arm. She slid close to him, her head on his shoulder, and they drove in silence to a little Italian restaurant in the North End.

David gave one of the tough kids who roamed the streets of the North End a couple of bucks to keep his eye on the car, knowing that if one of these kids weren't watching it, it would probably be stripped or, at minimum, damaged. It was cheap insurance.

They took a booth at the rear of the restaurant; David sat with his back to the door. The muted ambiance of the flickering candles that were the only illumination in the little restaurant completed his cover. More insurance.

They ate in silence, but their eyes spoke, and finally, when both were finished eating, they reached across the table and held hands, still talking with their eyes until the waiter broke the spell.

"Anything else?" the waiter asked.

"No, thank you, just a check, please."

David retrieved the car from the kid who was minding it. After he saw that the hubcaps and other incidentals were still attached he gave the kid an extra buck. They drove to Ginny's apartment and found a parking space on the first pass. A miracle. Ginny looked at him expectantly as he looked at his watch.

"Are you coming up?"

"It's almost ten. I ought to…"

Ginny opened her door and got out without a word and started toward the steps to her apartment.

"Wait a minute, dammit." David got out of the car and quickly overtook her. "For Christ's sake, don't you think I want to come up?"

Ginny turned to face him. "I really don't know what you want, and I don't think you do either."

David knew she was right. Ginny saw him hang his head, nodding side to side in hopeless frustration and a wave of pity swept over her. She took his hand and led him to her apartment. No sooner had they crossed the threshold than they were in each other's arms. Time stopped for them, but the clock kept ticking.

CHAPTER THIRTY-FOUR

JULY 1955

It was 1:30 in the morning when David slipped his key silently into the lock and opened the front door. He was sure Jessie was asleep, but he still worried that Ginny's perfume remained to betray him. He closed the door softly behind him and walked up the thickly carpeted stairs to Sarah's room. She was sleeping soundly with one arm hanging over the side of the bed. David tiptoed in and put her arm back under the covers. Kneeling by her bed he touched her cheek as a wave of guilt spread through him. He adjusted her quilt, pursed his lips and headed for the bedroom.

He undressed in the dark and finally slid into bed and stared into the darkness. Jessie's voice startled him. It was cold and not at all like her.

"Nice of you to come home at all."

David thanked the darkness for hiding him. He couldn't bear to look her in the eye. "Believe me, baby, I don't like these damn meetings anymore than you do," he answered, hating himself.

Jessie switched on the light and sat up in bed. Her eyes were red-rimmed and there was an extra touch of pink on the tip of her nose. He wanted to grab her, crush her into his arms and tell her he was sorry, that he couldn't bear to hurt her and that he loved her, but she was cold and remote.

She looked at him for what seemed a long time. "I don't know you anymore." She switched off the light and lay back in silence.

David found his voice and said softly, "Jessie, I don't know what you think is wrong but…"

Suddenly, she snapped the lights on again. She was already sitting up in bed, her voice almost a scream. "Stop it. Stop it. What do you think I'm made of? Don't you think I can tell? Do you think your kisses, your eyes, your body, are going to lie for you too? Do you think I'm so blind or naïve that my husband can fall out of love with me, and I wouldn't know it?"

"Jessie, Jessie. Please stop." He pulled her to him. She was sobbing uncontrollably. "Jessie, I love you. Please. I love you. There isn't anyone else." He despised himself for lying. How could he be such an idiot? How could he risk losing this woman he loved so much?

"Then what is it, David?" She dabbed at her nose with a tissue. "What's wrong? What did I do? I still love you." She cried between each word and he held her tighter, almost as if to stifle each sob, to stop each tear. He kissed her hair, her forehead, her eyes, nose and mouth. He used his finger to gently wipe the tears from her eyes. Then, as if to inspect his work, he moved back and looked at her.

She met David's eyes. "Please, darling, if there is anyone else, don't let me find out because I would just want to die. I love you so much."

He kissed her cheek, pulled her close to him again, and whispered into her ear, "There's no one but you. There's never going to be anyone but you." She moved back, looked into his face momentarily and then she kissed him. Her tongue slipped between his lips and he felt a thrill run through his body. He slipped her nightgown from her shoulder and kissed her breast while his other hand slid over the smoothness of her belly down to the softness between her legs. She was very excited now, and her hand was caressing him. Her body moved sensuously against him with her every breath. She kissed his neck and shoulders over and over until she felt him inside her. At first, it was a small thrill that ran through her. Then it was almost unbearable. She ground her hips wildly, and her nails dug into his arms. Suddenly she couldn't move anymore, but her whole body was vibrating. David had waited for her, and now he spent himself with her in a continued fury until she was sobbing, "I love you, my darling. I love you." Her forehead was covered with perspiration. Her eyes were closed. He kissed her softly on the lips and then she was asleep.

David got out of bed and went to the bathroom. Instead of going back to bed, he walked into the den without turning on the light and sat heavily into his favorite chair. Sarah's Barbie doll was on the floor next to the chair. He picked it up and held it close to his chest and then put it gently on the table beside him. He ran his hands over the soft leather arms of the chair and leaned his head back. *What the hell am I doing? Where is this going? I can't leave Jessie and Sarah, I love them, and yet, I can't leave Ginny either. I can't think clearly; I've got to straighten out my life or I'm going to lose them all and blow the business as well.* He swore he would never see Ginny again but he knew that he would. His eyes were heavy and he began to doze.

He was standing in the wreckage of the B-17. It was smoldering and wisps of smoke from the dying flames mixed with the morning mist. He floated through the wreckage, looking. Looking for Charlie. "Charlie, Charlie." He saw an arm that hung loosely from the wreckage. He began to pull the debris away. Slowly, he began to uncover a body. "Charlie!" he screamed. A few more pieces and he would free him. There, the last piece of charred fuselage. Charlie was face down. He took his shoulder and started to turn him over. His head lolled behind and then finally rolled over to face him. David fell back in horror, his hand to his mouth to try to stifle the scream that

*came from deep within his very soul. The charred face he saw
was not Charlie's; it was his own.*

His eyes flew open. He was disoriented. *The fire. Charlie.* He
tried to focus on his surroundings and realized that he had
fallen asleep in the big chair in the den. His body ached in
a thousand places as he wrenched himself from the chair.
He was drenched in a cold sweat. *The dream.* He tiptoed
hurriedly to the bedroom to shut off the alarm before it
would wake Jessie, picked out his clothes from the closet,
and took them into the bathroom, showered and dressed.
He looked into the mirror to make a correct little pleat in
his thin red-and-black striped tie and then stepped back
to check his entire appearance. He was wearing a black
pinstriped suit and a crisp white shirt. He combed back an
unruly lock of hair, straightened his tie, threw a kiss toward
Sarah's room and walked softly out to the garage.

As he drove to the office, the nightmare filtered back to
him. What did it mean? Who was the corpse in the dream?
Was it the part of him that had died? That his honor, his
integrity, everything he had fought for, everything his father
had taught him, lay in the burning wreckage of his dream?
What was the price for the power he strove for at Eastern,
their house, the fancy parties and, most of all, Ginny? He
knew the price. It was himself.

CHAPTER THIRTY-FIVE

AUGUST 1955

It was one of those mornings when David felt he should have stayed in bed. There had been one meeting after another and, when his secretary called on the intercom to tell him Jessie was on the phone, he was irritated.

"Hi, Jessie."

"Hi, honey. I'm sorry to bother you. Are you terribly busy?"

"No, no, go ahead, sweetheart," he said, straining to sound calm.

"Well, I'm sending out the invitations for the party, and I wanted to go over them with you. You know, like do you want to invite the Sanders, and what about Melvin?"

David's heart stopped. There it was. Melvin would bring Ginny. Jessie interrupted his thoughts.

"We really have to invite Melvin, David."

"Why? He'll only get drunk again, and make a damn fool of himself."

"David, he's your friend. You can't hurt him that way. You were the one who always said that friendship didn't stop with troubles, that helping someone like him was what real friendship was all about. He helped you, David…"

"Dammit, Jessie, I don't owe him anything. I've been putting up with him all these years. I…"

Jessie was surprised at David's attitude. She decided not to make any more of it. There was a pause on the line and then David said, "Alright, invite him."

"If you don't really want him, darling, we don't…"

"Jessie, invite him. Who else?"

"Well, I'm inviting the Donners, the Goldmans, Marsha and Ed; they'll mix well with your new people from Sunglow Oil. It will be nice."

"Okay, sweetheart." He snapped the pencil he was holding in half. "You do it your way."

After David hung up, he leaned over his desk, put his head down on his arms and mumbled, "This is going to be some party with Ginny, Doc Sanders, and Betty. Oh, yes, it's going to be a very interesting evening."

The Goldmans arrived early to give Betty a chance to help Jessie with the innumerable preparations that go with making a successful party. Betty went into the kitchen with Jessie, leaving Max and David to their Martinis.

David lit up a cigarette and spoke after a long silence, "You look great, Max."

Max started to sip his martini and then looked up at David. "You're a liar. You know damn well I look like hell."

"Alright, so you look lousy. What's wrong?"

"I dunno. I…"

"Are you sick? Is it money? Max, is there anything—?"

Max interrupted him. "No, no, it's not me. It's Betty, she's working now at a little boutique on Newbury Street, she's…"

The front door chimes sounded softly and Jessie called out from the kitchen, "David, would you get it, dear?"

"I'll be right back." David gave Max a worried look and went to the door. It was the Donners.

"We're early," Belle Donner said with her usual big smile.

"Don't be silly," David hugged her and shook hands with Will warmly. "Come in. Come in. The martinis will get warm."

Will was wearing a gray silk suit that showed off his silver gray hair. David put his arm around Belle and led them to the bar.

Max swirled the ice in his glass and waited for David to return, but David had forgotten him. A minute of conversation and then he was off to more fertile relationships.

Max knew that David's concern, not unlike others, was only courteous, and he realized that life was passing him by.

When the Sanders arrived, Jessie's party was already off to a good start. The record player was rocking with an Elvis song and Will Donner was failing miserably trying to rock and roll with Belle. He had everybody laughing. As a result, when Betty met Sanders' eyes and stayed there coldly for what seemed like an eternity, it went completely unnoticed. It was as if the room were a scene in a movie, and the projector had stopped all other action, except for those two, and then started again as Betty turned away.

Ginny and Melvin were the last to arrive. Ginny was wearing a red sheath that clung to every contour of her body. Her blond hair was up in a beehive, causing her to appear taller than she was. She surveyed the room as if she were royalty, waiting for her subjects to pay homage.

David saw them as they made their entrance into the living room. He flushed slightly as he saw Ginny and was momentarily embarrassed, thinking that she was overdressed for a simple house party. But, then again, he thought, she had a great figure, and what the hell, why not show it off? He started toward them, wishing he had fortified himself first with a stiff drink.

Jessie greeted Ginny at the door, kissed Melvin on the cheek and took Ginny's arm. "Come on, Ginny. Let's make all the wives jealous. I'm going to introduce you to every admiring male in the place." She saw David coming toward them. "We'll start with my wonderful husband, David."

"Hello, Ginny." David took her hand, looked for some hidden sign of recognition (which was, to his disappointment, not forthcoming) and turned to Jessie. "Ginny and I have already met. I drove her and Melvin home the night of the big snowstorm."

Jessie's face showed a glimmer of concern, but she kept her composure.

Ginny greeted David as she would any other host, and then, as if he didn't exist, moved on with Jessie to the next introduction.

When Jessie came to the Goldmans, she was surprised to find out that Ginny was the woman for whom Betty worked. Ginny embraced Betty warmly. "Well, fancy meeting you here." They both laughed and began to tell Jessie about Ginny's little boutique and what fun they had working together.

"What a small world," Jessie clichéd and they all laughed.

David knew Jessie was upset, and that he would have to explain why he had failed to tell her how he had met Ginny. He went to the bar and got another martini, sipped it and looked after the two women. Jessie had an oriental softness about her. Her raven black hair and her slim body in an emerald green Mandarin-style dress were in complete contrast to Ginny. *Damn her,* he thought, though he didn't really know which one he meant.

Melvin, nearby, noticed David's distress, and moved close to him. "What'sa matter lover boy, feeling a little guilty?"

David froze. He turned, looking for the voice that was vaguely familiar. *Melvin! Melvin knew!* He felt trapped in his own home.

"What did you say?"

"You know damn well what I said."

"I don't know what the hell you're talking about."

"Oh, yes, you do, and I'm not through with you yet, so watch your back, pal." Melvin sneered, turned on his heels and stalked off.

David broke into a sweat, opened his shirt collar and looked around to see if anyone had overheard Melvin. "That son of a bitch."

David, temporarily recovered, moved through his guests mechanically as if opening doors to rooms along a long corridor. Some rooms would be bare, empty of thought, others full of conversation, and some charged with electricity, but David absorbed nothing. His mind was too overloaded with Jessie and Ginny and he unconsciously scanned the smoky room for them. He saw Jessie with Betty, building a buffet on the dining room table and good-naturedly warding off those who were nibbling before it was ready. The food smelled delicious and they were having a hard time holding off the interlopers. David came over to the table, snitched a pickle, and danced away as Jessie admonished him. For a moment David felt relaxed and it felt good. Then he saw Ginny sitting with Belle Donner. Belle was just getting up. David decided to wait until she left, so that he could have a moment alone with Ginny.

Belle chatted with Ginny for a few extra moments and finally said, "Well, I had better find Will. It was so nice talking with you. One of these days I'm going to sneak out and pay a visit to your little boutique."

Ginny was drinking more than usual. When David sat down beside her she ignored him. Then she glared at him, lifted her glass and raised it to no one in particular. "To our hosts, Mister and Mrs."—she raised her voice on the Mister and Mrs.—"Jessie and David Livingston." Then she looked directly at David and, imitating Jessie, she whispered sarcastically, "My *wonderful* husband." She stood up, stuck out her chin and looked at him, her face filled with contempt. "Jesus," she said, turned on her heel and walked away.

David eyes stung as he tried to hold back the tears of frustration that should have come out in torrents. It seemed that his life, like the party, was unraveling at the seams. He wanted to get up and run, run away. He reached for another cigarette and changed his mind. He lifted the martini to his lips, grimaced and put it down. *Dammit.* He didn't know what he wanted. But that was the point wasn't it?

He got up from the couch and continued through the guests until he came upon Sanders, who eagerly pulled him aside.

"Listen, there's this great cruise on the Rotterdam to the Panama Canal. I want to take Ruth and I thought you might join us. I think we both could use a break and it would be a treat for the girls. What do you say?"

"I could never get away, but thanks for asking. Maybe we could do it some other time."

"I know you're busy but just promise me you'll think about it."

"I'll think about it, okay?" If it was a trip to the moon, he thought, he'd be standing in line to buy a ticket.

Sanders put his arm around David's shoulders and led him toward the bar. "C'mon, I'll buy you a drink. You look like you need one."

"Richard, I need a whole bottle."

"David, I don't want to pry into your personal life and this certainly isn't the time or the place, but I think you need some help."

The little bar that had an array of liquors, including a bottle of pre-mixed martinis, a bucket of ice and an assortment of glasses. Sanders poured them both martinis, just as Ruth joined them. Sanders put his arm around her and then turned back to David. "You'll call me and we'll get together, right?" Before David could answer, Betty walked over. She was wearing a cobalt blue, turtleneck jersey that set off her flaming red hair. David sensed trouble. "Hi, Betty. Having fun?"

"Having a ball," she lied.

"I don't think you've met Ruth and Richard Sanders." David flashed back to the night he saw Sanders with Betty at the Glass Slipper.

Sanders broke out in a sweat and almost choked on his drink. He took out his handkerchief and wiped his brow. Trying to regain his composure, he gave Betty his best smile and stuck out his hand. "Nice to meet you."

Betty took his hand and held it too long. There was an uncomfortable silence. Panic crept into Sanders' eyes.

Betty clung to Sanders' sweating hand and stared defiantly into his eyes. "Haven't we met before?"

"I don't...think so," Sanders stammered.

"Isn't that strange? I could swear that...was it the Glass Slipper?"

Sanders finally pulled his hand from Betty's grasp. He was visibly shaken. "I really think you have me mixed up with someone else...You know, the proverbial face on the barroom floor." He made an effort to laugh. "Well, it was nice meeting you." He turned slightly without loosing eye contact with Betty to take Ruth's arm.

Betty watched Sanders sweat as her eyes bore relentlessly into his. Ruth had looked confused at first, but now she stared at the ground, her face drawn and sad. Betty felt sorry for her and she was glad she had never called her as she had threatened. She forced a laugh. "You're right. Must be the booze, now I remember. You're not the *man* I thought you were." She continued to stare at Sanders and then, finally, turned to David. "So, are you going to get me a drink or what?" Then without waiting for David's answer or the drink, Betty ran to the powder room to repair the tears that she could no longer control.

David let out a long breath, shrugged his shoulders, and picked up his drink from the bar, thinking that he should give Sanders some space. He turned and almost bumped into Melvin, who was leading Will Donner toward the bar, to refill his many times emptied martini glass. Melvin was in a heated monologue about Eisenhower.

"No military man has ever made a good president or, for that matter, run a big corporation. Look good in their fancy uniforms, but they just don't have what it takes to do the job." Melvin looked in David's direction. "Well, if it isn't my old friend, David." Melvin slurred slightly. "Big time operator, but maybe a little short on principles. Know what I mean, Will?"

David grabbed Melvin's arm with an iron grip. "I think you've had enough to drink, Melvin."

Melvin twisted his arm from David's grip and smiled conspiratorially. "I'm just dandy and, besides, me and Will got a lot to talk about. Isn't that right, Willie?"

Will wasn't annoyed yet but it was only a matter of a few more moments. David looked for help. Ginny was sitting on a couch and talking with a couple of the men from Sunglow. Their eyes met momentarily. He thought she should have summed up his situation and come to his rescue, but instead Ginny's face froze in contempt as she turned away with a deliberate lack of concern.

Suddenly, Jessie was there. She separated Melvin from Will. "Melvin, where are your manners? You haven't said two words to your hostess all night." She smiled at Will. "Melvin very seldom visits with us anymore, and now that I have a chance, we're going to have a long-delayed talk. Would you excuse us, please?" She led Melvin away, leaving David with Will to try and repair the damage.

"I'm exhausted." Jessie wiped the last of the dishes, and passed it to David to put in the cabinet.

"It was a great party, sweetheart," David lied. He put his arms around her and held her close.

She looked up at him and he gave her a brief kiss. "I'm going to bed." As she started toward the bedroom, she looked back. "Are you coming?"

"I think I'll go out on the porch and have a smoke first. You go on. I'll be there shortly."

"Okay, but don't be long."

Obviously she either forgot about, or didn't think it was important enough, to discuss his meeting Ginny. Thank God for that little reprieve.

He stepped out on the porch and thought about Ginny, too angry to even say goodnight to him. He had to stop hurting her, hurting Jessie, hurting himself. Eventually he'd be found out and it would destroy them all. Even the business would be a casualty, he thought, wondering if Will had picked up on Melvin's remark. Things were way out of hand. Melvin had found him out, and there was no telling what the consequences would be. He took a deep breath. *"It was a great party, sweetheart."* Shit, it was a party from hell.

Sanders was probably getting it from Ruth and God knows what was going on with Betty and Max. Poor Max, he'd completely forgotten about him. He'd call him tomorrow and apologize. Hell, he probably could spend all day on the phone apologizing to the people he had hurt.

David ran his hands through his hair, took a deep breath and tried to relax. He could smell the sweet spring air. The sky was a mass of stars. He recognized the Northern Cross, and then traced the lip of the Dipper to the North Star. It was such an important star. It was true north and was the basis for all navigation throughout the ages. He had to find out what his true north was. What his direction was. He loved two women and hadn't done justice to either of them. He was happy when he was with each of them but he longed for continuity, which was impossible with either of them.

346

When he was with Ginny, they made plans that he knew would never be fulfilled. When he was with Jessie, it seemed like he was play-acting, knowing that Ginny was in a tug of war for his emotions. And Sarah. What about his little girl? She was getting lost in the shuffle. He had to make a decision. But deep in his heart he already knew the answer; he would never leave Jessie and Sarah.

He had to say good-bye to Ginny. Set her free. Stop lying to her, to Jessie, to himself. It was time to get away. Be with Jessie. Give them both another chance. He thought about the cruise he'd discussed with Sanders.

David checked his watch. It was one-thirty and he was emotionally and physically wiped out. He headed for bed.

A billow of red and orange flame burst into the tiny area like a firestorm from hell. Dense black smoke took the form of a corpse that had risen from the grave. It undulated and danced and weaved through the fire while everything it touched burned, and finally charred, black as death.

An agonizing scream, from deep inside the inferno, rose above the roar of the flames. Again and again the terrible screams continued. "David, help me, please help me. Help me!"

David moved toward the fire, his forearms in front of his face, the fire searing the hair on his arms. "I'm coming, hold on. I'm coming." But he had to stop; the heat was too intense; he could go no further.

Suddenly a figure burst out of the conflagration, the entire body aflame as it reached out a fiery hand toward David, and cried for help. David could see its eyes, begging, pleading, but he still couldn't move. He tried. It was impossible. He reached for the outstretched hand, but to no avail. He willed his legs to move. Nothing!

The body began to disintegrate. First the feet crumpled, and it fell to its knees, then the thighs and the torso followed and disappeared into the molten coals. Only the head remained.

David's hand flew to his mouth, as he stared with unbelievable horror. He could smell the stench of the burning flesh. He felt sick, and suddenly vomit spilled from his mouth. He caught his breath, wiped the vomit from his mouth, and looked again in disbelief. Was he going mad? It couldn't be. Charlie was dead! But it was, it was Charlie, and he was trying to say something. His lips moved slowly, agonizingly, yet formed each word clearly. David couldn't hear what he was saying, but he could read his lips.

"Help me. Don't let me die like this. Don't leave me! You fucking coward!"

David screamed and ran into the flames. His clothes caught fire, then his hair. The skin on his face began to shrivel as the fire licked at his cheeks; his whole body was aflame. When he reached Charlie, Charlie's head was dissolving, melting into the glowing embers. He was too late. He fell to his knees and

348

dug his hands into the red-hot coals looking for Charlie, who was no longer there, raised his head to God, who wasn't there either, and screamed, and screamed and screamed. "Charlie, Charlie, Charlie."

Jessie woke with a start. Her heart was beating wildly. David was sitting upright in their bed, his hands thrashing in front of him. He was crying and the tears ran down his cheeks. He kept repeating, "Charlie. Charlie."

Jessie grabbed his shoulders. "David, David. Wake up. Wake up! You're having a nightmare. Wake up."

Sarah came into the bedroom, rubbing her eyes. "Daddy! What's wrong? Why is Daddy yelling? I'm scared. What's wrong?"

Jessie got out of bed, took Sarah into her arms, and tried to calm her. She wanted to comfort David, but Sarah's eyes were wide with shock, and she was trembling. "It's okay, it's okay, sweetheart. Daddy was having a bad dream. That's all."

David was soaked with sweat. The dream hung on. He started to shiver violently. He squeezed his eyes shut again and held his ears, but he could still hear Charlie screaming, "You fucking coward!"

CHAPTER THIRTY-SIX

SEPTEMBER 1955

It was the end of a long day for David. The office had emptied out hours ago. He looked at his desk, still covered with work. *What a mess.* He ran his hands through his hair and leaned back in his chair, vacantly staring at the walls of his office. It had been a month since the party and he still hadn't talked with Ginny.

He wondered why he had risked his marriage and compromised his basic instincts of honesty and fidelity to be with another woman. It would be perfectly logical if he didn't love Jessie, but he loved both women with equal passion and intensity. Yet they were so different. What was it that attracted him to two such completely polarized women?

Ginny was independent, sometimes too much so. She had gone out on her own, albeit she had some help from Melvin, and now ran a very successful business. On the other hand, she was a slob, wouldn't know what to do with a kid and wouldn't think of having one. When they made love (she loved to say "fucking") it was equally anticipated and ferociously pursued. Was it sex? And would it continue with the same intensity if it weren't forbidden? Would it wear with familiarity and the loss of newness over time?

Jessie, by comparison, had a good education, was a homemaker—a damn good one—a good mother and an accomplished hostess, but she was needy. Was that it? Did he need to be needed?

Ginny only had to be Ginny. What would she wear? How to style her hair? Which perfume? Sexy underwear? High heels or flats? More blush, less blush, which ring, which necklace? She brimmed with excitement; her stock in trade was to be a woman. No male eye missed her. She was totally irresistible. Wasn't that enough for any man's ego?

Then there was Jessie, elegantly beautiful in a quiet, reserved way, soft and disarming. Ginny lived for Ginny. Jessie lived for her family and her home, and loved him fiercely. Still, David was only a part of Jessie's life, probably the greatest part, but it was shared with Sarah, the house and all that went with it. Was that enough?

There were no answers. Comparisons didn't work. Yet David knew that it was Jessie that he truly loved and that he had to find his way back to her. He had to reconstruct himself. He needed help. He knew he could not find the answers alone, but whom could he trust to give him another perspective, a more rational direction? He thought about calling Sanders, but didn't he have the same dilemma? Then again Sanders wasn't in love; he was just making conquests. David wondered what really got Sanders off, the sex or the conquest. Well, there was no one else that he could trust and at least Sanders would be a good sounding board. He looked at his watch. Sanders would be home now, and it wouldn't be right to disturb him at dinner. *What the hell,* he thought, *we're supposed to be friends and Sanders had suggested they have a talk.* He dialed the number and Sanders answered on the first ring.

"Richard, it's David. I'm sorry to call you at home. I—"

"Not a problem, what's happening?"

"I need to talk." David could feel his face get hot; he was embarrassed.

"Something you want to discuss in the office? I'll make some time and we can—"

"No. Listen, I know it's a terrible imposition, and friends shouldn't take advantage of each other this way, but could we meet for a drink or something? I just got to, I dunno, talk to somebody that I can trust. I…"

"Hey, I understand. Listen, there's a little café near my office, you know the one, Joe's. I'll meet you there in an hour. Fast enough? You grab a booth with a little privacy, and order me a nice martini, and you're paying."

After David arrived, he looked around the little café, but Sanders hadn't arrived yet. The place smelled of beer and stale cigarette smoke. It was empty except for a young couple that seemed completely disinterested in the food in front of them. They were oblivious to their surroundings, totally engrossed in one another. David envied them. They had had time to experiment, to date and to play. They had their yesterdays and would have their tomorrows. There was no war to steal their youth. They could take their time, sow their wild oats, do the normal growing-up things that young people did. He realized that he'd been robbed of all that, and that that was the biggest war wound of all. Lost in thought, he didn't see Sanders until he slid his bulk into the booth.

"So, where's my martini?" he said.

David signaled the waitress. "Jesus, I'm sorry to drag you out like this; it's just that I can't deal with this anymore."

"Deal with what?" Sanders wiped his brow with a wrinkled handkerchief as he waited for the waitress to serve the drinks.

David downed his drink in one gulp. "I'm cheating on Jessie."

"You're what, with who? Are you crazy?" Sanders thought, *Who am I to talk? But this was different. David was different. He was a good man and this was not like him.*

"It's Ginny and—"

"You're fucking Ginny?"

"For Christ's sake, Richard, I'm in love with her. What the hell am I going to do? I still love Jessie. I don't want

353

to hurt her. I don't know what to do." Tears sprung into David's eyes and he brushed them away with a sweep of his hand.

Sanders reached across the table and patted David's arm. "Look, you're not going to get any of that morality crap from me. You know how I feel about this kind of thing, but that's really not what you want to hear." Sanders took a sip of his martini. "You have to deal with your own issues of morality and all that other bullshit. I'm not interested in your immortal soul, but I am interested in not letting you tear yourself apart, which seems to be the case." Sanders wiped his forehead and signaled the waitress with the same handkerchief for another round. He took off his glasses to clean them. David twirled his martini glass and waited.

"You can screw around with a dozen women and keep 'em happy with a bunch of bullshit, but you can't love two women and get away with it. You are going to lose one or the other or both and worst of all, you're going to end up crazy, but you know that already."

"So, what's the answer?"

Sanders blew out a long breath. "There is no real answer. You have to ask yourself what you really want, because no matter what you do somebody is going to get hurt. You have to do what is best for you. My opinion is that you miss being eighteen and you still want a romance and—"

"I was never eighteen or nineteen or twenty."

"That's just the point, and you can't go back to where you never were, don't you see?"

"So, you're saying Ginny is a flip back and that I should go home to my wife and forget about her. Well, it just ain't that easy."

"First place, I said nothing of the kind; I just told you what I think is happening. You have to decide what to do. I will tell you one thing though: stop beating yourself up. You're a good guy and you're not alone with this dilemma. You will do what's best for you in the end but, unfortunately, you'll go to hell first."

"I'm already in hell."

"Listen, things have changed. The rules about sex and morals and what you can see or read and talk about are disappearing. Unfortunately the rules about monogamy in marriage, especially here in our country, still apply."

"So, what are you telling me?"

"Well, what I am *not* telling you, as hypocritical as it sounds coming from me, is that you did the right thing. You bit the forbidden fruit and now you're stuck with the consequences. I already told you that you can't love two women at the same time and you know that. What I am telling you is that you're on a big guilt trip. You want to go home to Jessie, bare your soul and throw up all over her so you can feel better; go ahead, but I don't advise it."

David took a cigarette, and offered the pack to Sanders who declined with a wave of his hand. David used his old

Zippo to fire it up, took a deep drag, coughed, and cursed. "So what do you advise, besides suicide?"

Sanders ignored the question. "Try to understand that what has happened to you is not unusual. Your basic instincts tell you to go out and fuck every woman in sight; of course you can't do that, unfortunately." Sanders smiled wickedly. "But you're pushed in that direction physiologically and psychologically, so you cheated. What a stupid word, cheated. You didn't cheat; you ignored the rules and now you're paying the price for it. Get rid of the guilt. Go home to Jessie and Sarah. Let Ginny stay in a secret place in your heart and get on with your life."

CHAPTER THIRTY-SEVEN

OCTOBER 1955

Jessie's eyes sparkled with excitement. "I still can't believe it. Tell me I'm not dreaming."

David started to answer her, but the ship's horn drowned out his words and they both laughed.

"No, you're not dreaming, my love," and with that David picked Jessie up, whirled her around and kissed her to the smiles and applause of the other passengers.

Sarah was with Jessie's mother and Jessie felt unencumbered and relaxed. "Now tell me how you pulled this thing off. And where are Ruth and Richard anyway?"

Just then, Ruth and Sanders saw them and squeezed through the crowds of other passengers standing at the rails, watching the ship pull out of port.

"Hey, you lovely people, we've been looking all over for you," Sanders said as he kissed Jessie on the cheek and shook hands with David.

Ruth was wearing a red-white-and-blue sailor suit. David looked her up and down. "Look at you, you gorgeous creature. What are you doing here with this ugly beast?"

Sanders gave an exaggerated pout. "Hey, hey, I resent that. Hell, we're probably the best-looking people on the whole damn ship, the youngest, for sure."

"You're so modest," Jessie said as she gave Sanders a big hug.

"Let's find a bar and get us some drinks." Sanders took Ruth's hand.

"Oh no you don't. We're going to stay right here until the ship pulls out. "Jessie said as she handed him a roll of streamers.

Jessie asked David again, "C'mon, tell me how you pulled off this miracle."

"Let Richard tell you. He's the guy that did it. Tell her, Richard."

"Well Harvard Travel does something every year for the alumni. They get great deals like this one. Two go for the price of one. I couldn't resist it. Of course, your stingy husband gave me a hard time, but I finally talked him into it."

"That's a dirty lie," David said indignantly, as he punched Sanders playfully on the arm.

The big ship started to move away from the dock, her horns sounding. Passengers threw streamers as they waved wildly at no one in particular. After a while the ship passed the Statue of Liberty and the passengers began to disperse.

After the two couples made plans to meet for drinks before dinner, they headed to their cabins to unpack.

Once in the cabin, Jessie fell into David's arms. She kissed him hotly, pushing her pelvis into him.

"Hey, what's this?"

"Just horny and in love with my man."

David kissed her lips, and then her neck. He started to unbutton her blouse. Her breasts were still firm. He slipped her blouse from her shoulders as she unzipped his fly and began to caress him, not that he needed any further stimulation. David slid her skirt and panties off, picked her up, carried her to the bed, finished undressing and finally had her in his arms.

"Sweetheart, I love you so much," she said breathlessly as he entered her.

That evening, David leaned over the railing, stared at the endless sea and inhaled the fresh salt air. He was happy and relaxed for the first time in what felt like years, yet Ginny crept into his thoughts. She had refused his calls. Simply hung up when she heard his voice. It was over. He didn't blame her. He would never leave Jessie and she knew it. Somehow the party had crystallized that for both of them.

Still he knew that he still needed to see her again, as if somehow, by being with her, he could wipe away the pain he had caused her and find some absolution. Since she wouldn't take his calls, he decided to write and beg to be heard.

Jessie finally joined him. She was wearing a white silk jacket with a Mandarin neck over a long black skirt that was slit up the side almost to her thigh. She twirled around so that he could appraise her gown. "What do you think?"

What do I think? I think that I am happy and that I love you more than ever.

Before dinner they headed for the casino and drifted over to the craps table. They squeezed their way in and watched the game for a few moments when suddenly the dice came to David. He bet ten dollars on the line and turned to Jessie. He put the dice into her reluctant hand and gave her a reassuring smile. "Just shake them and throw them. That's all you have to do."

"Oh, I don't know."

"You can do it, lady. You can do it," the huge fat man on the other side of the table said with a big smile. "Throw those dice, lady, and give us a seven."

Sanders bet five dollars and joined the chorus. "Do it, Jess. C'mon, seven."

Jessie threw the dice.

"Seven! Pay the line," the croupier said, as the crowd around the table cheered.

"You're beautiful," the fat man said as he took his winnings and put them right back on the line. "Can you throw an eleven?" He put another stack of chips on the eleven, an eight-to-one shot.

Jessie threw an eleven. The table cheered but the fat man screamed the loudest, "God dammit, you keep that up, sweetheart, and I'll own this ship!" He put all his chips on the line again, a small fortune. Jessie was into it now. She gave her biggest smile to the fat man and asked his name.

"Vernon, Howard Vernon," he answered.

"Well, Howard, this one's for you." She threw the dice. There was complete silence as the dice hit the back of the table and began to tumble to a stop.

"Come on eleven," Jessie screamed.

The dice finally settled and the croupier said, "Eleven!"

The table broke into pandemonium. "One more time," the table yelled.

"Sorry," Jessie shook her head, throwing her long black hair back and forth. "I'm quitting while I'm a winner."

"Good for you, princess, and besides, you are all going to join me for dinner and we're going to celebrate with the best champagne in the ship." Vernon walked over to Jessie and put out his arm. "May I?"

"I'm afraid you'll have to ask my husband." She turned to David, "Vernon, this is my husband, David."

"And what a lucky man you are to have married this beautiful princess."

Vernon led the way, as Jessie took in every detail, the crystal chandeliers, the elegant grand staircase and finally the huge dining room. She felt like a child on a visit to Oz.

Vernon became the fifth at the dinner table for the rest of the cruise and kept them in hysterics, as he told one joke after another. Most of them had Ruth and Jessie blushing and hiding behind their napkins.

It was the last night of the cruise. Vernon came to the table with mischief in his eyes, and two beautifully wrapped boxes. He put one in front of Jessie and the other in front of Ruth.

"A little thanks for making what would have been a lonely trip such a lovely experience. You will all have to come to Miami and meet my wife. She's a wonderful girl. You will love her."

"Your wife?" Jessie said and, without thinking that she might be rude, asked, "Why isn't...?"

"Why isn't she with me?" Vernon laughed. "Because she jumped ship just before we left. She's a little high strung and, well, you know, she thinks I swear too much and I guess I embarrassed her. We had a big fight. You know how those things go. I was damned if I was going to give her the satisfaction, so I just let her go and I stayed on. Damn glad I did too, thanks to you people."

Jessie realized her mouth was open and she clamped it shut in case she would say what was on her mind. There was a long, embarrassing silence that might have lasted through dinner but for more of Vernon's anecdotes and very dirty jokes. Dessert came and went and the girls hadn't opened their gifts.

"C'mon girls, open up your presents," Vernon prodded.

They both carefully unwrapped their gifts.

Each had a beautiful, solid gold watch. Ruth and Jessie looked up at Vernon at the same time, both at a loss for words. "Really, Vernon this is…"

"It's nothing." He started to leave the table. "It's nothing. And, by the way, you are all going to be invited to my birthday party. No, you don't have to go to Miami. It's going to be in New York at the Plaza." He got up, threw the ladies kisses and lumbered off to his stateroom.

Chapter Thirty-Eight

November 1955

David hadn't spoken to Ginny since the night of the party, nor had he mailed the letter that he had painstakingly written during the cruise. He knew it was over, but he just couldn't let go. He didn't want it to end this way. She just couldn't walk out of his life as she did at the party without even a good-bye. It felt like he was losing a part of his body. An arm or a leg would have been easier to give up. He had to see her again, to touch her face, and hold her in his arms one last time. Most of all he needed some kind of absolution. He picked up the phone and dialed her number hoping she wouldn't hang up before he had a chance to plead his case.

"Hi."

"Hello, David."

"I want to see you."

"Oh David. Let's not go through this again. It's time to say good-bye, I…"

"Ginny, I love you." His voice was choked.

"I love you too, David," she said solemnly. "But, it's no use. I want a man that's all mine. Not fifty-fifty. I want babies and a home of my own." She hesitated for a moment and let out a long sigh of resignation. "Go home, David. Make them happy, because you can't make me happy. I'm tired of your guilty good-byes. I want to be young and live again."

"Ginny, let me see you tonight, please."

"Why? What for? Are you going to leave your wife? Your precious business?"

"Look, we have to talk. I'm coming over. I'll be there at seven." David hung up without waiting for her response.

He opened the door to her apartment with his own key, but he knew before he crossed the threshold that the rooms would be empty. Yet, even in their emptiness, she was there. She was everywhere. He could smell her perfume. What was it, Joy?

He couldn't lose her. *I'll make her understand, write her a note and beg her to be patient, to come back, lie to her about marriage. Funny that I know it would be a lie. God, what's wrong with me? Why have I spent my whole life hurting people? I'll never leave Jessie. Ginny is right. I have to let her go.* He threw the key to her apartment on the lamp table. There could be no note.

He closed the door slowly after him and paused at the first landing. Ginny wasn't running down the stairs into his arms this time. They would never hold each other again. Make love again.

He couldn't go home. He drove to the Glass Slipper.

"Good evening, sir."

"Where's Al?"

"Vacation," the bartender answered with that patient look that meant, What can I get for you?

"CC manhattan, on the rocks. Make it a double."

A girl was silhouetted in the doorway. She had blond hair and wore it up in a beehive. His heart skipped a beat until she came into full focus and he realized that it wasn't Ginny. She was so embedded in his mind he knew he would be forever searching every face for her. He had to stop thinking about her, although he knew he would never stop loving her. She would always be in that secret place in his heart.

It was time to go home.

David pulled the car into the driveway and turned off the key. He sat in the darkness.

If there is a God, it seems that His rewards were just the reduction of pain, but not the elimination of it, and His punishments were simply an increase of pain to the various degrees that He sees fit.

Ginny, gone from my life. Increase pain. A new life with Jessie. Less pain. The nightmares and the memories. Eternal pain. Oh God, please reach into my brain and rip out the horror that lives there like a living thing. He won't listen. Eternal agony.

God has witnessed my sins. He knows about Charlie. I don't. What did I do? Why is Charlie haunting me? What about the little German and Sully? Does he know that I killed them? And did He hear the lies I told to Ginny; did He see how I manipulated her? Does He know how I lusted for power, betrayed Mrs. Bass and Melvin? Would there ever be forgiveness for the hurt I have caused Jessie and Sarah?

Go ahead, add pain, pile it on!

Well, I can't change what's done. I have to live with it, suffer with it, pray for forgiveness, but maybe, Jessie is the one sin that I could be absolved for, be forgiven for. Please, God, give me another chance and don't let it be too late.

Jessie heard the car in the driveway and she waited in the dark like an animal in the night watching its prey, waiting, patient, deadly.

David opened the front door to his home and his heart, anticipating a new start. The room was dark. He switched on the lights and started as he saw Jessie sitting on the couch. Her eyes were red rimmed, her face strained, and lips thin.

Jessie looked at her watch. "Would you believe 9:30 and you're home? Did you lose your way, darling?"

"Honey." David walked over and reached for her hand, which she withdrew vigorously.

"What the hell is wrong with you?"

"What the hell do you think is wrong?" Her eyes filled with tears.

"I don't know what you're talking about. Jessie, this isn't you."

"Well, baby, meet the new me." Her face was red with anger.

"Will you please calm down and tell me what is going on."

Her resolve broke and she started to cry. She got hold of herself, got up from the chair and faced him. She was trembling. This wasn't going the way she had anticipated. She wanted to have been calm, calculating. Give him a chance to explain, but she had lost it as her overwhelming anger took over. She fought back her tears. "I'll tell you what's going on. I got a call from an *anonymous friend* today. He told me about my cheating husband, but the son of a bitch didn't need to tell me, because I already knew." She reached into the pocket of her robe and withdrew a neatly folded paper. Her hand trembled as she waved in David's face. "Here, here's the letter I found in your pocket when I took your jacket to the cleaner." She crumpled the ship's stationary and threw it at David's face. "Now you can deliver it personally, you bastard." She lowered her voice. Her face was contorted in a mask of rage. "You used to be a man, a real man. But you're nothing. Nothing! Now get out of here and leave us alone. Just leave us alone."

David tried to take her into his arms, but she pushed him away.

"Leave me alone. Don't you understand? I don't want you here anymore."

David was dazed. He had never heard nor seen Jessie like this. It was useless to try to calm her. She was crying, her voice a hoarse whisper. "Get out! Get out!"

He started to reach for her, but she stepped back and, in a voice trembling with emotion, said, "You broke my heart, David. You broke my heart and I will never forgive you."

David dropped his outstretched hands, walked to the front door and stumbled down the front stairs as Jessie slammed the door behind him. He got into his car, leaned his head on the steering wheel and tried to cry, but nothing came out. He was empty.

Jessie listened to David's car start up and finally drive away. She leaned against the wall and slowly slumped down until she was sitting on the floor. *He is driving out of my life. Out of Sarah's life. Wasn't I enough for him? What did I do wrong? I tried so hard to be a good wife. Damn him! Why am I sitting here blaming myself? He's the one that cheated on me.*

"What's wrong, Mommy?" Sarah asked, peeking from the top of the stairs. "Are you crying?" She started down the stairs.

Jessie quickly pulled herself together. She blew her nose and took a deep breath just as Sarah reached her and came into her arms. Jessie choked back the sobs that filled her chest and pulled Sarah close to her breast.

"Were you crying, Mommy?"

"Just a little, honey."

"But, why?"

"I guess it's because Daddy has to go away for awhile." She couldn't hold back any longer. She pulled Sarah back into her arms as the tears flowed more freely.

"Please don't cry, Mommy."

Jessie sniffed. "Don't you worry, my love. I'm fine." She took her finger and wiped away the tears that still brimmed in Sarah's eyes. "Look at silly me, sitting on the floor crying." She got up and helped Sarah to her feet. "How about some hot cocoa and some pie?"

"Okay, but what about Daddy? When will he come home?" Sarah wiped her nose with the back of her hand.

Jessie didn't know how to answer Sarah's question. She wondered if she would ever let David come home. He was barely gone and she missed him. Was she so irrational that she had allowed herself to throw him away without even giving him a chance to speak? That wasn't her plan. Was this it? Would he even call? Try to explain? Maybe it was just a crazy fling. Dammit, why was she making excuses for him? She ran her hand down Sarah's smooth cheek, looked into her eyes and lied, "He'll be home before you know it, sweetheart, so stop crying and eat your pie."

It started to rain as David drove into the darkness. *How could I have been so stupid to have left that letter in my pocket? Well, it didn't matter. Melvin had already delivered the coup de grace. What a fool I've been.* He watched the speedometer needle creep up to seventy, then eighty. He thought how much this moment resembled his life. Going eighty miles an hour, leaving his whole world behind him and going nowhere. He'd lost Jessie. It was impossible to believe that he had loved two women, and had thrown them both away.

Rose hesitated before she knocked on Jessie's door, thinking back to Jessie's hysterical conversation earlier in the morning. What could she do to console her daughter? The standard phrases, "Don't worry, everything will turn out alright" or "It's all for the best," were useless drivel.

Her negative impression of David had disappeared. He had been hard-working, kind and considerate to Jessie and Sarah, and most respectful and attentive to her. She'd grown to both like and respect him. How could he have erred so badly? Harry had never cheated on her, at least she didn't think so, and if he had, what would she have done? Thrown him out? She would have been hurt, but would she have gone that far? Probably not, but that was because she would have been too frightened to go it alone. Oh, she would have made his life hell for a while, kept him out of her bed, but in the end of course, if he had been really repentant...But Jessie was different. She was strong-willed. What advise could she give her? "Take David back for Sarah's sake." "It isn't worth it to break up a marriage because of one mistake." Hardly. She knew her daughter. Her best bet was to keep her mouth shut and listen.

She knocked and held her breath. Sarah opened the door. Her eyes were red-rimmed and her greeting lacked the enthusiasm Rose was used to.

"So where are my hugs and kisses?" Rose asked, bending down with some difficulty to take Sarah into her arms.

"Daddy's gone away," Sarah choked out, the tears running down her cheeks. Rose took out her handkerchief, blotted Sarah's tears and then put it on her running nose. She said, "Blow." Sarah obediently blew her nose into her grandmother's handkerchief. "That's better." Rose caught herself before she was about to reply, "I'm sure he'll be back soon." Instead she simply held Sarah in her arms for an extra moment. Then, gathering herself together, she took Sarah's hand and said, "Let's go find Mama."

Jessie looked like a wreck. She was wearing a housecoat over her nightgown. Her hair was a mess. She was devoid of any makeup and it was easy to see she had been crying. When she saw Rose, she fell into her arms and sobbed. Sarah, not to be left out, joined them, and the three of them held on to each other as if in the middle of a terrible storm.

Jessie finally stepped out of her mother's embrace and knelt down beside Sarah. "I'm sorry, darling. I'm just not myself today. Terrible headache, you know how I get them sometimes? C'mon, let's find something on TV."

"You're crying because daddy went away."

"Well, yes, that too, but I told you it's just for a little while and…"

"I don't want to watch TV, and I don't believe you." Sarah stormed out of the room.

Jessie didn't have the strength to pursue her. Instead she sat on the side of her bed and spoke to no one in particular. "What did I do wrong? We loved each other, had something special. We were best friends. Why did he do it?" Her eyes were vacant. She folded her arms across her chest and rocked back and forth.

Rose sat down beside her and put her arm around her. "Well, certainly not because he doesn't love you. You have to believe that."

Jessie stopped rocking, dropped her arms to her side, and looked at her mother in disbelief.

You're supposed to listen, remember, Rose reminded herself.

Jessie stood, a little disoriented at first, and then started pacing back and forth in the small bedroom. Finally she walked to the mirror on her dresser and studied her reflection. Her eyes were red and puffy, cheeks still streaked from the tears that had barely dried, and her lips, a tight red slit. Anger was consuming her like a hungry beast. She had to pull herself together. There was Sarah to take care of and her own life had to go on. She took a deep breath and tried to relax, a hint of a smile softened her face. The anger slowly began to subside, left to simmer in her brain, lie dormant like a volcano waiting to erupt, unpredictable and dangerous. But then again the anger energized her; it was the loss of trust, something she might never be able to have with anyone again, that was defeating her. Still that was not all that ground her into depression like the heel of a giant boot. David's betrayal had humiliated her, robbed her of her self-esteem, sucked away the very heat from her body, leaving only a shivering shell of what once was a warm, living thing. She was cold and tired. The lying smile disappeared. Once again her eyes were blank, lifeless. She needed to be alone, to mourn for the life that had just died within her. "Can you take Sarah for the weekend?" she asked her mother. "I need a little time"

Chapter Thirty-Nine

November 1955

When Melvin reached the Boston Club, he was in high spirits. He was sober and he wanted to see Ginny. As he passed the desk on the way to the gym, he asked the telephone operator to get her on the line. The towel boy in the dressing room greeted him.

"Hello, Mr. Melvin. You look nice today, suh."

"Thank you, Paul. I feel good."

"That phone is for you, suh." He pointed to the phone off the hook.

"I know, Paul. Thank you."

Melvin took the phone. "Hi. Ginny?"

"Hello, Melvin. How are you?"

"Sober as a judge, believe it or not."

Ginny didn't respond.

"How about dinner tonight, maybe the Terrace Room or something?" He paused when there was no immediate answer, and then said, "I miss you, Ginny. I..."

"Mel, I'm sorry, sweetheart, but I've made other plans. Why didn't you call me earlier?"

"Ginny, break them, please. I really have to see you. I'm not going to drink anything stronger than ginger ale, and that's a promise. How about it, huh?"

Melvin sensed that slightest hesitation, that almost indeterminable moment that comes with an uncomfortable answer.

"I'd like to, Melvin, but I really have other plans, and I just can't break them. Maybe next week or…"

"It's David, isn't it?"

"What? What are you saying?" Ginny hoped her voice wouldn't betray the panic that gripped her like an iron vice.

"You think I don't know you're seeing David? What d'ya think I'm stupid or something? I thought you'd give it up, get tired of him. I mean he's married, for Christ's sake. He's got a kid. What the hell are you doing?"

"It's not what you think. It's, it's…" Ginny could hardly tell him that they were no longer seeing each other, and she was still mourning him.

"Yeah, it's what? It's bullshit. That's what it is." He hung up. *That son of a bitch, I've just begun to get you, just wait.*

He showered and shaved, slipped Paul a dollar bill and left. As he passed the door to the club lounge, he decided to have a drink and sauntered over to the bar with an air of nonchalance.

The bar was paneled in rich mahogany and smelled of cigar smoke. A couple of politicians from the Hill were sipping scotch and talking in subdued voices. They looked up when Melvin came in.

Melvin ignored them, sat down at the bar and ordered a drink.

"Here you are, Mr. Bass."

Melvin lifted his glass, paused and caught the bartender's eye. "Know what I'm gonna do tonight? I'm gonna have myself a drink in every goddamn bar in this lousy city." With that, he gulped down his drink, signed his tab and left. The bartender was impassive. He'd seen men try to drown their sorrows in whiskey before.

"Cab, sir?"

"Nope," he told the doorman. "I'm walking as long as I can under my own power. Plenty of time for cabs later." He headed down Beacon Street toward the Embassy bar.

The bar was in the Embassy Building. Most of its clientele were the lawyers and accountants that either had, or visited, offices in that building. Melvin always thought it was too high-class, and that the brown leather chairs with no contrast to the dark rug and mahogany walls gave the place the air of a mausoleum. He sank deeper into the sea of depression.

One drink, he said to himself. That completed, he continued on until he reached the Parker House bars. He had a drink in both.

By ten o'clock, Melvin had already bowed to the need of taxis and he was now at the Savannah Club on lower Massachusetts Avenue. He gave the cabby a buck tip. "Don't bother, old pal. I can get out by myself." He stumbled out of the cab.

"Look, buddy, it ain't none of my business, but this is a bad section to be in, in your condition. These niggers'll be on top of you before you know it. Why not be a smart guy and let me take you home?"

"Like you said," Melvin slurred, "it ain't none of your business." He headed for the Savannah Club.

The club was in the heart of the Boston colored section, which was rarely frequented by whites. Melvin entered the club, framed himself against the inner door, and peered into the smoke-filled room. There was a greenish glow to the dimly lighted, dark faces that inspected him. The music was very loud, and it pounded into Melvin's brain as he immersed himself into the smoky haze of the room.

The waiter appeared from nowhere. Melvin ordered and the waiter disappeared. A shadowy figure of a girl appeared at the table. Melvin could barely make out her dark face. Cheap perfume filled his nostrils as her velvety voice penetrated the gloom.

"Mind if I sit down, honey?"

"Yes, I mind but go ahead, you will anyway."

She sat down. "Wanna buy me a drink?"

"Nope."

"What are ya so angry 'bout? I just wanna be nice to ya." She reached for his hand but he pulled it away.

"Look." He took out a large roll of bills, peeled off a ten-dollar bill that didn't go unnoticed by other faces in the bar, and said, "Take this and give someone a free one."

"Well, thank you, love," She folded the bill into her brassiere. "You sure you...?"

"Yeah, I'm sure."

The waiter came back with his drink. Melvin paid and belted it down. His eyes were tearing from the smoke as he put the empty glass on the table and got up to leave. He felt dizzy and a little sick. The red exit sign at the door was blurred. Suddenly nausea overwhelmed him, and he began to vomit. Two big men took him roughly by the arms, dragged him to the door, and threw him sprawling to the sidewalk. He heard an oath behind him and then some high pitched giggles from a few onlookers as he struggled to his feet and zigzagged down the street. He felt sick again and he stumbled into an alley to avoid the eyes that followed him. Vomit spewed from his mouth. His heard the sounds of footsteps coming toward him. He looked around dizzily and saw two figures coming toward him out of the shadows. His heart quickened. He realized his danger. They were between him and the street. He started to run, stumbling in ruts grooved into the alley when, suddenly, he realized he was at a dead end. There was a large chain-link fence that separated the alley from the railroad tracks beyond it. He turned toward the two men.

"Wha' da ya want?" he yelled, racked with fear, his head swimming.

Then one of the men hit Melvin hard in the stomach, and as he grabbed at his middle and bent with the pain, the man raised his knee into Melvin's face. Blood ran from Melvin's shattered nose and, with the strength only a desperately frightened man could summon, he scrambled to his feet only to run into the second man. He felt a stabbing pain in his groin and then two lashing punches to his already battered face. He swung blindly at his foe only to feel another heavy blow to his ribs. Then they were both on him. He tried to scream but nothing came out. One man had pinned his arms behind his back, while the other was taking his time with hard, determined blows to his face and body. Melvin was crying and praying for oblivion. Then it came.

CHAPTER FORTY

NOVEMBER 1955

Melvin felt very calm, maybe even pretty good. It was as if he was floating and there was no more pain. He felt a little woozy, but his mind was clear. He thought about how he had been wasting his life; it all seemed so clear to him now. In his quest for love, for recognition that had never been forthcoming, he had buried himself in a bottle and alienated himself from all love. He could see Ginny's dim figure through the oxygen tent. Was she weeping? How he wanted her, and yet it seemed he never had a chance. The booze and his self-pity were too much competition. *Well, all that is going to change. Jesus, did I have to get the shit kicked out of me to wake up to the fact that I have a life, and that I'm going to live it? And that son of a bitch David stole my business, and now he's fucking Ginny, my Ginny. Well, we'll see about that. Things are going to change. That bastard's going to get his due.* He felt Ginny's hand giving him a reassuring squeeze. God, how he loved her. Was there still a chance, or would he drown himself in the bottle again? *No dammit! There was too much to do now.*

When David reached Melvin's room at the Mass General Hospital, Ginny was sitting beside Melvin's bed, holding his hand. The room had the usual hospital odor and for a moment memories of other hospitals rushed through David's mind. Melvin's labored breathing filled the room. David pulled up a chair and sat beside Ginny.

"I should have gone out with him that night. He sounded so desperate. I should have understood. I mean he called me, and I just couldn't…"

"Ginny." David touched her arm. "This is not your doing; you're not responsible."

"But if I had…" Her eyes were tearing.

"Ginny, it's just not your fault."

"Dear God, look at him. Look what they did to him!"

Melvin's nose was broken, his head was bandaged, he had multiple contusions, three broken ribs, one that had punctured a lung, and his bruised eyes seemed to stare unseeing through the oxygen tent.

David didn't think Melvin was aware, but he leaned close to his bedside. "How are you doing, trooper?" There was no response.

Melvin clenched his jaw. *Bastard.*

David turned to Ginny and shrugged his shoulders. "I checked with the police and of course got the usual bullshit response. Robbery and what the hell was he doing in that area anyway? Was he suicidal or just plain stupid?"

There was a knock on the door. Without waiting for a reply, a doctor dressed in his white coat entered, followed by a group of young interns. The doctor smiled, giving his silent message that it was time for Ginny and David to leave.

As they walked through the corridors to the elevator, David stopped and faced Ginny. "I missed—"

Ginny interrupted him. "Please don't."

"Ginny, I just wanted to…"

"Please." Her eyes were filled with tears. He wanted to take her into his arms and tell her what he knew she wanted to hear. Instead he looked down at the floor and felt a terrible sadness fall over him like a shroud.

As the elevator descended, Ginny said, "If God is good and lets him get well enough to get out of here, I'm going to take care of him."

Ginny saw to it that Melvin's apartment was cleaned and ready for his homecoming. She had visited Melvin daily in the hospital, and sat by his bedside for hours, sometimes in complete silence. Then, as he began to recover, they had long, serious discussions. At first they talked about politics, literature, and anything but themselves, but slowly they became more intimate.

"I don't think I have ever really been loved," Melvin said shyly. "I don't believe my parents loved me, especially my father."

"Oh, I think they loved you. They just didn't show it as much as you would have liked."

"No, my father hated me. I don't know why. Maybe I tried too hard for him to love me." Melvin paused and looked up at Ginny. "Is that what I did with you, tried too hard?"

Ginny didn't answer, but she touched Melvin's hand.

"I guess I needed love, needed you so much that I…I never believed that anyone would love me, especially you. Maybe I was so afraid of rejection that I hid in a closet, like I did when I was a kid. Only my closet was a bottle of booze. Well, I'm not hiding anymore. I love you, Ginny. I want you to give me another chance." There were tears in his eyes when he brought his index finger to her lips and said, "Don't say anything now. Just think about it for a while, okay?"

Ginny nodded affirmatively, leaned toward Melvin and kissed him lightly on the lips. "I'm going to leave now. Don't forget to take your medicine. I'll see you tomorrow."

As the weeks went tediously by, Melvin worked hard with the hospital therapist. Her sunny personality and consistent encouragement turned the painful and exhausting sessions into a lively banter and a serious challenge.

As she helped Melvin out of the wheelchair and he put his arm around her for support, he whispered, "So when are you going to let me make love to you?"

She got him settled into the wheelchair and rolled him over to the window. Melvin could see the Charles River winding its way from Cambridge through the locks to the ocean beyond. "Tell you what," she said. "When you can run along that river all the way to the ocean, you got a date. Right now let's get to work."

Finally he improved to a point where he would be able to complete his recovery at home.

Melvin finished shaving. He patted his face dry and stared at his reflection in the mirror. His hair had grown back from where it had been shaved, and it covered most of the ugly red scar that ran down past his left temple. He had refused plastic surgery for his nose, because he secretly liked the way he looked. It hardened his appearance and, along with the scar, it gave him a rather pugnacious look. He had combined his therapy with a strict weight-lifting regime, and was surprised at how quickly his body responded. He stepped back from the mirror, posed and liked what he saw. Best of all, he hadn't had a single drink. Although he was tempted, Ginny's comments on how well he looked had strengthened his resolve.

Ginny developed an easy relationship with Melvin. They spoke daily, and Melvin took it for granted that Ginny's answer to a new start to their relationship would be positive.

"Ginny, I want to spread my new wings. Have dinner with me."

This time Ginny didn't hesitate. "I'd love to. And besides, it's time for you to celebrate. When, where, and what time?"

Melvin was surprised by her quick and exuberant response; he took a deep breath. "Giovanni's, 7:30. Tomorrow night."

When Ginny stepped into the foyer of the little Italian restaurant, Melvin got up from the bar and started walking toward her. He had a glass in his hand. Ginny, seeing the glass, sucked in her breath and started to protest. Melvin saw her distress and quickly said, "Wait, wait, wait. It's just soda water, honest." They laughed as Melvin closed the gap between them, took Ginny's hand, and kissed her cheek. She pushed him away at arm's length and gave him an appraising look. "Melvin you look wonderful, just wonderful." She put her arms around him and gave him a quick, little kiss on the lips.

He smiled sheepishly, a little embarrassed and took her hand. "Thank you, and you know, I couldn't have done it without you."

They sat at a cozy table near the fireplace. "I called David today." He saw her begin to protest. "Wait, I know you don't like talking about him, but this is about me. I asked him if I could come in; you know, get started again, maybe help him out. God knows he could use some help. According to my mother, he's got a full-fledged rebellion going on. The board feels he's overextended, and he won't listen to them. He's alienating everyone, even his strongest supporters, the guys that always vote with him, and the people that give him control. She told me that he doesn't seem to give a damn. He's short-tempered and arrogant, and they don't like it. You know when you're on top you can get away with just about anything, but from what my mother has heard, Eastern's in trouble, and so is David. Anyway, guess what? He laughed at me. Well, I don't blame him. I haven't been much of a winner, have I?"

"Melvin, that was the past. After all, your father founded the company; David shouldn't treat you like that. I mean, you gave him his big chance. It seems to me that he's a little short on memory, don't you think?"

"Well, my mother has a seat on the board. Of course she often skips meetings, but anyway, she asked the board if they would allow me to take her place and they've agreed."

"Melvin, that's great. I'm so proud of you!"

Dinner came and went, and then coffee and dessert, almost without notice, as they talked and laughed.

At Ginny's door, Melvin held Ginny, searched her eyes as if trying to read her mind, leaned over, gave her a fleeting kiss, and waited anxiously for her response. He hoped this was the night that they would start their love affair again. But Ginny deftly turned out of Melvin's arms. She unlocked her door, slipped into her apartment, said a soft goodnight, and quietly shut the door behind her.

She sat down in the darkness and wept. *David, David what are you doing to yourself? Oh, my darling, how I would like to hold you again, to comfort you.* She folded her arms about herself, and rocked back and forth as the tears ran down her face.

CHAPTER FORTY-ONE

MARCH 1956

David brought the board to order in the smoke-filled boardroom and, after the usual preliminaries, introduced Melvin, who stood, smiled, and cleared his throat. Will Donner, who had recently retired from the bank and now sat on Eastern's board, gave Melvin a reassuring glance.

"Thank you for giving me this opportunity. I'm honored to be here, and hope that I can, in some small way, be of some value." He looked directly at David. "And I promise I will never put myself before the best interest of this corporation."

As Melvin sat down, David glanced at him coldly, took a sip of water from a crystal goblet and put it down on the polished mahogany conference table. "Well let's get down to business." He stood. "During our last meeting I passed out my proposal regarding the World Tanker investment. Melvin, I had my secretary drop off yours at your apartment."

"Yes, thank you, I received it," Melvin answered, staring back at David.

"Good. Well, as you know, I've spent an enormous amount of time on this project. I know there are risks here, but I think the rewards far outweigh the risks. Some of you have told me privately that you won't back this project, and I am hoping that when it comes to a vote today you will change your minds. I want to remind you that we have disagreed before, and although you might have thought that I bulldozed you into going along with me, the end results were always positive. Remember, the biggest risk is to take no risk. Gentlemen, I want this tanker! I've given you all the facts, I've answered all of your questions, and now I want your approval. This company must not stagnate or it will perish."

Bill Kelly put the unlit cigar he was chewing on in the ashtray in front of him and then stood. Bill graduated from Harvard Law and was still the toughest corporate lawyer in the East. He was a straight shooter, addicted to the bottom line, and impatient with small talk. "Excuse me, David, but aren't you losing sight of the fact that we decided that we can't afford to take on any more debt?"

David understood Bill's point that, in spite of the fact that they had successfully gone public and reduced a substantial amount of their debt, they needed more time in order for the shareholders to get back their stock that was still held by the bank. They would be taking on a great deal more debt for the moment, which, he had to admit, seemed counterproductive. But he knew that in a few years, with the price edge the tanker would provide, their stock would rise dramatically and their debt would disappear. He looked into Bill's piercing blue eyes. "Listen, Bill, you've fought me on every deal that I've brought before this board, and frankly I'm getting damned tired of fighting you every time I try to grow this corporation. If this board acted on your opinions, we'd still be a little oil company struggling to make the payroll."

"Hold on, David," Will Donner broke in. "You're being too tough on Bill."

David's face flushed and the veins stood out in his neck. "Will, you, of all people, know what I've done for this corporation. I run it, go to bed with it, and wake up every morning with it. You people meet here four times a year and you want to tell me how to run the business?"

"David, we all can use guidance. No one's trying to tell you how to run the business."

Bob Oliver slapped the table with the palm of his hand and stood up. His face contorted in an angry scowl. "I disagree with you, Will. We damn well better start telling him how to run this business. He's talked all of us into hocking our stock to cover debt that we're never going to get out of. I think it's about time we demand some consolidation, certainly not any more expansion."

"Hey, if you're not happy with my tanker project, that's one thing. But if you don't like the way I'm running this business, that's another." David felt his face burning. This was the final part of his expansion project. He was not going to take no for an answer. He resented having to be subjected to the views of the board, and he'd be damned if he let them tell him what to do.

"Gentlemen, gentlemen, let's all calm down." Will Donner rose from his seat in emphasis.

"No, let's not calm down; if you don't want the tanker project then you don't want me. Let's put this to a vote right now and get it over with." David knew he was out of line, but his temper had got the best of him, and it was too late to turn back.

Will looked at David in shock. "Are you telling us that if we don't approve this project, you will resign? C'mon, David, this is not like you. You don't mean this."

"Yes I do mean it, Will, because my intuition, my risk-taking, if that's what you want to call it, is what made this corporation. If this board thinks that now it's the wrong direction, then I'm not the man that should be running it. So, let's not belabor this any longer. I want an open vote, a simple show of hands." He was being arrogant and childish, and he knew it, but he pushed forward. "All those against the tanker project…"

Three of the six members of the board raised their hands, and looked about for the count. It was a dead heat until Melvin looked directly into David's eyes and slowly raised his hand.

CHAPTER FORTY-TWO

APRIL 1956

David looked around the cheap hotel room that he'd been living in since his separation from Jessie, let out a long sigh, and started to pack. It was hard to believe that all he had left of his life were the two suitcases that lay on the bed.

He had called and called Jessie to no avail. She was inconsolable. He had sat in the depressing hotel room for hours, maybe days, staring into nothingness. There were long walks to nowhere, a bottle of vodka that he brought to his room, only to pour it down the drain. Searching, searching for answers that didn't exist, something, anything, to quell the pain or erase the guilt that lived with him day and night. Nothing! He sat on the side of his bed, face in his hands, and let out long, uncontrollable sobs. There was no way he could be so close to Jessie and Sarah and not be able to be with them, but there was no alternative. It was time to get out of town.

In the last three weeks since he resigned from Eastern, there had been a few offers of employment, but they were far below David's abilities, and nowhere near the compensation that he had just given up. He decided that there would be more opportunity for a position in a bigger city, where he could distance himself from Jessie. After checking the want ads in the *New York Times*, he found three that appealed to him.

He took a cab to South Station and boarded the next train to New York. He threw his suitcases on the rack above his seat and settled in for the long trip. The whistle sounded its lonely song, and the train began to pull away from the station. David stared out the window as the train yards and back alleys of Boston began to slip by. He was leaving everything he had dreamed about and fought for. He'd never given up before, not even when there seemed to be no hope. Now there was nothing left to fight for. Ginny was gone. He had lost Jessie and Sarah, thrown away his career. The hopes and dreams that had kept him alive during the war had disappeared as if they had never existed. He could no longer face the remnants of his life that now lay in the ruins of his terrible mistakes. He was giving up, running away.

CHAPTER FORTY-THREE

MAY 1956

Spring was everywhere. The park was turning green and the trees and flowers were beginning to bloom. Women were carrying their jackets or sweaters, and they seemed to be blooming as well. Women always looked sexier in the spring, especially in New York, especially near the Plaza. And yet, David watched the cracks in the pavement instead. There was no joyous spring for him. There was just cold reality. He was alone in an unfamiliar city with a minimum of resources. He'd left almost everything behind, including his bank accounts. His job interviews had not been productive. He needed to get a job, a new start, but his prospects looked bleak.

The benches at the edge of Central Park beckoned his sore feet. He'd pounded the pavement since early morning, going from interview to fruitless interview, and he was tired and depressed. He dodged the heavy traffic that rumbled in a never-ending flow down Central Park South, crossed to an empty bench on the outskirts of Central Park and sat down. The sidewalks were crowded with smartly dressed men and women who hurried by to unknown destinations, filled with purpose and vitality. They contrasted with the tired old men who filled the benches around him, whose eyes stared into the memories of the past and to the hopelessness of their diminished futures. Some were dressed in suits that once had fit their now frail bodies; others were dirty, decrepit, and in rags that reflected the remnants of their hopeless lives. A little old man dressed in a suit that was at least two sizes too large for him walked over to David, and said in a heavy accent, "The other benches are full. May I sit?"

David realized that he was sitting in the middle of the bench. "Sure, I was just leaving anyway." He got up and started walking up Central Park South. Something nagged at him, and he turned back to look at the old man on the bench. He started to walk back, and then changed his mind. He stopped, something was trying to push its way into his memory, and then he remembered, the little German guard, his uniform two sizes too big for his small frame.

His mind slipped back to the past, when the guard was helping him to escape. They had both looked down on the little town in Germany that Patton had just stormed through. They could see the white sheets hanging outside the windows in total surrender, fluttering in the early spring breeze. David had hoped that some of Patton's soldiers had stayed behind to secure the town. His brow wrinkled, as he tried to remember what his guard—or was he his friend by then?—was saying.

The guard had tears in his eyes as he viewed the ravaged village. Young men still lay in the streets where they had fallen. A once-beautiful fountain now lay in ruin in the rubble of the crumbled buildings that had aged with the centuries of time, but couldn't resist Patton's thundering tanks that had crushed them and ground out their history and their existence forever.

There was a time, the German guard told him, when he had brought his family to this tiny village. Yes, his little boy was alive then; the war hadn't taken him yet. He had taken them to see the parade. Hitler himself would be there. The people had stood along the streets and had cheered as a division of proud soldiers goose-stepped by them in perfect time to the marching band that followed. Then the Hitler Youth had marched by, waving a sea of red banners that had snapped in the wind, emblazoned with the black swastika on a white background. Some of them might have been his students. They had been followed by an open, black Mercedes with Hitler standing in it, his right arm extended in the Nazi salute. The Tiger tanks of Germany's invincible Panzer divisions, the might of the Third Reich, had thundered after him. Pride and excitement had rushed through him as he recognized the power and glory that was Germany. The Germany that not many years ago lay in poverty and hopelessness from its last encounter with the Allies, the same countries that Hitler would now destroy. He had whispered, "Heil Hitler."

They stood there, staring at the ruins of the broken village, waiting to descend into the town where they hoped to find the Americans. The guard's voice broke when he told of when he, almost a year later, had looked down through a blur of tears at the face of his little boy, who had been killed when the American P-51 had strafed his school. The boy's eyes were closed and he looked like he was sleeping; he had brushed a wisp of blond hair from the forehead and tried not to look at the blood oozing from the holes in his chest. He knew then that he held his beloved Germany in his arms as well, and that Hitler had killed them both.

The noisy traffic and rushing humanity brought David back to the present. He thought of his own life's efforts, his drive for power, and his disregard for all else. Even Ginny fell into that category. Wasn't she, beautiful Ginny, a symbol of power, of conquest, that men strove for? And now, wasn't he facing the same consequences as the German village with his ruined life and broken dreams lying there like the dead that littered the streets of the little village?

Then he heard his name.

"David, I'll be damned! How the fuck are you, boy?" Vernon asked, as he signaled the six-door Mercedes limousine, following him, to stop.

"Terrific. Just terrific," David lied.

"You're full of shit. I heard you went broke. What the fuck happened? Don't answer, I already know. Your stock is hocked, and your old lady's got the bank accounts." He took a deep breath and put his big hand on David's shoulder. "Listen, I want to talk with you, but not now and not here. Where can I reach you later? Never mind. There's an 8:00 A.M. flight out of here tomorrow morning. Come to my office when you get in. I'll have a ticket and my address waiting for you at the Eastern information desk at LaGuardia. I'm going to save your ass, boy, so be there." Vernon walked to the car with incredible grace for his huge body, and without a second look drove off.

The girl at reception looked up apologetically. "He knows you're here. It's…it's one of those days."

Two hours and twenty minutes was enough, even for someone who is desperate. *Fuck it,* he thought, and started to get up. Then he heard the receptionist, "You may go in now, sir."

Vernon's office, a part of the penthouse suite that took an entire floor of one of Miami Beach's most prestigious residences, looked over a huge terrace that was exotically planted and blended with the white sands and azure waters of the beach below. It was exquisitely furnished in brown, beige and black colors. Three soft leather chairs fronted an enormous desk that unsuccessfully tried to hide the bulk of the man that sat behind it.

Vernon didn't look up as David sat down. There was something different. The good- natured clown wasn't there. Vernon was hardly recognizable here. The giant finally looked up. It was a natural transition, business to friendship, but it was too contrived, too perfect. *Like two different people,* David thought.

The giant spoke. "What do you need to get by, boy? I want you to work with me and not for charity either." His voice was level and almost kind. "I own real estate from Maine to Miami and from Mississippi to Athens, and I need help."

"But I don't know anything about real estate or about your business. Besides, I'm a loser. You know that, so why me?"

"That's the point," the giant's voice was hard again. "You went broke. You can teach me how not to, and besides you're a pretty smart cookie or you wouldn't have got as far as you did."

David knew he needed something, anything to get started, and he liked that Vernon had said, work with me, not for me. He had to get his life together again.

Vernon spoke again as if he'd read David's mind. "I own two pieces of property in Raleigh, North Carolina, that were built by the same builder. I just bought them from the bank that foreclosed. One's called The Heights and the other, Tiffany Estates. They're outside of the city and divided only by a rural road. The Heights has a waiting list of fifty yet, Tiffany has thirty vacancies, a loss to me of about $150,000 a year. I don't know what the fuck is going on up there, but sure as hell I got to get it fixed."

"And you think I can?" David chuckled. "I wouldn't know where to begin."

"Listen, boy, I didn't bring you all the way down here because I thought your mother had stupid children."

David's posture and eyes told Vernon he'd accepted the challenge, so he continued, "Okay, so what do you need, need to get by, to start?"

"About five hundred." He knew he was pushing it. The average guy on the street was making less than a hundred a week, but he remembered how many times in the last nightmarish weeks he'd asked himself how little he might get by with and still keep his commitment to support Jessie and Sarah. He knew he'd have to settle for much less, but it was worth a try.

"Okay," Vernon answered without hesitation, surprising David. "My secretary has a memo with more details, tickets and money." His voice grew hard again; his eyes became slits in his huge face. "Finish. That's the key word. Get it done or don't come back. Don't call me...just finish." Vernon looked down to what he had been doing before David had come in and David was dismissed. It was as simple as that.

CHAPTER FORTY-FOUR

JUNE 1956

It was nine o'clock. David sat in the darkness of his motel room. The Ed Sullivan show was on the black-and-white TV, but David wasn't listening. Instead he was trying to reconstruct the last three days that had told him nothing about the problem he'd come to solve. He'd met with the properties' management people, maintenance people, and the on-premise rental agents. He'd compared both properties' amenities, such as the pools, the clubhouses, the landscaping, etc. He'd checked the graphics, the advertising, the condition of the vacancies and the locations of the rental offices. Both properties seemed to be identical. Why did one property rent and the other didn't? He had done his best but he had failed to come up with an answer to the problem. There was no use continuing; he'd call Vernon in the morning, thank him for the opportunity and go home. But, there was no home to go to. Well, he'd take off somewhere. It wasn't important. Still, he couldn't stop thinking about the property. He wasn't used to failing. *What haven't I done?* He realized he'd never seen the property at night. Perhaps he'd missed something. The project was an easy walk from the motel, but the unlighted country road would be hazardous at night. David decided to take a taxi.

He picked up the phone. The sleepy manager, who was also the switchboard operator, bell captain, and whatever else was required, answered.

"Can you get me a cab?"

"A cab? Now? I don't think so." The manager paused and then, trying to help, said, "But, if it's really important, the sheriff comes by for coffee 'bout eleven. Maybe he'll take ya where you want to go, if it's local, that is."

The sheriff was a big, congenial man with a huge pearl-handled revolver hanging at his side. David told him his problem as they rode to the property. He didn't expect any answers, but he felt he owed the sheriff some sort of explanation for the ride. The sheriff listened quietly and then drawled, "Man, I know what's wrong."

"You do?" David looked at him incredulously.

"Sure, and you're going to know, too, when we get there."

And he was right. The Heights was lit up like a football field. Sodium vapor lamps illuminated each corner, disposing of every shadow. The Tiffany property was pitch black.

David compared the two properties, trying to comprehend the consequences of what he saw, when the sheriff's voice broke into his train of thought. "A rape, break-ins, muggings. Who'd want to live in that black hole?"

David was in a fury of work now. Although he'd worked through most of the night, he felt refreshed and strong again. He tried to call Vernon, but he refused to take his call. Then he remembered. *Don't call me, just finish.*

He called North Carolina Power and Light, and they confirmed what David had already surmised. Everything was in the ground, the poles and lamps were installed, but they had never been powered. It would take two days to bring on the lights, providing a check in the full amount was received first. The check would cover the unpaid bills of the bankrupt builder, whose property Vernon had bought from the bank that had foreclosed on it. It was blackmail, but it was good business too. David sent a telegram to Vernon with an explanation. The money was wired the next day and the lights went on two days later.

In quick, successive movements, David closed Tiffany's rental office and turned it back into a rental apartment. He replaced the signs with Tiffany's new name, The Heights II. Unhappily, he fired all of Tiffany's agents and offered a bonus to the Heights rental staff to convert their waiting list to the Heights II. The new advertisement in the local paper read, "The Heights II. Apartments in Raleigh's most prestigious residential community now available."

Twenty days later, David was sitting in Vernon's plush office and Vernon was smiling. He was counting out hundred-dollar bills, and putting them in little stacks of a thousand.

"Seven thousand, eight thousand, nine thousand, ten thousand," Vernon counted out loud and, finally, handed the bundle of bills to David.

"But, the deal was five hundred a week. This is…"

"Five hundred a day, that's what I'm paying you, times twenty equals ten thousand dollars, in case you can't count, boy."

"But I meant per week," David answered in shock.

"And, you would stay with me for about two months," Vernon said sagely. He knew David had been used to at least a hundred and fifty thousand a year and Vernon wanted to be sure that he wouldn't lose David to a better opportunity. After all, David had already made him his year's salary, and it had been less than three weeks.

Vernon continued warmly, "I got you an apartment. You'll like it. There's also a present for you downstairs with Victor, the doorman. The key to the apartment is with it.

Take a long weekend and rest up. I've got a new project for you on Monday." He looked away toward his reflection in the glass wall of the terrace and adjusted his tie. David was once again dismissed.

"Just a minute, sir. I'll get it." Victor ran toward the garage.

David was annoyed. He was tired; he wished Victor would give him the keys to his new apartment and the little gift that Vernon had talked about. But Victor was holding the door open to a shiny, new, cherry-red Mercedes. David looked around for its owner but he was the only person on the waiting platform. Victor had a broad smile on his face. "This is your car, Mr. Livingston."

"What? My car? Are you kidding me?"

"No, sir. Mr. Vernon said it was your car, a present."

David got into the car and Victor gave him the key to his new apartment and directions. David put both hands on the leather-covered steering wheel, breathed in the aroma of the new leather. *My God, this car must have cost over ten thousand dollars.*

The doorman at the apartment house took David's car and was obviously prepared for his arrival. "Welcome to Le Fleurs, sir."

The apartment overlooked the ocean on one side, up toward Lauderdale on another, and at the Indian River Creek on the other. The three views were breathtaking. It was furnished in subtle brown, beige, and black. David smiled and knew that Vernon had probably picked the décor himself, as it matched the same scheme as his office. He took a deep breath and thought that he was on his way once again. He walked through the apartment and wished Jessie could see it, could be here to share it with him. It was completely furnished with dishes, linens and even toiletries. Someone had done a good job, a perfect job.

David tried to reconstruct the day. It was completely overwhelming. He wanted to call Jessie and tell her all about it, but that wasn't part of their agreement. There were to be no calls. A terrible sense of loneliness and depression overwhelmed him. He was alone and he'd have to get used to it.

Monday came quickly and David sat in front of Vernon.

"How do you feel?"

"Great." David had slept for twelve hours and he felt rested and refreshed.

"Like your apartment?"

"Oh, yes, and thank you for the car and—"

"Forget it, my boy," Vernon broke in, waving his hand in dismissal. "You make me money. I make you money. Understand?" And, without waiting for an answer, he said,

"Here's the problem. The Chalet sits on the side of a hill of shale in Nashville. Every time it rains, the shale and mud from the top of the hill, where we couldn't lay foundations, slides down the road. It's costing us a fortune to clean up each time and we're losing tenants. We've got to figure out what to do. But, you will, my boy. I just know you will!"

David hated the way he kept calling him "boy," but Vernon had done that even when they were on the cruise together, so David decided not to take offense. "Just another easy job?" David mused.

Vernon smiled, picked a cigarette out of a silver box, and lit it with a gold lighter. He looked up, almost surprised to see David still sitting there.

The limo took David to Miami International. Vernon's Lear put him into Nashville two hours later. The property managers met him. They drove him to the apartment project and, as David had requested on the telephone, supplied him with a complete set of project plans. At the site, a young engineer that David had found, after telephone interviewing just about every engineer in the city, awaited him.

David had found out that the man had a reputation of being a maverick but had remarkable talent. He thought that might just be what he needed, someone possibly with an original—maybe even an unconventional—idea. David had spent days studying shale, the matter itself, the effects of stress, anything and everything that he could find. He was ready for the meeting.

After proper introductions and some small talk, David asked, "You know how we can stop this erosion?"

"Sure," the young engineer replied, having done his homework over the last week.

"Go ahead and tell me." He looked up the hill beyond the apartment complex to the wasteland that waited for the rain to send it down the streets below.

"Well, it's really simple. Just build on it." The engineer waved his hand in the direction of the shale.

"Are you shitting me? I thought you couldn't build on it."

The engineer's eyes twinkled like a little boy with a secret. "Not with foundations or slabs you can't."

"Well, what are you going to use, sky hooks?" David sat down on the fender of the rented car, thankful to get off his aching leg.

"Nope. Concrete pilings."

"Has anybody ever tried it before?"

"Not on shale."

"Why not?"

"No guts," the engineer said, smiling.

"I've got guts," David said as he slipped off the fender and faced the engineer.

"How about money?"

"That too. When can you start?"

"Do you mean it?" the young engineer asked incredulously. "Everybody but me says this can't be done. How come you're willing to take a chance?"

David put his hand on the engineer's shoulder and thought, *The Chalet has a waiting list. There's room for 50 more units.* It was a big gamble but it would be a *score,* as Vernon would put it. He had to chance it. The old intuition was back. He felt a revival of his self-confidence. Besides, he needed to be completely immersed in his work, so that he could stop thinking of Jessie and Sarah. He didn't care how hard or how long he worked. It was his panacea. Of course, if he was wrong…if he failed…

CHAPTER FORTY-FIVE

JULY 1956

The board, with the help of the best headhunters in New England, finally chose a new president to replace David. Melvin became Chief Executive Officer and Tim Fallon, a laid-back Irishman with see-through blue eyes, recruited from Eastern's biggest competitor, Gibbins Oil, became Chief Operating Officer. Melvin's newly acquired aggressiveness was a sharp contrast to Tim's quiet demeanor, creating a certain animosity between them from the start. Six months later, Tim had had it with Melvin, and tendered his resignation.

In his letter of resignation he wrote, "I cannot stand by and watch our CEO and this board sell off assets absolutely essential to the growth, stability and best interest of this company. Our CEO's pursuit of eliminating debt by selling off these assets weakens our ability to compete..."

But the board supported Melvin. For the first time in years they felt there was a possibility to get their escrowed stock back. The market also liked the CEO's new debt position reflecting higher values for the stock. While the stock flourished in the beginning, Melvin's continued sell-off of the company's best assets, just as Tim and David before him had predicted, now began a downward spiral. Profits disappeared, the board's stock was still escrowed, and the company floundered.

Melvin had traded his former obsessive drinking for an equally obsessive work ethic. He was the first in the office in the morning and the last to leave at the end of the day. His only diversion was Ginny, whom he pursued with equal intensity.

"Ginny? It's Melvin."

"My God, Melvin, it's six o'clock in the morning."

"I know, but…"

"Where are you at this ungodly hour?"

"I'm in the office."

"What the hell are you doing in the office at six in the morning?"

"I always get in early now. You know, new leaf, early bird gets the…"

"Well, don't you think you're overdoing it a little?"

"Ginny, that's not why I called you. I want to…" Melvin paused. Ginny could hear his breathing. "I'm in love with you. I've always been in love with you, and I thought, well I mean, I want us to. I want us to…"

"Melvin, are you proposing to me?"

"I guess I am, but wait! Don't answer me now. You know I'm not drinking anymore, and I'm working my butt off. I think I'm really making a difference here. The only thing missing is. Well, you know what I mean. Oh, hell, Ginny, will you, can we…?"

"Melvin, I'm half asleep and you're proposing to me on the phone. I…"

"Ginny, I will make the best husband…" Melvin's voice faded, as Ginny thought how much she had longed for David to leave Jessie and ask her to marry him. But that was never going to happen. How could she marry Melvin? She could never love anyone the way she loved David, but then…*Listen here, girl, there is no more David. Don't be stupid. This is your chance to get into the big money and you better take it.*

"Melvin, I'm sorry, this is really sweet. Let's meet for lunch. Can you make it? Maybe the Ritz-Carlton, the little bar downstairs?" *Why not get used to the best? The Ritz is a good start. Fuck you, David!*

Melvin had faith in his business tactics, in spite of the company's recent downturn. He felt strongly that he would be successful making the company profitable again, and best of all, now he had Ginny.

Ginny had changed a little, he thought. Well, she was settling down now, wasn't she? Sure, she was still mourning David. But, that would change. He'd get her pregnant as soon as they were married. That would tie the knot and she'd forget about that bastard, and if he so much as comes near her, I'll kill the son of a bitch.

Ginny's apartment was a walk-up in a historic Beacon Street townhouse. She occupied the top floor. She was hard-pressed to pay the exorbitant rent that Melvin had paid regularly before they had stopped seeing each other, but the view from the window seat in her bedroom that overlooked the Charles River was worth the struggle. She loved to sit there and watch the sun set over the river, the boats from the sailing club rushing back to the dock, and the gold domes topping the cupolas of Harvard in the distance.

She remembered the many times she sat with David looking out that window, leaning into each other's arms, each with a cold glass of white wine. God, how she missed him. His hand touching her hair, she had loved that; a kiss, not really a kiss, just a brush of his lips on hers, his smile, the crinkles on the sides of his eyes. And after the last rays went from gold to purple to dark they would be in bed, no rush, and no frenzy to their lovemaking. Little kisses, touches just in the right places, more kisses, hands and fingers moving quicker, pulling him on top of her. The rhythm of their bodies moving against each other, faster, faster, wild passion overwhelming them, and then—*oh God, was there anything more wonderful?* And afterwards in his arms, not much talking. They save that for before sleep when they will talk about the day in the dark. They are hungry now. A shower, a pair of jeans and sandals, the little restaurant hidden behind Harvard Square, another glass of wine, holding hands across the table, the candle casting dancing shadows across his face. His eyes, opaque, unreadable, unpredictable, now soft and yielding. This man with unflinching will, so hard, yet so gentle with her, who loves her, and lets her see through the black depths of his eyes to the pain that lurks behind them that she knows only she can quell. She loves him so much it hurts. But he is lost to her now, drowned in a sea of guilt. Gone but not forgotten.

Sure he loved Jessie and Sarah, but not the same way. *Maybe I'm kidding myself? How do I know? Did he leave my bed and go home and make love to her? Well, I guess I won't have to think about that now.*

She had said yes to Melvin.

He was so persistent and he did love her. He was a changed man. At first, when he was hurt, she felt sorry for him, but now...He'd been so good to her, like a big brother, kind and understanding, even knowing that she still mourned David. She wished he wouldn't carry that gun everywhere, but who could blame him after getting beaten up like that.

She still couldn't be with him in her apartment, there was too much of David there. Although she didn't love Melvin, she liked him, but was that enough? Their lovemaking was okay, just okay, lacking the passion and intensity that she felt with David. Would anyone be able to replace that? Poor Melvin, maybe she wasn't really giving him a chance. Well, she would try. She would make this marriage work. She would forget about David and be happy again. Fat chance.

Chapter Forty-Six

AUGUST 1956

His desk was strewn with papers, notes, and other miscellanea, which accumulated every day, the usual mess he didn't have time to file. He felt uncomfortable, not in control, until everything was put in its proper place. It was six o'clock and he was late for dinner with Ruth. She would be waiting for him at Barney's. Why they had to try every new restaurant that opened in Boston baffled him, but it was little enough to do to please her and ease his own conscience. He began to methodically enter notes, put away files and papers in their proper places until finally, with the exception of an invitation to the National Psychiatry Convention in Miami, only the green blotter covered his desk. He reread the invitation. It was a second notice. He'd already decided against going months ago. Who the hell wanted to be in Miami in September anyway? Hell, if it was in February... Just what he needed, Miami in September. He tossed the invitation in the wastebasket under his desk, snubbed out his cigarette in the ashtray, and got up to leave. Something nagged at him. He reached under his desk and took the invitation out of the wastebasket. David was in Miami. They talked on the phone at least every other week but…He left the invitation on the green blotter and left the office.

An easterly breeze wafted in from the open doors to the terrace of David's apartment. Puffy cumulus clouds stood like mountains of snow in the blue Miami sky. The ocean below sparkled with millions of flashes of reflected sun. Sanders stood on the terrace sniffing the salt air and at the same time wiping his brow with his handkerchief. He turned as David joined him on the terrace. "It's absolutely beautiful if only it wasn't so damn hot."

David sat down on a lounge chair. "You get used to it."

Sanders loosened his tie and sat down next to David. He took out a pack of cigarettes, offered one to David who declined, and lit up. "So, kid, what's new?" Sanders asked, still watching the clouds slowly floating by.

David got up and leaned against the balcony railing. "I miss Jessie and Sarah."

"I asked you what was new."

"Yeah, but that's always on my mind."

"Maybe you ought to get a life of your own. Y'know, find a nice lady, get laid. Go out and have some fun."

"I've thought about it. I have, but…I don't know; I just can't." David turned his back on Sanders and looked down at the beach below as he fought back the tears that lay behind his eyes.

Sanders got off the lounge and walked over to him. He put his arm around David's shoulders and gave him a little hug. "You are really beating yourself up, kid. I think it's time for you to go home. You're not going to get anywhere with Jessie 1500 miles away."

"Listen, I've tried. I've called but…"

"I'm telling you calling won't work. You have to do this face-to-face." Sanders looked at his watch. "Jesus, I'm gonna be late again. Got to get over to the convention. Meet you back here at six. Okay?" He grabbed his jacket and headed for the door.

David knew that Sanders cared little about the symposium he was about to attend and that his real motive for coming to Miami was to be with him, try to shore him up, but it had had a reverse effect, and had only made him more depressed and homesick. Maybe Sanders was right. It was time to go out, have some fun.

They ate at a little pub in the Mutiny Hotel in Coral Gables. The place was filled with singles and Sanders appraised a different woman between each bite. They finally finished, although David hardly ate, and they moved over to seats at the bar. Sanders lost no time striking up a conversation with a pretty blonde with too much makeup. David smiled as Sanders rolled out his standard line. He ordered a drink and swung around on his bar stool so that he could observe most of the room. As the swell of humanity in the crowded bar expanded and contracted with movement and newcomers, a young lady almost landed in his lap.

She recovered her balance but the crowd kept her pressed close to him. He looked into her liquid green eyes. He scanned her face, her black hair that fell like a satin sheet. She was a dead ringer for the Jessie that he had dated fifteen years ago.

She smiled Jessie's smile. "Oh, God, I am so sorry," she said and, just as abruptly as she had arrived, she melted back into the crowd.

David slid off the bar stool to find her but she had disappeared. That stark memory of his youth had blurred into the frenzy of the crowd and was lost. Yes, his youth, his life was slipping away like a receding tide and David felt he was being sucked into the undertow. The muscles twitched throughout his arms and legs as if he were flexing them to swim, to swim to the safety of the shore, to get his life back.

Sanders broke into his reverie. "Well, you look pretty glum."

"No, I'm fine."

"No you're not. You're sitting here feeling sorry for yourself."

"C'mon, get off my back. I told you I'm okay."

"Alright, if you're okay, then get off your ass and come with me. I got a couple of nice-looking kids lined up."

"Listen, be a good guy. Enjoy yourself. I'm going to get a cab. I got a really big day tomorrow and…"

"How did I know this wasn't going to work? Alright, if you're going back, I'm going with you."

"No, please stay."

"No way. You think I came all the way down here to go to a symposium? I'm here because my friend is hurting and, worst of all, I don't know how to help him."

David put his arm around Sander's heavy shoulders. "You're a good guy, Richard, and you have helped me by coming down here."

"Yeah, how?"

"Just being here means a lot."

The two girls Sanders had been romancing pushed their way toward them. "We thought we lost you."

Sanders looked at David and then back to the girls. They were both young and attractive. He knew he was about to lose a great catch, a great sailfish slipping off the hook.

One of the girls sidled up to David. "And who is this lovely man?"

To David's amusement he watched the young woman as she began the ancient dance that women went through to entice, and eventually capture, a man. She was attractive enough with light gray eyes, a little far apart, a straight nose, and although a little voluptuous, a nice body. A tempting morsel for a man who hadn't had sex, other than in his fist, for almost two years. Her name was Joy; it was too much.

"So are we going dancing or what?" she asked with a little pout.

Sanders looked at David for help, which was not forthcoming. "Well, I don't know. We..."

Joy reached across David and took a pretzel stick from a bowl on the bar. David could feel the warmth of her body as she pressed against him. She sucked on the pretzel seductively before she ate it. "C'mon, you guys. We'll have fun." She looked at Sanders accusingly. "What's the problem?"

David knew Sanders was trapped and for once at a loss for words. What the hell, Sanders had flown 1500 miles to cheer him up. What was the big deal if he went dancing? He gave the girls his biggest smile. "Okay, okay, let's go dancing."

Sanders' glasses slipped down his nose and he quickly adjusted them as he stared questioningly at David. He took out his handkerchief and wiped his brow, broke into a big smile and put his arm around both girls. "Let's get out of here."

David took the wheel and Joy slid over in the seat close to him. She smelled good.

"You're married?"

"Separated."

"So why are you still wearing a ring."

"Because I'm still in love with my wife."

"Well, that's encouraging."

David sat quietly and stared at the road.

"Would you rather we didn't do this? Was that the reason for all the 'Ring around the Rosie' back there?"

"Look, I'm sorry. I really would like to take you dancing. I haven't dated for a long time and I'm a little clumsy. So…"

Joy put her hand on David's arm.

They drove to Mucho a Rumba Club in Little Havana, the Cuban enclave of Miami.

Joy twirled back into David's arms. "You're a pretty good dancer. Did you take lessons?"

"We—I took lessons on a cruise ship a long time ago. A hundred years ago."

"Oh."

"Hey, let's not get into that again. I'm having a good time."

Joy pressed herself closer to David. As she moved against him to the beat of the rumba he became aroused. Embarrassed he pulled slightly away from her but she followed his body with hers.

"What do say we take a break," he said, and led Joy to a table and ordered drinks.

It was a hot night and when Sanders finally joined them he was sweating profusely. "Listen, me and my lovely friend here are going to cut out. You take the car and I'll see you for breakfast tomorrow morning. Okay?"

David watched Sanders leave with his arm around the blonde, whispering, he thought, the same old line into her ear as she giggled in response. David suddenly understood his imperfect friend and the finite difference between them. Sanders truly believed what he did was innocent. He wasn't cheating. He wasn't immoral. Sex was a natural phenomenon, like eating or drinking. There was no shame in it for him. He felt the ignorant world around him was simply behind the times and those prudish moralists that preached monogamy were no less ignorant than when scientists thought the world was flat. Love and fidelity just didn't have anything to do with one another. So if someone believes what he is doing is right and with no equivocation, like believing in a different God, is he wrong? Maybe not.

Joy broke into his thoughts. She was rubbing her hand on his thigh. A little rivulet of sweat ran down from her neck and disappeared in the cleavage of her breasts. "Do you live in Miami?"

"Yeah, on Collins Avenue."

"On the ocean?"

"Uh huh."

"I love to listen to the waves at night." She paused for a beat, and then continued. "Matter of fact I really don't know that because I actually never did it, but I sure would like to. Will you take me to your place so I can hear them?"

David watched another little river of sweat run between her breasts. He thought about all the tortured nights without Jessie, about how lonely and depressed he'd been.

Joy raised herself in her chair just enough to bring her lips close to David's. They were a breath apart.

So there's the fundamental difference between Sanders and me. I still think the world is flat. He took Joy by the shoulders and sat her back down. "We're leaving," he said. He rose and then gently took Joy's hand, helping her to her feet.

"No waves, huh?" she said with a sad little smile.

David bent down and kissed her briefly on the lips. "Nope, no waves."

Chapter Forty-Seven

October 1956 to July 1957

David stayed in an apartment within the project. It provided him with a bed where he slept fitfully, if at all, and an office that he shared with his secretary and the young engineer. He started at six in the morning and rarely finished before midnight. This was his baby and he'd be damned if he didn't succeed, yet he was haunted by thoughts of failure. He was betting on a theory and his intuition. What if he was wrong?

Weeks passed into months. The construction noise, especially the drilling for the pilings, was a cause for a resident's meeting. David attended, but there was no way to pacify the tenants, and he left as frustrated as did the group that attended the meeting. He promised that complaints about the noise would not be ignored and that he would call another meeting within a week.

A number of people had moved without notice, which was reflected in the reports sent to management, and finally to Vernon.

"Get Livingston on the phone, now!" The report in Vernon's hands trembled as if anticipating the storm to come.

The phone rang. David picked it up on the first ring "What?"

"I'll tell you *what*, you cocksucker. I sent you out there to make me money, not to scare all the tenants away. I'm fed up with all the complaints. Do you know that the mayor is ready to throw you and your crew out of town? They probably would like to tar and feather you and run you out on a rail. Now, listen to me, boy, you better straighten things out and damn soon." He hung up before David could respond.

David put the phone down slowly. There was at least another month of heavy drilling. The noise wasn't going to stop. There had to be an answer, but what was it?

Well, he could start drilling later in the morning and stop at five instead of six, but that would cause the project to bleed money. If he could only find a little more time.

He called another meeting. The answer lay with the tenants.

The meeting took place in the property's clubhouse. When David arrived, it was packed with angry people. Country music drifted from a radio. A big man who often spoke in behalf of the community was humming along with the music, waiting for David to speak.

"Look, I know how you feel about the noise; after all, I live here too."

"Shit, man, you get paid for living here." There was a murmur of agreement in support of the big man who spoke.

"That's true." An idea was formulating in David's brain. "Well, then let me ask you a question. What if you got paid to live here, too? Would you hang in here with me for another month or so until the drilling stops?"

"What do you mean *pay?*"

David searched his mind. He had half the idea. Sweat soaked the back of his shirt and under his arms. The rest of his initial thought began to germinate. "All right, here's the deal." David was formulating his ideas even as he spoke. "No rent until the drilling stops."

David knew that if he pushed, he could finish the drilling in a month. He would lose a month's rent, but the defections would stop. It was better than cutting hours from the work day, which would slow down the entire project. Vernon would have a fit when he found out, but he would face that when the time came.

There was still grumbling in the room as the tenants mulled over the proposition. David held his breath.

The big man discussed the proposition among the tenants. He spoke in a whisper, sometimes leaning close to a listening ear. He looked grim as he wandered through the room. There was interaction between different groups. Nobody looked happy. David's hopes dimmed. Finally the big man stood in the center of the room. He raised his hands to get attention and quiet. "This guy is playing it straight with us. I think we ought to go along with his idea. What do you think?"

It was a done deal.

The month passed without any defections. The drilling ended as David had hoped, and it wasn't long after that that the buildings miraculously began to rise above the pilings. He had tried to call Vernon to explain his idea, but Vernon never accepted his call. Instead his paychecks were discontinued. Typical Vernon. The project was finally complete. The renting process was in high gear and it wouldn't be long before the new buildings would be filled. He wrote Vernon. Still no response. He knew Vernon was weighing the results of more than a year's work. *Would he understand that I put everything on the line, my job, my pay, and a chance to redeem myself? Maybe go home? Get Jessie back?*

Finally he was summoned back to Miami. Esteban met him at the airport. "Mr. Vernon wants you to go directly to his office and have dinner with him there."

Julie awaited David's arrival. "He's in the dining room." Julie pursed her lips. "Good luck."

David limped through the office like it was the last mile. He mumbled a small prayer.

Vernon sat at the table as David entered. His expression was blank. "Sit down, boy."

David sat down, his eyes locked on Vernon. The cook served them and departed. They started to eat in silence. David's hand trembled more than usual. He waited as if he were watching a fuse sparkle down to a bundle of dynamite.

"You threw a lot of my money down the sewer. You didn't tell me about it. You just did it. Practically spit in my face."

"I tried to, but…"

"Never mind. It was a brilliant move. I'm proud of you, my boy."

David almost choked on his last bite. He finally composed himself. "Thank you, but the truth is, any accolades should go to the young engineer who not only figured out how to make it work, but broke his ass getting it done."

"Wrong. You put yourself on the line. You knew you were through if this thing failed, but you used your own initiative, and you succeeded. The engineer had nothing to lose. He was gambling with my money and your future. Fuck him. All he had was a good idea."

David started to protest, but he knew it would be fruitless.

They finished eating and smoked over a vintage port.

Vernon crushed out his cigarette and heaved his big body out of the chair. "Well, I'm tired, so let's get out of here."

As the doorman opened the heavy glass door, Vernon's eyes rose to the canopy. David followed his gaze to the dozens of bulbs that illuminated the drive. One bulb was out.

Vernon's face flushed with anger, his eyes bulged, suddenly a different man. He grabbed the doorman's arm, roughly dragged him into the drive, and pointed to the canopy.

The terrified doorman looked up at the dead bulb as Vernon continued his tirade. "If you can't see that a fucking bulb is out, you're either blind or you just don't give a shit."

"Yes, sir. I'm sorry, sir. It won't happen again."

"You bet your ass it won't happen again, because you're fired, now get the hell out of here!"

He turned and glared at David. "Where do you find these idiots? Why didn't you notice that the bulb was out?"

"Jesus, it was only a bulb. There must be a hundred of them up there. What's the big deal about one lousy bulb? This guy's one of the best doormen we have. I—"

"Listen, you stupid bastard, one light bulb out is the beginning of a creeping decay that erodes buildings and people alike. It's the beginning of apathy toward the responsibility I entrust in my people and I won't stand for it. Do you understand, boy?"

"I understand." David swallowed hard and looked down to avoid Vernon's eyes. *I am going to get away from this son of a bitch if it kills me.*

"I know what you're thinking. You hate me, don't you? Well, that's just fine with me, because I'm not running for a popularity contest. I don't give a shit what you or anyone else thinks of me as long as I get what I want."

David was silent. He could hear his father's voice admonishing him. *You bow down only before God.* He raised his head and looked into Vernon's eyes. "You think being a prick, kicking people around, humiliating them, makes you a big man. Well, in my eyes the only thing big about you is your mouth. I'm tired of patching things up after your tirades and I'm tired of watching you make people crawl to get their pay, or get their bills paid. I thought I needed this job at any cost, but you know what? It's just not worth it." David's face was red with the fury of his delivery, yet he inwardly chastened himself for losing his composure. *Now I've done it. There goes my job.*

Vernon glared at him and then broke into a huge smile. "Goddamn it, boy, that's what I like about you. You got balls."

It was three in the morning. The phone awakened and frightened him. He was alert instantly.

"David? Can you come over?"

"Is something wrong?"

"No, just want to talk." Vernon hung up with no further explanation.

David pulled on a pair of jeans, a loose cotton shirt and sneakers. He walked into the bathroom, brushed his teeth, and looked at himself in the mirror. He knew he was tired, exhausted from all the strain of the last few months. The tensions with Vernon should have taken their toll, yet although he'd shaved every day, he'd not really seen himself in all these months until tonight. His thirty-three years looked closer to mid twenties. There were no telltale bags under his eyes to underline his exhaustion. His face showed smile and squint creases and there was a little gray sneaking over his temples, but he was otherwise unmarred by age or exhaustion. Somehow he had managed to keep trim in spite of all the junk food that one invariably had to eat when on the road. Where were the circles and puffs under his eyes? Where were the stress lines? They just didn't show. *Dorian Gray?*

Vernon's Mercedes and Esteban, Vernon's chauffeur, were waiting for him downstairs. Esteban was dark as a walnut, short and muscular with an ever-present bulge under the left arm of his black jacket. David wondered what other chores Esteban did for Vernon besides driving the Mercedes.

"Good evening, sir." Esteban held the car door open for David. "Mister Vernon asked me to drive for you."

Vernon's property had thorough security. An electrically controlled gate, which swung on huge stone pillars, protected the entrance. A guardhouse accommodated two guards. One roamed with a Doberman while the other minded the gate. They carried sawed-off shotguns, all of which helped ease Vernon's paranoia that his children or his new young wife would be kidnapped. As the Mercedes stopped at the gate, Esteban rolled down the window.

"Who's with you, Esteban?" The guard peered into the back seat. When he saw David, he waved them through.

Alvarex, in full butler's dress, was already at the door. He showed David to Vernon's study.

Contrary to his work office, the study was small and compact. It seemed as if he could reach anything in the room by simply stretching out his long arm. As David sat down, Vernon flipped the cover of the cigarette box open with the back of his fingers and reached for a cigarette while, simultaneously, his other hand picked up a lighter. The box was empty. His eyes became slits and his lips had a strange smile. He picked up a little silver bell and shook it vigorously. And then at the top of his voice.

"Dorothy! Get your sweet ass in here."

Dorothy was twenty-five years younger than Vernon and, at twenty-three she was already a cool, mature beauty. She had short black hair, with cool gray eyes, and a perfect nose. Obviously she had been asleep. Her face was pale, but even without makeup she was beautiful and calm.

"What's wrong, darling?" she asked, as if it were nine in the morning instead of four.

"Seven fucking servants and they can't keep a cigarette box full?"

"I'm sorry, I'll…"

"Sorry, shit! It's like I told you about the light over the Van Gogh. If they couldn't see that the fucking bulb was out, what else are they ignoring? No cigarettes! The bulbs are out! You can see those things, but what about the things you can't see? If they're not doing the obvious, then what are they doing? If you can't see their fucking incapability, how can you tell them what to do? Fire every fucking one of them. No, I'll do it! Get their asses in here! Those lazy cocksuckers." The tirade went on and on, but Dorothy remained composed and, when Vernon stopped, she took a pack of Camels from the carton in one of the cabinets within easy reach of Vernon, opened it and filled the cigarette box.

"Can I get you something?" She looked at David.

"No. No, thank you," David stammered, still stunned by the violence of Vernon's verbal attack. He wondered why she took this shit from this brutal, abusive man. *Maybe for the same reason I do.* David vowed that it wouldn't last much longer.

Dorothy left the room without another word, ignoring Vernon's demand to see the help. Vernon watched her leave and went back to his controlled, smooth self as if nothing had happened.

"We've got this problem. I want you to go back to Nashville and get rid of the contractors and that fucking engineer. They're starting to sue, and they've already got mechanic liens on the buildings. Not that I give a shit, 'cause I'll put the fucking thing into Chapter 11 first, and they can get paid out of the proceeds. Of course, most of them will be willing to settle for a lot less to get their money right away. You got my point?"

"What are you telling me, that after these guys worked their asses off for me, you want me to screw them?"

"Listen to me, boy, these contractors screw us every chance they get, so if we're going to stay in business and make a profit, we've got to screw them back in spades. They'll give you all their sob stories, how they'll go out of business and all that shit, if we don't pay them. It's all bullshit. They've already made a killing and—"

"But we, I, accepted their bids. They were competitive bids and..."

Vernon glared at David. "Don't interrupt me, boy. You like your fancy office, the new Mercedes I gave you and the big bucks you take down each week? Well, stop bitching and go back there and make them kiss your ass and thank you if they get seventy cents on the dollar. You tell those motherfuckers that if they push us too hard we'll put that corporation into Chapter 11, and they'll get nothing."

David held up his hand, like a schoolboy asking permission to speak. Vernon's eyes gave him the go ahead.

"How do we do the next building project? Don't we run out of contractors?" David asked, controlling his anger and looking for any reason to change Vernon's mind.

Vernon waved off his objection with a sweep of his hand. "Believe me, they'll come back every time and beg to bid on the next job. Plus the fact, there are ten other guys waiting to take their place if they don't."

"Look, I worked with these people for over a year, most of them are pretty good guys. They trusted me; they've done their jobs. They're due their final payments as well as the late payments that I've been begging you to pay for the last six months. We've made a ton of money on this job; why can't we…"

Vernon leaned forward, his belly pushing against the big desk, his face florid. He narrowed his eyes and slammed his hand down on the desk so hard that David jumped in his seat.

"Listen, you stupid bastard, you think I built this business being a nice guy? You think I got where I am without being the biggest prick out there? Honesty is for little people, poor slobs that never made it and never will. Do you know an honest politician? Do you know a Fortune 500 CEO who didn't rape and plunder some little corporation? No, you don't, boy, because they don't exist. It's the strong—yes, the ruthless—that become the leaders, the same leaders that we depend on, that we look up to. So, don't give me that sanctimonious bullshit that you're different. We're all the same. We cheat on our wives." David winced. "We cheat the government, we steal from our employers. Then, we tell ourselves it's okay, because everybody does it. Well, let me tell you, boy, it is okay, because everybody does do it. Now, I'm paying you to make me money, and negotiating these bills is a part of your job, so stop this nonsense and get the next plane to Nashville. You hear me, boy?"

David stood up and, without a word, started to walk to the door.

Vernon squeezed himself out of his chair, his face beet red. "Don't you walk out on me when I'm talking, boy. What do you think you're doing?"

David turned, looked Vernon in the eyes, his face hard. "You want to screw contractors? Then you do it, and don't call me 'boy.'"

Vernon stepped around the desk and, like a chameleon, he changed his whole demeanor. "Listen, boy, I've tried to treat you like a son, be a good father to you. Give you good advice. I…"

"Be like a father to me? Advise me like a father? You couldn't polish my father's shoes."

439

Vernon realized he had to retreat or lose this man he had come to depend on. He walked over to David and blocked his way to the door. "Now, David, you've done well here and I've treated you right. Maybe this part of the business is too new to you and you just have to give it time. Listen, we're going to make a lot of money together and you know it. Why don't you take a few days off; go somewhere. I'll take care of paying the bills this time. What d'ya say?"

David didn't answer. He pushed by Vernon and walked back to Esteban and the waiting limousine.

Chapter Forty-Eight

July 1957

David saw himself in Vernon and remembered when he too thought that the only thing that mattered was to win, to make money, to cheat, or lie, or whatever it took, no matter whom it hurt, and that nothing else mattered. Fuck honesty, integrity, and decency. Anything was okay as long as it made you money or made you feel good. Well, that might have been yesterday, and he was ashamed of it, but this was a new day and he was learning.

He thought about his next move. His bank account was growing through the constant gifts, bonuses and raises that Vernon continued to heap on him. He only needed another year, but was it worth it? He was becoming the Devil's disciple, and he hated himself for it. He was nothing more than a whore and he knew he had to get out, no matter what the cost.

He had had nothing to do with a woman since he had left Jessie, although there were many opportunities. He couldn't even date casually, because he knew it would only depress him. It was his penance. There was little contact with Jessie, who seemed even more estranged and angry than ever. Although he had supported her well, it was hardly acknowledged. It was almost as if he didn't exist.

As the sun sank slowly into the horizon and the sky became one with the gray and almost motionless sea, he sat down on the couch, leaned back, lonely and tired, and fell into a troubled sleep.

He awoke, squinting at the sun streaking through the naked windows, got up, stretched, groaned, and walked out of the sliding doors to the terrace that looked down at Miami Beach. The sea was calm during these summer months and the beach was almost deserted. The tourists (everyone called them snowbirds) had fled to the cool shores of the north. A lone gull flew by and suddenly he thought back to the week he had spent in a little cabin at the Cape with Jessie and Sarah. It seemed like so many years ago yet, at the same time, like yesterday. He reached up and touched the little gold heart hanging from the chain around his neck. He had promised never to hurt her, yet he had betrayed her, and she would never forgive him.

He checked his watch and realized he was already late for a meeting with Vernon.

"Damn." He was a wrinkled mess. He tore off his clothes and changed into a clean shirt and a dark suit. He ran to the elevator holding his tie, pushed the button, and started to get his tie on while he waited.

"Nice of you to join us," Vernon said, shifting his massive hulk in David's direction.

"Sorry I'm late."

"You fucking well ought to be. You think we got nothing else to do but sit on our asses and wait for you?"

David took his seat. He met Vernon's glare evenly, but said nothing.

Vernon continued his eye contact with David, waiting for him to relent, but David kept contact defiantly until Vernon turned away, a red flush running from his collar into his face. "Alright, let's get this show on the road." And the meeting started.

David knew that this would not be the end of his confrontation with Vernon, but he just didn't give a damn any more. He thought that it wasn't too long ago that he was like this arrogant bastard.

The meeting went on and on until it finally broke up at seven thirty. David declined invitations for dinner, dodged Vernon, and slipped out of the conference room.

He was tired and hungry and decided to walk rather than drive to the Eden Roc Hotel a few blocks away. It had a good coffee shop and he felt like eating something light.

It was a cool night for a change, and the air smelled good. He thought about Vernon who, he knew, would be thinking about one of his little sadistic plans to get even with him. Well, he just wasn't going to worry about that right now. The walk was refreshing and each step brought new thoughts. He had learned a great deal from Vernon. Wealth bought power, and power corrupted men like Vernon, like himself, and took away their identity. Yes, David saw that in Vernon, and he learned from it. He had found humility again, but most of all he had rediscovered himself.

David sat down and picked up the menu. A skinny waitress came over and gave him a phony smile. She looked too old to be working the night shift but maybe, like him, she had nobody to go home to. David felt sorry for her.

"Coffee?"

"Sure, black, no sugar."

"You ready to order?"

David glanced at the menu, handed it back to her. "Yeah, okay, just bring me some scrambled eggs, toast and some French fries."

"Would you rather have a blueberry muffin instead of the toast? They're fresh."

"Okay, that would be nice, thank you." He thought how easily he had automatically written the waitress off as a nonentity. How wrong he had been in the past and, perhaps, still was, not realizing the worth of each individual.

He wished he'd brought a paper, anything to hide his self-consciousness. He scanned the other tables until his eyes rested on a young woman, also sitting alone. She was probably feeling as uncomfortable as he was. She was fidgeting with her hair and then adjusting her skirt. Sitting very erect and stiff, she looked straight ahead, seeing nothing. She was young, maybe in her late twenties, rather nondescript, but not unattractive. David wondered why she would be eating alone at such at late hour. Somehow, watching this seemingly lonely young woman reminded David of his own lonely life. He yearned to be home again, sitting at the table with Jessie and Sarah. Feeling the warmth of his family again. Listening to Sarah's little voice, watching Jessie sweeping back her hair, stopping for a moment on the way to the stove to give him a knowing smile. He had to go home. Get them back.

Chapter Forty-Nine

AUGUST 1957

"Hi, Jessie, it's Ruth."

"Ruth, what a surprise!"

"Well, it's about time I gave you a call. I want to know how you and Sarah are doing."

"We're okay, I guess." Jessie sat down on the chair beside the little telephone table.

"And David?"

"David? He calls every Saturday morning to speak with Sarah." Jessie squirmed in her chair; she knew where this was going.

"Just Sarah?"

"Ruth, dear, I know you mean well, but I'd rather not talk about David." Jessie stood up, not wanting to pursue the conversation further.

"I know, I know, it's just that I feel so badly for you. You two were so special. It's just, well, I shouldn't be saying this, but you know David talks to Richard. Jessie, David loves you. He's so sorry that he hurt you. It's a man thing, you know. They all have their little flings. It's just not important enough to ruin a marriage."

"Ruth! Please! I just don't want to discuss this any further." The tears streamed down Jessie's cheeks. Her hand clutched the receiver with such intensity that it hurt. "You don't understand. He betrayed me. He made a mockery of our marriage. He…"

"Yes, I do understand." Ruth paused. "I've gone through this, I've cried my eyes out, I've cursed Richard, maybe hated him, but we've stayed together, Richard and I." Her voice broke. "Yes, we've stayed together, for better or for worse, and I can tell you it's better than being alone. That's the reality." Ruth took a deep breath. "My God, I can't believe I'm saying this."

"Ruth, you're such a good friend, and I know that must have been very difficult for you, I mean, telling me that, just to help me." Jessie looked around the empty room and then to the stairs that led to her empty bedroom. "Believe me, I do miss David, but I'm just not ready to talk to him, or about him. I'm still hurting too much."

"I know, I understand, I just want you to think about giving him another chance. Letting Sarah have a daddy that she speaks to every day, not a telephone call once a week. You can heal. I did, or maybe I've just blocked. I didn't want to know where Richard was when he came home late. I ignored the other little suspicious things that were real or imagined. I know that he loves me. I know that. Please Jessie, just talk to him. Please, it is for the best."

Jessie was angry now. She could feel the heat rise in her body, and she was sweating. She wanted to yell into the phone, "Stop!" but she knew Ruth was innocently trying to help her. She had put herself on the line, embarrassed herself by confessing such a private matter. She was a good person, and she didn't deserve to be treated that way. "I'll try, Ruth. I'll try when I'm ready."

It was Saturday morning. When the phone rang, Jessie knew it was David. She hesitantly walked toward the phone, but Sarah came running down the stairs and grabbed it first.

"Daddy! I knew it was you. I miss you so much."

Jessie's heart ached, listening to Sarah. "When are you coming home?" *I miss him, I miss him too. Admit it. Tell him to come home. I can't keep waking up in the middle of the night, reaching for him, and then be up the rest of the night thinking about him, wondering if I am being too harsh. I want him back in my bed. How many evenings when Sarah was tucked into bed have I turned to ask him a question and have my heart sink when he wasn't there, wondering if he was in the arms of another woman.* Then she heard Sarah call her, "Mom, it's Daddy, he wants to talk to you."

Panic! Her heart was beating, pounding in her chest, her throat constricted, not ready to talk. Can't talk to him, especially in front of Sarah. But, she took the phone. Her hand trembling, her voice not her own. "You know, David, this is not part of our agreement."

"I know, Jessie, but I'm coming into town next week and I'd like to spend Saturday with Sarah."

Jessie panicked, but she knew he had a right to see Sarah. "Of course."

"I want to take her to the Swan Boats at the Public Gardens, but I don't want to put you out with the parking. I know how impossible it is to get a space, so I thought I'd just meet you outside the Ritz and you could just drop her off."

More panic. "No, that won't be necessary. I'll give the car to the doorman and bring her across the street." *I have to see him, just to look at him again,* she thought. "I'll meet you at the ticket office at the Swan Boats." She lowered her voice and said, "I appreciate it that you're not coming to the house as we agreed. I want to make this as normal as possible for Sarah. So, what time do you want to meet?"

It was amazing how two dollars could change the doorman's attitude from totally ignoring her at first, to almost groveling for the tip she finally displayed. As he took her car, she thought, if it had been a man that was driving, the doorman wouldn't have hesitated for a moment. It was still a man's world and she resented it. She walked across the street with Sarah to the Public Gardens.

The park was in its glory, the paths lined with flowers. It was a clear, pleasant day, a day to be happy, but her heart ached. Why had she kept them apart? Sarah needed her daddy. As they walked down the stone stairs to the ticket office, Sarah spotted David and ran into his arms. He swung her around as she screamed with delight. "Oh, Daddy, I've missed you so much."

"I've missed you too," he said, as he smothered her with kisses. He put her down and stepped back to appraise her. "Hey how old are you are you now? Let me guess? You must be twenty-one or twenty-two. Look how big you are."

"No, Daddy," she giggled. "I am going to be eleven next November."

"Well, you sure look absolutely beautiful, just like your mom," David said, as he turned to face Jessie.

She walked over to him and he took her hand and kissed her on the cheek. She moved her hand from David's without emotion. "Well, you guys have a great time." Sarah ran to her and took her hand. "Please, Mom, don't go, stay with us. Please?"

Jessie wrinkled her brow. She wanted to stay. Oh, God, she wanted them all to be together again.

David said, "Why don't you stay?"

"Please, mom."

David looked into Jessie's eyes. "Just for the Swan Boat ride?"

"Please, mom."

Jessie glared at David. "Okay, Sarah, but you know I told you I have important errands to run today."

They bought the tickets and stepped into the boat. It had a large replica of a swan in the back with white, curved wings and a long, graceful neck leading to the swan's head. As the driver slowly peddled the boat around the pond, Sarah sat between Jessie and David. She sat closer to David at first, holding on to his arm as if to prevent him from leaving her again. Then she moved to her mother, almost willing David and Jessie to become a family unit once again. David and Jessie exchanged glances, quite aware of what was happening.

"This is so nice, isn't it, Mom? Can we all go and get an ice cream after the ride?" She kissed David and then Jessie, and held both of their hands in hers. "I love you both so much."

David thought he saw Jessie's face soften.

On the way back to Jessie's car, Sarah lagged behind, feeding the pigeons with the peanuts that David had bought for her. David looked back to check on Sarah then back to Jessie. "I miss you."

There was no answer from Jessie.

"Why don't you stay and have lunch with us at the Ritz. It would be good for Sarah."

"David, you hurt me, you hurt me more than anything in my life, and I'm just not going to get better that easily," she said, even though she wanted to take him in her arms and never let him go.

"Jessie, it's been almost two years. I know this isn't the time or place but, please, let's have dinner together. I'll be here for a couple of weeks. Let's just talk."

"What's there to talk about, David?" She prayed that he would persist.

"That I'm sorry I hurt you, that it wasn't planned. I fell in love, but I never fell out of love with you. I almost went crazy, I was so confused, I couldn't function, I alienated everything and everyone around me and I lost everything. But, the worst loss was you and Sarah and I want you back. That's what there is to talk about."

Jessie noticed David's hand tremor had gotten much worse. His eyes were brimming with tears and he kept shooting glances at Sarah for fear she would return before he could finish his plea.

She swallowed her resentment and involuntarily touched his hand. "I'll think about it."

CHAPTER FIFTY

AUGUST 1957

When David's name showed up on Sanders' schedule, he was surprised David hadn't called him directly. He leaned back in his chair, thinking about the many times he had been to David's home. How Ruth and Jessie had hit it off at the start. The ocean cruise they took together. The secrets he and David had shared that they would not have parted with to another soul. There were even times when David became the psychiatrist and he became the patient. They had held nothing back from each other. They were good friends. There was no way, ethically, he could continue to treat him.

David was prompt with his four o'clock appointment. He shook hands warmly with Richard and sat down on one of the tufted leather chairs in front of Richard's enormous Victorian desk.

The room was paneled in dark mahogany and one wall was lined with leather-bound books in muted colors, their gold titles reflecting the light from Richard's desk lamp. There was what appeared to be a good copy of a Rubens, beautifully framed in gold leaf, on another wall. All the furniture was in dark-green, tufted leather and was enhanced by a deep-colored Oriental on the floor that added to the room's rich elegance.

"Nice digs, Doc."

"That's right; you've never been here," Richard said as he mopped his brow with a crumpled handkerchief.

"I'm impressed."

"You're supposed to be. Is this an official visit?"

"Yes." David took out a cigarette and lit it. His hand trembled and the match wavered. He dropped it in the ashtray on Sanders' desk

"Okay, but as your friend now, you know that it is unethical for me to continue therapy. I'll recommend someone for you. But, as long as you are here we'll talk as friends, so shoot. What's on your mind?" Sanders put his glasses on and gave David an official look.

"I'm still having the fucking nightmares, among other things." Somehow he couldn't bring up Jessie, although that was the reason he had come to see Richard.

Sanders took off his glasses, used them like a pointer and aimed them at David. "David, I've treated you off and on for a number of years—unsuccessfully, I must admit, because you never stuck it out. You told me everything but what I really needed to hear from you. What the hell are you hiding?"

"I'm not hiding anything." David got up, walked over to the Rubens.

"So are you telling me you want to start therapy again?"

"No, I just want to talk. "

"Okay, I'm listening." Sanders put his glasses on and leaned back in the big leather chair.

David rubbed his eye, which was tearing from the smoke that had drifted up from his cigarette. "I'm in hell. I still can't sleep without the nightmares, even after all of these years. I don't know what to do."

Sanders sat quietly but attentively.

"I dream I can see the women still clutching their children, the innocents, their limbs torn from their bleeding bodies, lying in the bomb craters, crippled or dead from the bombs we—I dropped. The schools, the hospitals that were bombed. I dream that I am screaming, 'That's not the way it's supposed to be. We just bomb military targets,' even though I know that I am lying."

Sanders sat quietly. He knew if he tried to push David, he'd lose him. He started to clean his glasses again and waited.

"And Sully; I dream about Sully."

Sanders had no idea who Sully was, but he waited patiently.

455

"I see that Irish grin break into a smile as he is running toward me. I know that he loves me. I see snow slide off of a pine branch. They're in the woods, the fucking Nazis. I yell at him. 'Get down! Get down!' But he just keeps coming. Everything goes into slow motion. I want to stop the bullets that tear into his back. I don't want him to die, but in my dream he always dies and, and..." The tears ran down David's face. Suddenly David slammed his fist down on Sanders' desk. Sanders flinched and his glasses slipped down his nose. "I couldn't save him anymore than I could save..." Charlie's pleading eyes stared at him.

"Who else couldn't you save, David?"

"I don't know it's..."

"It's the German, isn't it?"

David crinkled his brow, searching his memory. Wondering what were his dreams and what was reality. He looked down at his feet as the memory flooded into his brain. "He took us to his home. I can still taste the hot potato soup his wife cooked for us. We hadn't had any food for over a week. And his girls brought it to us where we hid in the attic. He knew they would execute his entire family if he got caught hiding us, but he did it anyway. We killed one of his kids, his only son, when a trigger happy P-51 pilot accidentally strafed a school, but he forgave us, and I paid him back by killing him."

"You didn't kill him, dammit, David. We've been over this a thousand times."

"You don't understand. He helped us because he was a human being, not for any reward or protection I might have given him. We had funny money that they gave us to use as a bribe if we ever got captured; he wouldn't take it. He knew, in his simple way, that the war was wrong, not just that Hitler was wrong, but that the war was wrong. Shit, I can still see him in that overcoat that was two sizes two big for him, carrying his Schmeisser. He hated the fucking thing like he hated the war itself, but he carried it. What choice did he have? So he rebelled in his own way; he took us home. He hid us in his attic and he fed us. Put his whole family in jeopardy. And what did I do? I tried to con him in my rotten high school German, that if he helped us to escape, I would see to it that his family would be safe after the Americans won the war."

David stood up and began pacing. It was as if Sanders wasn't there.

A summer shower pelted the high windows of Sanders' office, followed by a clap of thunder. David sat down, exhausted. His shirt was soaked through with sweat. "I need a cigarette." Sanders handed him his pack of Camels. David lit up and took a drag. He slumped back in his chair and Sanders worried that he might not continue.

"Go on, David."

David looked at Sanders as if he were a stranger. He crinkled his brow as if trying to remember something. He took another drag and ground out the cigarette in the ashtray on Sanders' desk. "Aw, what's the difference? What good is reliving all this crap? Hell, once was enough."

David took out his handkerchief and this time there was no smoke in his eyes; the tears flowed freely. "He looked up at me just before he died. I could see the life slowly fading from his eyes. I knew he was trying to say something, but I couldn't hear him. I could only see his eyes searching my face, asking me why. I see those eyes; I see eyes, not just his." Charlie's pleading eyes stared at him. "Goddamn it I can't stand to look at those eyes anymore."

"Other eyes?" Sanders asked expectantly.

"That's how I rewarded him. I got him killed."

"You didn't answer my question, David. What other eyes?"

"I want to leave now." David got up from the chair and headed for the door.

"Wait a minute," Sanders said. "We're not finished yet."

"No, I don't want to talk about it. Don't you understand? I don't want to talk about it." David was gasping for breath.

"Whose eyes, David?" Sanders voice rose as he stood and faced David. "Whose eyes, David?" he said, louder, staring into David's eyes, so close now, their faces nearly touching.

David slumped back into his chair, his head in his hands, sobbing. Sanders towered over him. He leaned forward and, in a whisper, he asked once again, "Whose eyes were they, David?"

"Charlie's, they were Charlie's," he almost screamed, "And I left him to die. Do you understand? I left him. He was pleading with me to help him but…" David's throat suddenly constricted as he remembered what he had suppressed all these years.

Sanders kneeled in front of David and searched his face. "But what? But what, David?"

"But I couldn't help it, I…"

"Go on."

"It was too late. It was too late. I had already jumped, but, but I didn't check him good enough. I didn't know he was still alive. Couldn't feel a pulse. He wasn't breathing. I…I remember now, just as I dropped through the hatch, I saw him. His eyes were pleading, and I could see his lips moving, begging, 'Help me, help me!' but it was too late."

Sanders put his hand on David's shoulder to steady him. They had opened the door that held the secret to David's nightmares, and now there was nothing left but to wait until all the demons left.

"He…he was bleeding from a big hole in his stomach; his arm was gone, just a stump. Oh, God. His face was burned black from the fire. I checked him. I checked him. I wouldn't have left him if I thought…Oh, God forgive me."

Sanders leaned down, put both of his hands on David's trembling shoulders. "God can't forgive you, David, until you forgive yourself. You didn't kill Charlie, nor did you kill your German, and you didn't kill Sully. The war killed them. That's right, David, the war killed them."

CHAPTER FIFTY-ONE

DECEMBER 1957

Eastern's future looked bleak. It had lost its competitive edge. Melvin had laid off help indiscriminately in order to cut expenses. Trucks lay idle for the lack of business.

Will Donner called a special meeting of the Board of Directors to order. He went through the preliminaries, cleared his throat, and leaned forward, both hands resting on the table. "Well, gentlemen, we have a problem, a damn big problem. Our stock is at an all-time low. Profits are nonexistent, and I'm not anticipating any changes to that condition unless we make some drastic moves now. Let's face it, we cut some debt, I'll give you that, but lost our ability to compete. We—"

Melvin broke in. "Wait one damn minute. I made this company liquid, I—"

"Melvin," Will interrupted, "no one is blaming you…"

"Well it certainly sounds like it."

Bill Kelley stood up, looked at Melvin, and said angrily, "Well, Melvin, who the hell else sold off the New Jersey bulk plant and fought like a tiger to sell, sell, sell. You would have sold your own grandmother if you could have brought in another dollar. It was you that killed the tanker deal…"

Melvin's face was purple with rage; he banged his fist on the table. His water goblet trembled and spilled a little bubble of water on the polished table. "You Goddamn hypocrite, you were the first to indict David, you…"

Bill Kelley's face turned red. He waved his finger in admonishment at Melvin. "That's absolutely not true. I worked with David on that project. I argued with him about it, agreed, but in the end, I supported him; you were the swing vote that—"

Will Donner interrupted them like an angry schoolteacher. "Melvin, sit down. Both of you, stop this; it's unproductive. Let's not lay this on Melvin. We all voted with him, we backed his ideas. He didn't work alone. The board is responsible, not just Melvin, so let's stop this nonsense and try to fix the problem."

Bill, still standing, opened his hands in a plea to the rest of the Board. "Fix it? How…?"

Will cut in. "Look, Bill, you worked with David on the Tanker Project that could put us back in business. Make us competitive again."

"Are you crazy?" Melvin interrupted, still angry. "Do you know what kind of dollars you're talking about? We killed that idea two years ago."

"Yes, we did," Bill said as he slumped back in his chair defeated, "and maybe we shouldn't have."

Will turned back to Bill and pursued his discussion of the Tanker Project. "Bill, you worked with David, what do you think?"

"Well, as a matter of fact, I've been following that project since inception. With rising oil prices and the way the whole industry has been in a shithouse, work's gone damn slow. She's still on the ways and there may be some bargain hunting there, but not for us, that's for damn sure."

Will raised his eyebrows. "What do you mean, not for us?"

"After we dumped the project and David resigned, the shipyard was left high and dry. I know, because David went to them. He felt guilty, thought he had led them on, so he got them together with Continental Oil. He didn't make a dime on it. Wouldn't take a finder's fee. They loved him for it. Well, anyway, Continental's not doing too good now and I think they'd love to get out. But, David's probably the only guy who could deal with them."

Melvin's face was red and contorted with anger. His eyes were slits. He stood. Spittle flew from his mouth as he spoke. "Let me tell you something. This is a lot of bullshit. Number one, we could never raise the funds to buy out Continental's position, and even if we could, there is no way we're going to bring fucking David back to this company. Number two, I think the rest of this board agrees with me, that all this talk is just a waste of time."

"I'm sorry you're taking this so personally," Will said, glad that Mrs. Bass was not in attendance to witness Melvin's outburst and profanity. "After all, we're just doing discovery here. Certainly there will be plenty of discussions before we bring any idea to the board for a vote."

And there was plenty of discussion, not to mention yelling and table-banging by Melvin but, in the end, it was voted to try to get David back. At least as a consultant to try to work out the tanker deal with Continental. The only negative vote was Melvin's.

David pulled up to the curb in the front of Eastern Airline's arrivals at Miami Airport and hoped the cop would let him stay there until Bill Kelley found him. He wondered what was so important that would make Bill fly all the way from Boston just to talk and why he couldn't have just told him what the problem was over the phone.

He saw Bill looking up and down the row of loading and unloading cars. David honked and flicked his lights until he got a nod from Bill who started in his direction. Bill was short and totally bald. He had a red button for a nose and his florid skin and scalp set off his piercing ice blue eyes. The back of his neck had rolls of fat that hung over his collar and then disappeared, until it merged with his powerful back and wide shoulders. A dark sweat stain was growing under his arms, giving testimony to the ninety-degree temperature.

David opened the trunk. Bill stowed his suitcase and got in the car. "Jesus, it's hot out there.," he said as he squinted at David. "It's like a fucking oven."

"Didn't you bring any sunglasses?"

"Now why would I think of bringing sunglasses? It's fucking snowing in Boston."

"You know, Bill, it's interesting that, for such a smart guy, you can't say four words without the F-word."

"Well, I sure as shit can't use it in the courtroom, so it's sort of like a verbal vacation when I'm not working."

David chuckled. "So what's on your mind, Bill?"

"What's on my mind? I'll tell you what's on my mind: a cold shower, a nap, a big steak, and three vodkas."

The best steak in town was at the Forge on 41st Street and David needed no reservation there.

The maitre d' gave David a firm handshake then snapped his fingers, beckoning to a waiter. "Take Mr. Livingston and his guest to his table and take good care of them."

Bill ordered vodka on the rocks, stone crabs and sirloin, medium rare. When he finished his first bite he smiled. "Best fucking steak I ever had."

Finally he finished the steak, patted his stomach, gave a silent belch, and reached for a cigar.

"So what's the story?" David asked, as Bill fiddled with his cigar and finally lit it.

"Eastern's in the crapper, that's the story."

"So what's that got to do with me?" David asked.

"Come on, David, stop the bullshit. How many shares you got, a hundred thousand, more? Don't tell me you're not interested."

David shrugged his shoulders and Bill continued. "The corporation needs help and needs it bad, or it's just not going to make it."

"That bad, huh?" David lit a cigarette, looked at it after the first puff and made a face.

"No, worse."

"So?"

"So, the tanker project we worked on…Continental can't handle it. There may be room for us there. That alone could make us competitive again. The bottom line, we need to get that tanker, and for Christ's sake don't tell me I told you so or I'll throw up."

"I told you so." David smiled wickedly. "So?"

"So, we want you to do the deal, maybe get the company back on its feet again. We want you—"

"Whoa, whoa, whoa, you guys have short memories; you voted against the tanker project, against me, and you knew I would leave, remember?" David's face was flushed. Realizing his voice was much louder than normal, he looked around to see if he had offended any of the other diners. Bill interrupted him.

"Hold it, my friend, I voted with you. I argued with you, but I never doubted you. Bill lowered his voice to a whisper. "Listen, David, I don't blame you for being bitter, but you can't just throw this corporation down the toilet because you're pissed off. Be reasonable and let's just explore this."

"Alright, Bill, I'll think about it," David said, as he pushed his chair back, ready to leave.

David dropped Bill off at his hotel and as Bill got out of the car he bent down to see David at the steering wheel. "David, sleep on this and let's have breakfast tomorrow morning, okay?"

"Yeah, see you tomorrow." He drove home, his mind racing, gave the Mercedes to the doorman, and walked to the elevator as if in a trance. His thoughts were filled with Bill's proposition. He locked the door to his apartment behind him and, without turning the lights on, walked over to the big picture window that looked over Indian River Creek and the lights of downtown Ft. Lauderdale. He thought that if he took Bill's offer, which he knew would be more than generous, he could be with Sarah on a regular basis and, maybe, just his proximity could bring him closer to Jessie.

David knew his relationship with Vernon was deteriorating. Vernon was never going to change. He would always be a bully. Worse, the more he became involved with Vernon's finances, the more he realized how devious the man was. Maybe this was his chance, a chance to get his self-respect back. He was on the verge of quitting anyway. Then there was Melvin to consider, now Ginny's husband. What would his reaction be? David knew there would be friction, to say the least, but there was no way he would hurt him and add him to his already long casualty list. Bill had assured David that he would have a free hand, but what did that mean? It was a dilemma. He'd sleep on it.

The phone rang. At first he thought he was dreaming. As he opened his eyes, bright sunlight streamed through his bedroom window and a tiny dust storm erupted in its rays. He was fully dressed except for his shoes. He remembered how drained he had been when he had kicked off his shoes and collapsed on the bed to fall into an exhausted sleep. *It must be Bill,* he thought. *Shit, I don't know what to say.* Suddenly Jessie's beautiful face materialized in his mind's eye. He wanted to reach out, touch her, caress her cheek, touch her hair, and tell her how sorry he was. A lump formed in his throat. God, how he missed her soft voice, the moments when they spoke in the dark before sleep and her soft lips on his when they kissed each other goodnight. Sarah, climbing into bed with them on Sunday morning, all of them giggling and laughing and loving each other. Sometimes there were tears, but they were important because they washed away the little agonies that come into all marriages. He thought of long talks, long walks, holding hands, making love, her gentle touch, all the wonder of the marriage that he no longer had. It was time to go home and get them back. He picked up the phone. It was Bill.

CHAPTER FIFTY-TWO

JANUARY 1958

Jessie sat on the little upholstered bench in front of her dressing table listening to the radio. Frank Sinatra was singing "All the Way." She was taking off her earrings, looking at her face in the mirror, when Sarah joined her reflection. "Hello, my darling," Jessie said quietly. "What brings you here after bedtime?"

"I tried, but I just couldn't sleep." She rubbed her eyes. "I was thinking about Daddy. I miss him, and I don't understand why you won't let him come back. He wants to, you know, and I just don't think it's fair."

Jessie saw the defiance flash in the green eyes that she had passed to her daughter. "Sarah, honey, Daddy and I need some time to figure some things out. We…"

Sarah's green eyes narrowed, her face flushed and her voice became harsh. "You've had enough time. He's been gone for too long. I don't see why he can't come back now. I just can't understand why you're being so mean."

Sarah started to cry. Jessie suppressed her own tears and swallowed hard; she felt as if her heart would break. She took Sarah into her arms to soothe her. She wanted David back more than Sarah could ever imagine. Was she punishing David or herself or, worse, Sarah? What was she gaining by keeping him away? She loved him and she knew he loved her.

"Mom."

"Yes, my darling."

"Are you going to make up with Daddy and let him come home?"

Jessie sat there in silence for a few moments, remembering that she had not yet agreed to the dinner date that David had proposed and thought that the next time David called she would accept his invitation. She hugged Sarah close to her. "Yes, honey, Daddy's going to come home."

"Promise?"

"Yes, I promise. Now you run off to bed, okay?"

"Okay, but remember you promised."

"I won't forget."

Sarah got off Jessie's lap after an abundance of good-night kisses and headed for bed. She stopped at the door and blew Jessie an extra kiss. "I love you."

Jessie blew a kiss back. "I love you too, sweetheart. Sweet dreams."

Sarah left the bedroom and shut the door behind her, leaving Jessie with her thoughts. The idea of David back home in her bed again sent a little chill through her. She was becoming aroused. She put her hand on her breast and felt her nipple growing hard. She half-closed her eyes, lifted her nightgown and put her hand between her legs. Her fingers began to move slowly.

Her mind drifted from David to the time she was a little girl of thirteen.

Her great uncle had died, and her parents had hired a young woman to sit with her while they paid a visit to show their respects to the mourning family. She had been in bed for about an hour when she awakened to hear muffled noises from downstairs. She got out of bed and went over to the little balcony that looked over the living room. The sounds became louder, mixed with some giggling and moans as she crept to the edge of the balcony and looked down. A young man was with the sitter. She was half undressed. The young man was trying to pull her panties down and she was giggling and pretending to stop him. He finally succeeded in getting her panties off of one leg. His hand was moving vigorously between her legs, and her giggling was turning to little moans of pleasure. His pants were unbuttoned and Jessie could see his hard erection. It was the first time Jessie had seen a man's penis, let alone an erect one. She was trembling with excitement. The young man was trying to get on top of the sitter and now she was accommodating him by spreading her legs. The narrow couch was impeding his efforts but he finally entered her. Jessie's eyes were wide with excitement now and she felt wet between her legs as she watched the boy pumping away at the wriggling and panting girl under him. Finally there was a grunting noise, a little scream and Jessie knew what had happened, because she too was trembling and panting as she removed her hand that had somehow found its way between her thighs.

Jessie's body stiffened suddenly as it strained in orgasm. She was in a complete sweat and her heart was beating wildly.

There was no doubt about it. It was time for David to come home.

BOOK FOUR

FINDING TRUE NORTH

CHAPTER FIFTY-THREE

JANUARY 1958

Vernon stood up, put both hands on his desk and leaned forward. His whole body trembled with rage. His eyes narrowed as he glared at David. When he finally spoke, his voice bellowed. "You ungrateful son of a bitch. You're giving me notice? You're quitting? You little shit. You think you can just up and walk out on me? You're going to quit and blow forty, fifty thousand dollars of bonus money? Are you fucking crazy?"

He had seen Vernon angry, very angry before, but the fury of this assault was frightening. Vernon's eyes bulged like those of a madman. David felt cowed sitting, so he stood and faced Vernon. "Look, I'm not leaving tomorrow. I will stay until I can break in a…"

Vernon suddenly went slack. He seemed to deflate as he slumped back into his chair. It seemed that the storm had come and gone. He smiled at David. The color of his face came back to normal. He was like a chameleon. There was a pleading melancholy to his voice. "David, my boy, I don't want a replacement. I've grown to think of you like a partner. You know, like a son."

David cringed.

"I was going to tell you at dinner tonight. Give you a piece of the action."

David sat down. "Look, it's not a question of money. I've got a kid, a wife. I got to straighten things out. Be a family again."

"So take a couple of weeks. Take a month, whatever it takes. Bring them down here to beautiful Miami."

"I'm sorry. Truly sorry, but it's time to go home. Get my life back together."

Vernon's face started to turn red, thick, blue veins swelled in his neck and forehead. Suddenly he stood. The fury of the storm was on the horizon. His eyes became slits. His voice rose to a hoarse scream. "You want to go? Okay, then get the fuck out of here. I mean now! Go back to your apartment and pack up. You're through here. You understand?" His head wobbled and his heavy lips trembled. "You'll find out that it doesn't pay to fuck Howard Vernon."

David stood and leaned across the desk toward Vernon. "Are you threatening me?"

"Damn right. You fuck me. I fuck you back."

David drew back, a slight smile on his lips. "Take your best shot."

Vernon calmed again. A broad smile crossed his face and he broke into a little chuckle. "Interesting choice of words, David."

David headed for the door. He knew what Vernon was capable of. It was time to get out of Dodge, and fast.

When he reached his apartment, he pulled out a big suitcase and started packing. His eyes wandered to the door. He walked over and double locked it. Shit. He was getting paranoid. Vernon was a bad guy, but he wasn't going to resort to violence. But, then again, he'd seen him in action. Vernon could be a madman if he got started.

He left most of his stuff behind. Suddenly he became unnerved, frightened. He called a cab. *Fuck the Mercedes,* he thought. He loved the car, but getting out of town seemed like the first priority. He took a last look around the apartment, caught a glimpse of the light blue sea from the picture window and thought it was too bad it had to end this way.

The cab was waiting. The doorman opened the door and gave David a little nod of recognition. David looked in all directions. Nothing. He sprinted to the cab. "Airport."

The cab took off with a jolt. David looked out the rear window. The big Mercedes limo pulled out and started to follow. "See that Mercedes behind us? Can you lose it? Never mind, forget it. Just step on it." He knew that Esteban or whoever was driving knew he was going to the airport. He'd have to play out the hand.

He sweated the thirty-minute ride to the airport and was out of the cab almost before it stopped. He grabbed his suitcase and ran to the ticket counter.

Trying to catch his breath, he listened to the reservation agent. "The next flight to Boston is Eastern's #233 leaving from Gate 5 at five-ten."

He looked at his watch. It was three-seventeen. Dammit. He looked around the crowded airport. He was sweating like a pig. No sign of Esteban. Could be anybody. He turned back to the agent. "Okay, one way to Boston."

He paced in front of Gate 5, his head on a swivel, searching every face.

Suddenly he heard an accented voice from behind. "Mister Livingston."

David turned in the direction of the accented voice. It was Esteban, wearing his black jacket, the same prominent bulge under his left arm. They were both motionless for a few seconds. David thought about hitting Esteban, but then he thought better of it. He could feel his heart slamming against his chest. There was no place to run. He was going to die. Esteban slowly reached inside his jacket. David froze. He wasn't going to get home after all.

Esteban's hand came out from under his jacket. There was no gun. Instead he held out an envelope. "Mister Vernon wanted you to have this, said you earned it. We'll all miss you, Mister Livingston." He left without further explanation.

David stood there with the envelope in his hand, trying to still his beating heart, dumbfounded, and watched Esteban disappear into the crowd.

Later, on the plane, David opened the envelope. There was a check for forty-five thousand dollars in it.

Chapter Fifty-Four

February 1958

David looked out of the window of his room at the YMCA and watched the students leaving the streetcars on their way to classes at Northeastern University. They were at the beginning of their lives, innocent of the tough world that lay ahead of them. He turned from the window and sat down on the one chair in the Spartan room. He had refused the offer to regain his old office, now occupied by Melvin, and a room at the Parker House Hotel. There was no need for fancy offices or elegant hotels any longer. He just needed the basics. Yes, just the basics: a job, a home to return to when the day was done, his family back. Those were the priorities. He would be back to work at Eastern on Monday, the beginning of the rest of his life.

The meeting with Continental was nothing like David's earlier conquests. It was held in Continental's glass-enclosed, soundproof conference room, which sat smack in the middle of their busy office space. David felt as if he were in a fish bowl. The massive workspace, filled with busy, bustling people, seemed to energize Continental's negotiators. They fought for every inch.

The meeting started at eight in the morning. They only broke for a sandwich lunch. And now David could see the people outside of the conference room putting the finishing touches on the day, straightening desks, picking up pocketbooks, and pulling on jackets. The day was done. He had argued fruitlessly about maintaining control of the newly formed merger but, in spite of the brilliance of his plan and the structure of the merger he had initiated, Continental wouldn't budge. Continental had the bulk plants to replace the ones that Melvin had sold off, as well as the additional land that would be needed for the storage of the cargo of the new oil tanker. On the other hand, Eastern would supply the sales and marketing and the enormous distribution that Continental lacked, as well as the balance of the credit needed to complete the tanker project. It was a merger made in heaven. Still, there was no way Continental would give control to Eastern; a split board was the best David could do. David was flattered to know one of the other considerations demanded by Continental was that he become COO and chairman of the board of the new corporation. His counterpart would be Continental's man, who would become president and CEO. Melvin's position was barely discussed. Secretly Eastern's board did not support him. He was demoted to senior vice president of administration.

Melvin was livid with rage. He blamed David no matter how many times he was told that it wasn't David's doing and it was the only way Continental would do the deal.

"You stole the business from my mother and now you're fucking me, you miserable bastard," he screamed as he wiped all the papers from the conference table in a wild sweep and charged out of the room.

David chased after him. "Melvin, wait up!" He caught up to him just as Melvin turned.

"What do you want, you son of a bitch."

"Listen, I know how you feel. This just isn't my doing. I…"

"You don't know how I feel. You've screwed me so many times it's a wonder I'm not pregnant." Melvin turned and started to walk away.

David grabbed him by the arm again. "Listen to me. Whatever you think, we are going to have to work together to make this thing happen. I'm going to need all the help I can get. I need you on my side." He knew Melvin would be nothing more than a hindrance. "Let's bury the hatchet, what do you say?" He reached out to shake Melvin's hand.

Melvin looked at David's outstretched hand. "Fuck you." He spat at David's feet and walked away.

David let his hand drop. Well, he'd tried. He didn't completely blame Melvin. After all, this was a big comedown for him. And then there was Ginny. Melvin was going to have to tell Ginny that he had, more or less, failed, and, worst of all, David had returned and was now his boss.

CHAPTER FIFTY-FIVE

APRIL 1958

Betty dried the last of the supper dishes and slammed the cabinet door shut. Max looked up from the work he had brought home.

"What's wrong?"

"Nothing. It's just this damn rain. It's been three days now. I'm sick of it."

It was another tedious night spent watching poor Max working his ass off. She wondered why he did it. He didn't get extra pay, never got a promotion, yet he plodded on. She thought about the time she could do anything. Be anything. All the ambition she'd had. Free to grow, and be, and do. Why had she settled for boring Max? True, he loved her, was sweet, caring and would do anything for her. And then, it was the right thing to do after the war. Get married, everybody did, but she had never followed the crowd, so why did she do it? She knew why. He was alive and vibrant then. They couldn't get enough of each other. He had great plans for them but then he lost it all. He lost his self-esteem in that fucking job. They never gave him a chance. Jews went nowhere in that goddamn WASP business. It broke him and their marriage along with it. *Maybe I didn't always help either, always bitching, even though I wanted to help him.*

"I'm going to get undressed and go to bed early; I've got a splitting headache." Max grunted an assent as she went into the bedroom.

Just then the phone rang. Betty waited for Max to pick it up in the kitchen. It was the third ring. "Damn," she muttered and picked it up. She took in a breath; it was Sanders.

"Hi, Doll, can you talk?"

She hissed, "Are you crazy, calling me at home?"

"Sorry, the damn rain, it's depressing me and I'm lonely. I'm sorry about last time. I really miss you. I want to make love to you again, fuck you until you beg me to stop."

"You're crazy and I am going to hang up."

"Wait." He chuckled. "This is the good Dr. Sanders with a prescription for—"

Betty cut him short and hung up, not knowing that Max had also picked up the phone on the third ring.

The doorbell rang urgently and Ruth started toward the door. "I'll get it."

She could see Max Goldman through the sidelights of the doorway and wondered what he would want at nine o'clock on a rainy night. A rainy night was putting it mildly. It was a deluge. She opened the door. Max stepped in out of the rain, soaking wet, looking a little wild-eyed as he searched the room. "Where's Richard? Is he home?"

Before Ruth could answer, Sanders came out of the study, holding a paperback book, his glasses down on his nose, forcing him to look over them to see Max. "Max, you're soaked; let me take your coat. What are you…?"

Max pushed by Ruth, leaving wet footprints on the marble foyer, and came in range of Sanders. He stared at him for a moment and then, without warning, punched him in the nose. Sanders fell backwards. His hand flew up to his bleeding nose in total surprise.

Ruth ran to him. "Oh my God," she screamed at Max. "What's wrong with you?"

Max stood there rubbing his fist; he'd never hit anyone before. He was crying, the tears making little rivulets down his face. He took a deep breath. "I hope I broke your nose, you bastard. I didn't have to listen to your dirty little telephone conversation to know there was something going on, but not with you. You're supposed to be my friend."

Sanders got to his feet. "Max, what are talking about?"

"Max, what are you talking about?" Max mimicked, moving closer as Sanders backed away. "I'm talking about you fucking my wife." Sanders saw Ruth's eyes fill with tears. Her face contorted as she turned away.

"I didn't know she was your wife when we started. I only knew it when we met at David's party, and by then I wasn't seeing her anymore. I swear it. I never touched her again after we met. I…"

Max had already turned, a beaten man, shoulders slumped forward; he walked out into the rain without closing the door behind him. Sanders slowly shut the door, thinking of what to say to Ruth. What could he say? She always suspected that he *ran around*. But now she had heard it from Max, that stupid bastard. He might just as well have been caught red-handed. He couldn't very well say, *Look, Ruth, all the guys fool around, it's not a big deal, I love you.* No way, she'd never buy that. He walked into the bedroom, looking for her. She was sitting in her favorite chair and appeared to be reading.

She lowered the book when she saw him. Her eyes were dry. She said in a quiet, calm voice, "I want you to pack your things and leave here tonight." She lifted the book and continued to read.

"You're taking this much too seriously. It meant nothing."

Ruth interrupted, "Yes, I know. Neither did all the others and I didn't need to have Max tell me about them. I've known all along." Now, the tears streamed down her face. "I've smelled the perfume, washed out the lipstick. I've known, but I just kept making excuses for you, told myself that was the way it is with men. Well, if it is, then I want no more of it. I've loved you. True, we couldn't have children. I blamed myself for that. It was even one of the excuses I made for you. But you never really loved me. I know that now and I'm through pretending, so just go, please just go. Just go."

Sanders went to her, kneeled beside her chair, trying to take her into his arms, but she rebuffed him violently and screamed, "Just get out. Do you hear me? Leave me alone and get out."

Sanders threw the two big suitcases into the trunk of the Caddy. He noticed that part of a shirtsleeve was hanging out of one of them. What the hell did he know about packing? Ruth always packed for them. Did a damn good job too. He backed the Caddy out of the garage into the rainy night. The garage doors were ajar. He started to get out of the car to close them. Then he looked at the pouring rain beating on the windshield and turned on the wipers. "Fuck it, I don't live here anymore." The steady beat of the wipers calmed him. He'd drive to the office and sleep on the leather couch. That is, if he could sleep. His mind was whirling through a thousand thoughts. *She'll want a divorce. It will drag through the courts. For Christ's sake, I'm a fucking psychiatrist. This*

will ruin my reputation, let alone leave me broke. Is it really my fault that I can't be faithful or is it one of God's little imperfections, maybe one of His little tests. We're put here on Earth to propagate so we are driven to copulation, married or not, and there's the big contradiction or maybe another of His tests. Society wants us to be faithful, monogamous, but physiologically we are driven in a different direction. It's not right. Great men, Roosevelt, God rest his soul, had a mistress. Eisenhower, big powerful men, full of testosterone and God's little imperfection, decent men, like David, strayed. It's not right that we should be punished.

The wipers thumped back and forth, but the downpour persevered and the lights from oncoming cars were blinding. Richard was crying. "Dammit, don't you understand Ruth? I love you. I never wanted to hurt you, I...what the..." He was blinded by the high beams of an oncoming truck. They turned the windshield into a splash of yellow glare. He thought the lights were coming right at him. He brushed the tears from his eyes with the back of his hand. *Oh, Ruth.* His last thought, as he slammed head-on into the Mack truck.

CHAPTER FIFTY-SIX

APRIL 1958

David made a screeching U-turn and headed for Sanders' house. The radio news reporter's voice was still giving the details of Sanders' spectacular accident and subsequent death the night before.

He ran up Sanders' front steps and rang the bell. He was surprised when Jessie opened the door.

"I just heard the news over the radio," he said breathlessly. "I came right over."

"I just got here a little while ago," Jessie said.

"How is she holding up?"

"I don't know. She's still a little hysterical. For some reason she feels responsible."

Jessie looked so distressed that, without thinking, David took her in his arms and tried to comfort her. The feeling of her body pressed against his was emotionally overwhelming and tears came to his eyes. After a moment Jessie gently stepped back and looked at his tear-stained face. She reached up with her forefinger and wiped a tear from his cheek. "You really cared for him."

"The tears aren't for Sanders, but, yes, I really cared for him."

"Oh, I…"

David reached out and put his hands on Jessie's arms while he examined her face. The tight lips and the cold green eyes that had greeted him the last time they had met had softened. When he had held her for that moment it seemed she had melted into his embrace that her body pressed into his. Was it just his imagination? "I've missed you so much, holding you again was like…"

Ruth's sobs broke the spell, but Jessie held David's gaze for an extra moment as if she were going to fall back into his arms. Instead she composed herself. "We should check on Ruth."

Ruth was still crying, her face buried in her hands. She looked up when they came into the room. David knelt down, took her hands into his, and kissed her on the forehead. "I'm so sorry."

David could see that she was in shock. Her eyes were vacant, staring into space, her mouth slightly agape as if she was stifling a scream. "I killed him. I sent him away. I sent him into the storm, I…"

David looked confused. "What are you talking about?"

"Max, he came here. He knocked Richard down."

David looked at Jessie quizzically and then turned back to Ruth.

"Richard was having an affair with Betty. Max found out. It was terrible." Tears washed down her cheeks; now her eyes were wild, darting about the room. "It wasn't the first time he's cheated. I looked the other way, but...I couldn't bear it any longer." She wiped her nose with a crushed handkerchief, more tears. "I...I loved him. I didn't care as long as he always came home to me." She took a gulp of air. "I thought it was just his way, that, no matter what, he still loved me..."

David squeezed her hand. "He did love you, Ruth. He made terrible choices and unforgivable mistakes." David glanced toward Jessie. "But he never stopped loving you."

"I threw him out, hated him, but I didn't want him to die. Oh, God, what did I do? I still love him, but it's too late. It's too late."

Jessie signaled David to leave as she helped Ruth up and led her to the bed. "C'mon, Ruth, you need to get some rest."

She clutched Jessie's hand like a drowning person. "Please don't leave me, not yet. I don't want to be alone."

"I'm not going anywhere; my mother's sitting with Sarah. Now you lie down and get some sleep."

David stood at the bedroom door feeling helpless until, finally, Ruth fell asleep from exhaustion, and Jessie came to him. "I'm going to stay with her tonight. Would you stop by and see Sarah in the morning? I'm going to help Ruth with the arrangements."

"Of course. I'll take the day off."

"Thanks, thanks for being here." She stood on her tiptoes and gave David a quick kiss on the cheek. Before David could say anything, she disappeared into Ruth's bedroom. David touched his cheek, watched the bedroom door close and left.

Jessie's mother answered the door.

"David."

"Hello, Mom. Jessie asked me to stop by and spend a little time with Sarah."

"Of course." She put her hand on David's arm. "How are you?"

"Miserable."

"I understand, but you...well, that's water under the bridge now; it's time for you two to get back together again. Sarah needs a Daddy."

"My sentiments, but Jessie, she..."

Sarah bounded down the stairs. "Daddy, you're here, you're here. I knew you'd come home." She ran into David's arms. "I missed you so much."

"Wait a minute. I don't know who you are," David said as he untangled Sarah and put her down. "Who is this gorgeous young lady?"

"Oh, Daddy."

"Well, I'll tell you what, if your Grandmother says its okay for you to skip school, how 'bout we spend the day together?"

"Grandma, is it okay? Please?"

"Well, it is a school day."

"Please, Grandma, please."

"I suppose if I said no, I would never hear the end of it."

Sarah kissed Rose and David and ran upstairs to get dressed.

Less than ten minutes later Sarah came down the steps. She twirled around twice. "How do I look?"

David picked her up and hugged her to him. "You look like...you look like a princess."

"Where are we going? Can we go to the movies? Can we see "South Pacific"?

As they drove home from the movies David knew he had to tell Sarah that he wasn't going to stay. Sarah was animated and happy with a never-ending dialogue of all the things she had saved up to tell her father when he came home again.

He hated to burst her bubble. "Listen, Princess, Daddy isn't going to stay at home yet, I…"

Sarah's face dropped. She seemed to deflate like a punctured balloon. "You lied to me. You…"

"I didn't lie, I…"

"Yes you did. You lied and I hate you. I don't want to be here with you." Sarah reached for the door handle and started to open the door.

"Sarah, what are you doing? Sarah, stop!" David reached for her, the car swerved out of control for a moment as the door flopped open. David had Sarah's arm. He pulled her away from the open door toward him and stopped the car. Sarah was hysterical. He tried to hold her but she tore herself away from him, her face contorted with rage.

"She said you were coming home soon. She was lying too. I hate you. I hate you both."

"Sweetheart, please listen to me. Your Mother and…"

"I hate her. It's her fault. She won't let you come home."

"That's not fair. Your Mother…we just have to work some things out. We…"

A police officer knocked on the car window. "You can't park here, buddy. Move it."

David started to drive. Tears streamed down Sarah's face; she wouldn't be consoled. He stopped in front of the house. Before he could say anything, Sarah got out of the car, ran to the house, and pounded on the door. Rose came out and gave David a knowing glance as Sarah rushed into her arms.

Max disappeared for two days. No one knew where he was. Betty was frantic and filled with guilt. God bless David, he'd spent the night with her waiting for Max to come home. But Max didn't show up that night or the next. Finally, on the third day after the accident, Max came home.

He stood in the little foyer, wet and disheveled. His eyes were red-rimmed and he bordered on exhaustion. He reached up to take off his hat and stopped midway, realizing that he wasn't wearing one. His raincoat dripped and formed little puddles on the tile floor.

Betty stood only a few feet away, still holding on to the doorknob, her eyes filled with tears. She reached out and took Max's hand. He stood there as if in a trance. Betty led him into the living room and he sat down on the couch. A wet stain crept around him. Betty fell on her knees in front of him.

"There aren't any more tears left, Max." Betty gulped a mouthful of air and swallowed hard. "I'm sorry, I'm sorry. I never wanted to hurt you. It was, I don't know." She looked around the room and took in another deep breath. "I have all I really ever wanted. I just didn't appreciate it. Appreciate you." She began to cry.

Max leaned over and brushed a lock of her hair from her forehead. "Betty, don't." He got off the couch and kneeled down beside her and put his arms around her.

She looked up, searching his eyes. "I'm not good enough for you."

"Betty, I love you. Don't you understand? I've spent two days in hell thinking about this. There are no answers. What happened, happened. It's over. I've never been good enough for you. Stuck in that miserable job, too scared to ask for a raise, too scared to quit and better myself. Well you can bet that's going to change. Just give me a chance. You'll see."

"Give you a chance? I'm the one who should be begging for another chance." She put her arms around Max and leaned her head on his shoulder. *He was so good. I never appreciated him. Never knew what I had. No, I didn't have all the luxuries, but what did it matter? To think I was in love with that snake, Sanders. Well, he's dead now, and he can rot in hell.*

Max wiped the tears away from Betty's cheeks with his thumb and lifted her to her feet. "We're going to start over. I'm quitting my job."

"What?"

"I'm quitting my job. Don't you see? The thing I feared most was losing you. I wouldn't measure up. I feel we have a second chance now. We've weathered a big storm, and now anything is possible."

"But, what will you do?"

"I'm not sure what I'm going to do yet, but I can tell you what *we* are going to do. We're going to go on our honeymoon, our second honeymoon."

David watched the pallbearers carry the casket through the great wooden doors of the Methodist church to the black hearse waiting in the rain, a rain that hadn't let up for the last five days. Sanders broken body lay inside.

Jessie and a church usher helped Ruth into a long, black limousine parked behind the hearse. Someone held a large umbrella over them, as if to protect them from the sorrows of death, as well as the pelting rain.

David saw Max and Betty standing under another umbrella across the street. Max held Betty's hand as the coffin was loaded into the back of the hearse.

David looked at the rainwater washing down the gutter toward the sewer. He wondered if the coursing water emulated life, rushing by to an ignominious end.

In a way, Sanders had touched all of their lives. David remembered Sanders wiping his brow, cleaning his glasses, waiting, waiting patiently for him to speak, to expunge his demons, to finally set him free. Sanders was a good doctor and an even better friend. Was there life after death? Perhaps one lived forever in the minds of those left behind.

Yes, Sanders almost destroyed the Goldmans, but was he not also the catalyst that saved their marriage? And poor Ruth, never her own person, set free to pursue a better life.

David knew he was looking for ways to excuse his imperfect friend, to justify his actions as well as his own, but what the hell, who was perfect? Who had nothing to hide? Which of us hadn't sinned against another? Which of us hadn't contributed to the other's wrongdoing? Who could throw the first stone?

He walked across the street. He was at a loss for words. He shook hands with Max and looked at Betty, wondering why she had come to the funeral. Betty seemed to read his mind. "You want to know why I'm here?" Without waiting for an answer she said, "I want to see that hearse drive away with that bastard in it on his way to hell, that's why."

David didn't meet Betty's eyes; he looked down at the wet pavement. Deep down, did Jessie hate him with the same intensity? Would she ever forgive him? He walked back across the street, and wondered if he could ever right the wrongs he'd committed. He vowed that he would try.

The hearse drove off into the rain. The limousine and cars of friends and family followed. David whispered, "Good-bye, my friend, and thank you. I'd rather say my good-bye here. There are too many memories buried in the graveyards of my mind, and you, of all people, would not want me to go back to them."

Chapter Fifty-Seven

October 1958

It was Saturday. David sat on a bench in the Public Gardens, surrounded by pigeons begging for the peanuts he was scattering aimlessly. It was a crisp autumn morning. The trees were shedding their red and gold crowns, filling the earth around them with all the brilliant colors of fall. It was a perfect day with a deep blue sky, a few puffy cumulus clouds scudding by on the northwest wind.

The pigeons fluttered around David and pecked at the empty peanut bag on the ground. Then, realizing the feast was over, they slowly drifted away. But that was life. If you give, you get in return, and when you stop giving, you stop getting. People were like the pigeons with the empty bag: they find out that you've deceived them and they want out. That's what he did to his family, wasn't it? He gave them an empty bag. He had lost years of Sarah's childhood and she had lost having a daddy. And Jessie—he never thought he deserved her anyway, and he certainly proved he was right.

He didn't deserve her, but he wanted her back. He would beg her on his hands and knees, if necessary.

He got up and started walking toward the Ritz-Carlton. There would be a phone there and he would call Jessie. When he got to the phone he realized he didn't have any change, so he went over to the little tobacco store in the lobby. There were a number of well-dressed women leaving one of the large function rooms. A sign beside the door read, "Gucci Trunk Show." He felt out of place in his jeans and sweatshirt among the fashionable women in the lobby. He was startled when he heard his name. "David, over here." It was Betty.

David looked in her direction in time to see Jessie shaking her head negatively as if chastising Betty. He walked over to them. Betty, who was obviously working the show for Ginny's boutique, gave David a quick peck. "Got to go get back to work." She turned to Jessie and said, conspiratorially, "See ya."

"I was just going to call you," David said.

Jessie looked at him. He looked healthy; he was tanned and he was smiling that wonderful smile that she could never resist.

"What are you doing here?"

"Well, like I said, I was in the park and I decided to call you, so I came here looking for a telephone."

"Well, I guess you saved a nickel."

"How are you?" he managed to mumble.

"I'm okay."

"You look wonderful."

"You look pretty good yourself," she said, looking at him appraisingly.

"But I'm not good at all. I'm sick inside. I miss you and Sarah so much." There were tears in his eyes. Jessie wanted to take him and comfort him. Instead she said, "Do you have a car here?"

"Yes, why?"

"Well, I came with Betty, but she's gone back to work, and I thought you might drive me home."

CHAPTER FIFTY-EIGHT

OCTOBER 1958

Although the merger had been finalized only nine months ago, David was pleased with the progress of the combined corporations. Work on the tanker had resumed and was nearing completion, sales were strong and, most of all, the transition had gone smoothly. He was about to make a call when Melvin pushed by his secretary, Julie, and barged into his office. Julie followed, protesting. He looked up from his desk with surprise. "Melvin, what—"

Before he could finish the sentence, Melvin grabbed him by his jacket lapels, his face inches from David's. "I want you to stay the fuck away from my wife, d'ya hear me?"

David could smell the liquor on his breath. He looked directly into Melvin's eyes, reached up and gently removed Melvin's hands. He steered Melvin, who was obviously very drunk, to one of his side chairs.

"Should I call Security?" Julie asked.

"No, just leave us," David said as he turned to face Melvin.

"You rotten bastard, can't you understand? I love her. If you don't leave her alone, I'm gonna kill you." Melvin slurred, his face bright red.

"Melvin, I haven't spoken to Ginny for a year, probably more. I don't know what you're talking about, and once more, I don't like you putting your hands on me. I don't like you threatening me. Most of all, I don't like that you're drunk at work."

"Fuck you, you arrogant bastard. You've been trying to kick me out of here since you got back. You stole the business; you want my wife, so I'll give you the finishing touch." He rose from the chair and pushed his face close to David's. "Stick your fucking job up your ass. I quit." He headed toward David's office door, almost tripped over another chair as he passed through the outer office. Julie was standing there with her mouth open. Melvin looked at her menacingly. "Fuck you, too."

Even before Ginny opened the door to their apartment, she had an uneasy feeling. Melvin had been drinking again and had gone from mean to quiet and brooding. She knew she had to find a way to help him out of his slump, but he resisted her every effort. She opened the door. The Chinese vase that normally sat on the little table in the foyer lay in pieces, scattered across the floor. She stepped around the shattered vase and held her breath. Melvin was in a heap on the floor in the living room in front of the big white couch that they had purchased only a few months ago. It appeared that somehow he had fallen off the couch. She ran over to him and knelt beside him. "Melvin, are you alright?"

She turned him so that she could see his face. His eyes were open but in an expressionless gaze. He smelled of liquor and urine. His pants were stained about his crotch.

"Look at me," Ginny screamed. "Look at me."

Melvin's eyes focused for a moment. He smiled and shut his eyes.

Ginny shook him. "Melvin, come on, wake up. What's wrong?"

He opened his eyes and slurred, "That fucker, he forced me out, no more job. Where's the fucking scotch? I need a drink."

"Who forced you out, what happened? What are you talking about?"

"Where's the fucking scotch?"

"No more scotch, Melvin. Let's get you off the floor."

"Good idea." He giggled and, with Ginny's help, he struggled to his feet and half-sat, half-fell back onto the couch.

"Now, tell me what happened," Ginny said anxiously.

"I'm through there, that's what happened. He finally got what he wanted. He stole the business, he screwed my mother and now he's got rid of me. What else is he going to take from me?" He stared at Ginny, but just for a moment and then he started to cry.

No matter how hard she tried, Ginny couldn't console him. He shook with deep, choking sobs. "He's going to take you away from me, too, isn't he?"

Ginny cradled him in her arms. "Shhh, nobody is taking me away from you, I…" Before she could finish Melvin passed out in her arms. She laid him back on the couch, picked his feet up, and covered him with a shawl.

I'm going to call David. She looked to see if Melvin was asleep. He appeared to be out cold. Little snorts now and then were the only sign of life. She crossed the room to the antique French desk, picked up the phone and dialed Eastern's number. She asked softly for David's office. David answered.

"I have to see you."

David was taken aback. A thousand thoughts and old memories rushed through his mind. He felt drawn to her voice, hungry for her, but he knew he could never succumb to those feelings again. He saw Jessie and Sarah in his mind's eye. Yet she sounded so desperate. His hand holding the phone trembled. "When and where?"

"Can you meet me at the Glass Slipper, tonight?"

"What time?"

"I'll be there at seven. Is that okay"

David hesitated for a moment, thinking that this was a bad idea but…"Yeah, that's fine. I'll see you there."

She was supposed to have dinner with the girls. Melvin wouldn't miss her.

David's name ricocheted off the wall and penetrated Melvin's saturated brain. *David. David.* The name screamed through the thick layers of fog that encompassed his brain. Anger grew within him like a terrible cancer. He gritted his teeth until his jaw ached. Ginny's voice pierced his heart like a like a hot poker. *I'll be there. I'll be there,* repeated and repeated until he put his hands over his ears in an effort to block it out. Then although his mind slipped in and out of focus he began to plot. "I'll be there too," he said to himself, as his muddled mind replayed Ginny's call to David. "I'll be there and I'm going to kill the both of you, the thief and the whore. I'm going to kill you both." Suddenly he felt at peace with the thought of his revenge. He smiled and feigned sleep again.

Ginny searched the bar at the Glass Slipper, but she didn't see David.

"Hi, Ginny, long time no see."

"Hi, Al."

"You're looking for...?"

"Yes," she interrupted.

Al pointed to the alcove in the darkest corner of the bar that led to the little private dining room. It served the bar and the main dining room, hidden from both rooms by tiny alcoves. Its only illumination was the light from a single candle that glowed through a crystal enclosure. The little room guaranteed total privacy and was usually taken by lovers or wise guys who didn't want to be seen. She and David had sat there before.

Ginny came out of the deep shadows and startled David. At first he didn't see her. When he did, she looked more beautiful than ever. She was wearing a simple black dress with a pearl choker. Her body was as slender and as provocative as ever. David rose and took her hand. She leaned over and kissed his cheek. "Hello, David." She smiled but her eyes filled with tears.

David held her at arm's length. "It's been a long time."

She wanted to say how much she missed him, how much she still loved him. She thought of the times they had both sat in this very same booth. She remembered that they had never really got to their food. How they had sat side by side, their backs to the world, and had whispered their love to each other. Their hands had touched and a fierce current had rushed through their bodies. Their eyes had spoken of their desires, their hopes and dreams. "I'm really not that hungry," she had said then, conspiratorially. He'd had taken her hand and they'd gone upstairs and...

But that was a long time ago. This was now, all that had to be over. She was married to Melvin now and he was in trouble. She had to save him. "He's drinking again. He's so angry. He thinks we're still lovers. Keeps cleaning that horrible gun and swearing that he's going to kill you. He..."

"Slow down." David took her hand. He could smell her perfume, feel the pulse of her energy. He wanted to hold her again but he restrained himself.

"Please, David, what he needs is his self-esteem back. He needs to feel in control again and only you can do that. I never realized how much I cared for him. We were really happy together until you came back. David, I'm carrying his child, and I can't even tell him about it. I just don't know how he'd take it. I know how much you hate him but you've got to help us."

"I don't hate him. I've known him since we were kids. I always took his side. Even though I suspected that he called Jessie and told her about us. There were other things, too. He tried to hurt me more than once. I still tried to help him. I swear to you, there were so many times I told myself not to come back, to be near you again. I didn't want to hurt

Melvin. I didn't want to hurt your marriage. I just wanted to get my life back, my kid and yes, Jessie. We're starting to heal now, Jessie and me."

David took Ginny's hands in his and looked into her eyes. "But I'll do whatever it takes, whatever it takes, I promise."

It took forever to find a cab. Melvin finally arrived at the Glass Slipper. He overpaid the cabbie for the short ride with a five-dollar bill. "Keep the change." The Glass Slipper's red blinking sign highlighted his face. He stood there in the red glow, wild-eyed, wanting to kill them both, but then he thought about Ginny. Did he want to kill her? His head was spinning. He stumbled and caught himself before he fell. Maybe he wasn't as sober as he thought he was. Maybe he ought to sit in the park for a while, get a grip. He walked into the park and sat on a slatted wooden bench. *Why would I kill Ginny? If I just killed David, she would be free of him. God, I'm tired.* He shut his eyes as his chin dropped to his chest, and he dozed.

He jumped as he felt a hand on his shoulder. It was a patrolman.

"Are you alright?"

Melvin assured him he was okay and then looked at his watch. He'd been in the park for only fifteen minutes, yet he felt he had been there for hours. His head throbbed. He walked across the street and up the stairs to the Glass Slipper. His eyes scanned the bar and then the busy dining room. He knew where they were. He got control of himself and headed for the little private dining room. He stepped into the dark alcove, unseen by the busy diners, and pressed his body into the darkest corner. He checked the .38. They were already there. Dammit. He wanted to be there first, to listen to their love talk and then…They were holding hands. He held the gun so tight he thought it might go off.

A ghost of a figure moved in the dark alcove. David could see a gun protruding from the darkness highlighted by the flickering candle on the table. He sat still, trying to remain calm. Melvin stepped into the little room. He was disheveled and his eyes were wild. He smelled of whiskey, sweat, and urine.

David tried to keep his voice neutral. "Melvin, what—?"

"Shut up! Shut up! You bastard. You took everything from me. My self-respect, my business, and the only thing that ever mattered, the only person I ever loved. You took my Ginny from me, and then when you got tired of her you threw her away. Now you want to take her away from me again. Well, I'll kill you first." He waved the gun wildly, screaming, "I'll kill you! I'll kill you!"

Ginny slowly rose from the table. She put herself in the line of fire between Melvin and David. "Melvin, put the gun down. No one is taking me away from you. I love you. For God's sake, I'm carrying your child." Her heart was pounding in her chest. She was frightened. She knew both of these men's lives as well as her own were in her hands and she had to be calm. "This is the first time I've seen David since we've been married. I came to ask him to help you."

Ginny walked over to Melvin so that her body still shielded David and looked into Melvin's eyes. "Please, Melvin, if you love me, put down the gun."

"You're having a baby? My baby?" Melvin's face went slack. He looked defeated. He dropped his hand and let the gun fall to the floor. He sank to his knees and put his face into his hands and cried deep, throaty sobs. His chest expanded and contracted with each new sob. Ginny knelt beside him. She took him into her arms and rocked back and forth with him, whispering to him as she would a child. "It's going to be alright, shush. I love you. I'll never leave you."

David felt as if he were watching a scene from a movie. He hadn't moved since Melvin had entered the room. He knew he wanted the scene to play itself out. He began to understand Melvin for the first time, his desperate need to be loved.

Weren't Melvin's needs the same as his own? Now, he knew what had been so elusive all these years. Why accumulation of money and power was meaningless. No matter how rich or how powerful a man was, without that special woman to love, he had nothing. The real quest was finding love and love was the ultimate goal. He thought that he had found love with Ginny, but in fact he had lost it by losing Jessie. He understood that a man could love two women, but what he hadn't realized was there could be no real fulfillment that way. Only guilt. Real love was monogamous. He knew that now. Although he loved Ginny, he wasn't *in love* with her, he was *in love* with Jessie. Somehow, she would forgive him and then, maybe, he could forgive himself. This was what Sanders was probing for, trying to make him understand. He had to forgive himself. That was the only way he would be whole again, would sleep again. Charlie, the German guard, Sully, Ginny, Melvin, Jessie, and Sarah were all casualties of his life, yet he had to go on living, had to repair what he could and forgive himself for what he could not. Going home to Jessie and Sarah was a good start.

He helped Ginny and Melvin to their feet and put his arms around them, "Melvin, you look like hell. Why don't you take Ginny home, get some rest, and then we'll talk. Tomorrow is another day."

ABOUT THE AUTHOR

Howard Kravets flew B-17s during WWII. He was shot down twice, once in occupied France where he escaped through the French underground and again when he parachuted over Germany and became a POW. He escaped once more and returned home to marry his childhood sweetheart. He is now retired from a successful business career and continues to write.

Made in the USA
Lexington, KY
30 June 2014